2 APR 1985

THE PHOENIX TREE

THE PHOENIX TREE is not a spy novel but a novel about spies, set in Japan during the dramatic closing months of World War II.

Early in 1945, Navy Lieutenant Kenji Minato is in internment in San Diego as a Japanese spy. When his offer to spy for US Intelligence is accepted, he asks that an old schoolfriend, Corporal Tom Okada, be his control. In Tokyo their mission is to identify members of a Peace Faction in Japan and estimate its strength. Natasha Cairns, mixed-blood widow of an English agent, becomes their wireless operator.

Amidst the dark terrors of the blanket bombing of Tokyo and the devastation of Hiroshima and Nagasaki, Minato and Okada find out more about themselves than they do about the Peace Faction. In doing so, each struggles to come to terms with the Japanese dogma that links death for Emperor with honour, surrender with dishonour.

THE PHOENIX TREE is a story of the tension of war, of secrecy, of disaster, and of love: a dramatic and compelling novel, original in concept, written with all the imagination and authenticity of a master story-teller.

by the same author

YOU CAN'T SEE ROUND CORNERS
THE LONG SHADOW
JUST LET ME BE
THE SUNDOWNERS
THE CLIMATE OF COURAGE
JUSTIN BAYARD
THE GREEN HELMET
BACK OF SUNSET
NORTH FROM THURSDAY
THE COUNTRY OF MARRIAGE
FORESTS OF THE NIGHT
A FLIGHT OF CHARIOTS
THE FALL OF AN EAGLE
THE PULSE OF DANGER
THE HIGH COMMISSIONER
THE LONG PURSUIT
SEASON OF DOUBT
REMEMBER JACK HOXIE
HELGA'S WEB
MASK OF THE ANDES
MAN'S ESTATE
RANSOM
PETER'S PENCE
THE SAFE HOUSE
A SOUND OF LIGHTNING
HIGH ROAD TO CHINA
VORTEX
THE BEAUFORT SISTERS
A VERY PRIVATE WAR
GOLDEN SABRE
THE FARAWAY DRUMS
SPEARFIELD'S DAUGHTER

THE PHOENIX TREE

JON CLEARY

COLLINS
8 Grafton Street, London W1
1984

William Collins Sons & Co. Ltd
London · Glasgow · Sydney · Auckland
Toronto · Johannesburg

BRITISH LIBRARY CATALOGUING IN PUBLICATION DATA

Cleary, Jon
The phoenix tree.
I. Title
823[F]   PR9619.3.C54

ISBN 0-00-222704-5

First published 1984
© Sundowner Productions Pty Ltd

Photoset in Linotron Plantin by
Rowland Phototypesetting Ltd, Bury St Edmunds, Suffolk
Made and printed in Great Britain by
William Collins Sons & Co. Ltd, Glasgow

To Judith and Arthur Morris

Certain historical persons appear
in this story, but all the main
characters are fictional and are
not meant to represent any actual
persons, living or dead.

Contrary to Japanese usage, I have
adopted the Western custom of
putting given names first and
family names last.

One

Kenji Minato's escape from the San Diego naval base did not go according to plan.

'We shall have to arrange your escape,' Commander Embury had said. 'It has to look genuine. You've got to land back in Japan without any chance of them thinking you've been planted. You make for the Mexican border and get out of the States, that's your first priority. As you know, there's no Japanese embassy in Mexico City – the Mexicans are theoretically at war with the Japanese.'

'The best way to be at war,' Tom Okada had said. Though he was the American he had been far less cooperative than Minato. But then, Minato remembered, Tom had always been a rebel, even at high school.

'That's enough, corporal,' Embury had said, not even glancing at Okada. I'm the important one here, Minato had thought, the real hero; and Tom doesn't like it. 'Lieutenant, there are Japanese and German businessmen down in Mexico who haven't been interned. We know they are part of the Japanese spy network – I'm sure you have contacts there.'

Minato nodded. 'And I'm sure you know who they are, Commander.'

Embury nodded in return. 'We do, but they don't worry us. You will have to persuade them to move you along their line back to Japan. It'll probably be down to an embassy in South America, one of the smaller countries. From there it will probably be by ship to Lisbon; then by plane the rest of the way, through Occupied Europe to Turkey. We're not sure what route the Japanese or Germans use from there on, but they do move personnel between themselves. It's a long way home, but there's no other way – it *has* to look as if you made it without any help from us. We'll allow six to eight weeks, but that will depend on how quickly you're moved along the line. We'll give you names of contacts in Mexico City and other possible stopovers, so that you can keep us informed of when you're being moved on. As for you, Corporal Okada—'

Okada sat up.

'You'll be going in by a much more direct route. We'll drop you by parachute. Or take you in by submarine. You have nothing to worry about.'

Okada, for the moment, had chosen to be more Japanese than American. He had looked inscrutable.

On 3 January, the night of the escape, all went well to begin with. At 10 p.m. Minato complained to the Shore Patrol guard on duty that he had a slight attack of diarrhoea and had to go to the head. In all the weeks he had been here at the Navy base he had given no trouble; he and his guards were on the friendliest of terms, though the guard detail still had no idea why he had been held here so long. The SP on duty that night had no reason to believe that this trip to the head was any different from all the other trips Minato had made. Nothing establishes a routine as much as certain natural functions.

The guard suspected nothing when Minato stopped to tie up a shoelace. He was all innocent curiosity when Minato said, 'What's going on over there?' He turned his head and was facing away from Minato when the latter hit him with a karate chop across the side of the neck. He went down in slow motion, allowing the Japanese to catch him and lower him into the shadows beside the latrine block. Minato took the guard's pistol and the scout's knife that was clipped to the man's belt; the knife was not general issue but had been a proud possession of Alvin Gellen, ex-Eagle Scout. Minato waited till he was certain he had not been observed by anyone still moving about on the base. Then, keeping to the shadows, he made his way to where he had been told the admiral's car would be parked.

He found the car, got into the boot and closed the lid, though making sure it could not be locked. Twenty minutes later the car was driven out of the base. The admiral, whose wife was keeping the home fires burning in Norfolk, Virginia, spent several nights a week being warmed by the wife of a commander absent on duty in the Pacific; keeping their adultery in the service, neither the admiral nor the commander's wife thought they were being too traitorous. The driver delivered the admiral to his rendezvous, then drove on to his own assignation with the wife of a yeoman first class who was also absent on duty in the Pacific. The celibate Minato removed himself from the boot after the driver had hurried off whistling 'Pistol Packin' Momma', a lover's serenade.

Minato had half an hour's walk through the darkened streets before he came to the alley off Market Street where he had been told the getaway car would be parked. He did not know San Diego well; he had not been in the city since before Pearl Harbor; so he had asked for the car to be parked where it could easily be found. Several times during the walk he had to slip into doorways to avoid being recognized as a Japanese. He sardonically wondered if the spies in Europe, from either side, appreciated the camouflage of looking no different from the enemy.

The car was a black 1938 Pontiac with California plates; the keys were taped under the front right-hand wing. He was just opening the driver's door when the escape plan went wrong. Embury and his fellow planners had, quite reasonably, not taken into account the perambulations of a half-drunken, off-duty SP mate third-class.

Clem Bateman was from a farm in Missouri, prone to seasickness and therefore confined to shore duty; but he was big and strong and he could wield a billy-stick with all the woundup efficiency of a corn thresher; he had broken more American heads than any Kraut or Jap ever had. He hated Japs, particularly because it seemed that he would never get the chance to fight any and he would go back home at the end of the war and have nothing to boast about to the folks in Pike's Corner. But if Japs had to go on living, then he reckoned the guy he had been guarding for weeks, l'il ole Kenny Minato, was as good as any to be given the chance. He had come to think that l'il ole Kenny was a real nice guy.

He was taking a short cut through the alley, heading for a

cathouse he had run aground on while on SP patrol, when he came on the Jap trying to open a car door. He was almost past him before he recognized that he was a Jap; he had taken two more stumbling paces before he recognized Minato. He turned round, fell against the car in his surprise.

'Hey, Minato! What the hell you doing here?'

'Nothing. I got a pass—'

'The hell you did!' He made a grab at Minato. 'Lemme buy you a drink! When'd you last have a good drink, eh?'

Minato did not want to kill the big American, but he had always been swift in deciding his options. He flicked open the scout's knife and stabbed Mate Third Class Bateman with it. He had a rudimentary knowledge of anatomy, but he knew that Americans were always boasting they were all heart and he took them at their word and stabbed in the general direction. Bateman died instantly, the best way to go, and had no time to be disappointed in the real nice guy.

The big farmer's boy slid down on to the front fender, lay there for a moment as if deciding whether he should go further, then slumped to the ground. Minato looked down at him dispassionately. The war was three years old and up till now he had killed no one; he was surprised at how little he was affected by the American's death. He had never expected to have to kill and now he had done it without compunction, as if it were part of his nature. There is a certain satisfaction in self-discovery, especially if you feel in command of what one has learned. Minato had no ambition to go on killing, but he knew that if he had to do it again he would kill without qualms.

He stepped over the body into the car, started up the engine and drove down the alley and into Market Street. He drove east out through Encanto and soon was in the desert, keeping his speed steady so that he would not attract the attention of a cruising police car. There was more traffic on Route 8 than he had expected at this time of night; then he realized it was mostly military traffic. But he took no notice of it; he was finished with spying here in the United States.

It came as something of a shock that he was finished in the United States, period. He had been here six years, at liberty more than half that time, and there had been times when he had felt himself becoming Americanized, a disease he had tried to avoid. But he knew how infectious America was; one could come to believe that all its propaganda was the reality. There was no discipline to the country, of course, but even that had begun to have its appeal; its vaunted democracy was riddled with holes, a political Swiss cheese, but it meant that anyone could rise to the top, something that was not possible in the Japan he had left six years ago. America had much to offer; it was a pity it could not be conquered.

Well out in the desert he at last turned south after checking the map that had been left for him in the glove box. He drove the Pontiac along a dirt road that wound between bare hillocks that looked like white buttocks in the bright moonlight. He had switched off the headlights and drove carefully along the twisting track. He stopped for a moment, switched on the car's interior light and looked again at the map; then he drove on, certain that he was on the right route to the weakest spot in the long surveillance by the Border Patrol. He drove for another ten minutes, then switched off the engine and let the car roll to a halt. He sat listening for a full minute; then he got quietly out of the car and listened again. He could hear a night bird of some sort; it had an unmusical cry, like a short cough of despair. He remembered from his time in the camp in Arizona how sound carried in the desert at night; the highway had to be at least five or six miles north of him, yet he could still hear the moan of trucks as they changed gears to climb a rise. But he heard no sound of motors close to him. Unless the Border Patrol was lying somewhere amongst the greasewood and cactus, he was safe.

He went to the boot of the car and took out the cheap suitcase he knew would be there; he had come to have a great deal of faith in Commander Embury. The suitcase contained a blue work-shirt, a pair of coveralls, work-boots and a woollen lumber jacket, all of them faded and worn; just the sort of outfit a farm worker would wear. He changed out of the Navy tans, then looked at what remained in the suitcase. Five hundred dollars in US bills and Mexican pesos, more than enough to get him to Mexico City and the contact there. He had always thought that Americans were far too generous with the taxpayers' money.

He headed south, leaving the track, which now swung east, and trudged along a dry watercourse. Occasionally he pulled up sharply as yucca trees or, once, a small Joshua tree took on the shape of a man in the moonlight; but no harsh voice hailed him, no light was flashed on him, and after a moment he would move on. Low cactus caught at his trouser-legs and once he jumped in the air as a jack-rabbit suddenly erupted almost beneath him. The watercourse began to drop, then he heard the trickle of water and soon he was walking through tule weeds besides a thin creek that reflected the moonlight like shards of polished shale.

Then the creek ran out, seeming to disappear into the ground. He came to a deep arroyo, slid down its bank and fell over the sleeping figure at the bottom.

He rolled aside, dropping his suitcase and grabbing at his pocket for the scout's knife. But there was no call to use it. The man he had fallen over sat up, grumbling at being disturbed; even in the moonlight it was possible to see, or anyway smell, that he was drunk, or had been. Two bottles lay near him on the pale sand and he smelled as if he had just climbed out of a wine vat. He was no danger to anyone but himself.

Minato stood up, then dropped down again with a sharp cry. His ankle felt as if it had been hit with an axe. Gingerly he moved his foot, wincing against the pain; he decided the ankle wasn't broken but sprained enough to make him a half-cripple. He looked at the man and wanted to kill him.

'Howdy,' said the man, and hiccupped. 'Who're you?'

'What the hell are you doing out here, you bum?' Minato tried to sound as American as he could.

'I live here. You new around here?' The man leaned forward, putting his breath on Minato like a dirty hand. 'Goddam, a fucking Jap!'

Minato was ready to kill him if he raised some sort of alarm, but the man just shook his head, almost dislodging the tall-crowned black hat he wore. Then Minato said, 'I'm Nisei, not Japanese. A Jap American, if you like.'

14

The man giggled, took off his hat and revealed the thick dark plaits hanging down by his ears. 'Only one sort Americans, buddy. Us. You ask General fucking Custer.'

Minato stared at the Indian, then looked around him, half-expecting to be surrounded. The man hiccupped and reached for one of the bottles. But it was empty, as was the second bottle; he threw them away with a curse. He sat in the sand of the arroyo bed, his shoulders slumped, looking ready to weep. But he and his sort had given up weeping years before: the struggle was long lost.

At last he looked up. 'You didn't oughta be here. White guys ain't allowed on the reservation. Yeller guys, neither. We're the last of the Apaches, western division.' He giggled again. 'The gov'ment tried to educate me once. They wanted an Apache bur'crat.'

'Reservation?' Embury hadn't mentioned any Indian reservation. Then Minato realized he must have taken the wrong turning off Route 8; he still had to go three-quarters of the way round the world and already he was lost. He cursed himself in Japanese, then reverted to English. 'A bureaucrat? You help run the reservation?'

The Indian laughed, more than just a giggle this time; as if with no drink left, he had decided to sober up. 'I lasted a week. They said I liked the fire-water too much. They was right, I do like it. Tequila, wine, whiskey, makes no difference. Where you heading?' he said abruptly, sounding very sober.

'Across the border.' Minato had begun to recognize a fellow enemy of the American government.

'What for?'

'I'm tired of being pushed around. You look different in this country, they want to knock the shit out of you.' He was trying to sound like some of the Nisei, the Japanese-American farm workers he had known in the camps.

'Didn't they intern all you guys?' The Indian was sounding more sober by the minute; and more intelligent.

'I spent two years in a camp over in Arizona. Then they let me out, guess they thought I could be trusted. I been working on a farm up in Utah.'

'Where you going when you get across the border?'

'I dunno. South America, maybe. They're not so fussy down there – what you look like, I mean.' It offended him to be talking like this, to have to act out this charade.

'Yeah.' The Indian nodded sympathetically. He was dressed in a dark shirt and coveralls and had an Indian blanket wrapped round his shoulders; but for the blanket and his plaits, he could have passed almost unnoticed in any American street crowd. But he was on the inside looking out of himself, the recognition of difference was in his own eyes. Then abruptly he sat up straight. 'Truck's coming!'

For a moment Minato heard nothing; then he caught the sound of a motor somewhere to the east. 'What is it?'

'The Patrol. They come along here every night. Dunno what they're looking for. Japs or Indians going out or Mex's coming in.' He laughed softly; he was no longer giggling. 'I'll take you to the border. How much?'

'Five dollars?'

'Five bucks? You a fucking Jewish Jap?' He had his prejudices; he didn't lump all white Americans together. 'Ten.'

'Okay, ten.' Minato stood up, listening to the truck getting closer. He put his injured foot to the ground and gasped with pain. 'You'll have to help me.'

'Another five bucks.' The Indian grinned in the moonlight. 'We give up taking beads. It's a cash economy.'

He offered his arm to Minato and the latter leaned on it. They set off along the arroyo, Minato hobbling painfully, the Indian slouching along; arm in arm they looked like old friends, or lovers, who had lost their way after a night out. To the east of them they could hear the grinding of the truck in low gear, as if it was ploughing its way towards them from the far end of the arroyo.

The Indian abruptly turned right, throwing Minato off-balance; the Japanese cried out with pain and the Indian gruffly muttered an apology. Minato clung to him as they stumbled up the bank of the arroyo. Like all Japanese he had always been meticulous in his bodily cleanliness and he was sickened by the smell of the Indian; but he had no other staff to lean on. They struggled up to the top of the bank and the Indian paused.

'There they are.' He spoke casually, as if he had been scouting for the enemy for over a century. Carleton, Sibley, Custer, the forces of the white man's law and order, were marked on the horizons of his mind.

Minato saw the slowly bouncing beam of the headlights some distance away: maybe five hundred yards, maybe more. He was short-sighted, a handicap for a spy, and at night he had no idea of distance. He just knew that the Border Patrol truck, probably a pick-up, was too close for comfort.

'Lay down,' said the Indian. 'You ain't gonna be able to run with that ankle.'

He pushed Minato to the ground, then walked off without another word, straight towards the approaching truck. Minato lay flat to the ground and watched the Indian through a spiky hedge of low cactus. The Indian stopped about fifty yards away and stood waiting on the top of the bank. The truck continued to approach, its headlights beam moving from side to side like a blind giant's white stick as it twisted its way along the arroyo. Then it pulled up immediately beneath the Indian.

The engine was switched off and a voice said, 'That you, Jerry? You out here again, drunk again?'

The Indian was silhouetted against the glare of the headlights beneath him; in his tall hat and with his blanket wrapped round him he all at once had a dignity about him, a dark monument. 'Just clearing my head, Mr Porter. I been celebrating Geronimo's birthday.'

Minato could imagine the Indian chuckling to himself. But he lay waiting for the Indian to give him away: in a cash economy, the reward for capturing an escaped Japanese prisoner must be more than five or ten dollars. Then Minato remembered he was supposed to be a Nisei; maybe the Indian knew that a Nisei was worth nothing.

The man down in the arroyo laughed without humour. 'You seen anyone around here while you been clearing your head?'

'Ain't no one here but us Indians, Mr Porter.' Again Minato could imagine the quiet chuckle. He began to feel easier, safe.

The Border Patrol man said something that Minato didn't

17

catch; then the engine was started up again and the truck drove slowly on along the arroyo. The Indian watched it go, raising his hand in a mock salute of peace. Then he came unhurriedly back to Minato as the latter got awkwardly to his feet.

'You gonna be okay now. We got about a mile to go.'

Minato looked steadily at him. 'Why is a guy like you still here on the reservation? There are plenty of Indians like you in the army.'

'The army don't want no drunk. Anyhow, they know I'm still fighting with the Chiricahuas. They think I'm crazy, a crazy drunk.' He laughed, not crazily but intelligently. 'What army wants a crazy drunken brave?'

Minato didn't know who the Chiricahuas were but he guessed they were warriors of long ago: maybe Indian *samurai*? He took the other man's arm again and they moved on. It was another half-hour, with Minato hobbling painfully, now clinging to the stinking Indian as if he loved him, before the Indian abruptly said, 'Okay, this is it. You're in Mexico.'

Minato sank down in the dust and looked up at him. 'Don't joke, I'm not in the mood for it.' He had forgotten that he was supposed to be a farm worker; the rough accent was gone. 'We should have come through a wire fence or something.'

'There's no fence, not around here, anyway. We've just crossed into Mexico, you take my word for it. Fifteen bucks.' He held out his hand.

Minato felt in the suitcase, took out the roll of notes and peeled off three fives. 'You're not going to leave me 'way out here? I'll give you another five to take me to the nearest road.'

The Indian put the bills in his pocket. 'This is as far as I go. You wanna be careful with that money. I could of took it off of you. You know what they used to say – never trust an Injun.'

'I'd kill you if you tried.' Minato stood up, awkwardly but quickly. The scout's knife was open in his hand, its blade a pale glint in the moonlight.

The Indian didn't back off. His right hand came out from under his blanket; it held a knife, one with a longer blade than Minato's. 'Don't try it, Jap. How many guys you killed with that potato-peeler?'

One: but what was that to boast about? Minato picked up his suitcase and backed away, on edge for the first hint that the Indian was about to plunge towards him. But the Indian didn't move; instead, he grinned and put his knife back under his blanket. He looked steadily at Minato, then he turned on his heel and walked slowly back into the moon-softened darkness, like a ghost retreating into the past.

Then his voice came floating back, as clear on the desert silence as if he were only a few yards away: 'You can't win, Jap. You're like us – the war's lost!'

Minato sat down suddenly in the dust; it was his spirit, not his ankle, that buckled. For six months, ever since he'd been picked up, he'd fooled the Americans. Slowly he had let them think they had turned him round, converted him into a double-agent, a traitor to Japan. It had not been easy to fool them; the Americans had a pathological suspicion of all Japanese, even the US-born ones like Tom Okada. But subtly, he thought, he had hinted at his six years' conversion to American thinking and institutions; but all the while he had remained as Japanese as ever. He was intelligent and objective enough to know that Japan was losing the war; but he wanted to go home to die in Japan, not live on, or at worst die, in America. And now it seemed that the long wait might end here in the Mexican desert.

He had twenty thousand miles to go, more than halfway round the world, and suddenly he wondered if it would all be worthwhile. Abruptly he began to giggle, almost drunkenly, sounding just like the Indian had when he had first stumbled on him. He was thinking of Tom Okada, the American, waiting for him in Japan and his own bleached bones lying here in the mean shade of a Joshua tree.

The joke was that Okada's code name was Joshua.

2

On St Valentine's Day Tom Okada hung in midair at midnight above the middle of Honshu. He had never felt so utterly alone; it was as if the whole universe were a vacuum and he, alive only on the air still in his lungs, were the only living thing in it. Already the sound of the aircraft that had dropped him had faded and above him the stars were dead white eyes that offered him no sympathy. Below him Japan was just a black hole hidden by cloud cover.

The feeling of being alone, at first not recognized, had begun as soon as Ken Minato had been allowed to escape; from then on Okada had realized there was no turning back, at least if shame was to be avoided. He had been surprised to find that he had a shame complex; that was a Japanese trait.

He had been sent to Corpus Christi Naval Air Base in Texas for, as Commander Embury sardonically described it, a crash course in parachuting. The instructors there had not been told why a Jap should be instructed in jumping; some of them had questioned Okada, but he, acting inscrutable, had told them he didn't know. They hadn't been inscrutable in showing their annoyance at this smiling, uppity Jap. He had made three jumps and been passed as satisfactory, though he himself felt far from satisfied with the situation.

He drifted down through the darkness, the air whispering along the cords of the parachute. He had little idea of what lay below him other than that it was mountainous country; there was the danger that he might land on the edge of a cliff, but it had been decided (by Embury and the others; he had been given no vote) that the danger would be greater if he landed in flat country where there would be villages or even troop concentrations. He began to sweat, wondering if he would be dead in the next few seconds.

'You're going to need luck,' Embury had said. 'But if you land safely, it should be a good omen for the rest of the mission. Do you believe in omens?'

'No,' said Okada, lying; lately he had begun to see everything as an omen, even a passing cloud.

Embury and Lieutenant Irvine had accompanied him to Saipan. Irvine had been of considerable help in assisting him to take on the character of a Saipan Japanese civilian. Okada had had to adjust his accent once again; thoroughly exposed to it now amongst the prisoners still held on the island, he had found

20

the Saipan civilians, the ones who had spent their life there, had a much coarser accent. Since he could not imitate it perfectly it was decided that, in the *persona* that was gradually being painted on him, he would have spent three years in Japan with his grandparents, folk who were now conveniently dead. He learned to say certain words and phrases the way the Saipanese did, the hint of local colour in the emerging portrait of Tamezo Okada, sawmill under-manager. It had been decided that he should keep his own name, the risk being taken that there were no records in Tokyo of all the civilians on Saipan. It comforted him to hold on to his name – an omen, if you liked.

'The thing to remember,' said Irvine, 'is that in a country as battered as Japan there is more confusion than suspicion. America is at war, but it isn't *in* the war – so forget all about how you felt at home. You'll be more at home in Japan—' He smiled as Okada looked at him quizzically. 'Well, you'll be less conspicuous, shall we say?'

But Okada had wondered if he would ever be at home in his father's homeland; he had certainly not been when he had been taken there as a child to stay with his grandparents. As a boy he had not come to terms with the Japanese mentality and now as a man he still felt uncomfortable with it.

Okada had been attached to a Marine battalion that had landed with the first invasion wave on the island of Saipan in the Marianas eight months ago. Like everyone else in the battalion he had been surprised at how, since World War I, the Japanese had colonized and developed the island. Besides the 30,000 soldiers on the island there were 25,000 civilians working in the sawmills, the sugar-cane fields and other light industries. Few military prisoners had been taken, but civilians had been captured in their hundreds and Okada had been kept busy as an interpreter. Then his battalion had been moved on, to the north of the island, picking their way through the countless, stinking corpses of the soldiers who had died for the Emperor in suicide attacks or by their own hand. Then, on the very northernmost tip of the island, he and the Marines had stood sickened and powerless as they had watched over 10,000 Japanese civilians take their own lives and those of their children. Babies had been

21

smashed against rocks, women and older children had been thrown from the high cliffs, men had hurled themselves, with long-drawn-out cries that would scar the aural memory of those who witnessed the scene; into the sea far below. The civilians had died because their Emperor had, at the last minute, promised them an equal place with soldiers in the after-life to which they all aspired. Hell was not for them, only for the Americans who saw them die.

'Jesus!' said the Marines and looked at Okada. 'What gets into you guys?'

Two days later Okada had been called back to the prison camps where there were still civilians, sensible though damned, waiting to be interrogated. Still haunted by what he had seen his father's countrymen do, he had tried for an explanation from those who had declined to die; but the survivors were struck dumb by shame, not at what the suicides had done but that they themselves had not followed the Emperor's call. He found himself in no man's land, shunned by the Japanese he was making fumbling attempts to help, suspected by the Americans as being sympathetic to the mass suicides.

In October he went with the first wave of the invasion force on to the island of Leyte, in the Philippines. A week after the landing, when a deep beachhead had been established, he was called back from a forward unit and told to report to headquarters.

'I got no idea what it's all about, corporal. All the order says is that you're being transferred. Permanently.'

He hadn't liked the sound of that. 'Can I protest, sir?'

'Corporal, I understand you've been protesting ever since Pearl Harbor. You must be the bitchingest soldier that's ever served in the US forces and I'd go back as far as the Revolutionary Army.'

Okada had smiled through his sweat. 'Just proving I'm an American, sir.'

Okada had been put on a plane and two days later, via Honolulu, he was put down in California, his home state which he hadn't seen in two long years.

'Welcome to San Diego,' said the Navy officer who looked as if he might have been starched inside his uniform. He was a good six inches taller than Okada, who was five feet nine, and he had a long nose that he appeared to use as a range-finder when looking down at men on a lower level of height and rank. 'I'm Lieutenant-Commander Reilly.'

Okada saluted, a sloppy effort due more to exhaustion than disrespect. 'I hope you can tell me why I'm here, sir. The Navy?' He looked around the base, as spick-and-span as an admiral's ribbons. This was the clean end of the war, the best end. 'Is there some sort of services merger going on?'

'God forbid,' said Reilly. 'Follow me.'

Okada, lugging his kitbag, followed the Navy officer across to a low building set aside from the main administration offices. He was conscious of being stared at by passing Navy personnel and he could read the question in their faces: who's the Jap bum, some prisoner they've brought back from the SWPA? Serves me right for looking like a bum, he thought. But then he hadn't expected to be dumped here in this naval base where even the lawns looked as if they were shaved daily.

Reilly led him into a room that, though spartan, was still far more comfortable than anything he had seen in the past two years. FDR smiled a toothy welcome to him from a photograph on the wall, but Okada ignored it. The President was not to know that he was no longer one of Okada's heroes.

'Sir, is this the usual accommodation for enlisted personnel in the Navy?'

'No, corporal, it's not. It's usually reserved for visiting officers – *certain* officers, that is. You will not leave it at any time, unless accompanied by a guard.' Reilly nodded at the mate second class of shore police who stood outside the door, all self-importance, muscle and gaiters. Okada hated police of any sort, service or civilian. 'You hear that, mate? If he wants to go to the head or the showers, someone goes with him every time. And he is not to communicate with anyone. *Anyone*, you understand?'

'Jesus!' said Okada.

Reilly looked at him. 'Are you a Christian?'

'Would it help?' Then he saw that Reilly had little sense of humour. 'Sorry, sir.'

Reilly gave him a look that, two years ago, Okada would have considered racist; but he no longer cared about such things. Not today, anyway; he was too exhausted. Reilly went away and Okada, letting his clothes lie where they fell, a most unnaval custom, went to bed and slept for twelve hours. If the war was over for him, he could have cared less.

Next morning, fed, shaved, showered and dressed in new tan drill, he presented himself, escorted by the SP detail, to Lieutenant-Commander Reilly. With the latter were two other officers, one American, the other British.

'Commander Embury. Lieutenant-Commander Irvine. You may sit down, corporal. For the moment there will be no formality.' It seemed to hurt Reilly to say it; his starch creaked as he tried to relax. 'Commander Embury will now take over.'

Embury was USN, but a reserve officer; the starch in him had never taken, or had been watered down. He had had a successful Oldsmobile dealership in Falmouth on Cape Cod; perhaps the Navy powers-that-be had decided that an auto salesman's shrewdness would be an asset in Intelligence. Not that he had a slick salesman's look, as if he'd only sold solid farm machinery. He was untidy, squat and ungainly, suggesting that he was shambling even when sitting down. He smoked a pipe that looked as if it might have been taken from one of the Indians who had greeted the Pilgrims and the tobacco he used smelled as if it were dried peat from the cranberry bogs on Cape Cod. Everything about him said he was a misfit, till one looked at his eyes. Okada had never seen such a coldly intelligent gaze.

Embury wasted no time: 'You speak Japanese fluently?'

'Yes, sir.'

'Read and write it?'

'Yes, sir. My father insisted that my sisters and I learn it. And I lived in Japan for two years with my grandparents.'

'We know that, corporal.'

'I thought you might, sir.' Okada was suddenly wary. 'Why am I here, sir?'

'You've worked with Detachment 101, of the OSS?'

'Just the once, sir, my first action. They were short of an interpreter and I was sent to Burma. I didn't volunteer, sir.'

24

Embury's gaze suddenly softened as he smiled. 'You didn't like it?'

'We were behind the enemy's lines for the whole of that month, just me and two other guys.'

'I thought Merrill's Marauders often worked behind Jap lines? Sorry, Japanese lines.'

Okada ignored the slip, wondering if it was deliberate. 'They did, sir. But usually in platoon strength, at least. It was pretty goddam lonely, just with those two OSS guys.'

'You may yet feel even more lonely.' But Embury didn't elaborate. Instead, he relit his pipe and went on: 'You have been under observation for quite some time, corporal. Not by us, but by Army Intelligence and before them the FBI. It was not your own record that caused suspicion, but your father's. As an anti-American Issei, he hasn't been trusted.'

Okada well knew that many of the Japan-born, the Issei, were strongly pro-American; but his father had never been, not even in the comfortable days before Pearl Harbor. He could not, however, leave his father undefended; to that extent, at least, he himself was Japanese. 'I don't think he'd go in for sabotage or anything like that, if that's what you mean.'

'Well, he is still under surveillance. Knowing the respect you Japanese, even the Nisei, the American-born ones, have for your elders—' Embury stopped for a moment to relight his pipe. The father of three bandit brats, he sighed inwardly for what the Orientals had achieved in family life. Then he went on: 'We couldn't be sure what influence he might have had on you. But your record with the Military Language School in Minnesota and then in the field with the Marauders and again with the Marines in the Pacific theatre – well, it showed you were prepared to prove you were at least one hundred per cent American.'

'At least that, sir.' Okada did not feel at ease, but he was not going to be humbly submissive to the Navy, USN or otherwise. He glanced at Lieutenant-Commander Irvine, RN, who surprised him by giving him a quiet smile. He wondered what the Englishman was doing here so far from any theatre where the British were operating, but he did his best to hide his curiosity.

25

While these three men were going to play the game close to their chests, he'd do the same.

Embury stood up and lumbered across to a narrow window, the only one, in the side wall of the office. Okada had noticed when he had come in that the room looked more like an interrogation cell than an office; there were no filing cabinets, just bare walls and a table and four chairs. Neither Embury nor the other two officers had offered any explanation of the room.

'This is a one-way window. We can see out, but those on the other side can only see a mirror. Take a look, corporal. Recognize anyone out there?'

Okada got up and moved to the window, curious and puzzled. All his life, being a Nisei, there had been times when he had felt off-balance; the supposed melting-pot that was America had thrown out Orientals like himself as non-absorbable. He was off-balance now, but not for racial reasons, and he felt cautious and, yes, a little afraid. He was being set up for something and he could only guess at what it might be. He fully expected to see his father sitting in the next room.

He looked through the window into a room as bare as the one in which he stood. One man, a Caucasian in Navy tans, sat at a table. The other, a Japanese in a checked shirt and grey flannel trousers, stood with his back against a wall, saying something to the Navy officer that was obviously defiant.

'Do you recognize the Japanese?' said Embury.

'He looks familiar, sort of.' Okada stared at the man in the next room; then he felt a stiffening of shock. 'It's Ken Minato!'

'Exactly. How long is it since you've seen him?'

'I don't know – six or seven years, I guess.' Okada looked in at the man who, when they were boys, had been his closest friend. But the friend was only dimly seen, as in a photograph that had been retouched and not for the better. A friendship soured does nothing for the objective view. 'It was in Japan, when I last went home with my father. 1937. He was in the Japanese Navy then. What's he doing here?'

'We'll come to that in a moment,' said Embury, dropping back to his game plan. But he did come out from behind the smokescreen of his pipe, leaning his head almost comically to

26

one side. 'Corporal, we'd like to send you back to Japan with Lieutenant Minato.'

'When?' Okada retreated behind his own smokescreen; Americans were always joking about Oriental inscrutability.

'Within the next three months.'

Okada forgot all about being inscrutable; he let out a cough of laughter. 'Commander, what sort of crap am I being fed? Did you bring me all the way from Saipan for something crazy like this?'

Embury looked at Reilly, who said, 'I told you he had a reputation for speaking his mind. It's all in his file.'

'No bad thing,' said Embury, and Reilly looked pained: Annapolis had never taught such heresy. That, of course, was a major problem of a war; one had to draw on the amateurs.

'Yes, corporal, we did bring you all this way for exactly that. We think the idea is worth exploring. All we have to do is convince you.'

'Fat chance.' Okada was openly rebellious now, American all the way. 'I'd like to be sent back to my outfit, sir. As far away from here as possible.'

'Sit down, corporal.' Embury resumed his own seat and after a moment Okada dropped into his chair. He eyed all three men like a trapped animal and he had the feeling that they were looking at him as animal trainers might have done. Clyde Beatty and his Japanese performing wild dog . . . Embury puffed on his pipe, which had now begun to look like a stage prop. 'Let me tell you about the man in the next room. You know some of it, but not all of it. He was born in Japan and brought here when he was a year old. He went back to Japan in 1929, the year of your first visit – he was then 13 years old. Unlike you, he stayed on – he *liked* the Japanese way of life. You didn't, we understand.'

'I hated it.'

'Well, Minato stayed on. He went to Echijima, the Naval Academy, then was posted to Naval Intelligence. He became a junior protégé of Admiral Tajiri, who was a senior member of the Navy General Staff. Minato's parents, his only relatives, were both killed in General Doolittle's air raid on Tokyo in March 1942.'

27

'My father would be upset to hear that. He was a close friend of Old Man Minato. Where did you take Ken prisoner?'

'Right here in the United States, at the Military Language School where you went. He's never been in action, except as a spy.'

Okada frowned. 'I find that hard to believe . . .'

The three officers waited for him to explain himself. Reilly fidgetted, but Embury and Irvine showed Oriental patience.

At last Okada said, 'Ken was a good guy, my best friend in junior high school. We fell out later, when I saw him on my second visit to Japan, that was in 1937, but it wasn't really serious. He just sounded like a younger version of his father. And my father too, I guess,' he added, and regretted at once that he had done so. He was still batting for his father, though the Old Man didn't deserve it.

'We understand the division between you and your father is very serious.'

'That came later,' said Okada abruptly. 'What about Minato?'

'He's been here in this country since March 1938. He came back here under the name Suzuki and enrolled as a student at Gonzaga University at Spokane in Washington State. He said he was a Catholic convert and they accepted him as such.'

'Why up there? Why didn't he come back to California?'

'We assume he didn't want to be recognized by you or any of the other Japanese he had gone to school with. Anyhow, within three months he had disappeared. He took on another identity, several in fact, and he's been here ever since. He's told us that he sent back to Tokyo enough information for the Japanese General Staff to know exactly the lay-out of all our West Coast shipyards, from Seattle down to here, San Diego, their capacity and our state of preparedness. Like the rest of you Japanese he was picked up at the time of the relocation order in February 1942 and he spent twelve months in a camp in Arizona. Then he volunteered for the Language School and was accepted – his idea, he's told us, was to get sent to the Pacific theatre as an interpreter. He'd pick up more information there and then at the first opportunity he'd sneak back through the Japanese lines. He made one mistake – he tried to tell his contacts here in the States what he intended doing and we intercepted the message. Or rather, Army Intelligence did. He's now volunteered to be turned around, as we say – to be sent back to Japan and spy for us. But we don't trust him, not entirely. In Intelligence we tend not to trust anyone. Though, of course, at the beginning of any game, that's all we can go on – trust. Right, gentlemen?'

The two gentlemen nodded, though Okada noticed that the Englishman smiled slightly, as if he thought trust were some sort of mild joke.

'You said you want me to go back to Japan. With Minato? Why would you trust me?'

'Why, indeed?' said Embury and relit his pipe once again. Okada was becoming irritated by the routine, then he wondered if it was some sort of punctuation to keep him off-balance. Neither Reilly nor Irvine seemed impatient with Embury's stop-go approach. 'We'll have to learn more about you, corporal, about your mental attitude. If you don't come up to scratch . . .'

Okada saw a small red light winking at him out of the future. 'If I don't come up to scratch, what happens to me? Am I going to be sent back to my outfit?'

Embury shook his head. 'No, we probably wouldn't let you go. We may have to keep you in protective custody for the rest of the war. In better conditions than those relocation camps you were sent to, of course.'

'Of course.' Okada sat up straighter. His athlete's body felt bruised, but it was really only his mind that was so. But this was still preferable to standing on the cliffs of Saipan, where his mind had almost suffered a knock-out blow. 'Go on, sir.'

'You're interested?'

'I'm interested, but that doesn't mean I'm volunteering for anything. If I'm going to be kept in protective custody for the rest of the war, you've got nothing to lose by telling me more. You'll have to tell me, if you want me to cooperate.'

Embury looked at Irvine. 'Do you have guys like this in the British services?'

29

'Occasionally. We exile them to the colonies or we send them out on commando raids and they become dead heroes.' Irvine smiled at Okada, like an angler who always landed *something* from troubled waters.

'I've heard of the British sense of humour, sir.'

'It helps us muddle through,' said Irvine, using a phrase that had become a British battle cry. Then he stopped smiling. 'I wish you would help us in this little venture, corporal. It could mean a great deal to both our countries, America and Britain.'

For some reason he couldn't fathom at the moment, Okada was suddenly receptive. Perhaps it was the friendliness in Irvine's manner; the Englishman, of course, had no authority to be as demanding as Embury or Reilly. But it was obvious that, for some reason or other, Irvine had a personal interest in the matter. He did not have the bored, indifferent look of a liaison officer.

Okada looked back at Embury. 'Tell me more, sir.'

Embury studied him for a moment through the smoke of his pipe. 'Okay, corporal. But the more I tell you, the more you're committed to going along with us . . . Admiral Tajiri was a leading member of the Strike-South faction in pre-war Japan. There were two factions – the Strike-South, the minority one, which had its eye on Southeast Asia and the Dutch East Indies, and the Strike-North faction, which thought it should prepare for an all-out war against communist Russia. Eventually the Strike-South lot won out. Admiral Tajiri knew the chances were high that America would come into the war if Japan struck south. So he set about preparing a spy ring. Minato was one of the first sent over here.'

'Have you picked up any of the others?'

'Several. They're all held in Federal prisons. None of them volunteered to be turned around. But Minato now loves our way of life, he's all for Mom and American apple pie and he thinks American democracy is the greatest system ever invented.'

'Really?' said Lieutenant-Commander Irvine, RN. Democracy was like original sin, anyone could lay claim to it.

30

Embury grinned at him, exposing teeth that looked as if they had been worn down by his pipe. 'I was quoting our friend next door, David. No offence . . . The trouble is, corporal, we think Minato's new-found love of America is just a bit too convenient. But we do believe that if we can smuggle him back to Tokyo, the risk is worthwhile. He may turn out to be very useful.'

'What if he feeds you false information? How will you know the difference?'

Embury nodded approvingly. 'You're sharp, corporal. You're right in step all the way, aren't you?'

'Let me say something, commander. I grew up in this country as a virtual outsider, no matter how much I loved Mom and apple pie and the American flag. You might almost say I was like a Jew in Nazi Germany. I *had* to be sharp to stay in step. You got no idea the number of times I stumbled, especially as a kid, and fell out of line. It was a question of survival – being sharp, I mean.'

Embury, Irvine and even Reilly looked suddenly sympathetic; as if, up till now, they had looked only in Caucasian mirrors. Reilly also looked disconcerted, as if he had not realized there had been another, earlier war going on.

'It'll be a question of survival in Japan,' said Embury. 'We won't try to hide that from you. You'll be our filter. Minato will give the information to you as his control and you'll assess it before passing it on. We hope to teach you how to assess that information before we send you off. Our main hope is that when we get Minato back into Japan, he'll go into Naval Intelligence on the staff of Admiral Tajiri. After six years in the field they're not going to waste his experience.'

'There's an awful lot of hope going on, sir. What hope do I have that I'll come out of this alive?'

'Oh, about fifty-fifty – we hope.'

Okada was surrounded by smiles. He felt suddenly angry; then he made himself relax. Getting angry with these men would get him nowhere; once again he was the outsider. Then his curiosity, if not yet his patriotism, began to get the better of him. There were drawbacks to having been trained as a lawyer; one enjoyed listening to argument.

31

'After I've assessed the information, how do I get it back to you? It seems to me that could be pretty hopeless, too.'

'David?' Embury looked at Irvine.

Irvine stood up, as if now that he had been invited to speak he had to stretch himself. He was about Okada's height, goodlooking but balding, with dark, and darkly amused, eyes; come Armageddon, he would treat it as the final, inevitable joke and accept it. He had what Okada, from meeting British officers in Burma, had come to know was a public school accent. British public schools, that is; Gardena High had never turned out an accent like Irvine's. He had the assurance of someone who would never feel an outsider, anywhere at all.

'I was in Tokyo before the war, as a junior naval attaché with the British embassy. We set up certain people as agents – we were working with our Secret Service, MI6. One of the agents was a man named Cairns. He was an authority on Oriental art, a professor at Tokyo University. He was very devoted to the Japanese in general, but not to their militarism, though he never said anything about that. He was highly regarded and he had access to a lot of top people. He was very valuable to us. He stayed on in Japan after war broke out in 1939 and even after Pearl Harbor – and the Japanese never suspected that he was an agent.'

Okada noticed that Irvine had not once used the word *spy*: the word was *agent*. Like most Americans of his time Okada knew little or nothing about spies and how they worked; he could remember seeing a couple of Alfred Hitchcock movies about British spies, but only one featuring an American. That had been *Above Suspicion*, which he had seen almost a year ago at the Language School: Joan Crawford had been an amateur, just as he would be if he agreed to go ahead with what was being suggested. He began to suspect that Irvine was the real professional in the room, at least in the field of espionage. He might be Royal Navy, but he was not just a sailor.

'Professor Cairns was interned. Not sent to a prison camp, but to a resort village about forty miles south of Tokyo. Friendly aliens, if they had the right connections, were kept in several places like that. Aliens who did not want to be repatri-

32

ated to their home countries or had no homelands to go to. Professor Cairns stayed on, ostensibly because he thought of Japan as his home – which he did. But he was also intent on continuing to work as an agent. He died in Nayora in May last year. Since then his wife has carried on in his place.'

'How? I mean how does she get in touch with you?'

'Cairns had a short-wave wireless somewhere in the village or nearby. Once a month, on a different day each month, his widow reports to a joint wireless station we run with the US Signal Corps in the Aleutians.'

'Why can't Mrs Cairns be Minato's – what did you call it? Control?'

'Yes, control. Two reasons. One, we're not entirely sure of Mrs Cairns. I met her in Tokyo, but she had only just married Professor Cairns and, as far as we know, she didn't know then that he was acting for us. Since his death she hasn't fed us any false information – again as far as we know. We have to go on trust there. If she is on our side, then we can't risk giving her away – I mean if Minato should doublecross us. You will, in effect, be the control for both of them.'

Okada gave his cough of laughter again. 'The meat in the sandwich, you mean.'

'Possibly,' said Irvine. 'I don't think any of us are trying to fool you about your chances.'

Okada had felt out of his depth ever since he had entered the room; he had tried to float with the current, but now he was being swirled around. 'You're lengthening the odds too much, sir. You haven't offered me one safe factor in this whole set-up.'

Embury took over again. 'That's true, corporal. Do you know of any safe factors in a war such as we're fighting now?'

'Yes, sir. Being posted to a base like this.'

'That's enough!' Reilly couldn't contain himself, rank or no rank.

Embury waved his pipe placatingly. 'It's okay, Roger. Corporal Okada is entitled to his opinion. I'm sure he feels the same way about the President being safe in the White House. The war is fought from many places.'

You son-of-a-bitch, thought Okada. He sat silent, putting on the mask he had inherited from his ancestors. At that moment, though he did not know it, he looked more Japanese than he ever had in his life before.

Okada sat staring at the one-way window in the wall. He was seated too low to be able to see into the next room. But Kenji Minato did not immediately interest him; the man next door was like himself, just a puppet in the game these men were playing. At last he said, 'I'd like to think about it. But first, one question. How did you pick me out for this – mission?'

'Your friend next door suggested you.'

So the course had been set and now he was on the last downward spiral of it; or at least of the first leg. He drifted through the cloud cover, which made him suddenly feel even more isolated; he was trapped in a nightmare. Panic grabbed at him, then let go; he dropped below the cloud into clear dark air. Japan rushed up at him out of the darkness; his stomach tightened and acid gushed up through his gullet and into his mouth. He caught a swift glimpse of pine trees that seemed to be jumping up at him like black sharks; the pale grey face of a precipice; and a snow-covered road that ran along the edge of the precipice. He jerked frantically on the cords of the parachute as he had been taught; but he was too inexperienced. It was luck, rather than skilful manoeuvring, that saved him. He sailed in above the cliff-face, hit a tree on the far side of the road, swung in hard against the tree-trunk and hung there twenty feet above the ground.

He was winded from hitting the tree and he felt sick from the acid in his mouth. But the overwhelming feeling was one of relief: he was alive. It was a good start: from now on he would have to learn to live by the hour.

He dropped the suitcase he carried, then awkwardly freed himself from the harness. He was wearing a flying-suit and flying-boots; he felt as cumbersome as a crippled bear. Somehow he got a foothold on the trunk of the tree and clambered up its branches to cut loose the tangled parachute. It took him another ten minutes to get the 'chute to the ground; it kept getting caught in the lower branches as he dropped it. At last he had it on the ground, folding it up so that it would serve as a sleeping-bag. Winter is no season for parachuting into enemy territory; but, he wryly told himself, war's calendar never waits for corporals. If he survived the war he hoped he might get retrospective promotion and back pay.

He dug a hole in the snow with a broken branch, wrapped himself in the 'chute and lay down. He took stock of himself: there was no point in taking stock of his surroundings, since he couldn't see any more than thirty yards in any direction. Behind him were the trees and in front of him, across the road, was a dark abyss. Black night, with the stars hidden by cloud, makes a joke of maps.

There was no turning back now: that was the first thing that had to be accepted. Agents dropped into Europe always had, dangerous though it might be, a landline to safety, to Switzerland or Spain or Sweden; it was Irvine who had pointed out the comparison. If he had to run he had virtually nowhere to run to but to continue circling within Japan itself. Rebellious as he had been, he had never practised philosophical resignation; but he had to practise it now. He was here to stay, probably till the end of the war. He shut out the thought that his own death might come first.

Abruptly he was exhausted; the tension of the last few days and hours caught up with him. He shivered with nerves; then the tension slipped out of him as if faucets had been opened in him. He lay back on the frozen ground and fell asleep. He stirred during the night with the cold, but better that than nightmares.

When he woke the clouds had gone and the sun was shining. He lay for a moment, wondering if his body was still alive: from the neck down he felt as if he was inhabiting an iron frame. Then, as if it had been waiting for him to wake, the sun began to warm him; he looked up into it and accepted it as another omen. At last he sat up, feeling like an old man; then got painfully to his feet, walked a few stiff paces and relieved himself. At least, he thought, I can piss like a young man.

He opened the suitcase. It contained a change of clothing, a faded blue kimono, a second pair of shoes, a cheap overcoat, and a battered cap: the wardrobe of a working man. There were also a thick wallet of yen notes, a package of sandwiches, a Japanese thermos of coffee, a map and a pair of Japanese binoculars he had picked up on Saipan. While he ate the sandwiches and drank the coffee, he studied the map, comparing its contours with what he could now see of the landscape.

The black abyss of last night on the other side of the road was now a valley; pine trees covered the upper half of the slopes like a green-black shawl, but the lower slopes were terraced. The snow-covered terraces were like giant steps of ice that caught the sun and flung it back up out of the valley in a white glare. A solitary peasant climbed like an ant up through the terraces; far below him stood two oxen, still as dark rocks. The valley was utterly silent and Okada, his mind straying for the moment, wondered where the war was.

When he had finished breakfast he took the parachute and the flying suit and boots further up into the timber. The ground was too hard to break, so he buried the 'chute, the flying gear and his map in the snow; by the time the snow melted he would be long gone and a long way away. Then he went back to the road, put on the overcoat and cap, hung the suitcase over his shoulder by a strap and set off down towards the valley floor. He had a rough idea where he now was, an hour or two's walk from the railroad that would take him to Tokyo.

By the time he reached the railroad line, following it north along the road that ran beside it, he had come down into the floor of the valley. He had passed through several hamlets and two large villages and no one had stopped him or, in most cases, even glanced at him. His apprehension, which had begun to rise as he had approached the first hamlet, had subsided; the people he had passed took him for one of themselves, he looked no different except that he was a little taller than most of them. Then he was coming into a town, larger than any of the villages he had passed through, and he began to feel apprehensive again. Here there would be police and military personnel; already he had been passed on the road by a dozen or more military vehicles, trucks and cars. He looked for a good omen, but saw none, so settled for some forced optimism, an American trait he had never shown at home.

The town was a light industrial one; evidently not an important one, because he saw no evidence of bomb damage. He walked through the factory area on the outskirts, aware more of the soldiers he saw than of the factories and other buildings he passed. There had to be a major military camp around here, but Embury and Irvine had given him no intelligence on that: he had to find his own hurdles and negotiate them. They were not interested in what happened to him before he got to Tokyo, only that he should survive and reach the city.

He saw very few private trucks or cars and those that were in the town had gas-bags or tanks fitted to their roofs or on the boots. He could not tell whether the people looked well-fed or hungry; as he remembered them, most Japanese had never run to plumpness. Very few were smiling or even relaxed-looking, but he could not remember if they had looked like that in 1929 or even 1937: boys of thirteen and even young men of twenty-one were not sociologically-minded in those days. The world was to be enjoyed, not studied, and the passing parade was only something that impeded one on the way to a movie or a ball-game or a date with a girl. Still, the people in this town, and even the soldiers he passed, did not have the buoyancy he had seen amongst the Americans on the bases at San Diego and Corpus Christi.

He had no firm idea where the railroad station was, but he knew it must be somewhere on his right. He turned a corner and two soldiers stood in his path. They were both young and had that arrogance that a uniform gives to some men, young and old.

'Where's the railroad station?' one of them demanded.

Each of them was shorter than Okada by at least five inches; they were twin dwarves of aggression, trying to intimidate him by horizontal merger. Though nervous, he wanted to laugh at them; but in Japan, the insult had less currency than in America. Especially so since this was enemy territory. He gestured down the street. 'I think it's down that way.'

'You don't know?' One of them was the spokesman; the

other, shorter one stood quiet. 'You're a civilian, you ought to know where your town's railroad station is.'

Why don't you hand me a white feather? Okada thought. 'I'm a farm worker from out of town. Someone has to grow the food to feed you soldiers.'

His tone was curter than it should have been; he would have to learn more courtesy. The spokesman looked at his companion, then back at Okada. 'You ought to have more respect for our uniform.'

Oh, come off it! Then again he realized he was not at home. 'I apologize. I was not disrespectful of your uniform.'

He bowed his head and went to step past the two soldiers. But the shorter of the two, the quiet one, stepped in front of him. He was thin and wizened and had a soul to match; though he did not admit to a soul. He had also been drinking, an indulgence that had kept him quiet up till now. He came out of a fog of *saké*. 'Someone as big and healthy as you should be wearing a uniform. Let the women and the old men work the farms.'

'There are no old men on our farm and my mother is too sick to work in the fields. The authorities decided I should stay and work the farm.'

Okada wanted to brush the two soldiers out of his way and escape towards the station. Passers-by were looking at them, though so far no crowd had gathered; Okada was grateful for Japanese politeness. Then he saw the two soldiers in helmets coming down the street, long sticks in their right hands; he could smell military police fifty yards away. He began to sweat and hoped it wasn't showing on his face.

He decided there was nothing to do but attack: 'Here come two military police. Perhaps you'd like to call them and have them arrest me? They'd appreciate a drunken soldier calling on them for help.'

The taller of the two soldiers looked over his shoulder, then grabbed his companion's arm and hustled him down the street. The half-drunken soldier snapped an obscenity at Okada, but allowed himself to be led away. Okada looked after them, pleased at how his attack had worked; then he turned to walk on and found the two military police coming towards him. One of them held up his stick to bar Okada's path.

'Were those two soldiers annoying you?' It was difficult to tell whether the man who had spoken, a corporal, was being courteous or sarcastic.

'They were just asking the way, corporal,' said Okada. 'They were not annoying me, not at all.'

'Where are you from? You have a different accent from the people around here.'

His own accent was middle class and Okada wondered if there was a different system for recruitment of Japanese military police. He decided now was as good a time as any to take the plunge. 'I am from Saipan. I escaped from there in September.'

'You ran away?' The corporal was as tall as Okada, met him eye to eye.

'Yes,' said Okada. 'I saw ten thousand die for the Emperor, but the Americans weren't impressed.'

It was a dangerous statement to make: he was still not thinking Japanese. But the corporal's expression didn't change. 'One doesn't die to impress the enemy. But maybe you Saipanese think differently. You may find it very difficult back here in the homeland.'

'I do,' said Okada with heartfelt emphasis.

Then the corporal unexpectedly smiled. 'You'll survive. How is the war going down there?'

You're losing it, just as you're losing it everywhere else. 'Not well. But all isn't lost yet.'

'Of course not.' But the corporal's smile suggested he might be thinking otherwise. He nodded to his partner and the two of them, acknowledging Okada's bow of the head with upraised sticks, moved on down the street. Okada, aware of the now not-so-polite stares of the passersby, moved quickly on his way towards the station, which he could now see at the end of the street.

He had cleared his first hurdle, but it was no more than a low brush fence in what might prove to be a marathon steeplechase, where the hurdles would get higher, would be topped with thorns and have deep ditches on the far side. He remembered a

Hearst Metrotone newsreel of the English Grand National and the frightening jumps that the horses had had to negotiate. The horses had had it easy.

When he got into the station he found it was crowded. A hospital train must have just come and gone; wounded soldiers lay on stretchers in neat rows like packing-house carcasses. Civilians would occasionally stop by one or two of the more conscious wounded and say a word, but no fuss was made; Okada could imagine the bright-smiled activity of Red Cross volunteers if these were American wounded coming home. He saw a few medics hovering near the men on the stretchers, but there did not appear to be any doctors. He had heard stories in the field of how Japanese doctors had neglected the wounded, as if the latter had shirked their duty as soldiers by getting in the way of a bullet or a piece of shrapnel.

He pushed his way through the crowd, joined a queue at the single ticket office. Twenty minutes passed before he reached the window. He asked for a ticket to Nayora.

'Where's your pass?' The clerk was old and tired and had a voice that sounded like a rusty-edged saw.

Okada had the quick wit not to say 'What pass?' He had seen the man in front of him push across a piece of paper, but he had thought it was some fare concession certificate. Now he realized that, for all their thoroughness in briefing him, Embury and the others had missed out on some small details; small but important. Okada decided to make use of his accent.

'I've just landed here. I'm from Saipan and Luzon. I came up on the same ship as those men along there.' He nodded towards the wounded beyond the line behind him. He had no idea where the soldiers had come from, but he took the risk that the ticket clerk also did not know. 'I still have to get all my papers.'

'Can't give a ticket without papers.' The clerk quickened the saw of his voice. 'Stand aside.'

Okada stood aside, feeling conspicuous; he glanced covertly around to see if there were any police nearby. He could see none, but he moved hastily away from the window before the clerk became too conscientious and started yelling for the arrest of a man trying to travel without a pass. Okada cursed San

Diego for its ignorance, but the cursing relieved neither his feelings nor the situation. He moved to the outskirts of the crowd, down towards one end of the platform.

He was standing there, debating his chances of crossing the tracks and trying to swing up into the train from the wrong side when it came in, when a voice beside him said, 'Want to buy a pass?'

He looked sideways at the man and had to choke the laugh in his chest. He *looked* like Joe Penner, or anyway a Japanese version; and though he had spoken in Japanese, he had exactly the same delivery as the comedian: 'Wanna buy a duck?' But this man would sell anything, the hustler at the world's railroad stations.

'Genuine or forged?' Okada said.

'Makes no difference. The old man in the ticket office wouldn't know – all he wants is a bit of paper.'

'How much?'

'Twenty yen.'

'You could sell me a girl for the night for that.' They had given him those sort of details, as if sex had a place in the price index.

'Of course. But she couldn't carry you to wherever you want to go.'

Okada looked around. No one was watching him and the hustler; then he saw the soldier on the nearest stretcher staring straight at him. For a moment he felt a sense of shame; then he put it out of his mind. He had no obligation to this soldier, the man had not been fighting for *him*. He took out a twenty-yen note and gave it to the hustler. The man, with a smile as forged as the pass, handed over a piece of paper.

'This had better work, or I'll come looking for you and break your neck.' Okada tried to sound menacing, but the hustler seemed unimpressed.

'Have a good journey,' he said, and went off with a bent-kneed walk that looked more like Groucho Marx's than Joe Penner's.

Okada looked at the pass; it looked genuine enough to be accepted. Then he turned back towards the line in front of the ticket office. As he passed the end of the stretcher line he looked down at the wounded soldier, who was still staring accusingly at him. He paused, wanting to say something to the man but unable to think of anything: scorn upset him, even that of an enemy. Then he saw that the soldier was beyond scorn or any other opinion: he was dead. Okada bent and gently closed the sightless eyes.

When he reached the ticket window again the old clerk barely looked at him as he presented the pass and asked for a ticket to Nayora. Maybe he knew the hustler and his black market in passes; or maybe he was just another very minor bureaucrat who would settle for any piece of paper so long as the system was not disrupted. He certainly was not looking for a spy travelling without the proper pass.

The train came in half an hour later. Okada caught it, stood in a crowded compartment and wondered if he would have any difficulty with Natasha Cairns when he made contact with her this evening. He felt exactly as he had as a boy and a young man: in his father's homeland but not at all at home.

3

'Every nation must be taught its proper place,' Chojiro Okada had said. 'If every country in the world were allowed its own sovereignty, there would be nothing but anarchy. Japan would not be at war with America if the Americans had only understood that.'

Tom had always been respectful in his arguments with his father; it was the only way the arguments could be continued. 'Dad, there's no natural hierarchy for nations—'

Chojiro Okada waved a hand of dismissal. He had a working man's hands, roughened and blunted by his early years in America, but they were capable of graceful movement. 'Of course there is. Why do you think the British and the French and the Dutch founded their empires?'

'I always thought it was for trade—'

'That was only part of it. They all three consider themselves superior to the people they colonized. They have no right to be in Asia. We Japanese are the superior ones in Asia, we are the ones who should be teaching the others their proper place.'

Chojiro Okada had been preaching the same doctrine to his son ever since the invasion of Manchuria in September 1931, when Tom had been fifteen years old. The boy, intent on his own small battles in high school, had listened politely but without interest. Chojiro had tried to tell him that his own private battles had been far worse. But one could never tell the young about the past, there was never any comparison in their eyes with the present, neither for good nor for ill.

'There's none so blind as the young,' he said.

'What?' Tsuchi, his wife, was busy cooking supper. She had become accustomed to his talking to himself, if only because she had forced him into the habit.

'Nothing.' Only a little less blind was a wife.

He walked out of the hut, pulling his hat down over his brow against the pale blue glare of the Wyoming sky. The mountain peak had the sharp outline of winter; much sharper than the peaks had been back home. When they had brought him and his family here to Blood Mountain relocation camp two years ago he had felt a bitter, masochistic joy at how the Americans had spun the wheel full circle to grind him under again. He had got out of the bus that had brought them from Green River, where they had been unloaded from the train that had brought them from California, and he had looked around at the wide landscape, thinking how little it seemed to have changed since he had first seen it forty-one years ago.

'Welcome back,' he had said sardonically, but he had said it to himself, a private joke that he knew was pointless to share with his family. None of them, not even Tsuchi, knew what he had endured here.

He had come to the United States from Nagasaki in 1901, when he was twenty-one years old. He was middle class, descendant of a long line of weapon makers who were more than artisans; the line could be traced back to one of the master swordsmiths of Tanega who were the first Japanese introduced to guns by Portuguese traders in the middle of the sixteenth

43

century. Okada guns and swords were bought and prized by army and naval officers; Chojiro had completed his apprenticeship when he got into trouble. He had never told his own family why he had left Japan: he had climbed into bed with his eldest brother's wife, something his brother's wife had liked but his brother hadn't. He had landed in San Francisco and, through one of the boarding-houses that also acted as employment agents, he had got one of the few jobs then available to Orientals: working on the railroad. He had worked for a year in Wyoming, never becoming accustomed to the vastness of the landscape; it had seemed to reduce himself in his own estimation, making him ridiculously small in any scheme of things. He had received poor pay, poor accommodation and poor food, had been abused day after day by the Irish foremen who, with the advent of the Chinese and Japanese labourers, had now moved up the social scale. It was the first time the Irish long upper lip had come close to being a patrician feature.

The day his contract ended he had left the railroad and gone down to Idaho to work on sugar-beet farms, where the pay was no better but where the farmers, Mormons who themselves knew a little about discrimination, treated him better than had the Irish foremen. Four years later, having saved a little money won at gambling, he had moved to Los Angeles. Since the Mafia and Bugsy Siegel had not yet arrived in California, there was little call for a gunsmith; men were shot dead occasionally, but a Colt .45 was usually sufficient for the deed and it could be bought on mail order. He drifted to Gardena, where there was a small Japanese community, and there he started a nursery, as much by chance as by choice. It had been a hard struggle for the first five years; then he had begun to prosper. He had dreamed of going home to Japan, but he was still in disgrace with the family and he would not return till his parents wrote him to come back. His brother had divorced his errant wife and taken another, but that hadn't altered his parents' opinion of Chojiro.

In 1914 he had married Tsuchi Yataba, a 'picture bride' he had chosen from a selection sent him by an agent. There had never been any love in the marriage, but there had been respect on both sides: it was enough for each of them. There had been

44

three children: Tamezo, born in 1916 after Tsuchi had had a miscarriage with her first pregnancy; then the two girls, Etsu and Masako, born two and three years later respectively. Their father never forgave them for calling themselves, Tom, Ettie and Madge when they started going to school and, despite their protests, he never called them anything but their Japanese names.

Ettie was now walking up the camp's main road towards him, picking her way carefully through the dust. The camp these days was half-empty and the camp authorities put in no more than was absolutely necessary to maintain the roads and huts. Earth was piled up against the walls of the huts as insulation against the bitter winds that blew down from the mountains in winter; they reminded him of the sod houses, built by the pioneer settlers, that he and some of the other railroad workers had lived in all those years ago. He regretted, more than he could tell them, that his wife and daughters had to live in such conditions. But it was not his fault: everything was to be blamed on the Americans.

'Another letter from Tom.' Ettie held up the letter, as she always did, though she knew her father, as he always did, would not ask what news it contained. But this time she did tell him: 'He is not in the fighting any more, he's safe somewhere. He said he can't say where, just that it was some sort of training school.'

Chojiro Okada said nothing, looking away from her.

'Dad—' Ettie was a pretty girl with a soft, sad voice that suggested she was ready to weep for the world; instead, she was an incurable optimist, an American trait her father found insufferable. 'I'm going to Chicago.'

'What for?'

'To work as a nurse. I'm tired of living here at Blood Mountain.'

Blood Mountain had been turned into a camp for incorrigibles, the 'disloyals' as they were called, those who had refused to take an oath of allegiance to the United States. Some of the women had been passed as trustworthy and were allowed to take jobs in nearby towns; Ettie worked for a dentist in Green

45

River and her sister Madge was a cook on a neighbouring ranch. They were looked upon as traitors by some of the more aggressive men in the camp, but they were never subjected to any abuse because of the respect in which Chojiro, a true patriot, was held.

'Madge is going with me.'

'You will not be allowed.'

'Permission has already been granted.'

'Not by me.'

Her voice was truly sad now. 'Dad, Madge and I are grown women. You don't try to understand that, just as you never tried to understand Tom's point of view—'

'Don't mention your brother.' He had stopped calling him *my son*. That implied some bond still existed between them, when there was none.

Ettie bowed her head. Whenever she was with her father, speaking in Japanese as he insisted, she automatically fell into certain Japanese gestures. 'Madge and I will be leaving in two days' time. We'd like to go with your blessing.'

He walked away from her, up towards the barbed wire that ran right round the camp. He was aware of the soldier, rifle slung over his shoulder, watching him from the nearest guard-tower, but he ignored him. There had been several escapes from the camp, including one attempt at a mass break-out; half a dozen of the escapers had been shot and all but three of the others had been recaptured. He had never himself attempted to escape, because he had known that his lot would not be improved: he would only have been at large in America. He was prepared to wait till the war was over, till Japan had won and he could go home again to the land of his ancestors. But lately he had been kept awake at night by doubts; if American propaganda could be believed the war was going badly for Japan. He was querulous with impotent rage at the gods. He had never been religious, but he had to blame someone other than the generals for the way things had gone. It did not occur to him to blame the Emperor.

In 1923, when his brother had died, Chojiro's parents had written to say he was forgiven and was no longer in disgrace. In

the late summer of that year he went home alone, leaving
Tsuchi and the children in Gardena. Getting off the ship in
Yokohama he went straight to a geisha house, determined to
plunge into old customs as soon as possible; if there were any
geishas in Gardena, he had never met any. He was still in the
house when the great earthquake of 1 September struck at just
over a minute before noon. He had been dressed and ready to
leave when the house suddenly fell down around him. He
survived, unhurt but for cuts and bruises, and for the next
seven days distinguished himself by his bravery and his devotion to the injured. Four hours after the earthquake struck, a
cyclone blew up, fanning the burning buildings and houses into
an inferno. Over 100,000 people died or were posted missing
and Chojiro would carry the memories of that week with him
forever. He was superstitious enough to wonder at first if it
meant some omen about his return to Japan.

But no: he went home to Nagasaki a hero. Both *Asahi* and
Mainichi ran stories on him and he went home to more than just
a prodigal son's welcome. From then on he had known he
would never be happy to die in America, that eventually he
would have to be laid to rest in the shadow of the hills outside
Nagasaki where he had grown up. He had gone back again in
1927, telling his father he would come home to stay when he had
made himself a rich man in America. He had become Wester-
nized to that extent: the prodigal son is even more welcome if he
brings home his own fatted calf. He had come to realize, though
reluctantly, that he lived better in America than his parents did
in Japan.

In 1929 he had returned to Japan once more, this time taking
Tamezo with him. The 13-year-old boy had not minded going;
after all, his best friend, Kenji Minato, was also going, with his
father. The two boys had been left with their respective grandparents; at the end of two years Tamezo had been glad to return
to America, but Kenji had stayed on, content to be thoroughly
Japanese. Chojiro had been bitterly disappointed and almost
uncomprehending when Tamezo, in his first fit of filial rebellion, told him how much he had hated Japan and everything
about it. He had taken Tamezo with him again in the summer of

47

1937, when Hideki and Mieko Minato had gone home to live in Japan for good. But the visit had not been a success. Tamezo had been politely respectful towards his grandparents, but adamant towards his father that Japan was not for him.

Tamezo had visited the Minatos in their new home in Tokyo and come away shocked. 'Ken's become one hundred per cent Japanese,' he told his father. 'Ken – he wouldn't let me call him that, like I used to. He insisted on Kenji—'

'As he should,' said Chojiro. 'You should take him as an example.'

'Dad, I don't want that sort of example. For Pete's sake, I just want to be an American – what's wrong with that?' As if to prove his point, Tamezo spoke in English. 'That's where we live, isn't it?'

'Only till the right time comes to leave,' said Chojiro in Japanese.

Over the next few years Chojiro talked of going home to Japan to stay. But, though he was not demonstrative, he loved his children and he came to realize that, if he and Tsuchi retired to Japan, Tamezo and his sisters would refuse to accompany them. They had become Americans, despite all his sometimes harsh discipline that was meant to make them Japanese.

He had welcomed the bombing of Pearl Harbor as if it were a blow for freedom. 'You will see now what Japan can teach the world. There are still too many barbarians masquerading as civilized people.'

'Hitler, for instance?' said Tamezo, now insisting on being called Tom.

'Germany is like Japan, it is entitled to its own sphere of influence. Do you think the barbarians we have in Washington are any better?'

They had argued, stiffly polite, with Tom choking on his anger at his father's attitude. Then the barbarians did start to emerge. Westbrook Pegler wrote in his column: 'The Japanese in California should be under armed guard to the last man and woman right now – and to hell with habeas corpus.' California's Attorney-General, Earl Warren, demonstrated that Justice could be as blind in one eye as any politician cared to make her.

The Western Defence commander, Lieutenant-General De-Witt, showed his stars as a racist; he took an overdose of patriotism, a bad thing for military men. There were no American-Japanese, as far as the bigots were concerned: they were Japs and nothing else, not even to be trusted as much as Germans. The Yellow Peril was peril indeed, and on 19 February 1942, President Roosevelt, one of Tom's heroes, signed Executive Order 9066, interning all Japanese from the West Coast.

'I told you so,' said Chojiro and packed his bags for the internment camp at Santa Anita racetrack, content to have been proven Japanese by the barbarians. Though they did not know it, he and his family were quartered in a horsestall that had once housed Phar Lap, an Australian national hero that had come to California and, according to Australian legend, been poisoned by the Americans. No one was safe from the barbarians, not even horses.

He had ignored Tamezo's vehement protests to the authorities at Santa Anita and then at Blood Mountain. It was shameful to have a son who so openly and loudly declared his allegiance to the American flag; so he went out of his way to shut America out of the family circle. In the camp he insisted that nothing but Japanese should be spoken amongst them. He had not taken part in any of the pro-Japanese demonstrations by the Issei and the Kibei, the Japan-educated Nisei, leaving that to the younger men; but he had sat in on the meetings that had planned the demonstrations. When a group of Kibei had attacked Tamezo, who had abused them for their treason to the land of their birth, he had turned his back and walked away, though it had hurt him more than he would ever confess, even to Tsuchi.

When in 1943 Tamezo had, after a number of applications, at last been accepted for army service, Chojiro had once more turned his back. This time he had moved out of the family hut and remained out of it till Tamezo had left for Camp Shelby, Mississippi. Once his son had gone he had joined all the demonstrations, as if he were fighting his own small private war. He had to wash away his shame in front of the other Issei.

'Okada-san—'

He came back from his reverie of the past, turned away from the barbed wire to see Yosuke Mazaki standing a few yards from him. 'I'm sorry, I was a long way away then— What is it?'

Mazaki was one of the Kibei, a young man whose fanaticism sometimes made even Chojiro uncomfortable. He was a hero who, fortunately, knew he would never be called upon to be heroic; such men are often more dangerous to their cause than to their enemies. Chojiro did not like him, but tolerated him.

'Okada-san, I've had a message. Kenji Minato has been held by American Naval Intelligence for the past six months down in San Diego.'

Chojiro Okada worked his lips up and down over his teeth, the only indication he ever showed that he was perturbed. As a young man he had been like his son, profligate with his emotions and the expression of them; but the years in America had taught him the dangers and non-profit in such indulgence. He had tried to look calm, but it was always the calm of a thinly frozen lake.

'What else did the message say?' He had no part in the espionage network that ran through the camps and through other channels of which he had no knowledge at all. But it had been he whom Kenji Minato had come to first.

Mazaki did not look at him directly, as if turning his face away from the steel of the wind. 'That he has now escaped.'

Chojiro Okada had been surprised when, two days after Pearl Harbor, Kenji Minato had phoned him. 'I should like to meet with you, Okada-san. But please do not mention me to your family, not even to Tamezo.'

He had driven all the way out to Santa Monica in the two-year-old Buick which he had to sell only three months later for two hundred dollars, the best offer he could get before he and his family were carted off to Santa Anita racetrack. The irony was that on that day of the enforced sale in Gardena there had been several vultures with German names.

He and Kenji Minato had walked up and down under the palm trees on the promenade. People looked at them suspiciously or, in the case of one man, accusingly. He was an elderly man, wearing a faded American Legion cap, and he stood at the promenade railing staring out to sea, towards Japan, then looking back at Okada and Minato as if expecting them to start signalling the invasion fleet just beyond the horizon of his dimly-sighted eyes.

'Why didn't you come to visit us?' Chojiro Okada had been circumspect in his greeting of the younger man, expressing no surprise. The war with Japan was only forty-eight hours old and already bricks had shattered the glasshouses in Gardena. Kenji Minato, wherever he had come from was not here just to pay his respects to his father's old friend.

'I had work to do. Seattle, San Francisco, San Diego. I very rarely came to Los Angeles.'

It was a moment or two before the significance of the three cities he had named besides Los Angeles sank in. 'You were attached to the US Navy?' Then he smiled at his own naivety; Minato mirrored his smile. Over by the railing the Legion veteran glared at them, then looked hurriedly out to sea again; he hated all Slant-Eyes, but especially ones who smiled as if the war was already won. Okada ignored the veteran of the war long gone; he nodded approvingly at the young man who was fighting the present war, albeit covertly. 'You started early.'

'Almost three years ago.'

'Why are you telling me this? Are you trying to recruit me? I'm too old for such a task, Kenji. In any case, I think it's too late.' He glanced across at the Legionnaire by the railing. 'They'll be watching us like hawks from now on.'

'Probably. But it wasn't you I wanted to recruit. I have to go back to Seattle. We need someone here in Los Angeles as a contact. Someone who can be trusted. Someone younger than you, Okada-san.'

Okada smiled again, bitterly this time. 'You're not thinking of Tamezo?'

'I was hoping . . . He won't be interned. He has a good reputation—'

'He is against *us*.' It shamed him to confess it to the younger man, the true Japanese. 'We argue . . . I wouldn't put it past him to betray you, Kenji.' They were speaking quietly, but in

English; there was no point in stirring up the natives too much. For the time being there was safety in appearing to be American. He wondered if the Mexicans down around Olvera Street would give up speaking Spanish for the duration. 'No, you could not trust Tamezo.'

Minato looked disappointed. 'I'm sorry about that. We were friends once – it would have been good to be working together . . . Do you know someone else?'

It had never occurred to him that he would be called upon to engage in such work. Spying (even the word was abhorrent) was for professionals. 'I can make enquiries—'

'Be discreet. Careful.' For the first time Minato showed some of the unease behind the relaxed exterior. Had bricks already been thrown at him?

'Of course. It will take a week or two.' He had immediately thought of two men he could approach. 'But I cannot help you myself. If ever Tamezo found out . . .'

'I understand,' said Minato and looked as if he did.

As they walked away the old Legionnaire hurled abuse after them, only grapeshot but it was a beginning. Chojiro Okada wondered if it were the veterans of the last war who always fired the first shot in the next. He would have to study more history.

Now Yosuke Mazaki was telling him that Kenji Minato had been arrested by US Navy Intelligence, though he had since escaped. 'Will he call on the network to help him?'

'Not here in the States. He is already in Mexico City, or was at last report.' Mazaki faced him, narrowing his eyes against the chilling wind. 'There is something else, Okada-san. Your son Tamezo Okada was also held by the Americans in San Diego. But he, too, has now disappeared.'

He felt a lift of hope; the war was lost but his son had been won over. 'You mean he has been working with Kenji Minato?'

'We don't think so, Okada-san. We think he is a spy, but for the Americans. The network will try to track him down. In the meantime it is informing Tokyo.'

TWO

I

Natasha Cairns had arrived in Japan by the most circuitous of routes, through the passions of randy forbears, her own ambitions and the love of a man she had come to love too late, after he was dead. Her mother Lily had been born in Harbin, the result of two roubles' worth of sex between a Chinese prostitute and a Russian soldier having a night off from the Russo-Japanese war of 1905. Lily Tolstoy, a surname she gave herself when she was fourteen, left Harbin on the same day that she left school. She went south to Shanghai, where she worked her way up various ladders and traders till she had established herself as one of Shanghai's better ladies of pleasure. Then she fell in love with one of her clients, an aberration that ladies of her profession should avoid at all costs; she married Henry Greenway, a manager for Jardine Matheson, and donned respectability, a gown that did not fit. She bore Henry a daughter, named her Natasha, gave her to the French nuns to educate and left for Saigon, still half in love with Henry but totally out of love with respectability and life on a Jardine Matheson manager's pay.

Natasha knew nothing of her mother's background; and those who did know it kept it from her. Henry did his meagre best to be a father to her; but expatriate Englishmen do not make good parents, especially of girls. Most of them were, at that time, afraid of females; to be responsible for one was too much. He would look at Natasha and see her mother and wonder, though he had genuinely loved Lily, what had ever possessed him to marry her. Of course, though he would not admit it to himself, he had married her because it had hurt him to share her with other men.

There was a great deal of her mother in Natasha; she had a

53

saint's name but the devil in her blood. Or so said the nuns, who knew more about the Blood of Christ than they did about the blood of young girls. It was they who had given her the saint's name, Therèse, one that Natasha never used. She already knew that the men she saw outside the convent walls weren't interested in saints.

In 1938, when she was sixteen, her father was killed. He was up-country, in Sikang, trying to sell Jardine Matheson goods to a warlord, when the warlord took a sudden dislike to Henry, Jardine Matheson, all things British or the goods themselves: the reason was never determined, but Henry was suddenly dead. He left Natasha a small inheritance, his cigarette card collection of English cricketers and a sense of loss that came as a surprise to her. Her true love for certain men, first her father and later Keith Cairns, was delayed. It was as if her absent mother had left behind the unspoken advice that nothing in her heart should ever be committed to men.

She ran away from the convent and went further south, to Hong Kong. She was already beautiful, her beauty apparent in the eyes of perhaps too many beholders; there was a certain coolness to her beauty, almost a remoteness which would suddenly be denied when she smiled. Men besieged her, and she recognized the pleasures of being a prize.

She did not become a prostitute, more a floating mistress: there is a difference of more than just price. In the middle class morality of the British colony, her mixed blood put a brand on her; even a girl with the blood of St Francis of Assisi and one of the better Sung princesses in her would have been looked upon as a half-caste. Though Natasha looked more Western than Eastern, there was a slant to her eyes, a tilt to her cheekbones and an ivory sheen to her skin that set her apart from the Roses and Daisies of Bournemouth, Scunthorpe and other respectable breeding grounds. She graced tea parties at Government House and receptions at the Repulse Bay Hotel, but she was never invited to dinner parties at private homes on the Peak. Then in March 1940 she met Keith Cairns when he came to Hong Kong for what was, supposedly, a conference on Oriental art. Only later did she learn that it was a conference of Intelligence agents.

Keith Cairns was that rare man, an academic with the proper flair for courting a woman. He was forty-two years old, roughly good-looking, had had no wives but a succession of mistresses and, at his first sight of Natasha, decided then was the time to settle down with a wife, one who would also be his mistress. He was a romantic, which was one reason he had become an agent for MI6, and though he did not sweep Natasha off her feet, since she was on her back beneath him when he asked her to marry him, he overwhelmed her with his passionate persistence. She married him for a variety of reasons: she liked him; she had a sudden, if fleeting, yearning for respectability; she knew that the war in Europe would soon spread to Asia. Keith Cairns told her that Japan would probably enter the war, but that he, and she, would be safe in Tokyo.

'Tokyo is my home,' he told her, 'even though I'm a Scot. I live there and I'll probably die there because, whatever the Japanese have done outside Japan, in their own country I find them honourable and admirable and I want to go on living amongst them.'

Later she would find that frame of mind at odds with his being a spy; but then she would also find him a mixture that, because of his early death, would always remain a puzzle to her. He was kind and cruel, romantic and hard-headed, daring and cautious; he was a mass of contradictions, which perhaps was why the Japanese, a nation of contradictions, liked him and he them. But he loved Natasha as none of her patrons ever had and eventually, but too late, she loved him. She took over from him as an MI6 agent as belated payment for what he had meant to her. Having no country of her own, she was neither friend of Britain nor enemy of Japan. She was, as Keith Cairns had been, a romantic, seduced by the thought of danger, trying to prove, without any hope that the proof would be made public, that life for her was more than bed, board and baubles. She was, in the most hazardous way, still looking for respectability.

'I got some extra fish on the black market,' said Yuri Suzuki, coming up from the village. 'But we are running out of money.'

She was a round little woman, a dumpling spiced with iron filings; Natasha had never discovered her age: she could have

55

been anything between forty and sixty. She had been Keith Cairns's housekeeper for five years when he had brought Natasha home; they had met like two wives over the still-warm body of a bigamist. But when Keith had died, Yuri had, as if there was no longer anything to fight over, abruptly changed her attitude; she had taken over as Natasha's surrogate mother. Short-tempered, ungracious, she nevertheless had a motherly instinct she could not deny: she had a need to take care of someone.

'I have nothing else to sell,' said Natasha.

She had already sold the jewelry that her admirers in Hong Kong had given her. She had always kept it hidden while Keith had been alive, not wanting to remind him blatantly of what she had been before she had met him. After his death she had brought it out and, piece by piece, had found buyers for it. Now all she and Yuri had to live on was the small pension that the university, with punctilious regard for its dead professor, still paid her. Keith had died after a bungled operation for appendicitis, a mundane death for an agent, and the university authorities had suffered a loss of face in that it was one of their own medical professors who had performed the fatal operation. The pension payment arrived each month like a penance.

'You should ask your friends to send money.'

Yuri knew of the short-wave radio hidden in the secret cellar of their house. She had never made any comment on Cairns-san's extracurricular work as a spy, as if it were just another bachelor's peccadillo, on a par with his drinking and his bringing home women who were no better than they should have been. When Natasha had taken over the broadcasting, Yuri had continued to make no comment, treating it as if it were the normal part of running a household. Natasha sometimes felt uneasy about her, but she had no alternative but to trust her.

'Yuri, how can they do that? Cable it to the General Post Office? One hundred pounds payable on the order of the British Government?'

'They should pay you for what you are doing,' said Yuri stubbornly. She was not thinking of the risk, but only of the actual work being done. 'Work should be paid for.'

'You sound like a trade unionist.' Natasha had learned from

Keith, a born Tory, of the blight one could find in Britain.

'What's that?' sniffed Yuri, and on the other side of the world Keir Hardie and company went on strike in their graves.

Then Natasha saw the local sergeant of police and a stout man in civilian clothes coming up the path towards them. Nayora was a private resort village that had been developed by a group of upper-middle-class professionals just before World War One: government officials, lawyers, doctors who did not want to have to mix in their holiday time with the rapidly expanding lower middle class. All the villas stood in what had once been carefully tended gardens; now, in the present war, one elderly gardener ran an arthritic-gaited race against galloping grass and exploding shrubs. Some of the old families still lived here, though they did not mix with the alien residents who had been foisted on them. Nayora had always been a law-abiding community and even with the advent of the aliens the authorities had seen no need to enlarge the village force of Sergeant Masuda and his rather dull-witted constable.

Sergeant Masuda, who had got where he was by being obsequious, almost contorted himself in his deference to the man he brought to the gate of Natasha's villa. 'Major Nagata is from Tokyo, a very important man. We are honoured that he should visit us.'

Nagata, who wrote bad poetry, saw all this as snow falling on Mount Fuji: praise, if taken with proper grace, can only make a man look better. He smiled at Natasha as if to make her feel she was properly honoured by his arrival. 'Mrs Cairns, forgive my manners. I should have warned you I was coming. But, unfortunately, in my profession warnings are often misunderstood. Or taken advantage of.'

'What is your profession, Major Nagata?'

'He is from the *kempei*,' said Sergeant Masuda, rolling his eyes as if he were introducing one of the Kuni-Tsu-Kami, the gods of the earth.

'It is difficult for the secret police to be secret when one is accompanied by a Greek chorus,' said Nagata. 'Go and arrest someone, sergeant. Leave me alone with Mrs Cairns.'

Masuda backed off with a bow that bent him double, then

went lolloping down the path with his peculiar loose-kneed gait. Nagata looked after him, then turned back to Natasha and Yuri.

'You may dismiss your servant.'

Yuri snorted, showing what she thought of the police, secret or otherwise, then, without a bow, she turned and marched up into the house. Nagata looked after her too.

'Does she give you any trouble?'

'If she does, I tolerate it.' Natasha felt far less comfortable than she sounded. 'What do you want, major?'

It suddenly struck her that, for all his fawning towards Nagata, Sergeant Masuda had taken a grave risk in identifying the secret policeman. The *kempei* was never spoken of openly; certainly not between an official and a woman like Natasha. The sergeant owed her nothing and she wondered why he had put himself at risk by warning her who Nagata was. Did *he* know about the radio set in the secret cellar?

'Do you have a pass to leave Nayora, Mrs Cairns?'

'Yes, a twelve-hour one, once a week. I report to Sergeant Masuda before I leave and when I return.'

'Where do you go to?'

'To Tokyo.'

'What do you do there?'

'Go shopping, mostly.'

'On the black market?' He smiled, to show he did not think it was a major crime. Though his teeth were not coated, they had a yellow tint, like an old man's.

'Of course.' She also smiled.

'Do you visit anyone? Friends?'

She thought of only Professor Kambe as a friend; the others had been friends of Keith's and still tolerated her, mainly because the men amongst them admired her beauty and some of them, she knew, had dreams that some day she might be their mistress. Her vanity was very clear-sighted, enabling her to see others' weaknesses as well as her own assets.

'Some people at the university.'

'Some who work for the government and the military?'

'They may.' She knew exactly who did; but she was certain

58

that Nagata also knew them. She had the sudden feeling that he knew all about her, that his questions were designed not to give him information but to trip her up. 'But you know, major, that men never discuss their work with women, especially women who are not their wives.'

'Did Professor Cairns ever discuss his work with you?'

'Never. He was Scottish – they are as bad as the Japanese. Do you discuss your work with your wife?' She was uneasy, but she had always believed that attack was the best form of defence. Especially if it was accompanied by what Keith used to call her whore's smile. In his cruel moments he could be as loving as a rugby forward, which he had once been.

'Hardly,' said Nagata, with a policeman's smile. Then, still showing his yellow teeth, like a bamboo blade, he said, 'Do you ever visit a woman called Eastern Pearl?'

Natasha frowned, wondering where this question was supposed to lead. 'Eastern Pearl? Is she a geisha or some sort of entertainer?'

'You might call her an entertainer. She is the mistress of one of our military leaders, General Imamaru. I thought you must have heard of her. People gossip about her.'

Natasha had indeed heard of the woman, but had paid no heed to the talk; Tokyo, she guessed, was like all capitals in wartime, full of mistresses. They were part of the fortunes, or misfortunes, of war, a compensation, for those who could afford them, for rationing and other inconveniences.

'I've heard of her vaguely. But my friends in Tokyo are not the sort who gossip.'

'Oh? I thought gossip was a major discipline amongst university people.'

'You never went to university, major?' Natasha had been well coached by Keith: she recognized the prejudice.

'Just once,' said Nagata. 'In Mukden. To arrest one of the professors.'

'I hope you got a good pass.' She knew she was being impolite, keeping this policeman out in the cold waste of the garden, but she could not bring herself to invite him into the house.

59

'I think so. The professor was executed.' Nagata was enjoying the company of this young woman, though he wished she would invite him into her house. He did not like standing out in the open; he suffered from agorophobia, the disease endemic to secret policemen. 'I believe you have Swedish papers, Mrs Cairns.'

The change of tack was too abrupt. Natasha felt that her eyes must have squinted, as if she had been slapped. 'Ye-es . . .'

'Your father was Swedish?'

Three months after he had brought her to Tokyo, Keith had come home one day with the papers. She had had none up till then other than a badly forged British passport given her by one of her benefactors in Hong Kong. She had queried Keith where he had got the papers and why she should be Swedish.

'Because before very long Japan is going to be in the war and if you and I are separated it will be best if you are a neutral.'

'But why should we be separated? If they send you back to England, why won't you take me with you?' For the first time she had wondered if England was like Hong Kong, where driftwood, no matter how beautiful, was not displayed in the best houses.

'I'll take you with me, darling heart – *if* they send me back—' It was another year before she had learned of his espionage work. 'In the meantime you had a Swedish father – a ship's captain—'

'Swedish? But I have black hair and brown eyes—'

Physical features Major Nagata now remarked upon: 'You don't look Swedish, Mrs Cairns.'

'My father came from the far north, Lapland.' Keith had told her to say that; she had no idea whether Laplanders were blond or brunette. 'Or so my mother said. I never knew him.'

'No, of course not.' Nagata was accustomed to liars; the secret police could be reduced by half if everyone told the truth. He did not resent the lying: he did not want to be put out of a job. He sighed contentedly, assured of a continuing supply of liars, including this charming one. 'Mrs Cairns, wc have made a few enquiries about Eastern Pearl. At one time she was married to an Englishman named Henry Greenway. We also have a file on you, courtesy of the Hong Kong police. They left so many things unattended to when we took over from them.' He made it sound as if the conquest and rape of Hong Kong had been a business merger. 'The file shows that your father was not a Swede. He was Henry Greenway and you were born in Shanghai, which was where Eastern Pearl married Mr Greenway and then left him.'

Natasha felt as if she were about to shatter into small pieces. She turned slowly, afraid that her legs would buckle under her, and went up the short wide steps to the verandah of the house. Beneath the steps she imagined she could see the small hole in the stone foundations through which she ran the aerial cable when she was broadcasting; everything was suddenly enlarged in her mind's eye, the hole a gaping tunnel into which Major Nagata was about to push her. She led Nagata into the house and into the drawing-room. She sat down, waited for Nagata to take off his overcoat and seat himself opposite her. It struck her, oddly, as if her mind were seeking distraction, that he was the first man to sit in that particular chair since Keith died.

'I've shocked you, haven't I, Mrs Cairns? What did that? Finding out that we know all about you?'

It had been partly that; she had never really thought about how efficient the secret police might be. But the major shock had been learning who her mother was. She had often thought of her mother, but her father had brusquely silenced any questions she had asked. He had let slip that her mother had deserted them both but he had told her no more than that. As she grew up she had dreamed of some day meeting her mother, who would be a rich beauty, perhaps a Mongolian princess who had run off with a Rumanian oil tycoon; the reunion would be tearful and happy and very profitable for herself, since she also dreamed of a rich life. Now the thought that she might be about to meet the woman who could be her mother had the chill of a dream that could prove to have gone all wrong. She was a tumble of curiosity, puzzlement and fear; but so far the thought of love hadn't entered her mind. She had always guarded against harbouring any love for a ghost.

'I suppose I should have realized that eventually you would

know all about me.' Sitting down, she felt a little stronger: there is great strength in the bum, Keith used to say. Sometimes she had thought a lot of his philosophy had come from a rugby scrum.

'Oh, we've known about you ever since Professor Cairns died.'

Natasha played for time. She called for Yuri to bring some *saké*, heard a grumpy response that told her the old woman would bring the drinks but in her own time. Natasha did not offer Nagata tea because that would have meant some ceremony and she was determined to keep his visit as short as possible.

She turned back to him. 'I know nothing about this woman Eastern Pearl.'

'Mrs Cairns, I am not suggesting you do. Madame Tolstoy knows nothing of you, I'm sure.'

'Madame Tolstoy?'

'It is the name she prefers to go by when she is with General Imamaru. It was down in Saigon, where he met her, that she was known as Eastern Pearl. Some people still use it about her in Tokyo. The gossipers, that is.'

'I've only heard the name Eastern Pearl, never Madame Tolstoy.'

'We must ask her if she has ever used Mrs Greenway.'

Yukio Nagata was an opportunist, a random spinner of webs. Not many babies are born to be secret policemen; he had been one of the very few. At school he had majored in intrigue; so devious was he that he was captain of the school before his fellow students realized how he had achieved it. Drafted into the army for his compulsory military training, he had spent more time studying the officers commanding him than on rudimentary military drill. When he was called back for service in Manchuria he had enough contacts to have himself placed in the secret police. If he had to fight a war, better to be out of range of the enemy. He had come to the conclusion that the present war was going so badly that Japan could not win it. So he had begun to gather evidence, most of it unrelated, that might stand him in good stead if and when the Americans came to claim victory.

'Are you suggesting, major, that I go and meet this – this Madame Tolstoy – and ask her if she is my mother?'

Round her the house creaked, as if it had shifted on its foundations; she felt that she had no foundations herself. The house was like her, a hybrid, part-European, part-Oriental. It had two storeys and had been built by a doctor who had lived in Germany for four years before World War One; there was a heaviness about it that made it look like a tugboat amongst the yacht-like villas that surrounded it. Inside, the furniture was heavy and dark; the beds were meant to accommodate Valkyries rather than doll-like geishas. Till Keith Cairns had been sent here for internment everything about the house had dwarfed everyone who had stayed in it. Still, Natasha had been fortunate to be able to keep the house for just herself and Yuri and not have other internees forced on her.

'I shouldn't want you to force yourself on this woman.' Nagata carefully arranged the creases in his trouser-legs. He usually wore uniform but today, calling on a beautiful woman, he had decided that his dark blue suit, bought at an English tailor's in Shanghai, would make him look less threatening and more presentable. Besides, he was not here on official business. 'I'd have thought you'd be curious to know about your mother.'

'She may not be my mother,' said Natasha, more stubborn against the prospect than against him.

'True. But I have seen her, Mrs Cairns – you haven't. I assure you there is a distinct resemblance between the two of you. She is a very beautiful woman. So are you.'

'Thank you.' His intimacy told her how confident he was. But then the *kempei* were perhaps always confident? 'No, I need time to think about it.'

'Of course.'

Yuri brought in the drinks, prompted more by curiosity than a desire to please. She looked at Natasha for some hint of what was going on, but Natasha was too preoccupied with her own thoughts to take any notice of her maid's curiosity. Yuri shuffled her feet for a moment, gave a loud sniff and went back into the house.

Nagata sipped his *saké*. 'It would be better, Mrs Cairns, if you didn't think about it too long. You could be very useful to me.'

'How?'

'If Madame Tolstoy is your mother – and I'm sure she is – if you could be reunited with her, there could be advantages for both of us. In return for any gossip you could pick up in your mother's circle, I can arrange that you have a pass to go into Tokyo any time you wish. That would help, wouldn't it? I mean if you want to buy a few things?'

Food had become very scarce in the past few months and the ration available in the village had been barely enough to ease Natasha's and Yuri's hunger. There was a general shortage of food throughout the country, but the alien internees had been the worst hit. Without the food they had managed to buy on the black market, Natasha and Yuri would have gone hungry more than half the time.

'I can't buy anything if I have no money, major.' She was stating a fact, not asking him for money.

He misunderstood her; or pretended to. He took a silk handkerchief from his pocket and opened it to show a heavy gold bracelet. Natasha recognized it at once; it had been given to her by a Chinese admirer in Hong Kong. She had sold it three months ago for three hundred yen, less than a third of its value.

'I'll continue to hold this as – shall we say, as collateral? I could have you arrested, Mrs Cairns, for dealing on the black market. I know every piece you've sold and what you got for it.'

'Everyone does it. I mean, buys on the black market.'

'Not everyone, Mrs Cairns, only those with spare cash. A lot of people commit murder, but it's still a crime. So is dealing on the black market, whether buying or selling. I don't want to see you in jail – you would be no use to me there. But if you just make yourself useful . . .'

'You want me to spy for you?' She suddenly wanted to laugh at the irony of what she was saying, but managed to restrain herself. All at once she no longer felt in any danger, Major Nagata was no longer threatening her.

'If you want to be melodramatic – yes.' He carefully wrapped the gold bracelet back in the handkerchief and put it away in his pocket. 'I'll see that you should not go hungry. Food for gossip.' He chuckled at his play on words and Natasha gave him the smile he expected. 'We'll meet once a week and you can tell me what you've heard. It should not be hard work for you. It may even be enjoyable, if your mother welcomes you. Life at General Imamaru's level is very comfortable, I'm told.'

Natasha had begun to feel a certain excitement at the prospect of meeting her mother after all these years; but she could not feel any enjoyment. She hesitated, then took the plunge, into the past as well as into the future: 'I'll work for you, Major Nagata. But I'll need money. I am penniless.'

Nagata smiled at her without smiling, then he took out his wallet and handed her a fifty-yen note. Years of corruption had taught him that his bank account had to have a debit as well as a credit side; he suffered the debit side because less went out than came in. He reached across and dropped the note into Natasha's lap, a further gesture of intimacy that told her exactly where she stood; or sat. She was his servant.

'We'll agree on the terms after your first month's work, Mrs Cairns. In the meantime that will be enough to be going on with. If your mother welcomes you to her bosom, I'm sure she will also welcome you to her table.'

He stood up, all at once became formal. He bowed, gave her a yellow smile, said goodbye. She escorted him out of the house and he went down the steps, walking with the light step of a man half his weight and one who had got what he had come for.

Yuri came out on the verandah. 'I was listening. He is a dangerous man. You should not encourage him.'

'It's not a question of encouraging him. Did you also hear what he said about my mother?'

'Yes.' Yuri was tough-minded, as one should be who wants to be a surrogate aunt. She tightened the sash of her brown work-kimono, making the action look as if she were tightening a noose round someone's neck. 'I had better come with you when you go to meet her. You will need my advice.'

She was a proprietary servant. She would have made a good trade union official. She went back into the house, leaving Natasha to contemplate the darkening day and, possibly, an

65

even more darkening future. The chrysanthemum bushes were like twisted balls of faggots. The maple tree beside the house was a many-armed crucifix. Out on the bay, on the leaden sea under the leaden sky, the fishing-boats, sails furled, looked like floating scarecrows in fields that no longer had crops. She felt utterly depressed, though not afraid.

She had never felt afraid of the future; living the life she had led, she had accepted there was only tomorrow to worry about. To think further, to next year, or the next ten, would have spoiled the present; even Keith's unexpected death had brought no fear of what might lie ahead. She could be afraid, terribly so, but the cause and its effect had to be immediate. She wore dreams like armour.

'Ah well,' she sighed, and folded the fifty-yen note Nagata had given her and put it in her pocket. At least she would be well fed if and when she went to meet her mother. She practised the word, but could hardly get her tongue round it: 'Mother . . . ?'

That night she made her monthly report to the US Signal Corps station in the Aleutians. She said she had nothing to report, but the station had a message for her. A man would soon be on his way to Japan and would contact her on arrival. His code name was Joshua. She took down the message, decoded it and sat wondering at how, on this otherwise ordinary day, the world was suddenly contracting.

2

'One should never waste one's time trying to impress those lower than oneself,' said Professor Kambe. 'One should only try to impress one's peers or above. That, as the commercial men say, is where the dividends are.'

Natasha had heard this sort of mock heresy at parties at the university, but she had not expected to hear it in a house as grand as General Imamaru's. The small group of men round the professor, however, raised their whisky glasses and laughed at his wisdom. One or two of them glanced at her to see how she had responded, but she kept her face blank and moved away to a safer distance; from the moment she had entered the general's mansion she had felt she was under intense scrutiny. Her beauty, her *different* beauty, was a handicap, like an ugly birthmark; she was an outsider, the one foreigner in the room. Except for Madame Tolstoy, who had greeted her politely and without surprise.

'We are pleased that Professor Kambe has brought you, Mrs Cairns. My friend, General Imamaru, is a great admirer of what your late husband did for Japanese art history. When Professor Kambe asked if he might bring you, the general was delighted.'

Natasha had been in a dilemma for several days before hitting on the idea of asking Professor Kambe if he would take her to a reception where she might meet Madame Tolstoy. She had shied away from the idea of going direct to Madame Tolstoy and introducing herself; the woman might just have refused to see her. Alternatively, if Madame Tolstoy had agreed to see her, there would have been no prior opportunity to study her and decide if she was a mother worth claiming. In the present circumstances there was as much decision in accepting a mother as deciding to be one, a sort of reverse pregnancy.

'Why do you want to meet her?' Professor Kambe was a widower, in his sixties and susceptible to pretty women. He had studied at Oxford and Heidelberg and had some Western attitudes; but he came of an aristocratic family and if anyone thought critically of him, they did not voice those thoughts. It was he who had brought Keith Cairns to Tokyo University and he had maintained an avuncular interest in Natasha since Keith's death. 'She is just another one of General Imamaru's fancy women.'

'I understand she is *the* one.'

'Well yes, I suppose so. She has lasted longer than most. But you still haven't told me why you want to meet her?' He looked at her reproachfully. Though he knew nothing of Natasha's background, he guessed that, since Keith Cairns had never mentioned it, it was not impeccable. 'I hope you are not looking for a model.'

Natasha tried to blush, but she had had difficulty doing that even as a child. 'Of course not, Kambe-san. It's just curiosity,

67

that's all. I have heard so much gossip about her . . .' Though she had never been disrespectful towards Kambe, she had never been able to practise the 'respect language': it always lay on her tongue like a mockery. So she spoke to him as she had always spoken to men, on their level but with just a hint of flattery when it was necessary. Though she knew that a woman's flattery always put her above the man. 'And she is like me, an outsider.'

He had smiled understandingly: like a true aristocrat he knew that most of the world was made up of outsiders. 'Tomorrow night then. General Imamaru is having a reception for a fellow general who has just come back from a glorious retreat somewhere in the Pacific.'

She was never sure whether to smile or not at Kambe's sardonic comments on the military; he came of a family that had supplied generals to the army for several centuries, but he seemed to have an academic's contempt of them; perhaps that was why he and Keith had always got on so well together. But she was not prepared to take the risk of sharing the joke.

Now, at the reception, she moved round the room towards where Madame Tolstoy was seated with two of the generals' wives. This was Natasha's first venture into Tokyo's high society and she was surprised at the lack of respect for the Palace's austerity policy. There was none of the depressingly drab dress one saw everywhere else; Professor Kambe had warned her that she did not need to look as if she were on her way to work in a coffin factory. Most of the women wore kimonos, but several of them, the younger ones, were in Western dress. Natasha had been careful about what she wore, choosing one of her more discreet dresses, a peach-coloured silk that threw colour up into her cheeks. She had come in by train from Nayora in the standard dress of baggy trousers and quilted jacket. She had brought the silk gown and her fur coat with her in a large cloth bag and changed at Professor Kambe's house.

Madame Tolstoy had also been discreet, though she had not been prepared to take discretion too far for fear of being disbelieved: she wore what could only be described as a missionary version of a *cheong-sam*. It was not too tight, the slit in the leg was not too high: even a priest would only have been aroused to venial sin.

Madame Tolstoy introduced her to the two women, one of whom was the wife of the general who had beaten a glorious retreat in the Pacific. She had the look of a woman who knew what a retreat, glorious or otherwise, was. The other woman, plump and pale as a thick rice ball in her kimono, was the wife of yet another general. Natasha felt like a novice camp follower.

'Mrs Cairns lives out at Nayora,' said Madame Tolstoy. 'She is so fortunate to be away from Tokyo. She is interned there.'

'How nice,' said the first general's wife and looked as if she wished she might beat a retreat to Nayora.

'I'd be just as happy here,' said the plump wife and looked around the large room where they sat. General Imamaru's mansion had been built for the general's father by a Japanese apostle of Frank Lloyd Wright's who had lost his nerve. Cohesiveness seemed to dribble away in corners; solidity and fragility confronted each other like figures in a Hall of Crazy Mirrors. The general had not improved the interior by furnishing it with what appeared to be a furniture album of his travels; some day it might be preserved as a museum of bad taste. The plump wife loved it. 'I don't know why you don't move in here, Madame Tolstoy.'

'One has to be discreet,' said Madame Tolstoy, and looked as coy as only a madame could. 'General Imamaru prefers me to live in the house across the garden.'

'Did you furnish the other house yourself?' said Natasha. 'I have heard you have beautiful taste.'

'People are so complimentary,' said Madame Tolstoy, and looked at her with benign suspicion.

'I should love to see it.' Natasha saw the other two women look at her with sudden cool disapproval. She knew she was being forward and disrespectful, but she was speaking to another outsider, not to them. Still, she backtracked, if only for Madame Tolstoy's sake: 'That is, if I should not be rudely intruding.'

She had spent the last half hour studying her alleged mother and had decided that she had to know more about her, even at the risk of – what? She had not even begun to contemplate her future with a newly-found mother. But she sensed now that Madame Tolstoy was puzzled and intrigued by her. Could it be that the mother in her had already recognized the daughter?

'Come to my house later,' said Madame Tolstoy. 'General Imamaru wants the ladies to retire early. He and the other gentlemen have matters to discuss.'

Natasha smiled her thanks, bowed to the three older women, though not as low as their position deserved, and moved away. She had never been able to bring herself to descend through the various bows of respect; a slight inclination of the head, more European than Oriental, was as far as she ever went. Though, if ever she met the Emperor, which was as unlikely as meeting God, she knew she would go right to the ground, even if only to save her neck. Having turned her back on the God the nuns had given her, she was still amazed at the reverence the Japanese gave to the Emperor.

She found a seat, a monstrous Victorian chair looted from a house in Hong Kong, and took note of the gathering; after all, she was supposed to be a spy, working for two bosses. She had never been to a reception as top-level as this, not even with Keith. Here were men who ran the country and the war. She recognized, from photos she had studied, Admiral Yonai, who was bigger than she had supposed and who seemed to be the life of the small group surrounding him; he was the Navy minister and had just been appointed assistant prime minister, but he looked as if he had no more worries than running a home for pensioned sailors. She saw others: Admiral Tajiri; the War minister General Sugiyama; Prince Mikasa, a brother of the Emperor: a bomb on this house tonight would be an exploding fuse that would blow out most of the power of Japan. She caught snatches of conversation from the various groups of men and was shocked at the frankness; defeats and retreats were being discussed here as they were never told to the public. She thrilled at the prospect of what she might hear and then pass on to the wireless operators in the Aleutians. But for this evening she had the more immediate, personal problem that had brought her here.

The groups of men began to break up and Professor Kambe came across to her. 'You have been a success, Natasha. All the men were most complimentary.'

'I did nothing but stand around.'

'It was enough. Military men, unless they are using them otherwise, like their women to stand around like regimental runners.'

Natasha glanced around nervously. 'One of these days, professor, the military men will stand you up against a wall and shoot you.'

'Possibly. Unless they are too busy avoiding being shot themselves by the Americans.'

'Are they all as pessimistic as that?'

But Professor Kambe wasn't going to stand himself up against the wall; he knew when enough was enough, especially in a general's own house. 'Don't worry your pretty head about it. Shall we go?'

'May I be excused, professor? Madame Tolstoy has asked me over to see her house.'

He gave her a quizzical look. 'Is that wise? You don't want the gossips painting you with the same brush they've used on her.'

'I shall be careful, Kambe-san.' She was grateful for his concern for her. With other men in other lands, she would have put a hand on his arm; but not here, not with so many in the room watching them. Such an intimacy would offend, though not Kambe himself. 'Thank you for bringing me.'

'Report to me tomorrow.' He was not a gossip, but he enjoyed hearing it. Like sex, it is one of the pleasures of all classes. 'And do be careful.'

How else could one be with a probable mother who was an almost total stranger? 'I shall be.'

A servant took her across the garden to Madame Tolstoy's house. The garden was large, one of the largest in the Koji-Machi district. Close to the Imperial Palace, which the Americans had evidently decided should not be bombed, General Imamaru's mansion and the smaller villa of his mistress were as intact as they had been since first built. Water trickled into pools, suggesting tranquillity; the white stones of the paths were raked each day so as not to offend the general's eye; a gardener worked here all day every day, as if flowers were an essential crop. But even as she walked through the garden, Natasha wondered if the general, from tonight's conversation, really believed it could all last.

Madame Tolstoy was waiting for her in the villa. The gossip about her taste was true: the rooms were an ideal marriage of comfort and formalism. Madame Tolstoy had learned from her travels, had done her own looting of ideas.

There was a man with her, Colonel Hayashi. Natasha had seen him at the reception, standing in the background, never intruding on any of the groups; she had assumed that he had been an aide to one of the generals. He was tall and muscular, a man who looked as if he would enjoy the physical side of life. But it would not be an extrovert enjoyment: his face would show nothing, even his eyes had a bony look.

'Colonel Hayashi has been admiring you all evening. He wanted to meet you.'

Dammit, surely she's not a procuress, too?

But if Colonel Hayashi had designs on her, he did not show them. In a soft yet harsh voice he said, 'Why haven't we seen you before, Mrs Cairns?'

'I am interned out at Nayora. I am allowed only one pass a week to come into Tokyo.' That was not true: she now had Major Nagata's promise of a pass any time she wished it. 'I usually spend the day with friends at the University.'

'We must see you more often at General Imamaru's.' He glanced at Madame Tolstoy, who tilted her head as if to say 'maybe'. Natasha wondered if he was Madame Tolstoy's lover; then she further wondered what General Imamaru would think of that. 'You are a close friend of Professor Kambe's, Mrs Cairns?'

She hedged on that one, suddenly wondering if he was one of Major Nagata's superiors from the *kempei*. But if he were he would not be wearing his present uniform; he was on the General Staff. 'The professor was a close friend of my husband.'

Hayashi nodded; not understandingly but more as if he

72

appreciated a shrewd noncommittal answer. He gazed steadily at her for a long moment, then abruptly picked up his cap from a nearby table and bowed to both women.

'I must be going,' he said and left, going out so quickly and without ceremony that he might have been alone when he had decided to leave.

Thrown off-balance by his abrupt departure, Natasha blurted out, 'Who is he?'

'A friend,' Madame Tolstoy had not even glanced at the door through which Colonel Hayashi had disappeared. She stood very still and composed, the straight lines of the *cheong-sam* seeming to accentuate her stillness. 'The point is, Mrs Cairns, who are you?'

It was a frontal attack and it made up Natasha's mind for her. All evening she had been wondering how she would approach Madame Tolstoy about their relationship. At every opportunity, when she had felt she herself was not being observed, she had looked closely at the other woman. She could see a resemblance to herself: they had been cut from the same fine but strong bone, their lips had the same fullness ('inviting kisses', Keith had said of hers), each had a trick of holding her head so that the curve of the neck was gracefully emphasized. Only the eyes were different: Madame Tolstoy's had more slant to them, they were darker and more calculating. Natasha did not think her own were calculating, but the last thing one ever did was look deeply into one's own eyes. Or at least she never had, and now she wondered if it had been cowardice, not wanting to see the truth.

'Madame Tolstoy, did you ever know a Mr Henry Greenway in Shanghai?'

It was as if they had collided, though the older woman did not move. But the impact was there in her face, the eyes were no longer calculating: they had had a calculated guess confirmed. Her lips thinned, then she nodded.

'You've been troubling me all evening. Yes, I knew Henry. You're his daughter.'

Natasha had had no experience of motherhood or mother love, but she had not expected an answer like *that*. As if

73

Madame Tolstoy, or Mrs Greenway, or whatever she had called herself in those days, had been no more than a vending machine, delivering a baby like those chocolate machines one found on railway stations. She laughed, though she did not feel in the least humoured.

'Yes, I'm his daughter. And yours too.'

It only struck Natasha later that, though neither of them wanted the relationship right then, neither of them denied it. Lily Tolstoy was capable of emotion, though for most of her life she had manufactured it as the occasion demanded. But she had never experienced an occasion like this, indeed had never even contemplated that it might arise. She had occasionally thought of the child she had abandoned, but never with a true mother's regret or grief. But now, if only for the moment, she felt what she had once felt, just as fleetingly, for Henry Greenway.

They had been speaking Japanese, though neither of them was really comfortable in the language. Now abruptly Lily said in Mandarin Chinese, 'Do you want some tea?'

'Not if we have to go through the ceremony,' Natasha replied in the same language. She was amused that her mother should have reverted to her native language, as if it was the tongue she had taught Natasha at her knee. Since Lily had deserted her when she was only three months old, it was hardly likely they had exchanged any intelligible words. 'Let's have it English style. As a gesture to Father.'

Lily's face had been almost masklike; but now she smiled. She liked ironic humour: she wore it as armour, to protect herself against some of the knights who had pursued her. She rang a bell for a servant. 'English tea it shall be. I believe I have a tin of Earl Grey somewhere.'

She led Natasha into a side room furnished with the proper austerity of a tasteful looter: some French elegance from a banker's home in Saigon. Only the walls were Japanese: Natasha, who had learned a little from Keith, recognized the two Sanraku prints. It was not a room for a warm reunion, and Natasha was glad.

'General Imamaru treats you well,' she said, looking about her.

'He is charming.' Never so much as when he was absent. Lily had early recognized the general's drawbacks, but he *was* a general and he had wealth. One, not even a high-class mistress, could not ask for everything. '*Mrs* Cairns? That means you were married?'

'My husband is dead. He worked with Professor Kambe. Father died too, you know. He was killed in 1938. A warlord up in Sikang shot him.'

'I'm sorry to hear that.' For a moment Lily was indeed sorry; not that she would miss Henry but that he should have died violently. He had never been a violent man. 'I liked Henry. I just should not have married him. If your husband is dead, what do you live on?'

'A small pension.' And, as of this week, an informer's pay from Major Nagata.

'You're very beautiful,' said Lily, and for a moment felt slightly queasy with a mother's pride. 'You could do better than that.'

Natasha had never thought of herself as a whore; consequently, she did not think of herself as a reformed whore. So she did not feel sanctimonious, a consequence of reform. 'Possibly – do you mind if I call you Mother?'

'I'd rather you didn't,' said Lily. 'I'd never get used to it. Call me Lily.'

Natasha didn't mind the rejection. She was still trying to sort out her feelings. She assumed she would have felt differently had her mother proved to be something like the romantic figure she had dreamed of; she might even have settled for one of the dull, motherly exiles from the Home Counties she had seen in Hong Kong. She could not, however, come to terms with the acceptance of Lily Tolstoy as her mother, though she knew now that it was a fact.

A servant, who must have had water boiling on call, brought in a silver tea service and exquisite bone-china cups and saucers: more loot. The tea was poured, without ceremony, and Lily offered a silver salver of Peek Frean's biscuits. Henry Greenway would have felt right at home in the family circle.

'I think I'd rather wait till the end of the war before I start

75

accepting any favours,' said Natasha. 'My late husband taught me to take the long view.'

'You think Japan will lose the war?' Lily sipped her tea, little finger raised: she was a good secondrate actress.

Natasha took a risk: after all, Lily was her mother. Besides, tomorrow Major Nagata would ask her what she had learned and she would have to give him something for his money. 'I listened to the men's conversation this evening. None of them sounded optimistic.'

'Natasha—' It was the first time she had called her by name; it suggested she was prepared to be a little more intimate. 'You probably have guessed what my life has been. Mistresses can never afford to take the long view. It is myopic for one to think one can.'

Natasha munched on a cream wafer; it was stale, but it tasted fresh and sweet to her after the years of wartime rations. 'So what will you do when the war ends? If Japan loses?'

'I still have my looks and my talents.' She had those, but no modesty. 'American generals, presumably, have mistresses.'

'Does General Imamaru know how you feel?' She sipped her tea, one part of her mind thinking of Keith. He had admired the Japanese style of living, but he had had a Scotsman's love of strong, sweet tea.

'Of course not.' Lily put down her cup and saucer and looked sternly at her daughter. 'I can understand that curiosity brought you to see me. But what had you in mind to follow? Blackmail?'

'Mother!' said Natasha mockingly. She felt suddenly at ease, deciding that she felt no love, not even repressed, for her mother. 'Of course not. As you say, it was curiosity . . .'

'Are you disappointed in me or not?'

'Ye-es,' Natasha said slowly; she had had her dreams for so long, if only intermittently. 'I used to picture you as a Mongolian princess who had run off with a Rumanian oil tycoon. Some day I was going to meet up with you on the French Riviera.'

Lily smiled. 'How flattering. I'm sorry I've disappointed you.'

Natasha put down her cup and saucer. 'I'd better be going. I have a long way to go, out to Nayora.'

For the first time Lily felt the situation was slippery. 'If we go on seeing each other . . .'

Natasha wasn't sure that that was what she wanted; but she had another role to play besides that of spurned daughter. She would never get another opportunity like this to move in the higher circles in Tokyo. She thought not of Major Nagata, but of Keith, who would have jumped at this same opportunity.

'Perhaps I could be your niece. Would General Imamaru believe that?'

'General Imamaru makes a pretence of believing anything I tell him.' She knew her men: she never believed anything they told *her*. 'I think he finds it easier, it leaves his mind free for problems of the war. The question is, will the women believe it?'

'The generals' wives I met this evening won't. They'd wonder why you didn't introduce me as your niece at once.'

'True. But if General Imamaru accepts you as my niece, then they will have to.' She had never bothered herself with respectable women's acceptance of her. 'Who is there to contradict us?'

No one but Major Nagata and the commandeered Hong Kong police files. 'As you say – who? Goodnight – Lily.'

'How are you getting back to Nayora?'

'By train. The last one goes at 10.30.'

'I can't have a niece of mine going all that way at night by train. A moment—'

Five minutes later Natasha was being driven back to Nayora in one of General Imamaru's two staff cars. The car had to go up a long curving driveway past General Imamaru's mansion to reach the gates. As it went past the wide steps leading up to the mansion she saw Colonel Hayashi coming down the steps with General Imamaru. Their heads were close together and Hayashi seemed to be doing the talking. She wondered if he was telling the general about her.

The driver, fortunately, was not talkative. He sat up front as isolated from her as he would have been had he been driving General Imamaru; she was glad that army drivers knew their place. She had him detour to Kambe's house, where without disturbing the professor, she collected the cloth bag containing her everyday clothes. She did not, however, change into them: that would be a too immediate drop from being Madame Tolstoy's 'niece'.

She lay back in the car, exhausted by emotion and the evening. Now, belatedly, she felt a deep disappointment at meeting Lily Tolstoy; she had really hoped for someone more like a mother. She was not disgusted at her mother's profession; she knew as well as anyone that in the Orient of the Twenties and Thirties any woman of mixed blood had to make her way as best she could; flexible morals only improved the opportunities. She was, however, deeply disappointed (not hurt: that would have implied some sudden love on her own part) that Lily had shown no affection for her at all. She was not a sprat, to deserve such a cold fish of a mother.

3

Tom Okada had had great difficulty in persuading the servant woman to allow him into the villa. To begin with, he was not accustomed to dealing with servants. The Okada household in Gardena, California, had had a cook and a woman who came in every day to do the chores; but he had never had to assert any authority over them and he had looked on them as part of the family. When he had graduated from his law studies at UCLA he had gone into the office of the nursery and run the business side for his father; the nursery by then had forty employees but it had always been his father who had given the orders. Faced this evening with a tiny servant, and a woman at that, as obdurate as a career army sergeant, he had felt for a while that he was fighting a losing battle. Then he had said, in a moment of inspiration, that he had been a student of Professor Cairns.

Yuri had eyed him suspiciously, but at least she had stopped shaking her head. 'Then why do you wish to see Mrs Cairns?'

'I have some information for her.'

Ever since the appearance of Major Nagata, Yuri had been

doubly wary. Was this good-looking young man also from the *kempei*?

'Where have you come from?'

'A long way.'

The distance had been nothing compared to distances in America; but he had had to change trains twice, waiting a long time in each case. Once he had had to walk six miles; the railroad tracks had been bombed out. As he had got further down out of the mountains he had seen more and more evidence of the American bombing; the war was being brought right home to the Japanese. He was tired and hungry and it was after dark before he reached Nayora.

'I haven't eaten since midday,' he said.

Yuri was torn between suspicion of the stranger and the thought of offending the ghost of Cairns-san, the one man she had come close to loving. At last she stood aside and gestured for the stranger to come into the villa. Later, she gave him supper, then went out on to the verandah to wait for Natasha's return, wrapping herself in two blankets against the cold. Once she crept into the house and saw the young man fast asleep on a couch. She decided that, in sleep at least, he looked honest.

Okada woke when he heard the car drive up; then he heard the voices out on the verandah. He had been exhausted when he had fallen asleep; he had had no more caution left than he had energy. If the woman servant had wanted to betray him, she could easily have done so; now, as he came awake, he knew he would have to be more careful in future. From now on trust might be an extravagant luxury.

He stood up, tensing as the door opened. When only the two women came in, he almost sighed with relief. There was only one lamp in the room, a small green-shaded table lamp in a corner; it threw enough illumination for him to see that the girl standing beside the servant woman was beautiful. Nobody in Intelligence at San Diego had told him what Mrs Cairns looked like; for some reason he had expected her to be older, tougher-looking, a woman whose mixed blood would have coarsened her looks. He had his own prejudices.

'Are you Mrs Cairns?' he said in Japanese.

'Yes. Who are you?' Natasha at once had guessed who he was, though she had not expected him so soon. She saw his questioning look at Yuri and she nodded reassuringly: 'I trust Yuri. I think you can too.'

'I'm Joshua. You should have been expecting me.' He still had one eye on the doorway, waiting for – soldiers? police? – to come bursting through. The day-long trip had been only prologue, from now on the real danger began.

'I have been.' She turned to Yuri. 'You may go to bed now, Yuri.'

'Will you be all right?' *With him*: she didn't say it but she nodded her head suspiciously at Okada.

'I'll call you if I'm not. Take a knife to bed with you.'

Yuri didn't think that was much of a joke; she snorted and backed out of the room, not respectfully but watchfully. Okada said, 'She doesn't trust me.'

'She's never trusted any man. Except my late husband.'

'They never mentioned her when they briefed me. They didn't tell me much about you.'

'What would they know about me, only that my husband had recommended me?' They were treading warily through the bramble-bush of suspicion and ignorance of each other. Natasha knew that she had not been able to send much information of value on her monthly radio transmissions; that feeling of inadequacy and the danger she was exposing herself to had weighed heavily on her. She welcomed someone who would share the burden with her, but she was not going to accept him blindly.

Okada, for his part, had been put off by Natasha's beauty. He was not averse to women and particularly beautiful women; but he had preferred them in the plural, taken singly only for a night or two and never with any commitment. But he would have to commit himself to this woman: it would be an affair, even if there was no romance to it. He was wary of her: a girl as beautiful and composed as this one must have received plenty of offers of commitment. She had a lot to sell besides secrets.

'They told me nothing about you,' she said. She had been

looking at him objectively, something she had always done ever since she had become aware of men. He was of medium height but tall for a Japanese, and muscular. He had a strong face, good-looking but for the dark suspicion in his eyes.

They had sat down opposite each other. The room, he had observed earlier, was furnished in Western style; which, for almost trivial reasons, made him for the moment feel more comfortable; he wanted to come back to Japan, to the style of living, a step at a time. Natasha, suddenly deciding the ice needed cracking, got up, went to a big ugly cabinet and came back with two drinks.

'Scotch whisky, the last of my husband's stock.' She took it for granted that he drank liquor; all the men she had known had been drinkers. 'Now tell me about you.'

But Embury and particularly Irvine had told him that an agent in the field should never know much about his or her control. 'I'm afraid you'll have to take me at face value. All I can tell you is that I'm a Nisei, a Japanese-American. For this mission –' he was still awkward with the jargon '– I'm supposed to have come from Saipan, where I was an under-manager at a sawmill. You'll report to me once a week – I may or may not have information for you to transmit. You'll be transmitting every week from now on, instead of monthly.'

'That increases the risk.' She didn't feel comfortable with the thought. Then, remembering Yuri's comment, she said, 'I'm not being paid for this.'

He caught the mercenary note in her voice. 'They didn't say anything about that. Was your husband paid?'

'I don't know. But with him it was different – he was a patriot.' She had never been sure that he was; he had seemed to have more love for Japan than for Scotland. 'It's very difficult trying to live without money.'

'You came home by car. Who paid for that?' The whisky, served without ice, hadn't broken any.

'It was a friend's.' She decided she wouldn't tell him about her mother, not yet.

'You're well dressed, too. A fur coat.' He had forgotten how cold an unheated house could be.

She put her glass down and said sharply, 'I don't have to answer to you like some servant.'

He had been studying her carefully. The male in him appreciated her looks; but he was unaccustomed to women of mixed blood. The Japanese he had known in California had been a tightly knit community; even amongst the whites he had known at school and university he could not remember any who had had any Negro or Oriental blood in them. He had grown up in a society that believed that any relationship between races had to be promiscuous and any child, especially a girl, born of that relationship would also be promiscuous. And being promiscuous, in that way of thinking, meant having less regard for other values. He would have to adapt to her and, tired as he was, that made him angry.

'You can raise the point with them in your next broadcast. I've got only enough to keep myself, till I get a job.'

'What are you going to do? Maybe I can help,' she said grudgingly. 'I have contacts at the university.'

He shook his head. 'No. If you were picked up and questioned, you would know where I could be found. It's better for both of us if you can't get in touch with me. I'll contact you each week.'

'You're not going to trust me, are you? What if I have something important to tell you in a hurry?'

He considered that, going over all the instructions Irvine, the experienced control, had given him. 'We'll settle on a mail drop, somewhere where you can leave a message for me. Or I can leave one for you, if I need you in a hurry. But we can't do that till I know my way around.'

'Will you stay around here?'

'No. It'll be easier to lose myself in Tokyo.' He could risk telling her that. He looked at his watch. 'I'm supposed to ask you a lot of questions, but I'm too tired. What time does the first train leave Nayora in the morning?'

'There's one comes through from Shizuoka at 7.15, if it's on time. They're not always on time these days, because of the bombings.'

'I'll get out of your house before daylight and go up to the station. I'll be in touch with you, where to meet me. Do you have a phone?'

'It was disconnected when we were interned.' She began to envy him. 'You seem to have had an easy war in America. Expecting the trains to run on time, telephones to work . . .'

He smiled, a tiny crack in the ice between them; she was quick to notice that with the smile his face changed, his eyes became livelier. 'Score one to you. Now may I get some sleep?'

She led him upstairs to one of the bedrooms, made up a bed for him and left him. 'I'll set an alarm to wake me at five,' she said. 'It's still dark then.'

'There's no need for that—'

'Yes, there is. You look worn out – if you're not wakened, you'll sleep right through to midday. Yuri will get up with me. She'll see that you have something to eat before you leave. It won't be an American breakfast, but it may be a long time before you have another one of those.' Then she said in English, 'Goodnight, Mr Joshua.'

'Goodnight,' he said in the same tongue. He took a risk, chipping away further at the ice: 'My name is Okada. Tamezo Okada.'

She smiled at him from the doorway. 'That could be a trap, speaking in English so carelessly. I think you are like me, Mr Okada. Not a very experienced spy.'

She closed the door, leaving him to sleep on that. He fell asleep wondering how long he would survive. He did not wonder about her: she looked a survivor, if ever he'd seen one.

4

Natasha lay in her own bed, wrapped in some wondering of her own. She had no doubt that Tamezo Okada was who he claimed to be; his arrival, however, had put sudden pressure on her, and, just as suddenly, she wondered if she could cope with it. Up till now she had been doing little more than playing at being a spy; keeping the transmitter oiled, as it were. From here on, if there was to be a transmission a week, it was obvious that the game was to be played seriously. She tried to think how Keith would have reacted; then knew he would have welcomed the pressure. But then he had been so much more experienced at the game than herself – or Tamezo Okada. She suddenly longed for the comfort of Keith's arms; but it was too late. She fell asleep, making love in her memory, which, like the real thing, is often disappointing.

In the morning she decided to tell Okada about Major Nagata but not about her mother: some relationships were, well, not *sacred* but suspicious. 'Major Nagata is working for himself more than for the *kempei*.'

'Jesus!' said Okada, thinking English so early in the morning. 'Does he suspect you're an agent for us?'

'I don't think so. But I have to report to him what I learned last night at General Imamaru's.'

Okada looked up from his plate of rice and cold fish. 'You were at a general's place? You move in high circles.'

'A friend of my husband's from the university took me. Professor Kambe.' She shook her head before he could ask the question: 'No, we are not lovers or anything like that. He's an old man.' Anyone over fifty was an old man to her; Keith had just escaped the description, dotage had been only four years away when he had died. 'He knows everyone in high circles, as you call it.'

'Have you been using him to get information?'

'The professor? No. Last night was the first time he'd taken me to a reception like that.'

He felt some excitement for the job now: with she and Minato both giving him information, the weekly transmission should raise some excitement back in San Diego, too. At the same time he realized that he would probably be transmitting no information of his own, that while Mrs Cairns and Minato moved in high circles, he'd be no more than the anonymous coach calling the signals. One hidden away in very low circles.

'Is Nagata having you watched?'

'I don't know. If he's working for himself, I shouldn't think so.'

'What makes you think he's working for himself?'

'Intuition.' She had done it for herself for so long.

He hadn't expected complications so soon. 'Well, we'll have to take a risk. We've got to meet at least once again, so that we can arrange the mail drop. The trouble is, you're conspicuous. Your looks, I mean.'

She was so accustomed to compliments that she took his remark as another one; and was surprised. 'Thank you.'

He looked at her blankly for a moment, then shook his head. 'I meant you're *different*. I'd pass in a crowd more easily than you would.'

She was rebuffed; but she saw his point. 'We'd better meet at night then. It will have to be an obvious place, till you get to know Tokyo better. Come to the university. There's a small garden next to the Art Department. There's no one in the Department now except some elderly gentlemen, like Professor Kambe, and they won't be there at night.'

They settled on a meeting at nine o'clock three nights hence. Then it was time for him to leave for the station. He held out his hand and she took it.

'Don't do that again,' she said, 'not in Japan. Good luck.'

He smiled, embarrassed at the small mistakes he was continuing to make. 'I hope we can work well together.'

This morning she liked him, despite his wariness of her. Though she didn't recognize it, she had the talent all good women spies should have: an ability to suffer men. 'I hope so, too.'

She let him out the side door of the house and he disappeared into the morning darkness.

Three hours later Major Nagata called on her again. His visit was prompted more by the desire to see her again as a woman than as one of his operatives. But she gave him a report on last night's reception at General Imamaru's and he was so pleased with it he was tempted to give her a bonus. But habit held him back: charity is not part of a secret policeman's make-up.

'And how was your mother?'

'Maternal,' she said and left it at that. After all, as a Japanese, he should appreciate there were some matters that were 'family'.

85

Three

It took Kenji Minato only five weeks to reach home. None of the contacts along the route wanted to hold him longer than was necessary. Those outside Japan and Germany knew how badly the war was going; they were planning escape routes of their own. Minato had managed to limp out of the desert to a dirt road where he had been picked up by a Mexican farmer who had charged him fifty dollars to drive him the two hundred miles to Hermosillo. It was almost as much as the farmer would earn in six months and he was not going to ask any questions of an enemy who was willing to pay so much. Mexico was officially at war with Japan, but not so the farmer.

Minato had gone on by bus to Mexico City and from there by plane to Caracas. There he had been put aboard a Swedish freighter that was bound for Lisbon. From the Portuguese capital he had been flown to Berne with a mixed bag of diplomats, couriers, businessmen and an exiled king's mistress going shopping in Zurich. There were two other Japanese on the flight, but they ignored him; he was not sure whether they knew who he was or whether they considered him socially inferior. He had been given a new wardrobe in Mexico City, but it was cheap and ill-fitting, as if spies on the run should not expect to be well-dressed. He longed to be back in naval uniform.

From Berne he travelled by no less than seven trains to Istanbul. On each leg of the journey he met other Japanese; these were more sociable, though none of them told him what their jobs were and he told them nothing of himself. But the number of Japanese travelling told him what he already knew, that the war was not going well. His fellow-travellers had a look of defeat about them.

He went all the way from Istanbul to Tokyo by plane, through Tashkent, Alma Ata: it was strange to see that the Russians were not yet at war with Japan. He stopped in Peking for two days when he had to wait for a seat on a plane, sleeping at the military airdrome and in his waking hours watching the military brass, none of them looking happy or victorious, trooping aboard the aircraft. He was closer to home than he had been in six years and suddenly he was more depressed than he had been in all that time. When he finally flew in over the huge bronze statue of Buddha at Kamakura and landed at Atsugi air base he felt it was more than just the end of a journey.

He was met by Lieutenants Sagawa and Nakasone. At the naval academy they had been close friends; but now they seemed like strangers. They bowed formally to him and he to them; then on an impulse he put out hands to both of them. They welcomed the intimacy, as if they had wanted proof that he had not changed. Did they know how one could be so insidiously corrupted in America?

'You must be glad to be back.' Haruo Sagawa hadn't changed, Minato decided. He still looked as he always had, a man so afraid of being thought vulgar that he had gone to the other extreme, primness. He had a round soft face and a mouth that was continually pursed. He still sounded as if he were preaching: 'There is no place like one's own country.'

What did I ever see in him? Minato wondered; and looked at Mikio Nakasone for relief. He was not disappointed: Nakasone was a jester, he would find a joke in any disaster.

'That's why the Christians are always aspiring to Heaven,' he said, his thin face widening with his smile. 'Unfortunately, I hear it's full of Americans.'

'That's what they claim. Unfortunately for them, God is an Englishman. Or so the English claim.'

The small jokes eased him; he felt better able to cope. But he was distressed at the bomb damage he saw on the drive into Tokyo. He made no comment, however, and his two friends said nothing. The fact that they did say nothing seemed to him a comment in itself and he sensed a feeling of shame in both of them. He wondered if Admiral Tajiri would be more forthcoming when he met him tomorrow.

'Admiral Tajiri is looking forward to greeting you,' said Sagawa, as if reading his thoughts. 'We work for him now in Intelligence. You'll be joining us.'

Minato felt a pang. Tomorrow he would have to reassume the burden of 'on', the sense of obligation that ruled an honourable man's life, something he hadn't felt obliged to do in six years. All at once he envied Tom Okada, wherever he was, who had always avoided such a load.

Nonetheless he slept well that night. In the morning he dressed in naval blues, looked at himself in a mirror and felt a surge of the old pride. Clothes made the man; or at least propped him up. He went to see Admiral Tajiri in better spirits than he had expected.

'Where are you staying?' the admiral asked him.

'For the moment I am at the Staff College, sir. I am to tell them everything I have learned in the past six years.'

'Don't rack your memory, lieutenant. Over there they accept fairy stories as the truth.'

Minato was shocked, but managed to hide it. Admiral Tajiri had always been frank in his opinions, an attitude that had endeared him to the young staff officers, but now he sounded careless. He certainly looked much older than Minato had expected; and pained, as if he suffered from wounds that did not show. He was short, bony and bald, the last of a long line of aristocrats in which the sperm had begun to turn to piss. He had no illusions, which was one of the few aristocratic traits he still had left. He squinted through his horn-rimmed glasses, an owl who had gone to sea and found little company amongst the seagulls.

He looked out the windows of his office in the Navy building across the square outside the main south gate of the Imperial Palace. He appeared to forget that Minato was still in the room with him and the younger man started to feel uncomfortable. Was the old man turning senile?

But then Tajiri looked back at him, eyes bright and shrewd behind his glasses. 'Did America change you, lieutenant?'

88

He decided to take a risk; he owed his mentor some honesty. 'Yes, sir.'

'For better or worse?'

Then all at once he was cautious again; he did not want to be banished to some remote, dull post. 'That's difficult to say, sir. I've been away too long to make a quick comparison.'

Tajiri smiled at him with crafty approval. 'A very circumspect answer, lieutenant. I'm sure you gave nothing away to the Americans while you were their prisoner.'

'Nothing at all, sir.'

Tajiri said nothing, appraising him as if he were some sort of report standing there to be read and assessed. At last he nodded and looked sad, as if he were sentencing Minato rather than offering him a plum post. 'You will join my staff. I have two personal aides, you will be the third.' Bound to a desk for too long, he had become a bureaucrat; if one couldn't conquer large empires, one built small ones. He had the honesty to smile at his own indulgences. 'We'll find something for you to do. If only to tell me all about America.'

Minato saluted and bowed his way out of the office. The admiral's – cynicism? resignation? Being young, he was still puzzled by old men's moods – the admiral's attitude had shocked him. He knew that Tajiri had never been an idealist nor a jingoist; he was too pragmatically minded for such fancies. But now the admiral sounded dangerously careless and Minato wondered if it would be safe to attach himself to Tajiri's staff; Sagawa and Nakasone had told him last night, bringing him up to date, of how frequently the cabinet ministers, generals and admirals were being changed. Yet Admiral Tajiri's attitude might put him amongst the Peace Faction, if there was such a group. Minato decided to take the risk and stay with his old mentor.

Just before he had been allowed to escape Commander Embury had told him the main point of his mission. 'There is a certain body of top men in Japan called the Peace Faction. We don't know who runs it and as far as we can gather it's a top secret group linked somehow to the Imperial Palace. Professor Cairns got a whisper of it just before he died, but he wasn't able to give us any information on it. But if it's really a peace movement, if Japan is starting to crumble at the top of the heap, maybe we can use it and bring us to the end of the war that much quicker. There have been peace feelers through Japanese emissaries in Switzerland, but they always break down. We want to know who runs the Peace Faction and if we can feed them enough ammunition for them to take over. They may even want to overthrow the Emperor. It's your job to find if the Peace Faction is a real force.'

Sagawa and Nakasone met him in the corridor and took him down to a large room where he was introduced to half a dozen other junior officers. These all knew where he had been and what he had been; they looked at him with the respect due a hero. Evidently Embury and his colleagues had done their job well; the publicity about his escape had, by various leaps, reached all the way here to the Navy building in Tokyo. After six years of anonymity Minato felt his new identity as a hero going to his head. He wanted to strut, but hobbled himself just in time.

'You must tell us all about America,' said Nakasone. 'What are the girls like? I saw some Andy Hardy films that were captured in the Philippines. All the girls looked and sounded like wound-up dolls.'

Minato had heard the same remark from Americans about Japanese girls. 'They *smell* differently. All that meat they eat—'

He was aware that a sudden silence had fallen on the group about him. He was the tallest of them and he looked over their heads and saw the army colonel standing in the doorway looking at him in the same way as Admiral Tajiri had, as a report to be studied. But this man would not read him with sympathy.

'You are Lieutenant Minato?'

Minato snapped to attention. 'Yes, sir.'

The colonel studied him a moment longer, nodded, said, 'Well, we know where you can be found', and was gone.

Minato looked at Sagawa and Nakasone. 'Who was that?'

'Colonel Hayashi,' Nakasone shrugged. 'Nobody knows anything about him, at least not at our level. He is some sort of liaison officer for the Imperial Household. He comes and goes as he pleases.'

'But why should he be interested in me?'

'You should be pleased,' said Sagawa; but Minato remembered that he had always aspired to be noticed by anyone of superior rank. He sounded envious as he said, 'Especially as you have been out of the picture for so long.'

But Minato did not want to be noticed by strangers, not so soon. He had been out of the Tokyo picture so long he had no idea of the size and weight of the frame that surrounded it. He knew something that, in his weeks of interrogation at the hands of Naval Intelligence in San Diego, he had realized the Americans had never guessed: that within the broad frame of who ran Japan there were smaller pictures of the true leaders. They were like the hidden portraits in the picture-puzzles one saw in the Sunday comics and he had never solved the puzzle. But the power-brokers were hidden there and, if the Peace Faction existed and had any strength at all, some of them must belong to it. Though he did not inflate his own importance, Minato guessed that any group interested in peace would want to question him about the mood of Americans in general. He began to wonder if that was why Colonel Hayashi was interested in him.

Two days later he received a phone call from Tamezo Okada. 'How did you know where to find me?' he said, hoping his own guarded tone would warn Okada to be equally guarded.

'Lieutenant Minato, this is the payroll division. We know where everyone can be found if they wish to be paid.' Suddenly he could imagine Okada smiling to himself at the other end of the phone. He smiled to himself, remembering how as boys they had tried to trick the school system at Gardena High. 'Is your parents' address still the same?'

'Yes.' He had given his parents' address as the spot where he and Okada should meet for the first time. Though the whole district may have disappeared beneath the bombing, it was still an address that could be found on a prewar map. He did not look forward to visiting his parents' deathplace, but both he and Okada had yet to learn their way about Tokyo again.

'Tomorrow evening at 8.30 then,' said Okada and hung up.

It was like a voice from the past, but measured in distance rather than time.

2

Okada had had less difficulty than he had expected in settling in. He had checked into a cheap hotel just east of the Sumida River in the Koto-ku district; it was a poor, crowded neighbourhood where a young civilian would be less likely to be questioned. He had been told by Lieutenant Irvine, the student of war, that the main concern of the poor in any war was their own survival.

He had asked the night clerk where he might find a job. 'I don't want to go to the employment office. They might send me anywhere.'

The clerk, an old man with one eye blank and the other rheumy with age and disillusion, nodded sagely. 'I don't blame you. Look after yourself in these times, I say. You're a strong young fellow. Why don't you try the docks? You'll have to see one of the *yakuza*, but they'll look after you.'

Okada had read how the Anastasia family and others had run the New York and New Jersey docks before the war; he had not imagined that gangsters would also run the Tokyo and Yokohama docks. He went down to the waterfront the following day, remarking bombed-out warehouses and wondering if he was looking for work in a prime target area for the American bombers. Then he told himself, even if it was no comfort, that if he chose a safe area there would be an equal risk of making himself conspicuous.

He asked directions of workers on the docks. Nobody mentioned anything about the *yakuza*; but the man he eventually reported to would have been ideally cast as a villain in a Japanese version of any James Cagney movie. He was as tall as Okada but burlier, had a broken nose and a voice that seemed to come up through a broken windpipe. The backs of his hands and fingers were totally covered with tattoos; when he clenched and unclenched his hands small dragons glared at Okada. Properly fused, he would be a bomb in himself.

'There is a contribution each week,' he said. 'To the war chest.'

Okada looked at the war chest, all forty-eight inches of it, and wondered if it, too, was tattooed. 'Naturally. I'm a patriot.'

'What accent is that?'

'I'm from Saipan.'

That seemed to satisfy the thug's curiosity; he asked no more questions. 'Start first shift in the morning.'

Okada worked from seven in the morning till seven in the evening, loading military equipment and supplies going out to the Philippines, food and timber coming in from China. Sometimes hospital ships, diverted from Yokosuka, the naval base further down the bay, berthed at the docks. But the civilian dockers were kept away from the ships till all the wounded had been taken away.

'They don't want us to know how bad things are,' one of the dockers told Okada.

On the night of his third day he had his second meeting with Natasha Cairns. He went out to the university and soon found the building that housed the Art Department. Natasha was waiting for him in the small garden beside it. The night was cold and she wore the fur coat and a fur hat. Scudding clouds kept darkening the moon, but beside her he felt shabby in his work-clothes and his cheap overcoat. He had come to the meeting wanting to impress her, as if they were on a date.

'It's too cold out here,' he said.

He let her lead the way in through a side door of the Arts building. She seemed to know her way around, taking him down a dark narrow corridor into a back room.

'This is a cleaners' storeroom. We can't risk a light.'

It was cold in the storeroom but not as chilly as it had been out in the garden. He hoped she was warm in her fur coat and he wondered why, if money was so short, she hadn't sold it. He was on the defensive again already, finding fault with her. She was even wearing perfume, dammit.

93

'You smell nice.' They were speaking Japanese, but not formally.

She guessed he was being sarcastic, but she didn't let it worry her. He was Japanese-American and he seemed to have the worst attributes of the men of both nationalities; or maybe he just had the arrogance of all men, or at least of those she had known. She might ask her mother about men some time.

'Chanel No. 5, my last bottle. I'm going to a reception tonight with Professor Kambe at the German embassy. Have you found a place to live?'

'Yes, and I have a job.' But he told her no more than that, though in the moonlight coming through the blindless window he saw her smile. He relented, because he knew he could not go on stiff-arming her like this. 'I'm sorry. But really, the less you know about me, the better.'

'How long are you going to be here? Are we going to go on being strangers for a year, a couple of years?' She wasn't flirting with him, just being practical. It was the only way to be with men, who were not always practical in relationships.

'Let's see how we make out. Are you likely to pick up any information tonight at the German embassy?'

'Only by accident, if I do.' She had learned from Professor Kambe that General Imamaru would be there; that meant Lily Tolstoy would probably also be there. 'When do you want me to broadcast?'

'Tomorrow night. Tell them I've arrived – use my code name. Tell them that I haven't yet contacted Wild Rice.'

He saw her smile again. 'Who is Wild Rice? Or shouldn't I ask?'

Suddenly he wished he was going with her to the German embassy; or anywhere, for that matter. He had not had a girl in almost two years, but it was not just sex that attracted him to her. He had never met anyone quite like her; she had an air – of mystery? He wasn't sure if that was her quality; women were always something of a mystery anyway. Even high school cheer-leaders, with their transparent extrovertism, had puzzled him in his youth. Possibly because they were always white Americans and he suspected their innocent exuberance.

'Better not to ask.' His tone was gentler this time.

She really didn't want to know about Wild Rice, whoever he or she was. Her life, which had never been simple, had suddenly become complicated by too many relationships that had too many questions to them. Nagata, her mother, this man; and he was the only one of the three who might prove a friend. Though he had not said as much she sensed that, like herself, he was an outsider. Outsiders have a sixth, seventh and eighth sense: they need them to survive.

'I think you should come out to the villa and look at the radio,' she said. 'I've had trouble with it the last couple of times I've broadcast. I know nothing about radios.'

'Do you have any spare parts?'

'None. But there are a lot of radio shops on the Ginza.'

The faulty radio gave him an excuse to visit her; after all, how could he claim to be running a professional game if he didn't supervise the equipment? 'I'll get some tomorrow before I come out.'

'Be careful. All radios are supposed to be registered. Ours is not.'

'I'll try and be at your place by nine o'clock, depending on the trains.' He was still getting accustomed to the twelve-hour shift. The Japanese seemed willing to work sweatshop hours; meanwhile he was sweating the American out of his system.

'You'll have to stay the night, catch the first train back in the morning.'

That made him pause. He had got through his first few days on the docks by being as inconspicuous as possible. He was learning that waterfront men minded their own business – they asked no questions, gave no answers, turned a blind eye: but they knew everything there was to know about keeping their jobs. One of them was never to break any of the rules without paying the *yakuza* for it. So far Okada had not spoken to Koga, the *yakuza*, since the first day he had been hired.

'I'm supposed to start work at seven.'

'You'll be late then.'

They looked at each other in the darkness. Their eyes were in shadow and they could not read each other's expression; but there was a tension between them that needed no light to be read. It was a mixture of suspicion and attraction, a chemistry found between lovers, politicians and opposing generals. To experiment with it is rarely denied.

'I'll see you tomorrow night,' he said.

They left the university, he to go back to his seedy hotel in the Koto-ku district, she to the German embassy just north-west of the Imperial Palace. He smiled wryly at the thought: he was the control but she got the fringe benefits.

Next morning he had his first brush with Koga. The *yakuza* swaggered; but it was not a natural gait with him and he always looked awkward and slightly comical. He wore the standard wartime civilian dress of mustard-green trousers and high-collared jacket; on his cannonball of a head he wore a derby hat. He looked ridiculous, but then Okada had always thought the same of Adolf Hitler.

'Okada! Over to Dock Three!'

Okada was helping an elderly docker stack boxes of dried fish for loading on to a ship due in this evening. The docker had hurt his back, but hadn't dared stop work – 'Koga-san will send me home and take my pay for himself.' Okada, working with him, had doubled his own efforts to make up for the older man's inability to lift the boxes. He had done it partly out of concern for the injured docker, partly because he figured he might some day need a friend on these docks; he was learning to look ahead, something he had rarely done in the past. At this moment, however, he forgot to look at the *yakuza*.

'In a minute, Koga-san. I'll finish up here—'

He fell against the stacked boxes under the force of the blow that hit him across the back of his neck. Anger boiled up inside him; he spun round ready to erupt. All that saved him was the vigorous shaking of his head by the elderly docker standing behind Koga. He drew a deep breath, straightened up and bowed his head almost to waist-level. It was a bow meant for someone of higher status than the *yakuza*: to a more sensitive and intelligent man than Koga it might have seemed satirical. But the *yakuza* was king here and he placed no limit on the depth of a bow.

Nonetheless, he had to put this Saipanese in his place. 'There is a war on!' he bellowed; the stay-at-homes, Okada thought, need to tell each other what's happening. Then he told himself he would have to stop thinking like a soldier: he was a civilian, just like the *yakuza*. 'Do what you're told when you're told! Get over to Dock 3!'

Okada bowed again, this time not so deeply, and hurried away; he did his best to look as if he were scurrying, but at UCLA he had been the top quarter-miler and no track star ever scurries. Still, he managed to look chastened and contrite, if not abjectly so.

On Dock 3 he had to work with a mixed gang of men and women. The women seemed to work more industriously than the men; or perhaps the men, more experienced at this sort of labour, cynically allowed them to do so. Several of the women looked appraisingly, with a candour he could not remember with pre-war Japanese women, at the goodlooking newcomer. But he put his head down and went to work. He did not want another brush with Koga.

At the meal break the elderly docker, Morishima, came over from the other dock and sat beside Okada. The dockers got a supplementary ration above the normal rations, but, being expert pilferers, they gave themselves a further supplement by picking and choosing from what was available in the dock-sheds. Okada had quickly fallen in with the practice and today was eating a choice of dried fish, plenty of rice and fresh fruit brought in from the Philippines. He longed for a steak, but to get the smell of animal fat out of his body he had given up eating meat a week after he had arrived at San Diego. Occasionally a fellow docker cocked a nostril at him, but no one had yet made any comment. Maybe they thought Saipanese smelled differently anyway.

'Okada, I don't know how things were down in Saipan,' said Morishima, 'but here nobody argues with the *yakuza*. They believe they are just as patriotic as the generals and the politicians. They make money out of the war, but that's the system.' He gestured at the food in his bowl. 'We get our share too.'

'There were bosses down in Saipan, but no *yakuza*.' Okada was not sure that was true, but he was certain that Morishima knew next to nothing about Saipan. He felt safe in the knowledge that the average Japanese working man was interested in nothing beyond his own small circle. 'You could explain things to our bosses.'

'You can explain nothing to Koga-san. But he has to explain things to the *yakuza* above him.'

'How far up do the *yakuza* go?' Okada made it sound like an idle question, small talk between mouthfuls.

Morishima clicked his false teeth, a metallic sound. 'As far as one could climb. Not as far as the Emperor, of course, but far enough. The politicians and the generals use them. But what they do up there—' He gestured above his head at a social level he could not even imagine. 'That doesn't concern you and me. We just have to worry about Koga-san.'

'Thanks, I'll remember that. How's your back?'

'I've been to see Koga-san. For half a day's pay he'll let me stay inside the shed this afternoon by the stove. I'll be poorer, but I'll be warmer.' He clicked his teeth again, a hollow note of resignation this time. 'What's it matter anyway?'

Okada had been a little surprised at the cynical attitude towards the war of the men amongst whom he worked. He had bought himself a cheap radio and each night listened to the propaganda, disguised as news, that came out of it, like a poison filtering into the ears of its audience. He had marvelled the first night that anyone could believe such blatant lies; but just three days on the docks told him that the workers knew the news was all lies. Their cynicism was as blatant as the propaganda fed them and he wondered why the secret police, about whom he had been told so much by Irvine, were not picking people up off the streets for their lack of patriotism. Unless, of course, the secret police were even more cynically resigned to defeat.

When he left work that evening Koga was waiting for him at the dock gates. He was tossing a silver coin in one hand and again Okada had the image of a character from a movie: George Raft tossing a silver dollar in *Scarface*, a film he had seen in his youth. The *yakuza* seemed to be playing at being tough, but

Okada did not smile. The blow on the back of his neck this morning had shown how tough Koga really was.

'Okada, you give me more cheek like you did this morning and you're out of a job.'

'I am sorry, Koga-san.' It almost choked him to be servile to this dumb thug. 'It won't happen again.'

Koga stared at him. Despite his rough accent, Okada knew that occasionally he had given himself away as being better educated than the other dockers; he had stayed out of the way of Koga, but someone must have passed on to the *yakuza* that this new one should be watched. He resisted the urge to stare back and kept his gaze below the level of Koga's. Come the end of the war he would come back here and throw this son-of-a-bitch off the end of the dock.

'Report to me direct in the morning. I've got a job for you.'

'Yes, Koga-san.'

Okada bowed and left, churning inside with anger and frustration. *This* was what he had always hated about Japan, this goddam obsequious respect towards guys whom, back home in the States, he would punch in the nose. He went back to his hotel wondering if he was going to be able to suffer this sort of humiliation till the Americans came to save him, wondering if he was the right man for the job that Embury and the others had in mind. At the same time he wondered what job Koga had in mind for him tomorrow. He would go out and see Natasha Cairns this evening, but somehow he would have to be back in Tokyo in time to start work tomorrow.

He had bought himself a standard civilian suit and back at the hotel he changed into it. In California before the war he had been a smart dresser; not flashy, but always better dressed than the other young men in Gardena. He looked at himself in the peeling mirror on the wall of his tiny bedroom and wished he looked better for this meeting with Mrs Cairns. He looked around the almost bare room, at the low stool, the bed mat and its hard pillow, and thought about coming back here after he had spent an hour or two with Mrs Cairns. It was no place for romantic dreams.

He went to the bomb-flattened Ginza, found a radio store still standing and bought a dozen valves, a set of dielectrics and a set of insulation coils. The sales clerk packed them in a box for him and passed them across the counter.

'You going to build a short-wave and listen to the Americans?' He was cheeky and sly, young and tiny, with thick-lensed glasses and a deformed hand. You poor bastard, Okada thought; then thought of all the healthy young men jumping off the cliffs of Saipan. 'They play good music, I'm told. Artie Shaw, people like that.'

'Never heard of them,' said Okada; but heard the echoes of Shaw on 'Begin the Beguine'. 'This is for the radio on my father's fishing boat. All he listens to is the weather.'

'Don't we all?' said the clerk and closed a giant eye behind the magnifying glasses he wore. Okada went out of the store wondering if some conspiracy was being built up around him, if everyone knew who he really was and was trying to tell him he was not alone.

He walked down to the main railroad station and caught a train out to Nayora. The evening was cold, with an ice-hinting wind blowing in from the sea, and he pulled the collar of his overcoat up round his neck. His cap was pulled low down over his ears and he guessed he looked like a bum, someone who shouldn't be calling upon a girl as beautiful as Mrs Cairns.

He felt no better when Yuri opened the front door to him and he was shown into the living room where Natasha waited for him. She was dressed in a pink sweater and dark blue skirt, an outfit that showed off her breasts and hips: she had what he thought of as an American figure. Her face had been carefully made up, not Japanese style but Western. Her black hair was drawn back into a chignon and, a man always with an eye for line, he admired the shape of her head. She looked overpoweringly beautiful and he felt like turning and walking out the door.

He took off his overcoat and, to steady himself, got down to business immediately. 'Where's the radio?'

Natasha was a little taken aback at his abruptness, she had expected better of him after their last meeting. She heard Yuri, both ears wide open, give a loud sniff out in the hallway.

Sometimes she felt Yuri was worse than a Mother Superior.

She led Okada down into the basement of the house. It was a small room, musty as a dungeon but kept meticulously clean by Yuri, as if she and her mistress might some day be confined there. The radio was hidden in the wall; a square of bricks mounted on a steel arm swung out to reveal it. Once again Okada had the feeling he was playing in some movie: he had seen such things in old horror pictures. In a moment Boris Karloff would step out of a hidden door in the wall.

'Very ingenious,' he said.

'We have to be careful. The security police have been out here several times to monitor for illegal radios.'

'How did you dodge them?'

'We have a very garrulous sergeant in the village. He tells everyone what's going on.'

'Let's hope he stays that way.'

He opened up the radio and was appalled at the condition of it. He looked around the spotless basement, then back at the radio's mildewed and dusty innards.

'It's a wonder it's still working. Haven't you ever done any housekeeping on it?' He had slipped into English, where he felt more comfortable with her.

'I was afraid to touch it. I don't know anything about machines.' She replied in English, determined to set him at his ease. She knew something about men, if not machines.

He took out all the valves, then the dielectrics in the capacitors. The dielectrics had almost dried out; the plates were so close together he knew there would have been no transmission tonight. He shook his head at the condition of the insulation coils; they had been saved only by the dryness of the winter: another summer's humidity and they would have been useless. It took him half an hour to clean and repair the radio; Natasha sat and watched him, saying little. But the smallness of the basement room made them sit close together and Okada felt a certain humidity rising in himself.

At last the radio was ready. 'I'll let you send, Mrs Cairns. They know your touch on the Morse key. If I send they might get suspicious. Have you got your code book?'

They exchanged seats, squeezing past each other in the narrow space. He smelled her perfume, felt her bosom brush his chest; she smelled the maleness of him, was as aware of his body as if he were naked. They were tentatively touching an invisible key, working their way into a code that each knew well in his or her own language.

The message was simple and direct: *Joshua arrived. No contact yet with Wild Rice. No further information. Message ends.* She encoded it and transmitted it; she might know nothing about machines but she had a naturally adept touch on the Morse key. The aerial cable was pulled in and the wall was closed up on the equipment. Only then did he relax.

'Why are you so tense?' she said. 'You must be more experienced at this than I am.'

'No, I'm not.' He felt relaxed enough to be honest with her. 'This is my first mission. But you don't look worried. Almost as if you thought it some sort of game.'

'Most of my life has been a game, in some way or other. It doesn't help, biting your nails.' She held up her hands, the fingernails long and shining. He could feel them stroking his belly, scratching his back; and she knew what he felt. They had both been without sex too long, they were swimming towards each other through a thick sea of desire. He thought wryly that he was no longer the control. 'I don't even think about the end of the war. I don't think about the end of anything.'

She sounds more Oriental than me, he thought. But she was smiling at her fatalism, as if she thought it, too, was a sort of game. He smiled in return, took one of the long-fingered hands and kissed it. It was something he had never done in his life before; but this was a new life. He might start being another person altogether.

'You did that very nicely,' she said, whose hand had been kissed by experts, all of them too old to thrill her. 'Is that the way Japanese-Americans treat their women?'

'All the time.' He was suddenly at ease with her, all his tension gone, waiting for her to make the important move; which he knew she would. He gave her back her hand, putting it on her breast like a rose. 'You're so goddam beautiful!'

'I know,' she said, leading him upstairs out of the basement. 'Aren't I lucky? Have you eaten yet?'

Then sanity, which has cooled more beds than it has warmed, returned, 'I've got to start back to Tokyo. I have to be at work at seven in the morning.'

'I told you, there's no train.'

'I'll try and pick up a lift on the road.'

'Then you can do it later. Yuri has prepared supper for us.'

Which Yuri served with as much lack of grace as she could muster. She still did not trust this new man and she was protective of her mistress. She recognized that Natasha was in need of a man, if only for tonight, and she did not blame her: low-born and now too old to have a man of her own, she had no squeamish morality about sex. But she wished her mistress had got the itch for some man about whom she knew more. She threw rice and fish on his plate as if she were throwing rocks at his crotch.

They sat at the high table in heavy mock-Jacobean chairs. The room's furniture was oppressive, but Okada hardly saw it. He continually looked at Natasha, the getting back to Tokyo forgotten.

'You may go to bed, Yuri,' Natasha said when the latter brought in the last dish.

Yuri went off with a sniff like the last whistle of a typhoon and Okada looked at the fruit on his plate. 'Pineapple?'

'I stole it last night from the German embassy. It stained all the inside of my handbag.'

'You did this for me?' He smiled, sure of her and of himself now.

She smiled back, too practised to be too coy.

From then on the pace quickened. They went upstairs to her bedroom, where the only light came from the fire in the grate.

'Where did you get the coal?'

'Yuri goes fossicking for it along the railway line. A few lumps at a time. I light the fire only for special occasions.'

He smiled at himself, a special occasion.

It was just as well the room was dimly lit, because the very weight of the furniture would have overcome Okada. But he saw it only out of the corner of an excited eye: Natasha took off her clothes and from then on he saw nothing else and her only dimly. There was no love between them nor was it mentioned: it was sex, impure and far from simple. He had never met a woman who knew so much: she found sensations in him that he had never dreamed of. For her part she was satisfied; his equipment was bigger than she had expected from a Japanese and he was not totally inexperienced. Finally he lay exhausted under her, his face covered by the black tent of her hair.

'Are you still my control?' she murmured.

He could feel her lips smiling against his cheek. 'Out of bed, yes. But here . . .' He blew away her hair, looked at the dying glow of the fire on the ceiling. 'Is this how we'll end every transmission?'

She sat up and he admired the way the firelight played on her body, choosing the perfect highlights and shadows. 'Don't let us make plans. Do you want a bath? Then we can come back to bed.'

'No,' he said reluctantly; his bottom half seemed to cling to the bed as he stood up. 'I've got to go. There'll be hell to pay tomorrow if I'm late.'

'You still haven't told me where you work.'

He shook his head, then kissed her gently. 'I'm out of bed now. I'm your control again.'

She returned his kiss, resisting the urge to pull him back on top of her. Though each shied away from it, there was a tenderness between them. She felt suddenly sad, remembering Keith, the last man who had made love to her. Okada couldn't remember the last girl he had had, so there was no sadness for him, just a growing feeling he would remember more of the past couple of hours than the wrestling bodies and the cries of passion.

'Do I call you Tom or Tamezo? I know – I'll call you Tom when we're up here. We'll be different people from what we are out there.' She gestured at the shuttered windows.

'Unfortunately, out there we have to be *real*.' He was dressed now. 'I'll take the valve boxes and the cans with me and ditch them somewhere. Meet me at the university, same place,

Sunday night. By then maybe I'll have found a mail-drop for us, where you can leave a message for me if you need me in a hurry.'

'What if you need me in a hurry?'

He smiled, deliberately misunderstanding her. 'I'll take a cold shower.'

He insisted that she remain in bed and he let himself out of the house. Snow had fallen, but the wind had dropped; he tried to keep himself warm with memories of the bedroom. He pulled his cap down over his ears, turned up his overcoat collar and trudged up to the main highway two miles away. He wondered what Embury and the others, safe and comfortable in the rising sunshine of San Diego, would think of tonight's adventure. Suddenly he laughed out aloud and jerked a thumb towards the east, an 8000-mile goose sign.

His luck was in. He had been on the highway no more than five minutes when a truck, laden with milk barrels, came down the pike. The driver pulled over and Okada climbed into the cabin with him.

'A man could freeze his arse off out there.' The driver was a farmer, glad of company on this cold lonely drive.

'Just what my arse was telling me when you came along.'

The farmer laughed and joked all the way into Tokyo; Okada, knowing no local jokes, laughed and listened. He got off the truck a few blocks from his hotel, found an alley where he discarded the radio parts containers. Then he walked light-heartedly on to his hotel, where he went to bed on his sleeping-mat, which he still found uncomfortable, and dreamed of a dozen women, all with Natasha's face, smothering him with their bodies.

In the morning he felt ready for anything Koga might have for him.

3 〜

Admiral Tajiri had asked for a detailed report on conditions in the United States and the thinking and morals of Americans. Minato had started work on it his second day at Navy Headquarters; he was eager to impress, to remain close to Admiral Tajiri till he had got his bearings. For six long years he had had no discipline other than his own mental attitude and he was finding it more difficult than he had imagined to settle back into Navy routine. He was surprised at how often he kept thinking of the discipline he had seen on the USN base at San Diego, strict and effective yet at the same time relaxed enough not to require any servility from the junior officers and other ranks. But then, he thought traitorously, the admirals there were confident of victory.

He, Sagawa and Nakasone worked in a small office just down the corridor from Admiral Tajiri's room. It was sparsely furnished: three desks, three chairs; visitors, if they came, were not encouraged to stay. A picture of the Emperor looked down on them through fly-speckled glass; Minato thought him a very ordinary looking man for someone of Divine descent; President Roosevelt and even Prime Minister Churchill looked more godlike, though the latter may have had difficulty finding a heaven. The most conspicuous item in the small room was the bank of steel drawers that took up one wall. It was full of reports: Admiral Tajiri, commander of a fleet of desks, was at war in a sea of paper.

Minato was aware of someone standing in the doorway; it was Colonel Hayashi. 'Lieutenant Minato, would you step outside?'

Sagawa's and Nakasone's heads were lowered over their papers, but Minato felt their eyes, like rats under a ledge, watching him as he rose and went out into the corridor. He bowed to Colonel Hayashi and hoped he didn't look as apprehensive as he felt. He had been a spy for six years and had become almost confidently careless in the role; but now he was home he felt curiously insecure. He was surprised to see Hayashi suddenly smile.

It was not a reassuring smile, though Hayashi probably meant it to be so. He had thin lips that folded back so tightly they seemed to be sutured together by his teeth; but he was one of those fortunate, secure persons who had never had to depend upon personality to advance him. He looked as if it would be difficult for him to be friendly, even to friends.

'Lieutenant Minato, I should like you to have lunch with me at the Army Club today.'

Colonel Hayashi would not take him to the Army Club to arrest him. 'Yes, Colonel Hayashi. I shall be honoured.'

'You do not need to broadcast it to anyone.'

'No, sir.'

So as soon as Hayashi had left he went straight along the corridor to Admiral Tajiri's room. The admiral squinted up at him through his horn-rimmed glasses and gave him a truly friendly smile.

'You are a very intelligent Intelligence officer, lieutenant. You have learned to cover all your options.'

Minato flushed. 'I thought you should know, sir—'

'I'm not criticizing you. After all, you do work for me, not for Colonel Hayashi. Have a good lunch and report back to me.'

A bitter wind was blowing as Minato and Hayashi walked from Navy Headquarters to the Army Club north of the Imperial Palace. Minato had expected that a car would be waiting for them, but Hayashi told him that he walked everywhere; and Minato, hurrying to keep pace with him, could well believe that the tall colonel would walk to the ends of the earth. He had an indomitable stride and Minato guessed he would never go for an aimless stroll but would always have a destination.

Over on their right there was ice on the water in the moat surrounding the palace. The sixteenth century granite walls loomed like low cliffs, pine trees adding a frieze on top; beyond them could be seen the tops of the tall hardwoods in the Fukiage Gardens, the Emperor's private park. When Minato had left here six years ago the watch-towers on the battlements had been white, with tile-and-copper roofs that curled as if the towers were about to be airborne. But now the palace was camouflaged, looked grey and dreary, no abode at all for an Emperor who had chosen as the title of his reign Showa, Peace Made Manifest.

The drab, poverty-stricken look of the city elsewhere had appalled Minato. The roadways and sidewalks were pockmarked with holes; bomb trenches were like water-filled graves. The wooden houses were rotting; even the better ones looked like patched-up shanties. There had been scrap metal drives but, for lack of transport, the scrap had not been collected: heaps of it lay in the streets like mounds of rusted bones. The street-cars were wrecks moving on screeching wheels, their windows broken, their seats ripped. But it was the people who shocked him most. Green-complexioned from the almost endemic diarrhoea due to their poor diet, clad in the dull crap-coloured standard dress, they looked like a shifting mass of mud moving on the surface of a city he no longer recognized.

Hayashi did not speak until they were in the Army Club and seated at their table. Junior officers were tolerated in the club, but Minato was beginning to feel he had been singled out for humiliation by Hayashi. Then the colonel smiled for the second time that day.

'Did you eat American style in America, lieutenant?'

'One had to, sir. Their meals are barbarous and wasteful, as if they are feeding a nation of hungry wolves.'

'Even in wartime? Such fortunate people.'

But the meal here was better than Minato had so far had at the Staff College. There was carrot soup, thinly sliced beef and plenty of vegetables; it was not sumptuous, but Minato guessed it added up to more than the daily ration of most of the citizens beyond the walls of the club. He was aware of Hayashi watching him closely, but he made no comment on the meal, just ate quietly and waited for the colonel to make the pace.

They were sipping tea when at last Hayashi said, 'You were very fortunate to survive so long, lieutenant. I mean as a spy. Have you ever heard of Richard Sorge? He first came here in 1933, ostensibly as a German journalist. But he was working for the Russians. He was arrested by the Thought Police in October 1941. We finally hanged him last November.'

Minato could feel the meal beginning to curdle in his stomach. Hayashi had mentioned the Thought Police, as they were called: the Special Higher Police which had been operating long before Minato himself had been sent to America. He had also said 'we finally hanged him': did that mean the colonel was a member of the Thought Police?

'Why didn't the Americans hang you, lieutenant?'

Minato had to get the sourness out of his mouth before he could speak. 'I don't know, sir. Except that American justice does tend to work slowly.' Then he added bravely: 'Why did they take so long to hang this Sorge?'

'Who knows?' said Hayashi; but Minato felt he was certainly one who did know. 'Tell me, lieutenant, what do the Americans think of the Emperor?'

'They don't respect him. They make jokes about him.' Then he added hastily, 'I mean the ordinary people. I don't know what the men in Washington think.'

'What ordinary people think doesn't mean anything in a war,' said Hayashi. 'It is a pity you were not able to find out what Washington thinks.'

'That would be impossible, sir, for a Japanese. But don't we have any agents there? Some Europeans? Germans?'

'The Germans probably do, but they don't share their secrets with us. By the same token, the Emperor has never really trusted Hitler. We're allies but not friends.'

Minato forbore to ask what friends Japan did have these days.

'Who do the ordinary people –' Hayashi made it sound like the name of a plague – 'think is responsible for the war?'

Minato hesitated, then said, 'General Tojo. That's the propaganda they are fed.'

Hayashi did not look annoyed that a senior officer of his own service should be branded the principal warmonger; instead, he appeared to nod with satisfaction. Whom am I dealing with here? Minato wondered. A secret policeman, a plotter? He glanced carefully around the big room where they sat, but no one seemed to be watching him and Colonel Hayashi. Yet he had the uncomfortable feeling that he was no safer here than he had been in America. He was a patriot, but he felt he was suspect because he had lived too long in the land of the enemy.

Hayashi abruptly stood up without a word and after a moment's bewilderment Minato realized the lunch was over. Hayashi marched out of the club and Minato followed him.

'Thank you for coming to lunch,' said the colonel and walked off, south along the moat behind the palace.

Minato knew that the direction Hayashi had taken was the

shorter route back to Navy Headquarters, if that was where he was headed; they had come to the Army Club by the longer route, up past all the government buildings. Minato chose to go back the way he had come. He did not want to be seen to be following the colonel and he also wanted time to think.

Sleet was falling as he walked back to his office; even the weather was making him feel more miserable. He had come home to Japan pessimistic about the future and uncertain of his place in it, but it had been preferable to the certainty of his death if he had remained in the United States. If he had refused to be a double agent, the Americans would surely have executed him as a spy. He would have died an honourable death, at least in the eyes of the Emperor and Admiral Tajiri; but to what purpose? The war was lost and if he had to die young it was preferable to die in one's own country amongst one's own kind. Yet already he was coming to realize that not everyone took him at face value, one of their own spies who had managed to escape the enemy; already he could feel the suspicion that he had not returned uncorrupted. He guessed he was being watched, though he had seen no evidence of it yet, and he further guessed that Colonel Hayashi was one of the watchers. He remembered the one-way mirror in the room in San Diego and felt less secure here in Tokyo than he had there in San Diego.

When he went in to see Admiral Tajiri he was still chilled, by the weather and his own feelings. Tajiri, who had never been a Spartan, saw how cold he looked and motioned him to stand by the coal fire that burned in the grate. There was no heating in the building, but Tajiri believed that admirals, like fleets, must never be icebound.

'I hope the colonel gave you a good lunch? The Army Club is not noted for good food.' Tajiri had spent two years in Paris as a naval attaché and still had a taste for *haute cuisine*. He hoped the French's disillusionment after the fall of France had not spoiled their cooking. 'But then I think Colonel Hayashi would have an iron stomach. The rest of him is metal.'

Minato couldn't remember senior officers discussing other officers like this, not with someone as junior as himself; some sort of rot had set in and he felt disappointed in his mentor. The warmth of the fire crept through him, but it made little difference.

'The colonel asked me about America, sir. He wanted to know how the Americans felt about the Emperor.' He explained the feeling; Tajiri just sat nodding his head, as if he already knew. 'He seemed pleased when I told him that General Tojo is looked upon as responsible for the war.'

'The Americans are being unjust,' said Tajiri and sounded as if he meant it. 'What did you think of Colonel Hayashi himself?'

Minato was surprised he should be asked such a question, and hesitated. But Tajiri looked encouraging and he said, 'The colonel is an odd man, sir. I can't fathom whom he is working for.'

'Would you care to guess?' Tajiri took off his glasses and polished them. He had very thick eyebrows which only accentuated the narrowness of his eyes. His voice was friendly, but Minato had the feeling he was being impaled by the admiral's squint.

'With all respect, sir, I don't think it is my place to do so.'

Tajiri put his glasses back on and nodded. 'As I said before, lieutenant, cover all your options. But you disappoint me. After six years in America, I thought you'd have opinions on everything. Isn't that the American way?'

Once again Minato hesitated; then he moved away from the fire and stood immediately in front of the admiral. 'Colonel Hayashi either works for the Thought Police or he is engaged in some plot. I think he is much more than just a liaison officer.'

'A plot against whom?'

'I don't know, sir. The General Staff, perhaps. Or even against the Emperor.' He had not expected to go so far, but now it was out he felt a certain relief. At least he would know from now on where he stood with Admiral Tajiri.

'America has done a lot for your imagination.' But Tajiri seemed to be talking more to himself than to Minato. He sat silent for a while, then he smiled. 'Lieutenant, forget about plots against the Emperor. And I can assure you that Colonel Hayashi is not a member of the Thought Police.'

Minato was disappointed. 'Then I seem to have learned nothing from the lunch with him.'

'Ah, but I have,' said Tajiri, but did not elaborate. 'Accept any further invitations Colonel Hayashi extends. You may yet learn something.'

'I hope you will not think I was presumptuous, sir, in suggesting there might be a plot—?'

'Not at all. But what made you think there might be one? Are the Americans expecting such a possibility?'

'I'm not sure, sir. While I was in custody in San Diego there was a suggestion one day—' He took the plunge: 'They asked me if I knew anything about something called the Peace Faction.'

Admiral Tajiri's face seemed to glaze over; the horn-rimmed glasses hung on a ceramic mask. 'Why didn't you mention this in your report?'

He spoke slowly, trying not to panic: 'It was an oversight, sir. At the time it didn't seem important. They asked me the question just once and when I said I knew nothing of it, they immediately dropped it.'

'What made you think it might be important now?'

'I'm not suggesting that it is, sir. But if there were a plot—'

Tajiri's face was still a mask; then it cracked slowly into a smile. 'I think you must be protected against yourself, lieutenant. If you have any more flights of imagination, tell them only to me. That way I am not likely to lose you. That will be all.'

Minato bowed his way out, wondering how far Tajiri would go to defend him. Especially since the Peace Faction, he was certain, did exist and that the admiral, and possibly Colonel Hayashi, belonged to it.

He worked impatiently throughout the rest of the day, waiting for the evening and his first meeting in Japan with Tamezo Okada.

If Koga, the *yakuza*, was trying to lay an *on* upon him, Okada felt no obligation at all. As soon as he had reported for work, still half-dreaming of Natasha and their lovemaking, he had been sent for by Koga.

'You can work out of the cold today, Okada.' He had two gold teeth, one at either end of his smile, like quotation marks. 'Get in the back of that truck over there. We've got some deliveries to make.'

As Okada walked across to the truck Morishima came out of a nearby shed, walking stiffly and carefully. 'My back still hurts. I asked Koga-san to give you this job.' He nodded at the truck, where two other men had already climbed aboard. 'I go out with him every month on this delivery. Our pay is extra food – this month it's a box of dried fish. I'll give you half.'

Okada suddenly wished he had not been so helpful towards Morishima yesterday. 'You shouldn't have done it, Morishima.'

The older man looked pained, and not because of his back. 'I thought you'd want it. We can all do with the extra food—'

Okada relented, smiled. 'It's all right. It's just that I wanted to settle in here slowly. I'm the outsider, all you men have been here so much longer . . . I'll see you get your box of fish. Where do we deliver the rest of the stuff?'

'You'll see,' said Morishima and hobbled away as Koga came swaggering down the dock.

Okada climbed into the back of the truck, sat with the other two dockers on the boxes stacked there. The two men nodded to him, but said nothing; they were from other work gangs and he had never seen them before. Koga got up into the cabin with the driver and the truck pulled out of the dock gates.

The first stop was outside a building in a narrow street behind the burnt-out Ginza. Four boxes of dried fish, two bags of rice, a case of tinned vegetables and a case of Scotch whisky (Okada wondered where that had come from) were unloaded and carried into the building. No crowd gathered to watch the food being unloaded, but Okada was aware of the covert glances of passers-by; but nobody made any remarks and as he went into the building for the second time he wondered if the passers-by knew whom the food and drink were intended for. The name on the door of the office where the boxes were stacked said: Segaki Company; but there was no indication of the company's line of business. There was only a middle-aged clerk in the office and he looked neither well fed nor affluent from trading on the black market.

As he got back into the truck Okada said, 'What does the Segaki Company do?'

The two dockers looked at each other, then one of them said, 'It's the *yakuza*. Koga-san's bosses.'

'It takes all sorts to win a war,' said Okada.

The two men looked at each other again and for a moment Okada thought he had said the wrong thing. Then they both grinned and nodded, and he knew he had been accepted as one of them.

There were three more stops, all of them at villas just west of the Imperial Palace. This was just behind the military and government administration area and Okada marvelled at the open effrontery of the deliveries. The villas were all large and their owners were obviously important men. The two dockers named them: one a general, the other a marquis. 'Now comes the big one.'

The truck drew into the grounds of the third villa. Okada noted there were two villas in these grounds, the larger a mansion that looked as if it might house half the government. But the truck pulled up behind the smaller villa.

'Who lives here?' said Okada.

Koga had got down and gone into the rear of the villa. Okada and the two dockers began to carry the cases into a small storeroom. He had remarked that there was more variety to the groceries being delivered here: tinned fruit, two sacks of flour, sugar, salt, besides the dried fish and the bags of rice. There were also four cases of Scotch whisky.

'General Imamaru likes his liquor,' said the docker who had

been doing all the talking. He was a wiry man, a twisted knot of muscles. 'He also likes other things.'

Okada caught the direction of his gaze and turned his head. Despite the coldness of the day a woman was walking in the garden. She wore a heavy fur coat, but her head was bare. He stared at her with shock; then he realized he was not looking at Natasha. The woman was beautiful but older and looked as if she would eat men raw.

'That's his mistress. Madame Tolstoy. They say he found her in Saigon.'

Madame Tolstoy glanced across at them, but they might as well have been shadows for all the notice she took of them. She went round the corner of the villa and was gone from sight as Koga came out of the villa kitchen.

'That's the lot,' he said. 'What's left is yours.'

Okada looked into the back of the truck and saw three small boxes of dried fish. 'No whisky?' Once again his tongue had slipped. Koga glared at him and he added hastily, 'Just a joke, Koga-san.'

Koga did not encourage joking; he bunched a fist and shoved a blue, red and green dragon into Okada's face. 'You Saipanese don't know your place! I'll teach you to be cheeky—'

Madame Tolstoy had come back round the corner of the villa, was standing watching them. Okada, removing his face from the close vicinity of the dragon-faced fist, bowed in her direction. Koga spun round, dropped his hands by his side and bowed; it was a much deeper bow than Okada's, more than a high-class whore deserved. The other two dockers also bowed, halfway between Okada's and Koga's. The four of them looked like backache cases in various stages of the affliction. In Saigon Lily Tolstoy might have shown her amusement, but here in Tokyo she was conscious of her position. An upright whore can be as stiffly formal as an elderly vestal virgin.

She gave a barely perceptible nod of her head and moved away through the garden. Okada and the two dockers hastily clambered up into the truck and drew up the tailboard. Koga glared up at Okada.

'One more joke out of you, Okada, and you're finished!'

He went round to the front of the truck and a moment later they moved off out of the Imamaru grounds. Tanabe, the talkative docker, grinned at Okada. 'Stay out of his way for a week and he'll forget you.'

But Okada doubted that the *yazuka* would forget him so easily.

On the way back to the docks the truck made a detour to drop off the three remaining boxes of fish at the homes of Morishima and the two dockers with Okada. Koga might be a thug, but he kept his part of a bargain. Nonetheless, each time he came to the back of the truck he ignored Okada, a neglect that the latter didn't mind. When they finally returned to the docks Koga got down from the truck and went into his office without a word.

Morishima came hobbling towards Okada. 'Everything went well?'

Okada nodded. 'Your box of fish is at your place.'

'I'll bring your share tomorrow.'

In other circumstances he would have accepted the fish, taken it out to Natasha; but she had better sources than Morishima or any of the other dockers. 'Keep it for your family. Some day, when I'm really hungry, I'll ask for a bite.'

Morishima bowed his head. 'You're a good man, Okada.'

'For a Saipanese?'

Morishima recognized a joke, he smiled broadly. 'There's room for improvement.'

'I'll do my best,' said Okada.

He went back to the hotel, crossed the street to the public baths and bathed, went back to the hotel and changed. He ate at a nearby stall, standing against a wall while the home-going crowd pushed past him in the near-darkness. There had been regular air raids since the middle of December, though the Americans did not come every night; though the Americans may not have realized the psychological value of their irregular raids, the seemingly random flights were tearing at the edges of the population's nerves. Okada could feel the brittle tension in the passing crowd, their spirit as dim as their faces in the darkness.

He caught a train out to the northern suburb of Tokyo where Minato's parents had lived. He lost his way several times in the blackout and had to ask directions; at the same time he was glad of the darkness. He was apprehensive of his first meeting with Kenji Minato and he could now feel the tension in himself. What if Minato turned up with the secret police? There was no guarantee that Minato could be trusted; he was safely back in his own country now, he could renege on all his promises. He had no *on* to the Americans, none to Okada himself.

He remembered one of the conversations he had had with Minato in their weeks together in San Diego. They had been in the room where Minato was always kept, with Embury and Irvine and Reilly on the other side of the one-way mirror.

He had said in Japanese, 'I don't believe a word of what you've told these Intelligence officers.'

Minato stopped smiling. Okada could only guess at the reaction of the three men in the next room at his suddenly speaking Japanese. Irvine could possibly speak the language, but he was certain that Embury and Reilly could not.

Minato replied in Japanese. Okada recognized at once that it was more formal than his own: Minato had moved up a class or two since the old days. 'I did not invite you to be my judge, Tamezo Okada. The Americans asked me to name someone *they* could trust. I thought you would leap at the opportunity to prove your old arguments you had with me, that you were an American and would never be anything else.'

'The Americans are asking me to prove it to them too.' That was a slip, to admit that, and Minato saw it at once.

'Then we are both on trial, one as much as the other.'

'No, I more than you.' Okada's own speech had become more formal. 'I shall be in Japan, where you can betray me and I shall have my head chopped off.'

'Do you think I would do that?' Then Minato said in English, 'No, Tom. We may no longer be friends, but we're not enemies.'

Okada was glad to speak English again. 'Maybe not, but you talked about *on*. I remember enough about that. You have an *on* to the Emperor and, I guess, one to Admiral Tajiri. You would never have one to me, you owe me no obligation, nothing. If it was your neck or mine, I know whose would go.'

'Probably yours,' Minato smiled again, but Okada found his charm in bad taste, something no honourable Japanese should indulge in.

'Have you any feelings about betraying the Emperor?'

Minato sat silent for a while, his bony face blank. At last he said, 'Shame I can hardly bear, but it must be done. The Emperor has been misled in this war by the generals.'

'And the admirals,' said Okada, giving discredit where it was due. 'How will you face Admiral Tajiri when you go back?'

'That must be done, too. I'm a good actor, Tom. One learns to be when you are a spy.'

'I better learn to be one, then.'

'You'd better. You wear your thoughts on your face too often. I can read them, if no one else can. I know that you still don't entirely trust me, do you?'

Okada stared at him. 'I'm being inscrutable now. Try and tell me what I'm thinking.'

But Minato wasn't to be drawn. 'We'll play this game right to the end of the war, Tom. Perhaps by then we'll trust each other.'

As Okada got closer to the meeting place he became more determined that, if Minato had betrayed him, he would turn and run and hope for the best in the darkness. He would rather die with a bullet in his back than with a rope round his neck. For the first time he realized that some people have a choice of deaths.

He found the street at last, turned down it. The clouds had cleared and the moon, a bomber's moon, rode high, bright and cold as a treacherous jester's eye. The houses here were middle-class, small and neat in their own small plots hidden behind thin walls. But there were gaps, three-year-old gaps, the results of General Doolittle's raid back in April 1942.

No houses had been rebuilt; but the debris had been totally cleared out. This was a neighbourhood that still had some pride left, if only as window-dressing. As he walked nervously down the narrow street Okada could see that gardens had been planted in the vacant lots: vegetable gardens, shrubs, even a plot of white pebbles that shone in the moonlight like an arrangement of hailstones. When he came to the fifth gap Minato was standing there in the shadow of a tree not much taller than himself.

Okada paused, looked around; but he could see no one hiding in the shadows. Then he moved closer to Minato. He said candidly, 'I wasn't sure you wouldn't have someone with you.'

Minato's smile was friendly. 'Tamezo' – he used the intimate first name, as if to prove his friendship. 'If I'm going to betray anyone, it won't be you.'

Okada, with no alternative here in this dark suburban street, took him at his word. He looked around the lot on which they stood. 'This was where your parents lived?'

Minato nodded. 'They were unlucky, they and the others in this street who were killed or injured. The Americans came over just after midday, I'm told, back in 1942. They dropped bombs downtown, near the Shinbashi station. But most of them were aiming for the steel factories and oil refineries over there—' He nodded towards the east. 'When they were leaving they must have had some bombs left. They jettisoned those around here. I don't know much about bombing, but they tell me you never can be sure which house is going to fall down when a bomb lands nearby. My parents' house fell down and they were killed instantly.'

'Did anyone put up a shrine to them?'

Minato nodded towards the back of the lot. 'A small one. It's now my responsibility. Someone also planted this tree for them.'

'A cypress. The tree of grief,' said Okada, the nurseryman. He was silent a while, then he sighed. 'Well, we better get down to business. Have you anything to report?'

'I don't think we can talk here.' Minato had lowered his voice. He nodded towards the houses on either side of them. 'Or have you forgotten how thin the walls of Japanese houses are? There's a café a couple of blocks away. Let's go there.'

Okada decided he would feel less uneasy in the smoky light of a café than here amongst these shadows. They walked back up the street, past houses where no lights shone but where voices laughed, argued, sang, where a radio told lies about the fighting on Iwo Jima, where people waited longingly for the end of the war. Jesus, Okada thought, why can't I knock on their doors and tell them the war is already lost? But no: only in ancient history, in the time of Jimmu, the first Emperor, could a man go from door to door with the news that a war was over. Now they listened to the radio which told them lies they half believed, but which they had no evidence to contradict.

They had turned the corner into a main road when Okada paused, put a hand on Minato's arm. 'Someone is following us!'

Minato looked back, then shook his head. 'You're imagining it, Okada. Please believe me – I haven't brought anyone with me.'

Okada stared down the moonlit street, tried to pierce the shadows. Then he shrugged. 'I guess I'm nervous.'

'You should be in control of yourself as well as me.' But Minato smiled to take the edge off his remark.

The café was one of a row of three shops, stood on a corner and had blackout blinds. Inside, most of the tables were occupied, but Okada and Minato found one in a corner at the rear. The café was noisy with talk and laughter and, by keeping their voices low, they would be able to converse unheard by those at the neighbouring tables.

Minato was in uniform, but there were several other servicemen in the café, two or three officers amongst them. This was a middle-class neighbourhood, but Okada noticed that the civilians seemed no better dressed than himself. In any event he hadn't come here to impress anyone. He thought of Natasha, but quickly put her out of his mind.

They ordered tea and while they sipped it Minato gave his report. 'I'm sure there *is* a Peace Faction and I think Admiral Tajiri belongs to it. But it is going to take time to find out who else belongs to it and how much influence it has. The important thing is I'm in the best place to find out – I'm back on Admiral Tajiri's staff. What are you doing?'

'That's classified information. All I can say is I'm not on any admiral's staff.' He wondered how much lower a minor *yakuza* boss was in the social scale.

'Have you been in touch with our chief back home?' Minato smiled again, but he knew the joke was weak. Home, he had realized tonight, was not America, never would be: it was where he had stood in the moonlight in the shadow of the tree of grief.

'Once. They had no message for either of us, just good luck.'

They talked further, mainly exchanging impressions on the low morale of the population; even here in the café the laughter, to their biassed ears, sounded false. When they rose to leave Okada felt more at ease with Minato, was beginning to believe he could be trusted. Minato would not believe the lies on the radio, he knew the truth.

They went out into the blackout, rode back together on the rattling, screeching train, an ice-box on square wheels, into the city. They got off at Tokyo main station and said goodnight, fixing another meeting for the same night next week. Minato went off to catch a bus to the Staff College.

Okada crossed the big square in front of the station, passed the granite cliff of the Marunouchi building and turned down one of the streets that led east towards his hotel. He had about a mile and a half to walk, but he wanted time to think. Minato's confirmation that a Peace Faction did exist was a message that had to be sent; but aside from the fact that Admiral Tajiri belonged to it the confirmation of the existence of the Faction was not going to cause any excitement in San Diego. He would have to put pressure on Minato for something more concrete.

He had walked no more than three blocks, careful of the holes in the pavement, before he realized he was being followed. He was not imagining it this time; as he paused on a corner, the man fifty yards behind him also stopped. He moved on, turning the corner, though it meant going away from his hotel, and halfway down the block, when he looked back he saw the man was still following him. What to do? He kept walking, wondering if he should suddenly burst into a run, confident that with his sprinter's pace he could lose the man in the dark streets. But if the man *had* been on his and Minato's tail out in the suburbs, had seen them go into the café together, then come back to

Tokyo together . . . Then that meant Minato was already exposed. And where would he have to run to?

Half-afraid of what he might have to do, if the worst came to the worst, he turned the next corner and waited. The man, as if afraid of losing contact, came hurrying round the corner. Okada stepped out in front of him, grabbed him by the shoulder and spun him around against a shuttered shop front. He bent his forefinger and shoved the hard pointed knuckle into the man's back. It was another movie trick, he had lived too close to Hollywood, but he could think of nothing else that would keep the man facing the wall.

'Try to run and I'll shoot.' Later he would laugh at the empty threat in his voice; but for the moment he sounded high-strung and dangerous, which he almost was. 'Who are you and why are you following me?'

Then someone came round the corner and Okada dropped his fist and prepared to run. Then Minato, the newcomer, spoke: 'Sagawa-san, what are you doing here?'

Lieutenant Sagawa turned from the wall, adjusted his overcoat with prim decorum. He ignored Okada, looked directly at Minato. Okada, watching him, had the sharp feeling that this naval lieutenant was in command of the situation.

'Who is this man, Minato-san? Why do you go right out to the suburbs to meet him, an inferior type of person like him? Is he a black market dealer?'

Minato sighed, showing great patience, Okada thought. 'Sagawa-san, you haven't told me why you are here. Were you following me out to Omiya?'

'Yes.'

Occasionally people passed them, wooden clogs clumping on the pavement, but nobody stopped or looked back. Okada was watching both Minato and Sagawa, but he was also watching every passer-by, waiting for them to turn back and reveal themselves as secret police brought here by Minato. He felt both disgust at, and disappointment in Minato: out at the café he had begun to feel a trace of the friendship they had known as boys.

'Why?' said Minato. 'Who sent you to follow me?' Sagawa

said nothing and after a moment Minato said softly, 'Was it Colonel Hayashi?'

Even in the dimness of the moonlight the answer was there in Sagawa's face. His mouth tightened, then he nodded. 'Yes. He came to me this afternoon and told me to watch you. I was honoured to be asked by the colonel.'

'Whom does Colonel Hayashi work for? The *kempei*?'

'I don't know. How could I, a lieutenant, ask a colonel such a question?'

'If I may intrude, though an inferior type of person' – Okada resorted to sarcasm: it was the language of the Devil, but this was a hell of a situation. 'How did *you* get here, Minato-san?'

'I saw Lieutenant Sagawa on the train. When he followed you, I followed him.'

'You still haven't told me who this person is,' said Sagawa, persisting, but no longer sounding in command of the situation.

'Nor am I going to,' said Minato. 'We are going for a walk. You walk between my friend and me.'

'He is a friend?'

'Yes, very much so. Now please let us walk.'

Sagawa seemed to have no idea of Minato's intentions; nor did Okada. The latter felt the situation had been taken out of his hands; Minato was now the control. As they began to walk down the narrow street the air-raid sirens began wailing.

There had been no raids on Tokyo since Okada's arrival and he was suddenly nervous. But Minato, the one who had never seen a shot fired nor a bomb dropped, who had had no experience of combat, was calm and composed. Or appeared so.

'We have half an hour – isn't that right, Sagawa-san? The early warning system gives us that much time, doesn't it?'

'Not any more,' said Sagawa. There seemed no antagonism between the two men; they were professionals discussing a military problem. 'Not since the Americans landed in the Philippines.'

'Well, perhaps that will be to our advantage,' said Minato. 'Mine and my friend's. Down here, please.'

He pushed Sagawa down an alley. Okada, taken by surprise, was left standing in the street; he recovered and followed the other two down the alley. The moon was directly overhead, splitting the middle of the narrow lane with a blade of dim blue light. The walls on either side were brick; the buildings, Okada guessed, were either offices or warehouses. People were now hurrying past the end of the alley, their clogs beating a hollow tattoo like sticks on bones.

Minato swung Sagawa up against the wall. Behind the latter's head was an old torn poster, faint as a ghostly image in the reflected moonlight. General Tojo, smiling with all the optimism of two years ago, a plague of bombers rising out of the background, called on all young men to fight for the Emperor. But tonight the wrong bombers were flying, the sirens had a different call.

'Why did you agree to do what the colonel asked without coming to warn me? I thought we were supposed to be friends?'

'That was a long time ago, Minato. You have changed. Everyone has noticed it.' Sagawa looked sideways at Okada, then back at Minato. 'I demand to know who this person is.'

'And if I tell you, will you give that information to the colonel?'

'Of course.' There was a simplicity about Sagawa's devotion to duty, or to Colonel Hayashi, that suddenly made Minato despair. He knew now that he was going to have to kill Sagawa. It surprised him that he would not be killing only for his own sake but for Tom Okada's. Out in the café in Omiya something of the past, of their boyhood together, had reached out and touched him.

Up till now he had been tense but still composed. Suddenly his composure broke. He ripped open Sagawa's overcoat, took out the American scout knife and flipped open the blade. He muttered, 'I'm sorry, Sagawa,' and drove the knife into the lieutenant's belly. Behind him Okada gasped, 'For Christ's sake!' Sagawa looked at Okada surprised to hear him speak English; then he fell against Minato, who gently lowered him to the ground. Minato wiped the knife on the dead man's overcoat, straightened up and only then looked at Okada.

'Jesus!' Okada said in English. 'Did you have to do that?'

'Yes,' said Minato in Japanese. Clouds were floating across

the moon, the alley had turned into a dark pit. The sirens were still wailing, moans out of hell, and the bone-clattering sound of the running clogs echoed down the narrow lane. 'He'd have reported me to Colonel Hayashi – he was that sort, I'd never have been able to explain anything to him. They'd have come looking for you and sooner or later they'd have found you. I had to kill a man getting out of San Diego. I didn't want to, but I had to—'

He looked at the knife, as if there might still be some flecks of the blood of Mate Third Class Bateman on it; then he snapped the blade shut and put the knife away, putting his hand away in the pocket with it. He could feel the hand trembling and he did not want the shame of Okada's noticing it.

'You may have to kill someone too, before all this is over. Maybe even me.'

Okada felt sick, but he knew he had no argument. He looked down at the dark heap in the darkness; the moon was completely obscured now, as if it had shut its face against what had just taken place. He wondered if, had he been in Minato's place, he would have killed Sagawa. And felt sure, though made uneasy by the realization, that he would not have.

'We'd better go,' said Minato.

'What about him?'

'He'll be found in the morning. Who knows, perhaps even a bomb may fall on him.' But Minato did not feel as callous as he sounded; he could feel himself still trembling. Though he had disliked Sagawa, he had had no personal urge to harm him. 'The point is, his death won't be traced to me. Why should I be in a district like this? They'll think it was some robber.'

'Then you better rob him,' said Okada, but made no move himself.

Minato could feel Okada's shock, even disgust, at what had been done. As boys Okada had always been the leader of the two of them, the one with initiative; but there had been no need to kill, no real danger threatening, in those days. He was hurt at Okada's reaction, but he kept his feelings to himself. He bent down, went through Sagawa's pockets, looked at his wrists. He came up with a wallet and a gold watch.

125

'Do you want the money? There's quite a lot here. Sagawa was a rich man's son.'

'Shit!' said Okada in disgust and turned away and went back up the alley.

Minato followed him. They stood in the shadows till the street was clear for a moment, then stepped out and walked back to the corner. The sirens were still wailing, but now they sounded tired (or was it the ear?), as if they were running automatically, unattended, as if the men who had pressed the buttons had deserted their posts and fled to safety. A few people were still hurrying home, but most of them had now gone.

'I *had* to kill him.' Minato spoke softly in English, though there was no one to listen to them.

'I know that!' Okada was angry, at Minato, at himself, at the whole damned situation; he had not been prepared, after all, for all emergencies. 'But Christ – did you have to be so goddam cold-blooded about it? The poor bastard trusted you—'

'He didn't trust me. He wouldn't have been working for Colonel Hayashi if he had. And we couldn't afford to trust him. Tom—' But the moment of intimacy died on his lips. There was no time now to explain that he was as concerned for Okada as for himself. Abruptly he said, 'We'll meet next week as arranged. In the meantime, find a mail-drop. You're not very well organized.'

5

The bombers came, Saturday night gate-crashers. They came in waves and the raid lasted an hour. Okada spent the time under the counter in the hotel lobby, he, the night clerk and three other loners; the counter would have been no protection at all if a bomb had dropped nearby, but it was like make-up to an ageing geisha. It gave a sort of brittle confidence, a desperate hope that they would last the night.

In the morning when they went out into the street everything was covered by a blanket of snow. Fires still burned, very pale in the morning light and against the snow; but the snow had been heavy and most of the fires had been doused; steam rose as from thermal springs. People wandered, wrapped in their quilted jackets, like dazed dark birds amongst the ruins; a man stood holding a bicycle with only one wheel, as if wondering whether he could unicycle somewhere to safety. Children cried, fire engines rang their bells, an old woman sat in the snow-covered wreckage of her home and wailed, an eerie shriek that had the sound of long-dead spirits in it. But Okada, standing in the street, could not but help remark how the snow had turned the ugly face of the neighbourhood into something resembling a beautiful abstract garden.

In the alley six blocks away Lieutenant Sagawa's body was hidden beneath a quilt of snow. During the day the temperature dropped sharply and the snow turned to ice. It was three days before his body was discovered, emerging out of the melting ice like a slowly developing three-dimensional photograph.

Four

I 〜

Natasha and Major Nagata walked along the beach, just below the overhang of the pine trees. Occasionally snow fell from the branches, scattering itself on the coarse dark sand like blossoms. Far across the bay Natasha could see thin pillars of smoke, like smudged drawings of the pines, rising from Yokosuka.

'Did they bomb the naval base last night?'

Nagata nodded. 'But it was worse in Tokyo. Things are bad. I'm afraid you are going to have an influx of evacuees soon. Everybody wants to get out of the city.'

Natasha looked up towards the villas ringed like neat ornaments round the contours of the hill overlooking the bay. She and the other internees had been miraculously fortunate in not having people from the city billeted on them; all that had saved them was that, as foreigners, they were always suspect as possible spies and good Japanese citizens should not be allowed near them. Nagata was not the first *kempei* officer to come to Nayora. Others had come regularly, arrogant, suspicious and hating the Europeans here. For herself she had felt they had only contempt, someone whose blood wasn't pure.

Two Italians, Arcadipane and Moroni, went striding by, hunched down in their dark, well-cut overcoats. They took off their hats and bowed to Natasha, Arcadipane giving her a Via Veneto smile, all invitation and shallow optimism. After the defeat of Italy most of the Italian embassy had been put in a concentration camp, but Arcadipane and Moroni and their wives, the only Italians with a summer home in Nayora, had been allowed to remain here. They did not mix with the Swedes and the other neutral internees, but each afternoon came for their walk along the beach and bowed politely to whomever they passed. They might be unhappy and homesick, but they looked relieved that, for them, the war was over.

Seeing the Italians, Nagata was reminded of another ally close to defeat. 'Did you learn anything at the German embassy the other night?'

'It was like a funeral party where none of the relatives like each other. The only cheerful man there was my friend Professor Kambe.'

'And your mother, Madame Tolstoy – was she cheerful?'

'How did you know she was there?'

He smiled, a cheerful secret policeman. 'We know where everyone goes. Everyone who counts, that is. Is General Imamaru cool towards the Germans too? He was once a great admirer of their army and the Luftwaffe. In the early years of the war, after Poland and France.'

'I think General Imamaru is one of those who would surrender tomorrow. But I got that only from listening to Madame Tolstoy.' She could not bring herself to say 'my mother'. 'She says he would like a posting to France as ambassador.'

'He's no diplomat.'

'This late in the war, does it matter?'

He smiled appreciatively at her cynicism. 'If the raids continue it may be more difficult for you to get into Tokyo.'

'Then I shan't be much use to you, shall I?'

'One never knows, Mrs Cairns.' She could always be kept in reserve, if only as a character witness when the Americans finally arrived.

He bowed and departed, walking up the hill towards the railway station. Once, his rank had entitled him to a staff car; but now staff cars and fuel were in short supply for all but the highest ranks. He wondered if the American secret police, in a nation devoted to the automobile, ever had to travel by decrepit train.

Natasha walked up and down the beach for another twenty minutes, twice passing Signori Arcadipane and Moroni but offering no encouragement to Arcadipane's smile; then she turned up the hill towards the villa. Sergeant Masuda, loose-

129

kneed legs looking as if they would fold beneath him at any moment, waited for her at the top of the narrow street.

He bowed, roughly courteous; if it were not for his obsequiousness, she would have liked him immensely. 'Mrs Cairns, I have bad news. Tokyo has instructed me to let them know what spare accommodation we have here in Nayora. I shall have to tell them about the spare rooms in your villa.'

At once she saw the complications and the danger. But outwardly she showed only the polite resignation of a foreigner who knew she had no rights. 'I understand, Sergeant Masuda. I just hope you can give me someone who is compatible.'

Sergeant Masuda thought he himself would have been highly compatible; unfortunately his wife and three children would have spoiled the atmosphere. He had all the extravagant dreams of a plain, ordinary man, extravagant because he would never have to cope with their fulfilment.

'I'll do my best, Mrs Cairns. But I'm afraid the authorities in Tokyo will be the ones to decide.'

Natasha went on up to the villa, wondering if she should start at once in dismantling the radio and getting rid of it. She was to meet Tamezo Okada tonight: she would accept his advice. She was rediscovering the womanly pleasure of allowing a man to think, mistakenly, that he was superior.

She had thought of him every day, and often several times a day, since their lovemaking last week. Sensuality had its own memory; her body wriggled with snakes of desire as she recalled the night. But she had been left with something else besides satiety; a feeling of comfort? No, she had never looked for that; and she was too experienced to think that one found it in a wild bed. All week she had searched for the exact description of what she felt. She did not delude herself that it was love; she was a romantic, but not a blind one. In the end being a romantic had helped her pin down what she felt towards Tamezo (or Tom, as she called him in her private thoughts). She saw herself as a boat adrift. First, there had been her father, a poor mooring post who had done his poor best. Then there had been Keith, solid as a rock, but in a sea the currents of which she was still learning when he had died. Now there was Tom, who hardly knew this sea at all, but, she thought, knew himself. He would be something to hold on to, and not just in a sexual way. The truth was, of course, that she had been looking for him before she had ever known that he existed.

Yuri joined her as she went up the last few yards of the path to the villa. The little woman held up a string bag. 'I've been up in the hills. Got some onions and watercress and potatoes. The prices—' She shook her head at the banditry of the peasants. Natasha knew that she must have walked miles to get the food; she was indefatigable and made Natasha ashamed. 'I'll make us a good soup. Are you going to see Madame Tolstoy again this evening?'

Even she did not use the word 'mother': Lily Tolstoy could have been barren. Natasha nodded. 'I have to see Okada-san, then there is a dinner at someone's villa.'

'How did you get invited? Through Kambe-san?'

'No, through Madame Tolstoy. Actually, I think she is beginning to feel proud of me, because I'm so beautiful.' She and Lily, daughter and mother, had at least one trait in common: they might be false in several things but never in modesty.

Yuri, a plain woman, spat into the snow. 'Looks can get you into trouble. Don't get carried away by your mirror.'

'Do you think I should shut my eyes against it?' She enjoyed her own simple conceit and she enjoyed these exchanges with Yuri, her real mother figure.

'Not if it's going to make you unhappy. But keep your willpower between your legs.'

Natasha packed a dress and her fur coat in the big cloth bag, put on her quilted jacket and a scarf and caught the train into Tokyo. She saw the other passengers looking slyly at her out of the corners of her eyes, but no one looked directly at her. She knew, from what some of the Swedes told her, that white people were often subjected to naked antagonism; for that reason few of the Europeans ever left Nayora. But the Oriental touch to her features had so far saved her from any public aggression; they might despise her as a mixed blood, but they could not be sure how much of her belonged to them. Dressed as she was in the cheap clothes similar to their own, they could not be sure what she was; though she had got on at Nayora, the foreigners' colony, she could be a servant. So they watched her covertly, their eyes like the hooded lamps in the blackout. She did not feel afraid, just uncomfortable. Soon people like this might be sent to live with her and Yuri in the villa.

Okada was waiting for her at their meeting place at the university. They stood for a moment in the bright moonlight of the garden, then he put out a hand and drew her into the shadows. He kissed her on the cheek, but she turned her lips to his and opened her mouth.

'There's no bed around here,' he said, smiling. 'And I've never made love in the snow.'

'That was just a sisterly kiss.' She too was smiling, so pleased to see him again.

'Incest.'

Natasha, who knew more about love, real and simulated, than he did, recognized how at ease they were with each other. She had not been sure how he would feel or, indeed, how she herself would be. She did not allow herself to think that she might be falling in love, but she did know she was glad to be here with him, that the anticipation she had felt on the train coming in had not been overblown. She did, however, admit to optimism and admitted, too, that optimism is necessary for true love.

Okada had been looking forward to their meeting. Part of the anticipation had been due to randiness; an erection is itself the flagstaff of anticipation. But commonsense had told him there would be no lovemaking this evening; so he was pleased at the pleasure he felt in merely being with her. He was too cautious, however, to think about any future with her. He had begun to appreciate that his own future might be very short.

He was still recovering from the killing of Lieutenant Sagawa. He had never thought of himself as squeamish; when he had been with the two OSS men in Burma there had been several times when he had had to draw a bead on a Japanese and, after only a moment's hesitation, had done so, though he had felt no elation when he had scored a hit on a man. But the killing of

Sagawa had been so unexpected; and he could not put out of his mind the thought that it had been murder. Minato had told him that it was not murder – 'in war, Okada-san, there is no murder. What is the difference between my killing Sagawa, who would have betrayed us, and the American bombers who kill women and children who just happen to be on the wrong side? Sagawa had to be killed. You had better accept that, Okada-san.'

He was accepting it; but it was going to take some time. He knew he was that worst of soldiers, one with a conscience; if Embury and the others had known, perhaps they would not have chosen him for this job. Still, the job had to be kept in mind: 'I've picked a mail drop for us. It hasn't been easy – I looked at three other spots and found them bombed out the next day.'

'The safest spot would be the Imperial Palace. The Americans seem to be avoiding that.'

He laughed drily. 'That would be a nice joke, hiding our notes somewhere there. But the Palace is overrun with guards.' He had spent most of his time when not working walking about central Tokyo. After the first day he had felt like an archaeologist, one too impatient for the ruins to age; occasionally he had felt like a ghoul, but that had only been when he had come unexpectedly on rescue parties digging bodies out of the wreckage of homes and buildings. He had soon recognized that the least bombed area was that around the Palace. 'No, you know the Marunouchi building opposite the main station? At the southern end there's a small wooden structure – it looks like a cross between a hut and a coal bin. The street workers use it to store tools. It has only one door to it. At the opposite end there's a rusted drainpipe coming down from the roof. It's not connected to the roof, so no water runs down it. Nobody will take any notice of a piece of paper shoved in there.'

She giggled, though she knew they were engaged in serious business. 'It all sounds so elaborate.'

He nodded: they were both novices. 'I know. But that's what they taught me – to be both elaborate and simple. Elaborately simple, they said.'

'Well, they know best,' she said, sounding unconvinced.

133

'We'll only use it in an emergency.' He had to find another mail drop for Minato; he was like a bigamist trying to keep his wives apart. He ran his hands over her quilted jacket. 'I think I prefer you in the mink. It feels sexier.'

She gestured at her bag. 'It's in there. I'm going to a dinner.'

'Where are you going to change? In there?' He nodded at the building in whose shadow they stood.

'No, at a friend's.' It was on the tip of her tongue to tell him about her mother; but something held her back. Their relationship at present was simple; or elaborately simple, as their masters might have called it. Till she was sure exactly how she felt about him, she did not want to complicate matters by mentioning her mother. Not even by calling Lily her aunt.

'How are you going to get there?' The street-cars had stopped running till their tracks, torn up by the bombing, were repaired. Bus services were restricted and taxis had virtually gone off the road. He wondered if Berlin or any of the other German cities were as devastated as Tokyo.

'I'll walk.'

'I'll walk you there.'

'I'll be all right—' But he wouldn't take no for an answer and she didn't want to spoil the mood between them by protesting too much.

It was a long walk and he was surprised that she should have been attempting it. Though it was through one of the best areas of the city and there was not much bomb damage here, the streets were dark and he got angry and worried that she should take the risk of being set upon and assaulted.

'I'd rather you didn't do this. Walk around the streets on your own, I mean. How will you get back to Nayora?'

Lily had told her there would be a staff car to take her home. 'That has been arranged by my friend.'

He sensed that she was holding back; now he felt angry and hurt. They walked in silence for a while, their steps silent in the snow.

Then she stopped abruptly, only now recognizing where they were. 'This is it.'

He looked at the high walls surrounding the garden, saw the

sentry standing inside the big gates. 'Your friend lives *here*?'

'She is General Imamaru's mistress. I'll explain next time I see you. Out at Nayora, same day as usual.' She was aware of the sentry watching them closely. She could not risk kissing Okada, not Western style. She bowed her head in a short jerk and left him quickly, like a sister leaving a brother with whom she had quarrelled. The guard stepped in front of her, but she gave her name and, when he had checked a list with a small flashlight, he saluted her and let her walk on up the driveway to Madame Tolstoy's villa. She resisted the urge to look back at Okada and prayed that he would be sensible enough to move off at once.

Which he had done. Women have been known to say that grown men are like babies: it is true. They hate being abandoned on doorsteps.

23

Lily Tolstoy looked at her daughter and wondered if maternal pride could do any harm to amorality. She marvelled at the beauty she and Henry Greenway had produced; though she had difficulty in remembering exactly what Henry looked like and so gave him little credit. So she sang her own praises, *sotto voce*, which is the best way, in case the chorus doesn't join in.

'Your father would have been proud of you, my dear. Did he leave you anything?' She would think better of him if he had.

'You mean money? Just a little. And a few oddments. All I have left is his cigarette card collection of cricketers.'

'How English. I don't remember much about him – just odd things. His particular hero was someone named Jack Hobbs. Other men have heroes like Tamerlane and Genghis Khan, romantic names. His was called Jack Hobbs. Still, he was nice.' She said it as if Henry had been afflicted with leprosy.

'Too nice, really.' They were speaking English, as if Henry were listening. 'You shouldn't have left him, Lily.'

'If I hadn't he would have finished up hating me. Then he wouldn't have been nice at all.' She smiled as if she had made some saintly sacrifice for Henry's sake. 'Now don't let us spoil our evening by talking of what's done.'

'Who is my dinner partner? Some old general?' She would feel safer with an elderly man; though she had noticed that at the top level *all* the men were elderly. General Imamaru was, she guessed, only in his fifties, but then he was not absolutely top level.

'No, you will have a young man. Well, *younger*. I'm not sure how old he is.'

'Colonel Hayashi?' She felt excited at the thought: she would perhaps have something of value to report to Tom. She wanted to please *him* now, not the masters he worked for.

But then there was a knock at the door and General Imamaru came in.

Sakichi Imamaru was the son of a prosperous coal baron from Hokkaido. Hisaichi Imamaru had come to Tokyo and tried to buy his way into society and failed; he had committed suicide, but slowly, by drinking himself to death. He had, however, managed to enter his son in the Japanese Military Academy, where Sakichi had been a classmate of another general-to-be, Chiang Kai-Shek. He had graduated with average marks in tactics and strategy, but top of the class in *kendo*, liquor consumption and arrogance. He was built like a weight-lifter and Lily sometimes felt during their lovemaking that she was a barbell. He looked like a man who knew only victories, but for the past year he had presided over nothing but defeats. He felt that eventually honour would dictate that he would have to commit *seppuku*, but he had turned honour into a deferred mortgage. He had no religion but hoped for miracles.

He looked admiringly at his mistress and her niece, smacking his lips in approval. 'You will embarrass all the other women with your looks! Oh, you make life worthwhile for an old soldier!'

'General, you're not old,' said Lily, who knew her lines.

Imamaru nodded, as if he had suddenly been regenerated. 'No, not while you are here to keep me young.'

Natasha felt uncomfortable while her mother and her lover went through their middle-age routine. Though she had had middle-aged and elderly lovers (though one of them had called himself her patron and she had preferred that), she had never been coyly subservient to them. She would have made a terrible geisha.

A minute of coyness was about all Lily could stand. 'All right,' she said briskly. 'Let's go up to the main house and be ready for our guests.'

'My guests,' said the general, just as briskly, putting flattery behind him.

Lily gave him a small mocking nod, took Natasha by the hand and led her out of the villa and up through the garden to the main house. The general strutted along in front of them, bulging from his uniform, his thick thighs hissing like short pythons as his trouser-legs rubbed against each other.

There were thirteen other guests at the dinner besides Imamaru, Lily and Natasha. They were all men and women who have lived in or travelled to Europe or America; the women, then, demanded a certain freedom, though they were careful not to go too far. The men all had titles, of rank if not of nobility; besides generals and admirals there were a marquis, a viscount and a prince. The only exception was Natasha's dinner partner, Lieutenant Minato.

'You and I appear to be the only common folk here,' she said.

They were standing in a corner, like children at an adults' party, waiting for the two servants to work their way down the scale and bring them cocktails.

'I understand Madame Tolstoy is common,' said Minato.

'Not really.' Natasha bridled at the insult to her mother, though she was momentarily stuck for another word to describe Lily. 'In Bangkok she had a title – Princess Eastern Pearl.'

'How do you know that?'

'She is my aunt.'

A servant arrived with cocktails: Manhattans. Minato suddenly wished that was where he was: Manhattan, Philadelphia, Sioux City, anywhere on the other side of the Pacific Ocean. He had never been comfortable with girls and certainly not with beautiful girls who looked at him as if he were a dog that was not house-trained. He drained his cocktail in one gulp, hoping it would loosen his tongue, which had tied itself in a knot.

'Are you a diplomat, lieutenant? I understand you've just come back from abroad.'

Minato recovered, managed a smile. 'No, I think I just proved I'm not a diplomat. But yes, I've been abroad.'

'Fighting?'

'In a way.'

Minato was still unsure why Admiral Tajiri had brought him to this dinner. But then Tajiri had always been a little eccentric; he liked to throw his protégés in at the deep end. What the generals and statesmen in the deep end thought of having a mere lieutenant thrown in with them didn't bother Tajiri; but it bothered Minato. This girl bothered him too.

He was saved by the gong: dinner was served. He and Natasha fell in at the end of the line as it filed into the big Western-style dining room. The menu made no concession to austerity. Minato had been shocked at the scarcity of food in Japan; in comparison America had been a glutton's paradise. Foolishly, he now realized, he had dreamed of coming home to all the foods he had once relished; the first day home had told him that those dishes were just memories to everyone else besides himself. But not to the diners sitting down at General Imamaru's table.

There was *tempura*, fish and lobster fritters; shell fish; raw fish dipped in soya vinegar laced with thyme; French wines; it had all the extravagance of a condemned man's last meal. For Minato had now begun to sense the pessimism that pervaded the capital, as if the *kamikaze*, being a wind of the gods and therefore prone to the gods' whimsy, had turned back on itself, bringing with it a bad smell.

The *kamikaze* pilots, the heroes of the wind of the gods, were being discussed by Prince Kagoshima. He was a gentle man, now in his seventies, known to be writing his autobiography, which would be full of the lives of his friends and virtually nothing of his own.

'I am horrified at the sacrifice of these young men. They are not *samurai*, one can't equate an airplane with the sword. We shan't impress the Americans with these suicide attacks; they will just think we are atavistic.'

'While they are thinking that, we are sinking their ships,' said Viscount Hatori. 'Is that not so, Admiral Tajiri?'

'Indeed, indeed.' Tajiri nodded, the light flashing on his glasses like a semaphore trying to contradict the verbal message. Minato knew that the admiral had little faith in the *kamikaze* pilots' efforts to win the war. 'But my information is that the Americans have more ships than we have planes.'

If any of the men at the table knew that Tajiri's protégé had spent the last six years in America reporting on shipping, they gave no hint. None of the men had even looked at him after he had been presented to them, though several of their wives gave him covert glances, wondering if Madame Tolstoy was sponsoring him as a possible fiancé for her niece. They preferred gossip to the sinking of ships: it floated better and, if sunk, could always be raised again.

'What news from Berne?' The viscount's wife was a woman who used her tongue in her husband's interests; or so she thought. Her husband winced at her gaffes and secretly regretted the freedom he had encouraged. She looked around the table at the other women and explained to them what she took for granted that they didn't know.

'The peace mission. It's been there since Pearl Harbor and never seems to get anywhere.'

Sitting beside each other, Natasha and Minato independently wondered if the mission in Switzerland was part of the Peace Faction. Their attention sat up, if not their bodies.

'Nothing on which to base any hopes,' said Tajiri, the senior of the two admirals at the table. The Navy had set up the peace mission in Berne, but he knew now that it was doomed to failure; the peace overtures were now being conducted through Moscow where the reception of them was as freezing as the weather. He sipped his wine, remembering his first taste of Chablis and the golden peace of 1910 when, on leave from the embassy, he had driven south-east out of Paris in his first car, a Daimler 38. It had been a grand car for a junior naval attaché, but already in those days he had been careless of protocol. One could be, if one was more noble than any of one's senior officers. 'Still, the Americans may grow tired of the war.'

'Never,' said General Imamaru, who knew how victories could become a way of life to military men and even statesmen; though he had almost forgotten how one felt after a victory. 'They'll go on till they've conquered everyone, including the Russians. In the meantime eat, drink and be merry . . .'

'For tomorrow we die,' said the viscountess, helping out.

After dinner Lily took Natasha aside. 'You were not very polite to Lieutenant Minato. You should cultivate him.'

'Is he important? Or rich?'

'Neither, I gather. But some day he may be. He is a favourite of Admiral Tajiri's. The admiral and his wife have no children. If they should adopt Lieutenant Minato . . .'

'Lily, you are starting to sound like a real Japanese mother. Matchmaking.' She shook her head. 'I'm sorry, I'm not interested. When the end of the war comes, I'll probably be like you. Looking for a husband amongst the Americans.' Perhaps a Japanese-American: the thought startled her with its precocity. 'I don't think Lieutenant Minato would be what they call a very eligible bachelor. It would be like being engaged to a bankrupt with a rope round his neck.'

'You have a nice turn of phrase, my dear. What sort of education did those nuns give you?'

'They used to pray for you, Lily.'

'Then their prayers were answered,' said Lily satisfied with what she had achieved. 'You'd better go now. There may be another air raid tonight. I'll make your excuses.'

The staff car would take Natasha home. She went down to Lily's villa, collected her everyday clothes in her big bag and waited for the car to pick her up. As they drove out the gates the sirens began. The driver speeded up to get out of the city. As they went through the devastated southern section she saw people dropping into the air-raid trenches like animals going underground. She knew that many of them, their houses obliterated, now lived in the trenches, sheets of galvanized iron drawn over them as roofs, human rats surviving as best they could in a hopeless world. Suddenly the rich food in her stomach turned sour and she wanted to vomit. She felt something she could not remember feeling before: guilt. The nuns, with their sense of sin, had taught her better than they knew.

3

On the eighth day of every month, the celebration of 8 December 1941, there was a public reading over the radio of the Emperor's text, 'Greater Asia Day'. This day Minato listened to it for the first time, wondering at this national self-delusion. He stood at his office window, listening to the radio on the shelf behind Nakasone's desk, and looked out at the yellow-grey crowd down in the street. Did they ever listen?

'We, by the grace of Heaven Emperor of Nippon . . . rely upon the loyalty and courage of Our subjects . . .'

He turned as Nakasone came bursting into the room. He bounced across the small room, switched off the radio as if it were broadcasting nothing more than some inconsequential song, and blinked excitedly at Minato.

'They've found Sagawa – dead! The police say he was probably stabbed and robbed by some gang!'

There had been plenty of talk about Sagawa's mysterious absence: he had never been known to miss even a day's work. Minato had stayed out of the speculation, withdrawing into the protection of being the only newcomer.

'The admiral is sending me over to identify the body. Do you want to come?'

'I – I'd rather not. He was your friend.'

Nakasone shook his head. 'No, he was never anybody's friend. Not the way – not the way you and I were.' He sounded apologetic that he had spoken in the past tense and Minato was quick to sense it.

'The way we *are*.'

Nakasone smiled in relief. 'I was hoping you would say that. I was afraid you had changed.'

'Of course not. I'm still – well, I suppose I'm still coming home. A step at a time.'

'You should write a poem about it,' said Nakasone, who did write poetry but never read it to anyone. Then he looked at the doorway behind Minato's back. 'Good morning, Colonel Hayashi.'

Minato had spent an anxious three days waiting for Hayashi to send for him to interrogate him. But the colonel had made no appearance; not until now. He stood in the doorway and smiled his cold smile, bleak as the day outside.

'Will you excuse us, Lieutenant Nakasone?'

Even though he was suddenly afraid, Minato remarked the arrogance of the man: an army colonel, he had come into the staff office of a Navy admiral and told one of the admiral's aides to step outside and leave him alone with Minato, another of the admiral's aides.

But Nakasone seemed neither to be offended nor surprised by the request. 'Of course, colonel.'

He jammed his cap on his head, bowed and was gone. Minato found his voice: 'Did you wish to see the admiral, sir?'

It was almost an impertinent question, but Hayashi recognized it as a ploy and seemed amused. 'Not if you give me the answers I want, lieutenant. I don't think we need to trouble the admiral.'

'What answers, colonel?' In his own ears it sounded to Minato that his voice was vibrating.

'Did Lieutenant Sagawa speak to you on Saturday night?'

Minato made a pretence of frowning. 'Saturday night? No, sir. I haven't seen Lieutenant Sagawa since mid-afternoon on Saturday. He's just been found—'

'Yes, I know his body has been found. Where were you on Saturday night, lieutenant?'

'I went out to Omiya, to where my parents used to live. They were killed in the air raid in 1942—'

'I know,' said Hayashi, but did not sound sympathetic.

Minato showed no surprise that the colonel should know that; he was coming to feel that he would not be surprised at anything Hayashi knew. 'The neighbours had put up a small shrine to them. I went to pay my respects.'

'Were you a good son to them?'

'I hope so, sir.' He had been; and wondered what sort of son Hayashi had been. If, indeed, he had ever had parents: it was hard to imagine his having any ties to anyone, as if he had been created whole and adult, just as he was now.

'Are you a good son to Nippon?'

'I hope so, sir.' For the first time he felt the doubt within himself, a tiny crack in the edifice he had built. But he put it out of his mind at once; it must not be allowed to show.

Hayashi, no crack showing in *his* edifice, all metal and just as expressionless, stared at him for what seemed an unbearably long moment. Then he said, 'We shall see', and was abruptly gone.

Minato shrank inside his uniform. He leaned back against a desk, glad of its support. He started up, trying to put strength back into his legs, as he heard Hayashi returning down the corridor. But it was not Hayashi, just an orderly.

'Admiral Tajiri wishes to see you, sir.'

Minato stood stiff and tall, willing himself to be composed. He straightened his tunic, wished that there was a mirror in the office: normally a most unconceited man, he suddenly wanted reassurance that he looked all right. Hollow legs slowly refilling, he went down the corridor and knocked on the admiral's door. When he entered he saw that Tajiri was not alone.

'Ah, lieutenant. This is Colonel Nitobe of the *kempei*. He has my permission to ask you some questions.'

Minato suddenly felt sick; he could not understand why he did not keel over. They were about to question him regarding Sagawa; he wondered if Hayashi had known that the secret police were already waiting for him. He bowed, kept quiet.

'Lieutenant Minato—' Colonel Nitobe was a squat little man with a grey moustache and an abstract air, as if he were trying to remember something he had forgotten. Or trying to forget something that persisted in being remembered: the rape of Nanking. He was that rare man, a secret policeman with a conscience. 'You have been in America for the past six years?'

'Yes, sir. I was sent there by Admiral Tajiri.' He was aware of

Tajiri watching him, but the admiral was offering him no encouragement.

'And I understand you did an excellent job.' Nitobe had a habit of scratching his moustache with his middle finger, a delicate movement like that of a geisha applying make-up. 'While you were in custody did you ever meet a man named Tamezo Okada, a Nisei corporal in the American Army?'

Minato had learned that when being interrogated it was better to tell part of the truth than deny it all. He furrowed his brow: it was both simulated and genuine puzzlement. Had the discovery of Sagawa's body somehow led them to Okada?

'Yes, sir. He was one of my interrogators at San Diego.'

'Why did they need him when they knew you could speak English so well?'

The air of puzzlement made him look sincere. 'I don't know, sir. The Americans have a lot to learn about interrogation.'

Nitobe scratched his moustache a little harder, as if he would have preferred not to be reminded how well the *kempei* could interrogate people. 'Yes.'

'They are still young,' said Tajiri, but it was difficult to tell whether he was praising the Americans or deriding them.

'Did Okada spend much time with you, lieutenant?'

'No more than any of the others, sir.'

'Yet you and he were friends as boys, weren't you? He came to Japan at the same time as you, back in 1929. You stayed on, but he went home.'

Minato carefully paid out a little more of the truth, like a man fishing round a crumbling hole in the ice. 'We quarrelled about Japan, sir. We stopped being friends then. When they brought him in to see me in San Diego, I thought then that they were hoping our friendship would be revived.'

'And was it?'

'No, sir. We were as far apart as ever.'

'Why didn't you mention this encounter to Admiral Tajiri when you wrote your report?'

Minato, feeling panic creeping through him, glanced at Tajiri. But the admiral had swung round in his chair, sat facing the window; his profile showed nothing, his face could have been no more than a bas-relief mask hung in the air. Minato wondered if they already had Okada in custody and how much he had told the *kempei* under interrogation.

He could feel the ice crumbling around him. He began to tie knots in the truth, hoping he could unravel them if he had to use the same line again. 'I had a *giri* to Okada's father, sir. Okada-san is a true patriot, always has been. It was he who helped me build up my contacts after Pearl Harbor. He hopes, when the war is won, to return to Japan. I could not shame him by naming his son as a traitor in my report. I did wrong, sir, but I did it for the best of reasons.'

In his six years in the United States he had almost forgotten the obligations of *giri*. It was the debt, less an inheritance than *on*, that one could incur to those outside one's family; one could bear it unwillingly, which one never did with an *on*. It had once been a *samurai* virtue, but now, more often than not, it was a burden. It was a hire purchase drain on one's spirit; nonetheless, it could also be borne honourably. He hoped he sounded honourable now.

Tajiri swung his chair back. 'I think that is a good enough explanation, colonel.'

Nitobe's finger seemed glued to his moustache now, 'Of course, sir. But may I put one more question to Lieutenant Minato?' Tajiri nodded and the colonel looked at Minato. 'Lieutenant, did Tamezo Okada ever give you a hint that, like his father, he wanted to return to Japan?'

Another knot in the truth: 'Only if America won the war, sir. He hates everything his father believes in. May I be presumptuous, sir – why do you ask?'

Nitobe dropped his finger. 'We have word from the United States, lieutenant, that after you escaped he was sent to Corpus Christi in Texas to do a parachute course. Since then there has been no trace of him.'

Minato kept his voice steady. 'Does that mean, sir, you think he has been parachuted here into Japan?'

'It's a possibility, lieutenant, don't you think?'

Minato looked at Tajiri, but the old man was giving him no help now. At last he nodded. 'I suppose so, colonel.'

'Did they attempt to convert you, lieutenant? Have you come back here to spy for them?'

He unravelled a knot in the truth. 'Yes, sir, the first week. I said no and I continued to say no, but they kept at me. That was why they kept me so long in San Diego instead of sending me to trial, I think they kept hoping I'd change my mind.'

'And you didn't?'

'No, sir.' He should have said no more than that, but he had been too long in America, the land of free speech: 'Am I under suspicion of being a double agent?'

He caught a glimpse of Tajiri's lips twitching in a slight smile: the old man, a rebel himself, admired a little rebellion. Of course virtually everyone not in the secret police was rebellious of the *kempei*. Colonel Nitobe knew he was the odd man out in this room, so he took the easy way out. He smiled.

'Of course not, lieutenant. But if Okada has landed here in Japan, do you think he will try to contact you?'

'I doubt it, sir. We were not very friendly towards each other in San Diego.'

'If he did, would you turn him over to us, the son of a patriot to whom you had a *giri*?' Minato said nothing while he tried to think of an answer that would not sound too glib. 'You hesitate, lieutenant. Why is that?'

The truth now was a mess of knots. 'Yes, I'd turn him over to you, colonel. But it would hurt me because I know it would hurt the name of Okada-san, his father.'

There was silence for a moment, then Admiral Tajiri said, 'I think that will be all, Colonel Nitobe. I'm satisfied that Lieutenant Minato is loyal to the Emperor and Japan and to me. If this Tamezo Okada does appear, I personally guarantee that Lieutenant Minato will hand him over to you. He will have that *on* to me.'

Minato looked bleakly at the old man, wondering why he should have been so explicit. He had come home, not a step at a time, but suddenly in one giant leap.

Spring came overnight, as it often does in Japan, like a messenger who knocks on the door before one is awake. There were few trees left in the inner city, but the surviving ones suddenly were spotted with pale green buds, as yet hardly discernible against the black-grey trunks. Out in the hills beyond the city wildflowers magically appeared; the stretched cold air loosened and softened and sounds were not as sharp. Hope blossomed weakly in the faces of the people, as if the air raids were seasonal, concomitant with snow and ice and freezing weather. To some, the despairing whose only sustenance was a desperate optimism, even the ashes that covered the city looked like fertilizer.

'At least it will be good to be warm again,' said Morishima. He was still favouring his bad back, but he and Okada were working together stacking bags of rice that had been shipped from Shanghai. 'I am tired of sleeping in a trench full of water that freezes my balls and arse.'

'At your age it should preserve them.' Okada liked these rough, hardy men on the docks with whom one could joke without fear of being thought too familiar. Morishima was close to the sort of men who had worked for Okada and his father in the nursery.

Then the sirens began wailing and Morishima looked hurt and disappointed. 'Ah, why do they have to come on such a day?'

They stopped working and waited; then Koga came out of his shed and blew a whistle. The dock workers began to move quickly but without panic towards the air raid trenches in the streets outside. The docks had already been badly damaged and timber and iron roofing from the wrecked sheds had been used to reinforce the shelter trenches. Okada knew that there were very few safe places in the city, unless one lived within the Imperial Palace compound, but he felt a little more protected in the trenches with the extra roofing over his head. A bomb directly on his head was too terrible to contemplate, so he did his head no premature harm by not thinking about it.

The men crowded together in the trenches. Okada found himself next to Koga, who took up enough room for two men, feeling himself entitled to die in comfort. He stank, and it was a moment or two before Okada realized it was the stink of fear. 'The chances of a direct hit, Koga-san,' he said, 'are one in ten thousand.'

'Who's afraid?' said Koga, shivering with bravado. 'You knew nothing about air raids on Saipan. There's never been anything as terrible as the raids on Tokyo. The Americans are barbarians, like they've always been.'

There were murmurs of assent from the rest of the trench residents. Okada wanted to tell them about the German raids on Coventry and London and Rotterdam; but this was not the place nor the time. Besides, he was not really up to date on the quality and quantity of air raids. It is difficult to get an overall view when one's head is well down in a trench.

Then the all-clear siren went without any bombs having been dropped. Okada was first out of the trench. He stretched himself to ease his cramped muscles, wiped the mud from his trousers and looked up at the clear blue sky. There had been only two aircraft: probably photographic reconnaissance planes, he thought. Two chalk-marks were drawn in a beautiful curve across the blue, as if the pilots were taking an aesthetic delight in showing off their calligraphy. Okada watched them with hidden pride, feeling safe again. The planes would be Superfortresses, a type of aircraft the Japanese could not match.

The other men came up out of the trenches, hawking and spitting. Tuberculosis had become rife and Okada, always careful of his health, had become as much afraid of contracting the disease as of the bombs. Diarrhoea, a malady caused by a combination of fear and bad diet, was even more endemic and as soon as they were above ground at least half the men hurried towards the latrine bins at the end of the docks. Okada looked back up at the sky where rode danger which at least was clean and noninfectious.

'No bombs,' said Morishima beside him. 'Do you think they were looking to see if we wanted to surrender?'

'Did you wave your white flag?'

'Do you think the Americans would take any notice of just me?'

He shook his head in good-humoured resignation. The poor, thought Okada, who was turning philosophical, have an investment in resignation.

In the afternoon the wind began to rise. Ash blew over the city like a grey dust-storm, soft against the skin but irritating in the nostrils. In certain areas the wind turned into eddies; ash and dust spun like giant smeared perspex tops. By the time Okada left work the small signs of spring had been buried under a grey film and the guerilla wind came and went in spasmodic assault. All he wanted was to get back to the hotel and out of the provoking wind. But first he had to go to the two mail drops.

He went first to the drop outside the Marunouchi building; but there was no message from Natasha. He felt a certain disappointment, more personal than official; had he come expecting a love note? He walked on towards the second drop; he noticed that the wind had eased a little. The drop was behind a telephone box beneath the elevated railroad tracks two blocks north of the main station; an angle in the iron pillars that supported the tracks provided an almost perfect hiding place. Okada had to wait till two men left the phone booth, then he went behind it and groped in the angle of the ironwork.

Minato had been there. Okada lit a match and read the message: *Phone me at once.* He stepped into the booth and called the Navy building; but Lieutenant Minato had left for the day. Then he called the Staff College; but Lieutenant Minato could not be found. The man who answered the phone asked him his name and if there was any message, but Okada said no and hung up without saying who he was.

He stepped out into the night. The wind was blowing again, but in gusts, acrid with the smell of ash. A fire engine went past, its bell jangling, headed for a dead fire that the wind had bellowed into life again. Okada went home to the hotel, feeling irritated by the wind and grit, worried by Minato's urgent message and lonely because he wished he were seeing Natasha this evening. He had a sense of isolation, and felt that he had caught some malady far worse than tuberculosis or diarrhoea.

He changed his clothes, went to the public baths, soaked in the water, felt even more isolated amongst the crowd in the bath; then he dressed again and went down to the cheap café where he ate each evening. He had learned that the restaurants and cafés had been closed for a long period and had only reopened late last year. Though he was managing, like all the other dock workers, to pilfer some food from the docks, he was continually on the edge of hunger. There was no rationing system, a fact that had surprised him; he had expected that the Japanese, with their regimentation, would have had a strict systematized approach to the handing out of food. Instead, the distribution of food was left to the *tonarigumi*, the neighbourhood associations; he was reminded of what he had read regarding the ward bosses in American cities. The method, however, worked and each week he drew his quota of whatever was available.

But each evening, tired after his twelve-hour shift, he did not feel like cooking his own meal and always came here to the Gilded Lily café. It was a place where one served oneself, but it was no Automat. One stood in line, the food was plopped into one's bowls: tonight there was a little dried fish, balls made of rice, wheat, potatoes and beans, and a small apple for each customer.

Okada found a place at a table crowded with a family: a young couple and their four children. He recognized them for what they were, peasants brought in from the countryside to work in the metropolitan factories. One saw them every day, thousands of them: out of their element, overwhelmed completely by the war and life in the city, stunned into a retreat behind a mask of idiocy. The young parents looked at Okada sullenly and he looked at the four children with compassion. The children stared back at him, tiny battered dolls in their shapeless quilted jackets: their mother looked so young that they might have been her toys.

Three of the children dropped their heads, but the youngest, a girl of about three, continued to stare at Okada. He picked up his small apple, cut it into four pieces and handed three of the pieces to the other children, all of whom took it shyly. He held out the fourth piece to the little girl, but she made no move, just stared at him out of her tiny, narrow eyes.

Then her mother said, 'She is blind.'

Oh Jesus, Okada said silently; and wanted to weep. Emotion choked him, he looked at the parents, tears welling in his eyes. They saw his concern and suddenly the look of sullen idiocy melted from their faces.

'We are going back home,' said the father. 'The war is too much for us. We are going back to Akita.'

Akita, Okada knew, was in the north, a long way from the bombs. 'You are fortunate.'

'Our train leaves at six o'clock tomorrow morning. We shall sleep at the station to be sure of getting on it. Everybody wants to go back to the country. The children have almost forgotten what it looks like.'

Okada was sorry when they got up and left the café. He had enjoyed their company; he had little in common with them, but they had relieved his loneliness. He sat at the table a while longer, then he rose and made his slow way back to the hotel. He went up to his room, lay down on his sleeping mat and tried to read the cheap edition of *The Tale of Genji* which he had bought a week ago. But he was not in the mood for the love affairs of Prince Genji and the indulgences of a medieval royal court. He put down the book, lay thinking of Natasha and the pleasures of her flesh, looked around him at the drab austerity of his room, and finally got up, put on his jacket and went out again.

The wind was still gusting and he turned away from it, walking without direction just so long as he did not have to face the grit and ash flying through the air. He had never felt so aimless as he did tonight; his thoughts and his feet were at a loss; he felt as if he were adrift even from the war itself. He had no idea where he was when the sirens began to wail. He stopped on a corner, looked around him in bewilderment as if he had just come awake after sleep-walking.

He was down by the Sumida River, not far from the Fukaga-wa docks. This was one of the poorest areas of the city; as he stood there the people came pouring out of their wooden tenements and began to hurry towards the air raid shelters. Many of them, as if knowing there would not be enough room for them in the public shelters, scrambled down into the trenches in the street, pulling sheets of iron over them. He wondered if there was time to get back to his hotel, decided there wasn't and joined the stream moving towards the public shelter at the far end of the street.

He used his weight and height to push his way down the steps and find a place against one wall of the shelter. People crowded in against him, their fear and tension increasing their smell. Their chatter drowned the sound of the sirens; then someone began to laugh and the laughter spread through the shelter, a nervous giggle that silenced the chatter but did little to relieve the tension.

Okada heard a voice and strained his ears to hear what was being said; then he realized what had caused the laughter. From a loud-speaker up in one corner of the shelter's ceiling a mechanically enthusiastic voice from Radio Tokyo was telling the crushed crowd that calisthenics could make them all strong and vigorous again. Okada, too, began to laugh; he freed his arms from the pressure of those around him and lifted them high. He waved them in a stiff, slow parody of exercises; those near him, still giggling, lifted their arms and imitated him. The pantomime spread, the giggling turned to open laughter and drowned out the stupid mechanical voice. In the dim light of the dirty electric bulbs hundreds of hands moved slowly like the heads of dancing cobras; fingers turned into horns that made rude gestures; and all the while the laughter went on like that of happy madmen who had at last realized who was truly sane. Then the first bomb fell.

It landed in the street upstairs; the floor of the shelter shuddered with the concussion. Okada, his arms still raised, looked at his watch: 11 o'clock. He wondered how long the night would last: the bombing always stretched the hours.

The loud-speaker had suddenly shut up; the laughter just as

abruptly stopped. In the silence a child cried, but was quickly hushed. Another bomb burst somewhere up above, then another and another.

A man standing beside Okada, his face only inches away, said, 'Why are they bombing *here*? There are no factories around here.'

'They could be aiming for the docks,' said Okada.

'They've bombed those before. We've got only the odd bomb, the one or two that missed the docks. But listen to *that*!'

There was a pattern to the bombing; Okada could hear it. Twice more the floor of the shelter trembled beneath his feet; the bombs that caused it were not random misses. The people around him started to stir; children began to whimper and at the far end of the shelter an old woman suddenly shrieked. Then the door at the top of the steps swung open.

A screaming figure stood there: it was impossible to tell whether it was a man or woman. Flames enveloped it; it stood at the top of the steps like some avenging angel. Then it fell headlong down the steps.

Okada pushed his way through the crowd, was the first to reach the burning figure: it was a man. Okada grabbed a piece of sacking and flung it over the man, but he knew the poor wretch was already dead. He wrapped the body in the sacking, shutting his nostrils against the burning flesh, and carried the man up the steps and out into the street. He put the body down, turned away from it in shamed disgust; he had felt the charred flesh coming away through the sacking. He wanted to be sick; he opened his mouth but nothing came up. Then his lungs felt the searing air he drew in and suddenly he saw the horror about him.

Bombs were still falling, but farther away. In the short pauses between their explosions he could hear the planes in the red-tinged darkness above; they sounded much lower than on previous raids; these were not the high-flying Superfortresses, but probably B-29s. And the bombs they were dropping were not high explosives but incendiaries.

Okada's first reaction was to plunge back down the steps out of the rapidly gathering inferno. Then he saw the woman with

153

two small children, one of them carried in a satchel on her back, run past. The quilted hood of her jacket was on fire but she didn't seem to realize it; the baby on her back was screaming as the smouldering flames flickered at it. Okada raced after the woman, grabbed the baby from her back and snatched at the burning jacket. He wrenched the woman off her feet; she fell back against him with a shriek. The second child screamed and fell on the mother. Okada was assaulted by bedlam: the screams, the crash of the bombs, the roaring of the flames. The heat was increasing; even as he tried to get his balance he saw a wooden house opposite him explode into flames. He dragged the mother to her feet, picked up the second child under his free arm and began to stumble rather than run, towards the canal he could see at the end of the street.

This district was crisscrossed with canals, most of them no more than open sewage drains. Okada didn't know that till he reached the first canal; he looked down into its stinking surface and then ran on over the iron bridge that crossed it. The wind was continuing to rise and several blocks away he saw the flames being sucked up into it like giant yellow lilies shooting up out of the ground. As he crossed the canal he looked up its length and saw people, flames herding them, already jumping into the filth below.

He was in another street of tumbledown houses, dark and fragile as cardboard cutouts against the flames in the street beyond. Suddenly there was a giant roar and a fierce crackling; the houses blew up into one giant furnace. The heat was a physical blow that stopped him in his tracks; he shut his eyes, fearing his eyeballs would boil, and felt the skin on his cheeks tighten as if about to split. He swung round, holding the children against his chest, protecting them from the blast with his own body, and started running away from it, pushing the mother ahead of him.

He could no longer hear the planes for the roar of the flames; but he could hear the explosion of the bombs. Still running, he shouted in English at the top of his voice, 'Go home, you bastards!', but not even the woman running in front of him heard him and least of all did the men in the planes, his countrymen, up there in the red swirling vortex of impenetrable smoke. He was running now at the head of a herd of people; it was a moment or two before it struck him that, for some reason or other, they wanted him as their leader. When he swung to the right, down towards the river, they followed him, running with a sort of blind faith, as if all they wanted was someone, anyone, to lead them out of the holocaust that surrounded them.

The wind was almost a gale, a storm of heat that was creating whirlpools of fire; on the far side of the river a whole street of houses suddenly was sucked up into the huge fireball above it; the houses went up into it like firewood being thrown into a giant bonfire in the sky. Okada ran on, but behind him people, their lungs burned out by the searing air, fell down and died with horrible moans that only their own terrified ears heard. Looking back, Okada saw a red dragon in the air, a thermal tornado: it leapt high, then arched over and struck at a street two blocks away. The street went up with a red roar.

There was a narrow canal to be crossed before the river could be reached. Okada, seeing people stumble and fall, abruptly pulled up as he reached the iron bridge over the canal. It was a foot-bridge, wide enough only for two people to cross side by side; the crowd behind him, panicstricken, rushed at it as if it were a four-lane highway. He stepped in front of them, thrust the baby and the small child at their mother and told her to run ahead down to the edge of the river. The crowd pushed against him, but he fought them, hurling his fist at a man who tried to push through and knocking him to his knees. Alternately swinging his fists and then turning his fists into hands to push the terrified people through in an orderly line, he somehow got them over the bridge.

He looked back to see if there were any stragglers, saw the old woman sitting in the middle of the street, head bent, waiting to die by fire. He ran back, slung her up over his shoulder and turned once more towards the bridge. And saw the ironwork turning a glowing red.

Okada could feel his clothes beginning to smoulder. His face felt as if it were one huge cracked blister; his eyes were tiny fireballs in the grate of his skull. He had stopped breathing; he was surviving on a last lungful of air that had no fire in it. He knew he was going to die the next moment, but he was not going to die standing still.

He took off, running faster, or so it seemed, than he had ever run in his life before. He went over the red-hot bridge, the wooden floor burning beneath him, the ironwork on either side scorching him like branding irons. It seemed for a few moments that his whole body was smouldering; the old woman bounced on his shoulder like a burning log. Then he was across the bridge, running full tilt into a gust of wind that, miraculously, was not lung-searing. He opened his mouth in one great gulp, then ran on down towards the river.

The fire had already raged along here; there was nothing left to burn. There were no banks to the river, just piers and warehouses, still blazing fiercely; but below them was a line of lighters covered with tarpaulins, some of them beginning to smoulder as hot ash fell on them. Men were pulling off the tarpaulins and throwing them into the river. Okada gently handed the old woman to two women, paused to see that she was still alive, then clambered down on to one of the lighters. He reached up and took a child from its mother and put it down; he was yelling at the people as they pushed forward to get away from the heat and flames behind them. Two men joined him and between the three of them they managed to bring all the children down on to the lighter. Then the adults, careless of each other, driven to selfishness by panic, started to tumble down from the pier.

Okada, trying to protect the children from being trampled on or pushed into the water, was ruthless. He hurled two men into the water, punched a third in the face. Yet even as he fought the men he couldn't blame them for their self-interest; indeed, the back of one man's jacket was on fire as Okada threw him into the river. His anger was as hot as the flames on the riverside but not at the desperate men trying to save themselves from being burned to death. Every blow he struck was a blow at the invisible pilots and bombardiers above him and at the generals, safe on some island hundreds of miles away, who had ordered this holocaust. He was burning with shame and anger, glad only that his father was not here to see what the barbarians were doing.

The lighter was now a packed mass of people. Okada grabbed a pole, shouted for someone to cast off the ropes that tied it to the pier, and pushed the lighter out into the river. It drifted slowly into mid-stream, then began to move just as slowly down towards the distant harbour. The Sumida was a river running through Hell. On either side of it an inferno raged, fire leaping hundreds of feet into the air, turning the thick swirling smoke above it into red-and-black banners of a dark victory that, Okada furiously hoped, would forever haunt the victors riding high above it. The wind gusted and eddied, creating giant revolving cones of flame; the wind fed the fires and the heat from them fed the wind in a terrible cycle of horror. Everyone on the lighter stood or sat facing inwards, their faces away from the heat. They looked like a prayer group, but Hell already surrounded them.

The river was now bearing a fleet of lighters and small boats down towards the harbour. The water was a bright red mirror on which charred bodies, steam rising from them, floated like black flowers in a morning mist. Okada, lifting his face for a moment, felt his eyes burn with the bright red glare: the world, it seemed, now had only two colours, red and black. Spring, born that morning, was dead forever: the only perfume was that of ash and smoke and burning flesh.

Then at last the river widened. The small fleet, a long dark line between the flames on either side, drifted out into the inner harbour, past the burning docks and the blazing ships moored there, out into water that no longer threatened to boil, into air that, still thick with smoke and ash, was cool enough not to sear the lungs. The people raised their heads, as if their prayers were finished, and looked back at the tornados of fire still consuming what had once been their homes. Children began to cry, women to moan, and a man stood up and screamed a long-drawn-out obscenity at the planes above the burning roof of smoke above his head.

Okada, crouched holding two children close to him, stood

up, half-expecting his roasted body to fall apart like a well-cooked chicken. He turned his face seawards and took a deep breath; the air was acrid but he could smell salt on it. He opened his mouth to it; it tasted of life. He looked down at the two children and smiled. They stared at him, then, reassured, the blank round plates of their faces opened in smiles that touched his heart.

In that moment a ship, four hundred yards away at a pier, blew up. The explosion was deafening, the blaze blinding. The air seemed to be pressed into a solid mass; it came across the harbour, pushing a wave ahead of it. It hit the lighter and the people on it; the crowd fell back before it, the lighter tilted. Okada felt his feet going from under him, then he went backwards into the water. In the moment before he went under he saw the children above him, still smiling.

He struggled to the surface, hampered by his jacket. He managed to get out of it, fighting off people who were grabbing at him as they fought to stay afloat. But most of them could not swim and their heavy quilted jackets kept them afloat only for moments; then the jackets were soaked, started to drag down those who wore them. Okada saw the lighter drifting away on the still turbulent water; he swam after it, hauled himself up on to it. A few people were still aboard, lying flat on their stomachs, screaming as they reached out to help those struggling in the water.

Okada knelt down, grabbed a despairing hand and, with strength he didn't realize he had, lifted a woman out of the water and up on to the lighter. He grabbed another hand, pulled a man aboard. Then he saw the two small children floating on their backs, their faces already being lapped by water as the soaked weight of their clothes pulled them down. He didn't know if they were the children he had been holding before; he just pushed himself forward and went overboard into the water. He grabbed them both, keeping himself afloat with his feet, and pushed them up the side of the lighter. Someone above him took the children and pulled them to safety.

Okada would never know how long he remained in the water. It was very cold, a contrast to the very warm air still being blown

158

from the fires onshore. He swam from body to body, never certain which one was a corpse and which not. He would push them towards the lighter, let the helping hands there decide whether to pull them aboard; he swam round and round, like a sheepdog bringing in the remnants of a flock. Once he paused to rest, lying on his back and looking across at the blazing waterfront and the devastated districts beyond. The scene was so awesome it somehow could not be believed; there was a terrifying beauty to it that turned it into a nightmare from which he knew he would awake safe and sound. He could see no people onshore and that only added to the unreality of the scene. He was looking at the end of the world, too weary to be anything but resigned to it.

At last there were no more bodies to be saved; at least not live ones. A blackened corpse drifted past, both arms sticking up stiffly like the stumps of masts; he turned away from it and, exhausted, hauled himself up on to the lighter. He lay on his back and looked up at the grateful faces above him. He was one of them: a Japanese.

53

The all-clear went at five o'clock in the morning. The fires were still burning, but not as fiercely; there was nothing left for them to feed on. The wind had dropped, but a black storm of smoke blotted out the sky. The lighter had drifted inshore and half an hour after the sirens went quiet, it bumped up against a jetty.

Okada jumped ashore, helped tie up the lighter. Across the street from the jetty there was nothing but a black, smoking wasteland; but there were no fires here. He lifted children up to safety, helped the elderly back on to land; they all did what he told them, even the men. He was their leader, their saviour, and he was embarrassed by their gratitude.

'We must find something to eat and drink,' he said, but hoped they did not expect miracles of him.

He led them away from the jetty, which was wooden and still smouldering, towards a cobblestoned square standing in the middle of burnt-out warehouses. He sent men into the ruins of the warehouses and small miracles were found: a sack of rice, a cask of tea. They found receptacles, twisted but still usable; in one corner of the square a water main had burst and water gushed freely. Moses, Okada thought, might have found no more than a Sinai water system when he tapped the rock. There was no shortage of heating to cook the rice and make the tea: small fires burned obligingly all around.

They were eating the rice and drinking the tea when two men, blackened by smoke and ash, one of them carrying a camera, came across the square towards them.

'We are from *Mainichi*,' said the man without the camera, producing a notebook and pen. 'Have you been here all night?'

Everyone stopped eating and looked at Okada. He hesitated, one eye on the camera. His mind had begun working again: he was *not* one of these people. 'No,' he said slowly. 'We came down the river.'

'He saved us all.' She was a little old lady, toothless, dark with smoke, her head singed almost bald; but she looked at Okada with eyes made bright and young with admiration and gratitude. 'If it wasn't for him, we wouldn't be here.'

There was a sudden chorus of agreement. The reporter moved in on Okada. 'May I have your name, sir?'

Okada, sharp now as a fox, already seeing the trap closing in on him, turned his back on the photographer, shook his head at the reporter. 'No, please. I was just one of them – we all helped each other—'

'No!' shouted the crowd, lauding him, endangering him. 'Tell them your name!'

'Fujita, Tamezo Fujita,' he said, grabbing a name out of the past, that of the foreman at the nursery in Gardena. He turned again but this time the photographer was too quick for him. The flashlight blazed and Okada, caught offguard, looked directly into the camera.

Five

1

'How could you be so foolish as to let them do it?' said Minato. 'You should have taken his camera and smashed it.'

'How could I do that?'

'Your photograph in the papers! Don't you know they are looking for heroes? The country needs them – and you let them make you one!'

'It's a pretty poor photo – the printing quality is terrible. No one will recognize me.' But he said it without confidence, though he smiled.

'What are you smiling at?'

'My father had his photo in both *Asahi* and *Mainichi* twenty-two years ago. They said he was a hero too. No one would have recognized him either, from the photos.'

It had been a long day, a sick, disturbing, worrying one. Just after daylight he had left the group in the square, all of them rising and standing in ranks to bow to him; he had bowed in return and then, feeling embarrassed and even something of a fake, he had headed back towards the centre of the city. He knew now, as well as any other brave man, that heroes often become so out of hopelessness. He had wanted desperately to live and he could not have lived knowing he had let other people die.

He walked through the smoking, still burning devastation. Fire crews turned their hoses on burning ruins, but the hope on their blackened faces was as weak as the flow of water trickling from their hoses. Families sat in the middle of streets outside the ruins of their homes, their eyes blank with shock; a woman, looking like a roughly carved statue, sat with a dead baby in her lap. Ash drifted in the air like black snowflakes; smoke, caught

...ies of stray wind, turned into grinning grey devils. And over it all hung the acrid yet sickening smell of smoke, ash and burning flesh. This part of the city was one vast crematorium.

He had rung Minato at the Staff College before he left for the Navy building. 'I tried to get you last night.'

'I was with Admiral Tajiri. How did you get on in last night's raid?'

'Okay. I'll see you tonight. Same place?'

'No, they tell me all the trains are out after the raid. I'll meet you where I left my note. Seven-thirty.'

Okada had gone down to the docks to work; but there was no work to be done. The docks had all gone up in flames; the hulks of ships burned at the burnt-out wharves and out in the harbour; the water was black with ash, a great lake of ink. Debris floated on it, some of it obscene; bloated carcases of dogs, a woman's corpse. There seemed to be no living soul in sight: he was alone on the morrow of Judgment Day.

There was no sign of Morishima or any of the other dockers. As he walked away from the smouldering skeletons of the sheds he saw Koga coming down the street towards him. The *yakuza* wasn't swaggering this morning; the night had knocked the bounce out of him. The derby hat had gone and his closely-shaven head was covered with a fine grey ash. He looked old and beaten and unthreatening, a heavyweight in the last of all rounds. Okada almost felt sorry for him, but there is a limit to how much one can cheapen sympathy.

'Go home.' Koga's hands were hanging at his sides, the dragons on them shrunken and wrinkled. 'There's no work today.'

Okada looked back at the ruins. 'There won't be any work for weeks. Where do I go?'

Koga shrugged. 'They'll want us to help with the cleaning up. I'll have to find new crews. A lot of 'em died last night. Fujioka, Inagaki, Morishima—'

'No!' The whole night and morning seem to fall in on Okada. He hardly knew the little man with his bad back, but all at once he was the face of all the people Okada had seen die last night. Morishima had never been the 'enemy': he had been a friendly

little man who, in his awkward way, had made Okada welcome. He had not deserved to die by incineration. 'His family
too?'

Koga nodded. 'All of them. His wife and five kids.'

There was not even someone left to whom he could go and
give sympathy.

'Come and see me tomorrow.' Koga gave him an address. 'I'll
talk to the boss. We can give you a job cleaning up. There'll be
plenty to clean up.'

Okada left him, his mind already made up that he would have
nothing further to do with the *yakuza*. He went back to his
hotel; but there was no hotel. The whole area was just a black,
smoking dump, as if the houses and buildings had been no more
than garbage thrown there to be burned. He stood in the street
and watched people picking amongst the ruins like giant crows,
searching for the carrion of their own lives. He felt an odd
identification with them and none at all with the Americans who
had caused all this destruction. Several times he thought he saw
Morishima amongst the ruins, but he was just conjuring up a
ghost to haunt himself.

He joined the line at the tables where the *tonarigumi* had set
up its emergency food supply and drew a ration of rice. But he
was not hungry, just exhausted. He went back to the docks,
found a space between two charred packing cases, lay down and
fell asleep. He was so utterly depressed he did not care if he did
not wake again.

But he did wake, seven hours later. He rolled over on his
back, feeling his muscles grinding, and looked up at a sky where
smoke still drifted like the remnants of a storm. The smell of the
city was still thick and sickening in his nostrils. He tried to
remember sweeter, fresher odours; and out of the peaceful past
came memories of his mother's herb garden. He had planted it
for her in the back yard of their house in Gardena, herbs from
foreign lands that he had nurtured in the hot California sun. He
savoured in his mind the perfume of fennel, calamint, thyme
and rosemary. But he knew they could not shut out the smell of
death.

He had thought of Natasha just before he had dropped off;

now abruptly she was live in his thoughts. He sat up too quickly; every muscle in his body objected and he winced. He looked around wildly, as if expecting to see her. But all he saw was a big dark limousine, followed by three other cars, driving slowly across the square behind the docks.

People were dropping to their knees, putting their palms flat on the ground and lowering their heads till their foreheads touched the backs of their hands. He got stiffly to his feet, walked hurriedly towards the gathering crowd. He saw the limousine come to a halt, the other cars pulling in close behind it. A chauffeur and an aide jumped out of the limousine as men, in drab suits and awkward dignity, got out of the cars at the rear. Then the rear door of the limousine was opened and Emperor Hirohito stepped out.

There was a hissing gasp from the crowd. Okada still not fully awake, still American, stood and stared; then he heard the angry murmur beside him. He bowed, dropped to his knees, bowing his head but not so far that, under his brows, he could not see the small figure of the Emperor. This unprepossessing man, with his rimless glasses and small, thin moustache, his dark unadorned uniform and nondescript cap, dignified but not grandly so, looking more like a desk soldier than a field-marshal emperor, was the Son of Heaven.

No one spoke, no one called to the crowd to hail their Emperor. In the distance there were noises: the bells of fire engines, the grinding moan of trucks in low gear, far away an explosion. But here there was silence, as if the Emperor had brought with him the hushed atmosphere of his court. He looked at his kneeling subjects, then beyond them at what had been part of his domain. Okada, watching him from his awkward angle, saw the bland, smooth-cheeked face suddenly crumble; but only for a moment, so swiftly that it might have been no more than the shadow of a flying bird passing across it. Except that there were no birds here.

No words were exchanged between the Emperor and his staff. He took one last look around, shut his eyes for a moment behind the rimless glasses, then got slowly back into the big limousine. It went on its way, the other cars following it. Okada

164

was left with the impression that he was seeing a funeral procession drawing away from a vast open grave.

The crowd straightened up, began to chatter amongst themselves. They went about their business; then Okada, for the first time, saw what their business was. In the time he had been asleep these people had recovered from their shock, were getting ready to abandon the ruins of their homes. They had set up a flea market; blackened salvage was laid out for anyone who cared to buy. The goods offered were pathetic: pieces of charred furniture, twisted cooking utensils, clothing with holes burned in it, bicycle frames with no wheels, wooden pillows that looked like logs from a grate. Okada turned away, bumped into a man bent over under everything he possessed, a heavy bundle wrapped in oilskin.

'Where are you going?' Okada said.

'To the country. Everybody is. We'll never let the Americans do that to us again, not here. They'll have to come to the mountains to kill us now.'

He went trudging off, joining a gathering line of refugees heading towards the city centre and the railroad that would take them to the mountains, their last bastion.

At 7.30 Okada was waiting for Minato by the phone booth beneath the elevated railroad. He had not bothered to buy a copy of *Mainichi*, as if he were afraid to face himself in its pages. It was Minato who produced the newspaper and slapped it angrily against the iron stanchion beside him.

'It's the last thing we want – especially now!'

Okada decided it was time to get off the subject of his unwanted fame. 'What did you want to see me about? Something urgent?'

'Let's walk.' Minato looked around him for spies. The blackout had been turned into a ghastly farce; fires still burned and the evening wind was fanning glowing embers into bright red illuminations. The night was a less horrifying repeat of last night's pattern of black and red, an ideal camouflage in which anyone spying on him could hide. 'If you see anyone following us, tell me.'

165

Okada was not surprised at Minato's warning; it was an ending to the day that he might have expected. He fell in beside Minato, eyes alert, and they walked down towards the main station. If the trains were running south, he would go out and see Natasha. Tomorrow, indeed the rest of the war, could look after itself.

'They know you're in Japan,' said Minato. 'Or anyway, they suspect you are. They must have had someone planted in San Diego.'

Okada cursed quietly. 'Do they suspect you?'

'I don't know.' Minato told of the visit of Colonel Nitobe. 'You never can tell with the *kempei*. I don't even know if Admiral Tajiri suspects me. He hasn't spoken to me since Colonel Nitobe questioned me, I mean about whether I told the colonel the truth or not. I was with him last night and again today, but he just ignores the subject.'

'If he did suspect you and I were working together, would he throw you to the *kempei*?' Okada's voice was calm, dispassionate. They were walking through a battlefield (a truck went by, carting away last night's dead decently under the cover of darkness); he had expended all his fear last night, he had none left. 'You're his protégé, aren't you?'

'That's all that's saving me, I think. I just don't know—' Minato sounded distraught, and knew it. He tried to calm himself. 'I don't know that I want to go through with our mission.'

Okada felt he couldn't press him; at least not now. He couldn't tell Minato that he had lost his own enthusiasm for the war. He abruptly made up his mind: after he had seen Natasha tonight, he would make for the mountains with the other refugees. He might even go all the way down to Nagasaki, his father's home town, and lose himself there.

'You've got no closer to finding out what the Peace Faction is about?'

'I found out that last month the *kempei* arrested several hundred men – they're still being held. They're supposed to be supporters of a peace move, but as far as I can gather, there are very few big names amongst them. Except one, Shigeru Yoshida – he was a top diplomat. But there are no top military men held and they are the ones who got us into the war and are still running the country.'

'What do you want me to tell San Diego?'

Minato sighed, opened the newspaper and looked at Okada's picture. 'At least you had the sense not to give your real name . . . Don't send any message yet. Give me time to think things over.'

'I'd like to tell them a few things about that raid last night. They nearly killed me.'

'Nobody knows how many were killed in the raid – it could be as high as a hundred thousand. We got the word in Intelligence this afternoon that it may have had the wrong effect. The workers are saying it's pointless surrendering, that the Americans just want to exterminate them all.'

Okada remembered the man heading out of the city – 'They'll have to come to the mountains to kill us now.' Should he give that message to San Diego? Or would the air force generals who had ordered the raids not want to hear about such defiance?

'The civil defence people found an unexploded bomb. It contained half gelignite jelly, half gasoline,' Minato said.

'That doesn't seem to upset you.'

'It's war. You don't win battles moralizing about what the other side is doing.'

Goddam, thought Okada, should I be in this war at all? Maybe I should have stayed at Blood Mountain.

'I'll meet you at the same place in three days' time,' said Minato. 'What are you going to do in the meantime?'

Okada grinned sourly, 'Stay out of the limelight. You better make sure the *kempei* haven't got a tail on you.'

They were in the big square outside the station now. It was packed with people sitting or lying on their belongings; in the smoke-streaked moonlight the square looked like a plaza of huge dark cobbles. There were plenty of policemen about, but they were too conspicuous to be secret police.

'I'll be careful,' said Minato. 'You be the same.'

They parted then. Okada went into the station, wondering if the family he had met last night, the one with the tiny blind girl,

167

had managed to get away before the trains to the north were bombed out. Some trains to the south were still running; one was leaving for Nayora in twenty minutes. There was no chance that he could jump the long queues waiting outside the ticket offices; he had to find another way on to the train. He wondered if a hero should be given right of way, but he was not tempted to find out. One could be too brave.

He found an entrance to the freight section, went in unchecked. He crossed several sets of tracks, once being almost run down by an engine that suddenly started up, as if it had been lying in ambush for him. Then he came to a train standing at a platform, looked up at the driver hanging out of the cabin of his engine.

'This train going to Nayora?'

'Yes. Who are you?'

'A train examiner,' said Okada, and went down along the train banging at the wheels with his fist. The train driver looked after him, shaking his head in wonder at the mentally retarded who could now get a job on the railroads. He blew his whistle and started up the train to get away from the dregs of war.

But Okada had swung aboard, pushing his way into a crowded compartment, using fists and elbows.

'Who are you?' said a man whose kidneys had just been bruised.

'A train examiner,' said Okada, and glared at the man as if *he* shouldn't be aboard.

He had as much trouble getting out of the train at Nayora as he had had getting on it. He punched his way out, stood on the narrow platform and watched the long dark beast clang its way on into the night. Then he walked down through the pine trees towards the village, drinking in the sea-tinged air as if it were an elixir. There was no ash or smoke here and suddenly he wanted to sing with happiness that Natasha had been spared last night in Tokyo. Far across the bay to the north there was a faint glow in the bottom of the sky, like a hint of red dawn that remained static; he couldn't tell whether it was the city or a town farther down Tokyo Bay. It didn't matter: all of that was behind him.

He was so happy and eager to see Natasha he was careless; he banged on the front door of the villa as if he called here openly every night. Yuri, all belligerence, opened the door; then, though she didn't smile, her face relaxed with relief. She ushered him in and closed the door.

'The mistress will be so pleased to see you.'

Natasha came to the top of the stairs, saw him, then sat down suddenly on the top step and began to weep. He went up to her, two stairs at a time, took her hands and kissed the top of her head.

'I've been sick all day with worry—' She lifted her head, looked at him and smiled through her tears. 'You look dreadful!'

'I looked worse last night.' He leaned forward and kissed her on the lips; Yuri watched from below, from the stalls. He said softly, 'I love you, Natasha.'

She nodded, kissed him in return. She wanted to go to bed with him at once; but she had to be sensible. She looked down past him. 'Make him a meal, Yuri. And find some hot water so that he can have a bath.'

'Of course,' said Yuri in the tone of voice of someone who was expected to produce hot water out of cold rocks.

Natasha thought she had never spent such a long day. There had often been anxious moments, even hours; there had also been moments of danger. Such a life as she had led could not have been bland; nor would she have wanted it to be. She believed in herself, if not in her invulnerability: she had always had a cheerful resignation to fate.

There had been no suspense about Keith's death; he had died suddenly and unexpectedly. She had no recollection of the day following his death, whether it was short or long: grief had stopped the clock.

Today, however, the clock had seemed to move only a minute every hour. There had been little information on the radio about the raid on Tokyo; but by mid-morning the village had received enough news to know how bad the bombing had been. At midday Major Nagata had arrived. Though he carried no evidence of the fire with him, having spent the night in one of the *kempei*'s concrete shelters near the Imperial Palace, he was ashen-faced. He had begun to doubt whether, come the war's end, the barbaric Americans would have any need for him. They would just eliminate everyone above a certain rank. The bottom rank, he was afraid, would be below his own.

'Evacuation has already started,' he told Natasha. 'People will be moved in here tomorrow. Don't worry' – he saw the look of concern on her face, misunderstood it. 'You will not have people forced on you. I shall see to that. You see, I have had myself transferred here.'

'You? But why would they send a *kempei* officer here?'

'They are moving the rest of the foreigners out here, the diplomats and the businessmen. I shan't be the only *kempei* officer – there will be others. We shall have to be careful, Mrs Cairns.'

Doubly so; but he didn't know that. 'Where will you stay, major?'

He would have been pleased if she had made it sound more like an invitation; but if it had been, he would not have been able to accept it. 'My wife and children are coming. I have requisitioned a villa down by the beach. My wife loves the sea.' He wished she would drown in it. 'We must see you get someone congenial.'

'Please do that, major.' Then she said, 'How bad was it in Tokyo last night?'

'Nothing could have been worse.' He had spent the whole of the raid in the shelter; his wife had described it to him, as she had seen it from their apartment in Shibuys. She was a foolishly curious woman, which sometimes helped him in his profession. 'Nobody knows how many thousands died. All of them the poor, the workers,' he added piously.

That meant nothing to her: she had no idea whether Tom (she thought of him constantly as Tom, never as Tamezo) could be classed as one of the poor or where he worked or lived. So she went back to her own immediate problem.

'Please do see I get someone congenial billeted with me, major.' Someone blind and deaf and confined to a wheelchair, who would never go down to the cellar and discover the radio transceiver. 'Otherwise it might be difficult for you and me.'

170

He left then, to go down and make sure that the best available house on the beach was still his; the village had become like a new nesting ground with migratory birds coming in to fight over the best spots. He might write a cynical poem about it, one to be saved for postwar publication. It might even impress the Americans, though he doubted it. From what he had read of American poetry, it was mostly sentimental.

Natasha had somehow got through the rest of the day; she was certain that if Tom was alive, he would let her know. Having no phone was just part of the torture; she knew it would only have rung if there had been good news. There would have been no one to ring her if Tom were dead. The long agonizing wait had had one crystallizing effect; she knew now that she loved Tom Okada.

So tonight, weak with relief, hungry for love, a mess of emotions not necessarily more feminine than masculine (Okada felt the same way), she sat opposite him while he ate the meal Yuri had prepared. It was better than anything he could have got in Tokyo that evening; Natasha was still bringing home scraps from rich men's tables. Or anyway from General Imamaru's table: Lily was determined her 'niece' should not go hungry.

When Okada had finished his meal they went up to the main bedroom. It struck Natasha that tonight might be the last time she could have him up here; but she did not want to spoil their lovemaking by telling him so. For his part he looked at the small fire in the grate, then turned his back on it: he had seen enough flames to last him a lifetime. When he took off his clothes, which still smelled of the city's smoke, he felt as if he were shedding another reminder of last night's horror.

Their lovemaking, though as sensual, athletic and at times violent as previously, this time had another atmosphere to it; there were zones to them that were not all erogenous. They had the urge to discover in each other something other than their physical reactions. Their limbs were a cage for more than just the wild sex that consumed them.

In a quiet moment she said, 'Tell me about your life in America.'

171

'What do I compare it with?' He stroked her black hair, which had a shine to it that ashes never would. 'Your life here? Or in Hong Kong?'

'I don't want comparisons.' She was sensible enough not to be ashamed of what had gone before: perhaps she was more Japanese than he in that regard, though she had no Japanese blood. But she sensed that he would be jealous of the men in her life if she told him about them, no matter how indirectly. It was Keith, the renegade Presbyterian, the only man who had made an honest woman of her, who had told her that America was founded by Puritans and the country had never got over it. 'I want to know what to look forward to.'

Discrimination? But he couldn't tell her that, not while locked in her trusting arms. 'I lived better than most people here in Japan. I had an automobile and money and my parents had a good home—'

'Better than this house?'

'Yes.'

'Your parents are rich?'

'No. Well off, I suppose you'd call it.' They were speaking English, the language for bed; or at least they knew more erotic words in it. 'But not now. They've got nothing now.'

'Because of the internment?' He had told her about that on their first night together. 'But they'll get everything back after the war, surely?'

He smiled at her, his face so close to hers that she saw it only in his eyes. 'You're mercenary.'

'I know.' She was unashamed of that, too. She knew her faults and another one didn't matter. In her thesaurus, venality was only another name for foresight; she was happy in her ignorance that it also meant corruption. She had never felt corrupt, never in the least. 'But I'm not greedy. I don't mind if you're not a millionaire.' She had known one or two and they had been as mean as any beggar. 'Will your family like me?'

'My mother and sisters will. I don't know about my father. He doesn't like me.' He told her about his father and was surprised when he felt her tears dropping on his own cheeks. 'What's the matter?'

172

'I hate the thought of anyone not liking you. Especially your own father.' Coming from a home that had never been more than a shell, she had the romantic's idea of what a true family home should be.

'What about your father? Did he like you?'

She had told him nothing about Henry Greenway. But now she thought of that quiet, rather bemused man who came every weekend to the convent in Shanghai and took her for a drive in his car, a bull-nosed Morris-Cowley that, in retrospect, she believed typified her father: he lived in the immediate past. They would drive along the Bund, passing the Chinese millionaires in their bullet-proof Rolls-Royces and Cadillacs; they would pass side streets, down which she would glance and see the child labourers going home from their shifts at the foreign owned textile companies. They would finish up at the Cathay Hotel, where they would have tea in air-conditioned comfort, and strangers, those who didn't know Henry Greenway, would throw disgusted glances at the Englishman parading his teenage, half-caste concubine. Then on the way back to the convent they would stop off at a music shop and he would buy her a Bing Crosby record and, his own favourite band, a Harry Roy. The nuns would let her place Bing Crosby on the school Victrola, but they confiscated Harry Roy. There was sedition and hints of sin in such songs as *Does Santa Claus Sleep With His Whiskers Over Or Under The Sheet?* Yes, her father had liked her, but she had never been sure that he loved her.

Suddenly she was misty eyed about him. She got out of bed, went to a chest of drawers, came back and sat naked on the side of the bed. She opened a small lacquered box and took out a pile of cigarette cards.

'These were my father's heroes. It's all I have left of him.'

Okada sat up against the pillows, looked at the unfamiliar faces under the narrow-peaked caps, like schoolboys' headgear, read the unfamiliar names. 'I've never heard of them. Were they famous?'

'I only heard of them from him. Famous cricketers.' She read the names on the bottom of the cards. 'Maurice Tate – Father used to tell me he was the greatest bowler of all time. Frank

Woolley – he used to say he was just so beautiful to watch, so graceful. I think I fell in love with Frank Woolley myself when I was a girl, just listening to Father talk about him. George Gunn. Herbert Sutcliffe. Walter Hammond. And Jack Hobbs, his real hero.'

She dropped the cricketers, with their good, solid English names, into her lap. He looked at them lying there.

'Do you think that would please your father, putting them there on the doorstep of that temple?'

She looked at him, puzzled; then she laughed and swept the cricketers on to the floor. 'I don't think Father ever thought of his heroes having sex. He was an innocent in lots of ways.' Or so Lily had told her; but then what man would Lily not consider an innocent? 'I wish I'd known him better. At least you knew your father.'

'Too well,' he said and drew her back into bed, not wanting Chojiro Okada between them, here least of all.

It was a splendid night for both of them, all loving violence and tenderness; tomorrow was shut out. And for him, so was yesterday: there was only the present and it was Natasha. But when he woke in the morning he knew that was an illusion. She lay beside him, a beautiful reality; but she would have no influence at all on the future. That lay with factors outside this bed and this house. The war was the reality and he had no illusions about that.

They had just finished breakfast downstairs in the kitchen when there was a knock on the front door. Yuri had gone down to the village to collect what food was available from the *tonarigumi*; if evacuees were to start arriving today, the locals wanted to make sure of their own quota; charity was to begin at home, before their homes were invaded by unwelcome visitors. The knock on the door was loud and peremptory. Natasha, still in a silk house kimono, looked at Okada in alarm.

'Don't tell me they're bringing people here so early! Go down to the basement – I'll try and hold them off till you can get out of the house!'

He went quickly down to the cellar as she went through to

the front of the house. She had woken exhausted but happy, tender in more ways than one; at breakfast she had barely begun to think about today. As she reached the door there was another loud knock and she pulled up sharply, startled as if someone had fired a gun right in front of her face. She did her best to remain calm; then she opened the front door. The day had begun far worse than she could have imagined.

On the verandah stood Major Nagata and Lily.

2

'I have brought you your house guest,' said Nagata, beaming as if he were presenting Natasha with the Empress herself; or perhaps his own favourite, Greta Garbo. 'Madame Tolstoy. I believe you know each other. Better to have a friend staying with you than a stranger, isn't that so?'

'We are better than friends,' said Lily, a mink-wrapped evacuee; she had worn the coat because she knew that even in General Imamaru's circle there were looters. 'We are aunt and niece.'

Nagata did a beautiful act of surprise. 'What a coincidence! What a stroke of good fortune! I had no idea—' He shook his head in wonder at the workings of fate; and at the information in *kempei* files. 'Well, I shall see that no one else is billeted here. We can't have intrusions on a family reunion.'

'I shall tell General Imamaru,' said Lily. 'He will be appreciative.'

Nagata bowed, gave a yellow smile. 'Perhaps I could arrange something in Nayora for the General?'

Lily gave him a small smile. 'I think the General has made his own arrangements, major.'

Nagata bowed and backed away; he knew when to make an exit. 'I shall come back this evening to make sure you are properly settled in. I shall see that the other officers don't trouble you.'

He went down the path and Lily looked at Natasha. 'Are you

175

going to ask me in or am I to be – "billeted" – out here on the verandah?'

Natasha, her mind almost blank, had said not a word while Nagata had been with them. Beneath her feet she could almost *feel* the presence of Okada in the cellar. 'What? Oh – I'm sorry—'

She stood aside and Lily walked into the front hall. 'Tell your servant to have the driver bring up my bags. There are only three. The rest will be arriving tomorrow.'

'My servant is down in the village—'

'Then who is this?' said Lily, looking past her.

'I am the handyman and gardener, madame,' said Okada, coming forward. 'I shall get your baggage.'

He bowed and stood aside to let the two women pass him and go into the living room. Natasha, dumbfounded that he should have chosen this moment to appear, managed not to look at him; she wanted nothing, not even puzzlement, to show in her face. Lily paused at the door of the living room and looked after Okada as he went out on to the verandah and down the path.

'The handyman? A handsome, healthy young man like that? How do you manage to keep him out of the army or some essential industry?'

'I think you'd better ask him that.' Natasha's control was tightening. She was a long way from being calm, but she was not going to fall over, as she had thought she might when she had first opened the front door. 'He comes only once a week.'

Lily gave her daughter a long appraising look; then she looked casually about the big room. 'I hope this isn't your taste, my dear. Who furnished it – Queen Victoria?'

'It was all there when my late husband bought the house. Why did you choose to come to Nayora? Did Major Nagata suggest it?'

'I didn't meet the major till my car was stopped at the entrance to the village – the *kempei* appears to be checking everyone in and out. He is *kempei*, isn't he? I thought so. Though he is more charming than most – or maybe smarmy is the word. He seemed to know you very well.'

'This is a small village. All the foreigners in it are known to the police.'

Okada appeared at the door with the three bags on the floor behind him in the hall. 'Where shall I put them, Mrs Cairns?'

'Leave them for the moment.' Natasha thought quickly. 'You can go back to cleaning up the garden at the rear.'

'Yes, madame.' Okada bowed his way backwards, the perfect servant.

'He knows his place,' said Lily approvingly.

I wonder? thought Natasha; she certainly didn't know what his place was right now. She went back to her question: 'Why did you come to Nayora?'

'Surely you've heard about the bombing the night before last? They didn't drop any bombs near the Palace, but the general thinks it must come. Everyone is moving out.'

'The general too? He's coming *here*?'

'Not to stay. His wife and children are up at Miyanoshita.' That was a spa in the mountains immediately behind Nayora; Natasha knew that the German embassy staff had a retreat there. 'He wanted me close by, so I at once thought of Nayora.'

Natasha suddenly smiled; she had regained her sense of humour, if not yet all her composure. 'You mean I'm to run a love nest for my mother and her lover?'

'Prettily put,' said Lily. 'But no, I don't think so – Who's this?'

Yuri, carrying a string bag, had come into the hall. Natasha said, 'This is my housekeeper, Yuri Suzuki. This is my – my aunt, Madame Tolstoy.'

Yuri knew at once who she was: aunt, indeed! She had a gossip's double vision, she could read between the lines. Still, better an aunt than a suddenly exhumed mother; she had respect for the proprieties, though she'd never heard the word. She bowed, halfway between a bob and a curtsey, nicely sardonic. Then she went on out to the kitchen and Lily said, 'She resents me. You'll have to get rid of her.'

Natasha was shocked at her gall. 'Lily – this is *my* house! You're here as my guest. Yuri is not just my servant – she is my friend!'

She was as surprised as Lily at her own outburst; she could not remember ever having been so passionate out of bed. Lily stared at her, then put out a placating hand. She smiled a motherly smile, as if she were tasting curdled cream.

'I'm sorry, Natasha. Of course it's your house. I shan't interfere, not in the least.'

Natasha was mollified, but only slightly. 'I'll take you up to your room. Then I'll have to tell Yuri you'll be staying here. She will need to register you with the *tonarigumi*.'

'There'll be no need for that,' said Lily sharply. She had a high class whore's snobbery, she did not wish to be classed with *hoi polloi*, especially for hand-outs. 'There'll be food coming with the rest of my luggage. The general has promised I shan't go short. Nor will you,' she added maternally. She really would have to cure herself of this growing habit, she told herself. 'There'll be enough for all of us. Even the handyman.'

Natasha ignored that; but only because she had no answer to it. She led the way upstairs to the second bedroom, a room as big as her own and just as lumpily furnished. Lily inspected it without moving from the doorway.

'I've never been comfortable in a Japanese-style house – sitting and sleeping on the floor is for children. But do Europeans find *this* comfortable?'

'Lily, this was all bought by a Japanese who really knew nothing about European taste – or so my husband told me.'

'I'm surprised that your husband, an art expert, could live amongst this. Or was he a masochist?'

'No. He just liked big solid beds. He was a big man and very energetic.'

'In bed? So was your father. All the British are – it must have something to do with the sports they play.'

'I understand the general was a champion at *kendo*. Does he take his staff to bed with him?'

Lily took off her mink, shivered. 'I'll need the room heated . . . Don't let's discuss our love life, my dear. Otherwise you will find yourself in the novice class.'

Natasha left her on that, turning sharply and clattering down the stairs in her high-heeled slippers. She went into the kitchen, where Yuri, chopping up seaweed, bailed her up with a knife.

'Is that *her*? Your mother?'

'Yes. But she's supposed to be my aunt.'

'She's like all the *narikin*.' It was a derisive nickname, a Japanese chess term meaning a pawn promoted to a queen. 'They never know their proper place.'

'Her place is *here* now. We'll just have to accept that. She'll be bringing her own food.'

'The best of everything, I'm sure.'

'Of course. And I'll see you get your share of it.'

She knew she was being too sour with Yuri, but she was still trying to get her bearings. Through the kitchen window she could see the handyman, as unworried-looking as a crippled octogenarian safe from any call-up, digging a spade into the hard winter's earth of the neglected garden. She went out to him, stood amongst the weeds and wild grass and dead cabbage stalks. The community gardener never bothered with the back yards of the villa.

'Why did you come up out of the basement? You could have stayed there till I'd got her upstairs. Then you could have got away—'

'Where to?' He stopped digging, rested his foot on the spade. 'Who is she?'

'Madame Tolstoy. She is General Imamaru's – mistress.' She wondered how many other girls would have to describe their mother like that to the men they loved. Then she decided to tell him the whole truth. She was a good liar, but after last night she knew she could not lie to him. 'She is also my mother.'

His foot slipped off the spade, he almost fell over. 'Jesus!' he said in English. 'Does she know about us? I mean, why I'm here?'

She shook her head. 'Why would I have told her? She's one of – *them*.'

'Who does she think I am then? I saw her looking at me. She doesn't believe I'm the handyman—' He was speaking Japanese again, his voice low. 'I'll have to think of somewhere else to hide.'

'Where? The trouble is, you look too strong and healthy.' She

179

had been deliriously glad of that last night; but a bed was no fortress nor even a hiding place. She remembered another of her father's heroes, Lord Nelson: 'You'd be better off with only one arm and one eye.' The thought horrified her and she touched him to make sure he was whole.

'We're being watched,' he said, and gestured with an eyebrow towards an upstairs window. 'Your mother mightn't like you being familiar with the handyman.'

'She suspects it anyway,' Natasha said recklessly. 'She has that sort of mind. My mother has been a whore all her life,' she added just as recklessly. She put out of her mind what *she* had been: even Lily had said she was no more than a novice. 'Don't leave here till I've talked to her.'

'What are you going to tell her?' He was alarmed.

'I don't know. I'll make up something—'

But she didn't know what. She had always been adept at inventing fantasies: the mother, for instance, who was a Mongolian princess. But this was no time for fantasy. She went inside and upstairs. Yuri brought up hot water, tipped it into the big bath in the villa's one bathroom.

'Shall I heat more water for *her*?'

'You'd better, just in case.'

'Ask her if she can get us more coal or wood. She looks as if she could get anything.'

Yuri went downstairs, grumbling to herself, but already scheming to make the most of their unwelcome guest. She had a servant's pragmatism: you never turned your nose up at a bargain, no matter how tainted.

Natasha got into the bath. It was another Japanese pleasure Keith had taught her; she loved the pleasure of soaking in hot water. The French nuns hadn't encouraged indulgence in the bath; a sponge down, a quick leap over the bidet, and God and the Church were satisfied with her cleanliness. She had learned to do better than that in Hong Kong, but till she had come to Japan she had not known what a pleasurable ritual it could be. She usually bathed in the late afternoon or early evening, when most people did, but now she sank down in the hot water as a retreat where she might think.

Her mind was tossing between invention and the truth when there was a knock on the door. 'May I come in?' said Lily, and did come in.

She sat on a stool and looked at what she could see of her daughter's body through the steaming water. 'You're very beautiful. But I've told you that, haven't I? Does your handyman tell you that?'

That, at least, gave her a start, put her thoughts on some sort of track. 'Yes. Do you want me to tell you about him?'

'I think it might be wise. May I join you? Your servant tells me there is a shortage of fuel for heating the water. I'll have to arrange something.'

It was a huge bath, a German spa, as Keith had said, for an hussar, horse and all. It stood on clawed feet that would have held up an elephantine dragon; its sides were like those of a small dam. It was built for company.

Lily slid out of her clothes; Natasha remarked admiringly how she did so, like a beautiful snake shedding its skin. She soaped herself on the stone slab in one corner of the bathroom, poured water over her shining body, then stepped into the bath and slipped down opposite Natasha. Natasha made room for her legs, keeping her own modestly together. She could not remember the number of naked men she had seen, but she also could not remember when she had last seen a naked woman; she had never gone to the public baths here in Japan. She suddenly felt remarkably innocent.

'You still have a beautiful figure.'

'Still? Don't make me feel middle-aged. If you look after yourself, yours will be just as good. We're fortunate.' They were like water-lilies pushing Narcissus' reflection out of the way. Then Lily got down to business: 'Who is your young man and why is he here?'

Natasha gently sponged her shoulders and arms, taking her time. 'He is from Saipan. He had a terrible time there and he deserted.'

Lily was sensible about war: any man who ran away from it was also sensible. Unlike Henry Greenway, she had never had any heroes, least of all military men. As lovers, yes, but never as heroes. 'They'll catch up with him eventually, especially if the *kempei* are now here in the village. Where did you meet him?'

'He came looking for my husband, Keith. He had been a student of his before the war.'

'Do you love him?'

'Yes.' It was strange to hear herself confess it; doubly strange to confess it to her mother. She felt almost pious, as if she and Lily belonged to a respectable middle-class family.

Lily let her arms float on the water, graceful as long white eels. Her breasts were just below the surface, curved and light as large lotus buds. She had noticed that Natasha's breasts were heavier, but that was Natasha's problem. She contemplated herself for a moment or two, then looked up as if satisfied.

'Well then, if you love him, we have to protect him. I shall have a word with the general.'

'Oh no!' Natasha made waves in the bath. 'He'll have him arrested at once! A military man—'

'My dear, the general is a military man who knows the war is lost. He doesn't want to go back to it and I think I can persuade him that my niece's fiancé also shouldn't go back to it.'

'Fiancé? We're not engaged—'

'Hasn't he asked you?'

'Not yet. We haven't talked about marriage—'

'For our purpose, you'll be engaged.' Lily felt disgusted at her maternal spirit; she shouldn't feel so warm and – decent? She would have to be careful, or soon she would be picking up babies and kissing them. She almost sank beneath the surface at the sudden, scuttling thought of being a grandmother.

'I'll have to tell him. Though it will be like me proposing to him—'

'He should be flattered. But he will have to be sensible, do whatever the general suggests. Does he have nerve?' She didn't believe that because a man deserted from a war, he didn't have nerve. She knew that to desert from a love affair required nerve; there was no difference in her mind. 'He'll need to play a part, whatever it is.'

'Oh, he can do that!' All at once she was excited by the idea, vague as it might be. She had faith in Tom, as if he were a god; Keith had told her who the Japanese gods were, but she could never remember them; she had had only two gods up till now, the nuns' God and Keith. But now she had another and she had a deep romantic faith in him. He just had to be saved from being mortal, that was all. 'He's very resourceful.'

'The general will be coming to see me this evening. I'll talk to him then.' She got out of the bath, ran her hands down over her body, as much to enjoy herself as to dry herself. 'Let me dry you.'

She took the big, threadbare towel and waited till Natasha got out of the bath. Then she dried her, gently, as if Natasha were still the baby she had deserted; even then she had never bathed her daughter, had left that to their *amah*. Natasha let the towelled hands move over her, her eyes following every movement.

'Relax,' said Lily. 'I'm not going to seduce my own daughter.'

'Lily – can I trust you? I don't mean *this*—' But she took the towel and held it in front of her as if for protection. 'I mean about Tamezo. I couldn't bear to have something happen to him.'

'Tamezo? That's his name?'

'Tamezo Okada.'

'You can trust me. I'm a neutral in the war. All one has to do is take care of oneself.' She might have added 'of one's own', but she was not prepared for that commitment. 'Let me talk to him.'

When they were dressed they went downstairs and Natasha told Yuri to bring Okada inside. Yuri looked at her enquiringly and warningly, then shrugged: it was none of her business. She could already feel that things were going to be very different with that other woman about the house.

Okada came into the living room, not meekly but with stiff wariness. Natasha gestured to him to sit down.

'I'm only the handyman,' he said, testing the water.

'No, you're not. My mother knows who you are. Up to a point,' she added in her own wariness.

183

'I think,' Lily told Okada, 'that you had better think of me as Natasha's aunt. That's the story we have told everyone else. Now what's your story?'

'I gather Natasha has told you that.'

Lily recognized a shrewd, cautious man. 'You're not giving anything away, are you? I heard what Natasha said. "Up to a point." Up to what point, Mr Okada?'

'Madame Tolstoy, I love your daughter – or your niece. That, I'm perfectly honest about. But till the war is over, I think it better if I don't tell you about certain things. I am not a criminal, I can say that.'

Lily was looking at him with the steady, penetrating gaze of a recruiting sergeant. Then she turned to Natasha. 'There's a copy of yesterday's *Mainichi* on the table beside my bed. Send your servant up to get it.'

'Maybe I can get it,' said Okada. 'I know what's in it.'

'No, Mr Okada. I am not going to have my niece's fiancé running errands. Let the servant get it.'

'Fiancé?' Okada looked at Natasha, but she had gone to the door and told Yuri to go up and get the newspaper. As she came back to her chair he got up and went across and kissed her on the forehead. 'I'm glad we're engaged. It would have happened eventually anyway.'

'Lily thought it best. It gives you more standing.' Natasha smiled at him lovingly as he went back to his own chair.

'I'm sure it will. Madame Tolstoy's nephew-by-marriage-to-be.'

'Don't be impertinent, Mr Okada. I'm trying to help you and Natasha.'

'I appreciate that. But I've never liked arranged marriages, it's just a matter of principle.' Then he looked at Natasha, as deeply in love with her as he could possibly be. 'No offence.'

'None taken.'

'Such love talk,' said Lily, and took the newspaper that Yuri brought in. She waited till the old woman had gone back to the kitchen, then she opened up the paper. 'There is a photograph of you here. But it says your name is Tamezo Fujita.'

'Let me see that!' Natasha grabbed the paper, looked at

184

Okada's picture, quickly read the story. 'A hero! And you let me talk to you last night about Jack Hobbs and Frank Woolley!'

'Jack and Frank?' Lily frowned in puzzlement. 'Who are they?'

'Nobodies.' Natasha got up, took Okada's head between her hands and kissed him on the lips. She was on the point of tears. 'You might have been killed!'

'But I wasn't. Sit down, sweetheart.' He gently pressed her back towards her chair. 'Let's get everything straight with your – your aunt.'

'Well, almost everything,' said Lily, who had begun to expect no more. 'I understand you are from Saipan?'

Okada had been wondering up to what point his story had been told; now he knew that Natasha had kept secret his true identity. That meant she trusted her mother only up to a point. 'Yes. I was a sawmill foreman there. I got away after the Americans came. I've been working on the docks in Tokyo since I arrived here. I didn't want my photo in the paper, I wasn't looking for that sort of thing. In fact, I was trying to avoid it. That's why I gave the name Fujita.'

'Then you're stuck with it,' said Lily. 'I'll introduce you to General Imamaru as Tamezo Fujita, the air raid hero.'

'General Imamaru?' Okada looked enquiringly at Natasha. 'Lily is his—'

She hesitated, as if, with a new fiancé, she had suddenly become very proper. Lily said, 'I'm the General's mistress, Mr Fujita. Not his geisha, though.'

He knew the difference. He couldn't see her pandering flatteringly to any man.

'I hope you're not a moralist, Mr Fujita,' she said, mistakening the reason for his silence.

'Only occasionally. But never about relationships.' He winked fondly at Natasha.

'What can you do, Mr Fujita? I mean besides rescue people from fires. And run a sawmill?'

He pondered a moment, decided to draw on the past: 'I have been a nurseryman – I know plants and shrubs.'

'I don't know there is much call for nurserymen at this stage of the war. Or even ordinary gardeners. Can you drive?' He nodded. 'I'll suggest that to the general.'

'But he has an army driver, hasn't he?' said Natasha. 'The one who's been driving me home.'

'I was thinking about a driver for his wife.' She seemed amused at the idea. 'I believe she is a meek little woman who needs someone to take care of her. But you'll have to be discreet about your relationship with Natasha. Madame Imamaru is meek, but she gossips.'

'Does she know about you and the general?' said Natasha.

'Of course. We're her prime item of gossip.'

Later, when Okada and Natasha were alone together, they discussed the proposition. Natasha said, 'I think it's a perfect solution.'

He drew her out of the house, up through the tangled garden to the pines that ran up the hill to the main highway. From here they could look down over the house into the village. Trucks and buses and a few cars were already arriving, people spilling out of them with the bewildered look of shipwrecked passengers tossed up on a strange, wild shore. Sergeant Masuda and his constable were doing their best to be a welcoming committee, but it was obvious they were overwhelmed. On a corner Natasha could see Major Nagata and two other men standing apart, making no attempt to help the two local policemen. But Natasha knew they would not be standing there out of idle curiosity. The *kempei* were never idly curious. And suddenly she was even more afraid for Tom.

'Look,' said Okada, 'I think there's something you should know. The *kempei* know I'm here in Japan. There must have been a spy back in San Diego who spilled the beans on me.'

'Who told you this?'

'Someone.' He wanted to tell her about Minato; but knew that he couldn't. Though in the past twenty-four hours he had almost forgotten what he was here for, to be the control for her and Minato. 'He says the *kempei* are asking questions about me.'

'I wonder if Major Nagata knows about it? That's him down there, the stout one.' She nodded down towards the distant

186

figure on the street corner. 'Those men with him are *kempei* too, I should think.'

'Then I can't stay around here, not even up in Miyanoshita with Mrs Imamaru. It'll be too close to you, I can't put you in danger.'

'You have to stay close!' she said vehemently; she couldn't be separated from him, not now. But she was cunning, disguising love as duty. 'How else can we send our messages? You can't leave me to take that risk on my own.'

'You sent them on your own before I got here.' Then he realized they were on the point of arguing; perversely, he felt it made them more certain of each other. 'I'm sorry. I'm only thinking of you—'

'Then stay close to me – please.' Above them the pines creaked in the morning breeze. She heard a *kak-ko* call and she wondered why any bird should choose this spring to come back to a war-torn land. But then Keith had told her that the cuckoo was a parasite bird and the parasites seemed to be doing well in Japan right now. They seemed to be the safest people to be around. 'The general will look after you, if Lily asks him. He's looking after himself, I can tell you that.'

'I don't know—' He didn't want to be away from her; he wanted to be within reach if she needed him. And perhaps there might be a crazy logic to being right in the centre of the vortex of danger. 'All right. We'll see if Lily can persuade the general. There's one other thing – how do we get Lily out of the house so we can transmit?'

'The general is coming tonight, but I don't think he'll be coming every night. He'll take Lily somewhere else to entertain her. She told me she wasn't going to use my house as a love nest.' She giggled at the phrase.

He took her in his arms and kissed her; high above them the *kak-ko* told them they were crazy. The breeze whispered its warning, too. But they were deaf.

Major Nagata came to the villa again in the late afternoon.
Natasha, who had been waiting for him, went out to meet him
on the front verandah. They sat down on the dusty cane chairs;
Nagata dusted his chair with a handkerchief before he sat. He
was wearing his best uniform, hoping to impress Madame
Tolstoy, and was disappointed when she did not appear.

'Madame Tolstoy is not well?' He knew she hadn't left the
villa; his two junior men had been patrolling the village constantly.

'She is resting.'

'Does she know that I know who she is?'

'I haven't told her.' Not yet: that might need to be explained
later. But for the present she did not want Lily to know the
extent of her arrangement with Major Nagata. She wanted a
card or two up her sleeve, though she did not know how she
would use them. She had always been able to handle men (she
supposed she had inherited that talent from Lily); but she had
never had any serious dealings with a woman, certainly not one
as clever and experienced as Lily. A little Chinese patience
(from her grandmother? Though no one had ever spoken of her
grandmother) might come in handy. 'Do you want me to?'

Nagata had decks of cards up both sleeves: he was a crooked
poker tournament in himself. 'Let's wait and see. Is General
Imamaru coming to visit her?'

'This evening. Shall I mention you're in charge of the
village?'

'Better not.' His vanity responded only to the highest bids; he
knew no general would be impressed by a *kempei* major's being
in charge of such a small place. But he looked down at the
village and thought of the distinguished company now under its
roofs: 'You have some very superior neighbours now. An
ambassador, some rich businessmen, the families of two other
generals, some foreign correspondents – you could create a very
interesting social circle, if you wished.'

'You mean bring them together so that I can spy on them for you?'

He was not offended. 'Why else do we have our arrangement?'

'Whom do you want watched?'

He shrugged. 'All of them. Don't limit yourself. Perhaps Madame Tolstoy will help you entertain them.'

Natasha didn't think so; but she didn't tell him that. She stood up. 'We'll see.'

He too stood up, but reluctantly: he had really come to see Eastern Pearl. 'I shan't come up every day,' he said grudgingly, but sensibly. 'We don't want people gossiping about us.'

'Of course not,' said Natasha, hiding a smile at the thought. Then: 'Haven't you forgotten something, major?'

'What's that?' He turned on the top of the steps.

'It's pay day.'

'I brought you Madame Tolstoy. Who else would get a guest who could pay as well as her?' But he saw she was unimpressed and he took out his wallet and passed over some notes. 'You're very mercenary, Mrs Cairns.'

'So I've been told,' she said, smiling, not at him but at Tom's remark. 'Goodbye, major. When I have something to report, I'll let you know. But please keep your officers away from here. We don't want them finding out more than they should know, do we?'

He went down the path and, looking after him, Natasha all of a sudden had the feeling that their relationship had been reversed, that she was now in control. It paid to have a mother with influence.

Lily, Natasha and Okada had an early supper. During the day the rest of Lily's baggage had arrived by military truck; there were also boxes of food. Yuri, presented with an opportunity such as she had not experienced since the war began, prepared a meal that brought a smiling look of approval even to her own face. She could put up with the Tolstoy woman if the kitchen continued to be supplied as well as this. She had grown tired of being hungry.

It was Lily who suggested that Okada should eat with her and Natasha. 'We must feed him up. We don't know how Madame Imamaru treats her servants.'

Okada was impressed by what was presented to him, but then remembered the almost empty plates in the queues down in the docks area. 'I have a conscience about eating this. The workers are almost starving.'

'Are you a communist, Mr Fujita?' Lily had accepted his new *persona*, even if he still felt strange in it.

'No. Just a Democrat.' It was safe to say it: there were no capital letters in the spoken word.

Neither mother nor daughter confessed to being democrats, big 'D' or little 'd'. Their hypocrisy was impeccable.

'I often think of the poor,' said Natasha, but neglected to say in what way.

'If you wish to indulge your conscience, Mr Fujita, then feed it,' said Lily with a hypocrite's logic. 'I can tell you there are far more self-indulgent people than ourselves. Marquis Kido, the Lord Privy Seal, feeds his dogs every day on red meat.'

Natasha noted that item, to be passed on to Major Nagata.

'It's wartime, Mr Fujita. Democracy is something that should be saved for peacetime.'

Okada threw back his head and laughed, wondered where Lily had heard that one but didn't ask. Then he fed his stomach, which was stronger but emptier than his conscience. At the end of the meal he excused himself and went up to Natasha's bedroom.

'I think it better that I be out of the way till you see how the general feels about me.'

General Imamaru arrived half an hour later, with muted pomp and ceremony; he hated to be inconspicuous, but this was new territory and he already knew the *kempei* were here. He kissed Lily's hand, a gesture she had taught him; her movie heroes had been Conrad Veidt and Erich von Stroheim and Adolph Menjour, villains all. Then, because Lily told him to with her eyes, he also kissed Natasha's hand, something he hadn't done on previous occasions.

When Lily at last mentioned Okada, or Tamezo Fujita, as she called him, the general shook his head. 'An able-bodied young man who's not in the army? It's out of the question.'

'He's no coward,' said Lily. 'Haven't you seen the newspapers?'

Imamaru never read the newspapers; he knew they were all propaganda and how valueless it was. But he looked at the copy of *Mainichi* that Lily gave him, then nodded in appreciation of what he read.

'But what's he been doing that he isn't in the army?'

Lily let Natasha take over: 'He was in a reserved industry on Saipan – that's where he comes from. He ran a sawmill. He escaped after the Americans landed and managed to get to Japan. He's been working on the docks.'

'They need able-bodied men there,' said Lily.

Imamaru didn't ask why the able-bodied young man, contrary to what the Emperor expected, hadn't stayed on to fight the enemy or, in the last resort, commit *hara-kiri*. He knew the good sense in retreat.

'Why can't he go on working on the docks?'

Lily took over again: 'He doesn't like playing the hero – the people won't leave him alone. If you gave him a job—'

Imamaru looked at Natasha, disappointed in her. 'How did you meet such a common man? A worker on the docks?'

'He is educated,' said Natasha. 'He studied here in Japan under my husband. He was caught in Saipan when he went home to help his parents with their sawmill. When he came back to Japan, he came to pay his respects to my husband, not knowing Professor Cairns was dead.'

'And fell in love with his widow.' But Imamaru liked sentimental romances and was not being sarcastically critical. It was Lily who had taken the sentiment out of his romance with her. 'Well, what do you suggest I do?'

'Employ him as a chauffeur and bodyguard for your wife,' said Lily.

'Bodyguard? Who's threatening my wife?' He laughed at the idea; but wished it were true. 'And she doesn't need a chauffeur. Where would he drive her?'

191

'She needs a bodyguard because very soon this area is going to be full of thieves and looters. Not only the best of us are leaving the city,' she said; and Natasha, almost a spectator now, admired her mother's conceit. 'As for needing a chauffeur, perhaps she can be driven down here to Nayora. There may be some interesting social life here now.'

'You're not thinking of entertaining her?' said Imamaru drily.

'No. One must have a proper sense of the decencies.' Lily sounded as pious as a fallen prioress. 'I have my niece to think of.'

'Will you and this Fujita meet in secret?' Imamaru asked Natasha. 'I can't have people talking about my wife's chauffeur and my – Madame Tolstoy's niece.'

'We'll be most discreet,' said Natasha, wondering how much he cared about the gossip about Lily and himself.

Then Okada, who had made himself look as presentable as possible, was brought downstairs. Imamaru looked him up and down, sideways and diagonally: he might have been inspecting a new piece of military equipment. Then he nodded as if satisfied.

But said, 'You should have joined the army, young man. A fine type like you.'

'I wanted to, sir. But the army didn't have a high regard for Saipanese – they didn't put us much above the Koreans. I didn't want to be just a guard in some prison camp.'

Imamaru nodded understandingly. In the Greater East Asia concept the Koreans were the menials. He knew of their excesses as guards in the prisoner-of-war camps and he could not see this young man amongst them. Besides, a chauffeur might be a nice present for his wife, a change from the teak carvings, elephant tusks and stuffed birds which had heralded his homecoming. Up till now the second car, his father-in-law's, had only been used when a spare army driver had been available.

'Report for duty tomorrow morning at nine at Miyanoshita. Madame Tolstoy will give you the address.'

Then General Imamaru took Lily out for the evening.

Natasha did not ask if they were going to a reception or just being driven somewhere where they could be alone: she shut out of her mind the image of her mother and the general canoodling (one of Keith's words) in the back of a staff car. When they had gone, Natasha took Okada up to bed.

'One last night,' he said.

'Don't talk like that!' She had very rarely spoken in exclamation marks; he seemed to fire her to expressive punctuation. All the dormant passion of the almost two years since Keith's death was bursting its way out of her; lust and love, which can go hand in hand or even more intimately closer, were making her more emotional than she had ever been. Then she sobered down, fell on him and wept. 'I like to think we'll both live forever. All we have to do is stay out here till the war is over.'

'The war isn't over, darling, not by a long way.' He gently pushed her off him, sat up. 'We better go down and use the radio. We may not get many chances now, with Lily in the house.'

'It's not our regular night for transmission.'

'They're always on stand-by, just in case of emergency. Let's hope they're standing by tonight.'

They went down to the basement. While Natasha prepared the radio transceiver, Okada encoded his messages. There were three of them and when he handed them to Natasha she looked at them with concern.

'This will mean we'll be on the air for ten minutes, perhaps more.' She was not his lover now, but his co-worker; her emotionalism was for the bedroom. 'It's too dangerous – we could be picked up—'

'We'll have to take that risk. Tell them to take the messages and ask no questions, at least not tonight. I'll go upstairs and keep watch.'

She was slowly reading the messages, decoding them in her mind; she knew the code better than he. It was a mathematical code and she had always been good at mental arithmetic; she sometimes wondered if she had inherited that from her unknown Chinese grandmother. The messages, once decoded, were stark and simple.

'At last we're giving them some real meat. But they're not going to like what you're saying.'

'I'm not here to send them birthday greetings.' Now they were down here in front of the exposed radio set he was on edge, fearful for her rather than for himself. He wished that he could move the radio elsewhere, out of this house where its presence would be a constant danger to her. 'Get started. I'll be upstairs.'

She saw his tenseness. She kissed him gently on the lips, then sat down in front of the transceiver. He kissed the back of her head, loving her deeply, turned quickly and went up to the main floor. He prowled the house, front rooms, back rooms, side rooms, watching for any approach. The night was dark and the darkness seemed to be full of barely moving shapes; his imagination gave him eye-strain. Once he stepped out of the back door and listened for movement; but all he heard was the night breeze in the pines, the whine of truck tyres up on the highway and, somewhere down in the village, a drunken voice shouting '*Au secours, au secours!*' He hoped the Frenchman needing help would distract any patrolling *kempei*.

He went back inside, kept checking his watch every minute or so. Fourteen minutes passed before Natasha came upstairs. 'It took me almost five minutes to raise them. I gave them a piece of my mind.'

Jesus, women! 'In code, I hope.'

'Don't be sarcastic. You said they should be standing by each night. I just reminded them of that.'

'I'm sorry.' He took her hand. 'Those guys should have been ready. It's just – I'm worried for you. We should look for another place for the radio. Sooner or later, with your mother in the house, it's going to be discovered. There's no guarantee she'll protect you, not if it means her own neck.'

Natasha felt a twinge of shame that she should allow her mother's maternal loyalty to be doubted like this; despite her own suspicions, she had come to like Lily, though she did not love her. Besides, someone had said that blood was thicker than water, though she had never known exactly what that meant.

194

'I don't think she'd hand me over to Major Nagata,' she said defensively.

'I wouldn't bet on it,' said Okada, who still didn't see Lily Tolstoy as a mother, no matter whom she had borne. 'Let's go to bed.'

She had no argument against that suggestion; bed was her bunker. She devoured him as if, without him, she would be like an empty cupboard. She did not consciously think of sex and love in food terms, but she could live on both if that were all that was available.

They were lying exhausted when they heard Lily come in. She came upstairs and paused outside Natasha's door; Okada, more modest than Natasha, willed her not to knock and enter. After a moment she went on to her own room and they heard her door close.

'I wonder if she and the general made love tonight?' said Natasha.

Okada laughed softly, marvelling at her one-track mind. Then he dozed off; but Natasha, her body still experiencing him, lay looking at the darkness. She said a prayer, something she hadn't done since she had fled the convent: she prayed for the end of the war. Her prayer, which must have startled the Virgin Mary, who wouldn't have been expecting any word from that quarter, was only spoiled by her selfishness: she was praying only for herself and Tom.

She got up, put on a kimono and went to the window. The moon had now risen and out beyond the village the sea stretched away, a boundless steel plain; there were no waves, nothing at all to break the cold loneliness; even the fishing boats had disappeared. Suddenly she shivered, wondering if she was looking at the future.

Then she saw the man standing in the shadows watching the villa.

'I don't like it,' said Reilly. 'We ought to recall him. Okada, I mean.'

'How?' said Embury and lit his pipe for the fifth time in five minutes.

Reilly gestured awkwardly, knowing how stupid the suggestion had been. But, like Embury, he was worried for Okada, whom he had reluctantly come to respect. He had not thought about Minato, who was half-enemy and therefore not to be pitied.

'Should you try to trace the leak here on the base?' Irvine was diffident about *his* suggestion; it was not his place to comment, no matter how indirectly, on US Navy security. The Americans, even after three-and-a-half years of war, were still inexperienced. But, being a natural gentleman and not a manufactured one, he hid his feeling of superiority.

'Where do we start?' said Reilly. 'There are goddam civilians coming and going all the time—'

'It won't hurt to start an investigation.' Embury had at last got his pipe going. 'But keep it low key. We don't want the FBI sticking their nose into this.'

'We could lose control of the operation,' said Reilly, sounding as if he had just discovered they had lost the Battle of Midway. He said determinedly, leading a charge uphill, 'We can't let that happen!'

'We won't,' said Embury, puffing on his pipe. 'We won't let the FBI or anyone else know what's happened. But we'll tighten security right here in our own outfit. I want the code clerks screened again.'

'I think we shouldn't take any more personnel on board. Admin. has been trying to press two Waves on me.'

'Lucky you,' said Irvine, then apologized; he really should not joke about the Americans' problem. He saw it as theirs, not his: there were advantages to being no more than a liaison officer.

'Women are security risks.' Reilly never told his wife *anything*. But then she never told *him* anything and that worried him. Sometimes he wondered if she had a lover.

'What about Okada then?' said Irvine. He had liked the Japanese-American and he did not like the thought of his being abandoned. But of course there was little or nothing that could be done; one had to accept that. For a moment he was ashamed of his own professionalism.

'We just have to hope for the best,' said Embury and let his pipe go out. 'What we also have to hope is that Minato won't doublecross us and him.'

'There is also Mrs Cairns. She may be in danger too.'

'Christ, do you think I don't know that?' Embury looked as if he was going to snap his pipe in two. Then he shook his head at his burst of temper. 'I'm sorry, David. Yes, we have to hope for the best for her too. At least Minato doesn't know about her.'

Reilly changed the subject; or anyway went on to another section of Okada's message. He jabbed at the sheet of paper with his Parker pen, almost breaking the nib; he could feel himself becoming infected by Embury's anxiety for their agents. He thought of them now as agents, had begun to enjoy the operation once it had started. He had already started to dream of the future, of espionage in the postwar peace, had cautiously questioned Irvine about the British Secret Service. He had no urge to go into the field, but he could see himself in Washington in charge of a dozen agents operating in the trouble spots that would continue when the war was ended. He just had not thought of the mental anguish one might experience when it was known that an agent was in peril.

'This bit about the Peace Faction members being in jail? What do you think of that?'

Embury looked at Irvine and the latter said, 'I'm suspicious of it. Several hundred? How many is that? In any case it's far too many. A week ago Okada was unable to report anything further on the Faction, that Minato hadn't been able to come up with anything. That meant it must have been what we've thought all along, that it was made up of only a few top people. Now all of a sudden we have several hundred supposedly belonging to it and

197

all in prison. In prison? Why haven't they been executed? The Japanese aren't going to hold treason trials at a time like this. No, it doesn't smell right. We'd better ask Okada for more information before we try to make something of this. If Washington or London get hold of this, they could start making propaganda of it. And if it turns out they're in prison for some other reason, black market or something like that, we're going to look fools. The OSS might want to take the operation away from us. Let's wait till Okada can send us more.'

Embury was silent for a while, then he nodded. 'You know the Japs better than we do. Okay, we wait till Okada can send us more.'

Reilly looked at the message paper again. 'What do you think of his comments on the bombing raid, that it's strengthened the people's will?'

'I suggest we keep that to ourselves too,' said Irvine.

'Sure,' said Embury and once more lit his pipe. 'I don't think General Le May or the other Air Force generals would be too happy to know an Army corporal was telling them they'd done the wrong thing.'

Six

4

Minato had the uneasy feeling that he had been sent across Hibiya Park to the Dai Ichi Insurance building as some sort of test. He knew already that the Japan Broadcasting Corporation had its secret emergency station in the basement; at least five people among the juniors on the Navy Staff had told him that secret. He knew also that on the sixth floor were the headquarters of the Tokyo Area Army and the Army's switchboard controlled direct lines to the Imperial Palace, to police headquarters and all the military barracks in the city. But Admiral Tajiri had sent him to neither of those two places.

The offices on the fourth floor were not large and there was no sign on the main door. There were four middle-aged men at desks in the outer office and they all looked up, with what Minato thought of as impolite curiosity, as he entered. Perhaps not too many unexpected visitors came to his office.

'I have a letter for Prince Konoye from Admiral Tajiri.'

One of the men, baldheaded and bespectacled, a career clerk – his face as pale as the paper that had surrounded him all his life, rose and took the letter Minato handed him. He bowed, then knocked on an inner door and entered. The other clerks lowered their heads over their desks, deciding that Minato was not worth their curiosity.

He stood at ease, since there was no spare chair to invite him to do otherwise, and wondered what business was conducted from these offices. The admiral had given him no hint, just handed him the letter with what had seemed a secret smile and told him to wait on Prince Konoye for an answer. It was the smile, almost sly, not in Tajiri's character, that had made Minato uneasy.

After five minutes the inner door opened. 'His Highness will see you, lieutenant.'

Minato had not expected to meet Prince Konoye. He was a lowly lieutenant, a commoner, and he wondered why the prince should see him. Konoye was the head of the Fujiwara clan, an extended family that could trace its heritage back to service under the Emperor Tenji in the seventh century AD. The women of the clan had been the wives and concubines of emperors: marrying well or, if marriage wasn't offered, then bedding well; one way and another, they had served under emperors for centuries. Fujiwara princes, more upright, if only in stance, had served as advisors to the Son of Heaven for thirteen centuries. Such long servitude, Minato knew, would never be understood by Americans. Two generations, they thought, constituted a power dynasty.

He went into the office, bowed low, heard the door close behind him as the clerk went out. Then he straightened up and stood at attention. The prince behind the big oak desk gazed at him with what Minato took to be a princely stare – cynical, superior, capable of demolition of lesser beings.

'So you are the one who has spent six years in America?'

'Yes, Your Highness.'

'You are to be commended for your fortitude.'

'I did it for The Emperor and my country, Your Highness.'

'Of course. Why else?'

Konoye brushed his small moustache with a knuckle. He stood up, clasped his hands behind his back and walked to a window that looked out on the park. He was as tall as Minato, lean and bony, had high cheekbones and a habit of tilting his head back as if the rest of the world were beneath his nose. Minato had already heard the gossip about him, that he had a taste for deviant sex and liked in particular lower-class women. Minato, who was prudish about sex, wondered how such an elegant, dignified aristocrat could lower himself, socially and physically, to the level of the coarse women he was supposed to like.

'Colonel Hayashi tells me you say that the Americans don't respect the Emperor. That's a dangerous opinion, lieutenant.'

Hayashi? Did he belong to the Prince's staff? 'With respect, Your Highness, I was reporting the facts.'

Konoye had altered the direction of his gaze, was staring across the palace plaza at the Palace itself. 'You haven't expressed those facts to any of your colleagues?'

'No, Your Highness. Only to Admiral Tajiri and Colonel Hayashi. And only after they had asked me for an opinion.'

'You speak up for yourself, lieutenant. Did you learn that in America?' Konoye turned back from the window. 'I understand you have shown some interest in the Peace Faction.'

Minato could feel the foundations shifting, as if he stood on sand. But why should Prince Konoye interest himself in a lowly double agent, if that was what they had decided he was? He tried to keep his voice steady: 'The Americans mentioned it when they were interrogating me, Your Highness.'

'Did they appear to know much about it?'

'I don't know, Your Highness. When I said I'd never heard of it, they dropped the subject immediately.'

Konoye came back to his desk, sat down. For three years during the 1930s he had been Prime Minister; he had the languidly magisterial air of a man who might think of himself still holding the post; he certainly did not have to depend, like common politicians, on the whim of the voters. Minato, perhaps a little too long in America, had forgotten the boxes within the boxes of the hierarchy who ruled his own country. The Fujiwaras, he guessed, would still be close to the Emperor for another thirteen centuries.

'Lieutenant, did the Americans ever try to persuade you to work for them?'

For a moment Minato thought he might faint. 'Yes. Yes, sir.' He hadn't enough breath to say Your Highness.

'And what did you say to their proposition?'

'I refused.'

'A pity,' said Konoye. 'I don't suppose there's any way you could get in touch with them and tell them you've changed your mind. That you would supply them with information?'

You know better than that, thought Minato; but one didn't tell a prince that he was naive. He knew damn well that Prince

Konoye was not naive; those cynical eyes, hard as marbles, had never underestimated an enemy or a friend. What was he getting at? Did even he know about Okada?

'I don't think the Americans would trust me, Your Highness. They are simple-minded people, but not all of them are naive.'

For the first time Konoye smiled, but it had little warmth to it; Minato felt like a beggar who had been tossed a coin. 'You do have your opinions, don't you, lieutenant?'

Minato bowed his head, not sure what answer the prince wanted.

'Who do you think are the principal opinion makers in America?'

Minato hesitated at being asked for another opinion. 'The newspaper columnists, Your Highness. Those and certain politicians.'

'Forget the politicians.' He had a true aristocrat's contempt for elected representatives of the people; inherited power was the only safeguard against hypocrisy. 'Name the columnists.'

'Walter Lippmann. Dorothy Thompson. Drew Pearson.'

Konoye nodded. 'Yes, our mission in Switzerland always quotes those. Did any of them ever mention the Peace Faction in their writings?'

'Not that I recall, Your Highness.' He had been a good spy, had known that as much information could be gleaned from a newspaper as from observing a shipyard.

Abruptly Konoye nodded. 'That will be all, lieutenant. Give this letter to Admiral Tajiri.'

Minato bowed his way out, still wondering why Prince Konoye had called him in, still no wiser what the Peace Faction was and who ran it. He could not bring himself to believe that the prince, so close to the Emperor, would be involved in a plot to go behind the Emperor's back to seek peace with the Americans.

He walked back across Hibiya Park. The trees and shrubs were loaded with the slow green bullets of spring; but there was still the dead perfume of ash in the air. Office workers sat in the park having their lunch; they all looked gloomy, he thought, as if they were having their last meal. Since he was a boy he had

been destined for the Navy and he had never really given much
thought to civilians; they were almost a foreign race; he had
grown up in the time of militarism and had been thoroughly
indoctrinated. Even in America, though he had been infected
by the way of life there, and indeed had masqueraded as a
civilian, he had never thought of himself as one of them. Now
he looked at these office workers, women as well as men, and for
the first time began to see them as part of Japan, as much part of
it as the ruling class and the military who had taken the country
to war. He suddenly felt a welling of pity and quickened his
step, as if afraid that, like a leprosy sore, the pity might show.

Admiral Tajiri was lunching from a tray at his desk: rice, fruit
and a glass of green tea. He invited Minato to bring in his lunch
and smiled pleasantly when he saw that his aide was having
almost the same meal.

'Did you ever become accustomed to American food?'

He was certainly being pressed about America; his lunch
suddenly soured in front of him. 'No, sir . . . Prince Konoye
had me into his office for ten minutes.'

'Really?' Tajiri's glasses glinted as he moved his head, but his
voice contained no surprise. 'Well, he's an odd man in many
ways. What did he talk about?'

Minato took a chance: 'The Peace Faction. He asked me if
the Americans knew about it.'

Tajiri nodded. 'That's another of his oddities – he has some
sort of faith in the future. Perhaps I'm too old for such an
indulgence. Did you ever read the Greek poets at the Academy,
lieutenant? Of course not – they would have distracted you. I
read them in an earlier time, when I was in France before the
last war. There's a similarity to our own poetry. More –
voluptuous, perhaps, but dreams just like ours.'

Minato was at a total loss; the day was spinning round him
and he felt he was going in the opposite direction. But he
ventured: 'You have dreams, sir?'

'Don't you?' Tajiri looked over the top of his glasses.

'Of course, sir.' But, still dizzy, he couldn't think of even
one.

'And so do I. They are of peace – but a different peace from the one Prince Konoye dreams of. My favourite lines are from a Greek poet, Euripides:

> *O, for a deep and dewy spring*
> *With runlets cool to draw and drink,*
> *And a great meadow blossoming,*
> *Long-grassed, and poplars in a ring,*
> *To rest me by the brink . . .*

They were meant for a young god, but I've taken them as an old man's dream. I'm tired, lieutenant, I'm at the brink.'

Minato was trying to find his footing in the spinning day. 'Are you thinking of retiring, sir?'

Tajiri sipped his tea. 'No, lieutenant. Where would I go? All the long-grassed meadows are full of civilians who have fled from Tokyo and the other cities.' His dreams allowed no room for the plebs. 'I shall remain here and watch Prince Konoye and his colleagues in the Peace Faction hatch their plots.'

'So there is a plot, sir?' The day stopped spinning; he stood his ground feeling safe. For the moment, anyway.

'Oh, there are dozens of plots.' He finished his tea and smiled. 'We shall just keep our eye on them, shall we, lieutenant?'

'Yes, sir,' said Minato, no longer dizzy but now blind.

2

Okada, for the first time since he had lived with his grandparents in Nagasaki, was back in a typical Japanese household. The Imamaru villa in Miyanoshita had been built at the turn of the century by Madame Imamaru's father; the old man, still alive, came from the merchant class that had prospered after the arrival of Commander Perry in the middle of the nineteenth century and the opening up of trade. The villa was a traditional one, built of materials natural to its surroundings – timber, paper and tiles. It was raised on a platform, stood at the edge of a large pond; in the morning and evening light it looked no more substantial than its own reflection in the still water. The garden was large, designed in that self-consciously irregular pattern that, perversely, suggests an almost stiff formalism. Stone lanterns stood beside the paths like fossilized robots. Maples, chestnuts and a single big tree that Okada didn't recognize stood amongst gentle waves of bamboo; loquat bushes, camellias and chrysanthemums caught the eye at a lower level; a lone cherry tree stood at a carefully measured casual angle from the main house. Okada fell in love with it all, if not with Madame Imamaru.

She was an ideal wife for a general; she would have driven a pacifist off to war. She was pernickety; she reduced the world to tiny detail and when that was not possible she ignored it; the war, unmanageable in her tight, ordered mind was shut out completely. Okada, manageable and close at hand, was polished till he shone.

'Your hair must be cut shorter. Those clothes must go. You will wear gloves when driving the motor car. Do not smile so much, it distracts me.'

She was a short dumpy woman who no longer resembled the attractive girl she had once been. The wartime dress she affected did nothing to enhance her; Okada, still thinking American when it came to women, compared her most un favourably with Natasha and Lily. Being American in his thinking and also male, it did not occur to him to blame General Imamaru for his wife's lack of pride in her own looks. He naturally assumed that the general, though he did not like the man himself, had taken up with Lily Tolstoy because his wife did nothing to make herself attractive to him. But if Madame Imamaru had lost her looks, nothing else must be allowed to do the same.

The villa was clinically immaculate; the two maids fluttered about the rooms with dusters and brooms constantly in action; the *tatami* mats fitted together with mathematical precision. The garden and the car had been neglected, but with the arrival of Okada they were to be put right immediately.

'You will also be the gardener as well as chauffeur. Everything must be trimmed, the paths raked, the pond cleaned out. By summer it must look like the Garden of Eden.' She saw herself as Eve still in residence; Adam had fallen and been kicked out. 'Have you heard of the Garden of Eden.'

'Yes, madame.'

'You're not a Christian, I hope?' She only borrowed Christian images; she would never want to own them.

'No, madame. It's all too complicated for me.'

'Yes.' She nodded, as if that gave her a reason for her own incomprehension of it. 'Now the car. It must be polished till I can see my face in it. The leather must be polished, too. Also the silver vases by the side windows – they must have a fresh flower in them each time we go motoring. It must delight my father when he returns home.'

The car was not hers but her father's: a 1932 black Rolls-Royce, now made cumbersome-looking by the gas-producers mounted on the rear. Okada could not remember the economic conditions in Japan when he had been here as a boy, but he wondered at the confidence, or the gall, of Otozo Toshiaki, who had bought a Rolls-Royce in the worst year of the Depression.

'You are too big to wear our previous chauffeur's uniform,' said Madame Imamaru. 'We shall have to make do with your civilian suit. See that it is pressed and neat at all times. The chauffeur's cap should fit you.' It did. 'He too had a big head.'

'Thank you, Madame Imamaru.'

He had been working on the car and in the garden for three days before he asked about Madame Imamaru's father. 'When is he coming back?'

'Who knows?' Shigeru Hara was the butler, a wisp of a man who had been worn away by years of service with the family.

'Where is he? Working for the government?'

Hara smiled, something he rarely did: his false teeth always seemed in danger of falling out. 'Hardly. Well, yes, perhaps he is. He is in prison.'

Okada was pruning double buds from a camellia bush. He stopped and looked at Hara. 'In prison?'

'With his friend Shigeru Yoshida. The police came here one day and took away Toshiaki-san. It was all very strange – it was as if he was expecting them. He told me the night before to pack a bag. The police came and were very polite. It was as if he were going off to hospital or something, rather than prison.'

'Was it in the newspapers?'

'Just a small bit. They didn't mention Toshiaki-san's name. We have heard nothing since.'

'Do I have to drive Madame Imamaru to visit him?'

'I don't think so. She doesn't seem to be very upset by it all. As I said, it's all very strange.'

'What about the chauffeur and gardener before me? Has he gone to prison too?'

Hara's lips twitched, but he held his teeth in place. 'He went home at once to Kobe. He was afraid the army might call him up, as soon as Toshiaki-san went to prison.'

'Do you think I'll be safe?'

'That will depend on Madame Imamaru, won't it? Watch your step and you should be all right. Otherwise . . .'

'Otherwise I'm likely to be kicked out of the Garden of Eden?'

But Hara knew nothing of Eden. He went off into the immaculate house, taking off his shoes at the door and lifting his feet to inspect his socks, as if afraid that they might be dusty.

Okada went back to the camellias, but his fingers were fumbling with the buds. Shigeru Yoshida: he was one of the imprisoned Peace Faction leaders. Did Otozo Toshiaki also belong to the organization, was he another plotter against the Emperor and the military?

He could not believe how his luck, with that irony which God or the gods delight in, had turned. Five days ago he had been cursing at how chance had made him a hero, exposing him to publicity, sending him running from his cover. He had come here to Madame Imamaru with the utmost reluctance, only because the job offered safety of a sort and put him relatively close to Natasha. He was convinced that his effectiveness as an agent and control was finished.

He had not yet readjusted after the impact of the fire bomb-ing. He was like a jig-saw puzzle from which small but important pieces were missing; anger and shame (or was it guilt?) were large segments that had forced out pride and elation. Maybe Minato was right: that in war there should be no moralizing. The morning after the raid he had wanted to turn his back and walk away from the war. For twelve hours he had stopped being an American; Chojiro Okada would have been proud of him. It was Natasha, with her artless questions about life in America, who had brought him back into himself. It was, ironically, the Japanese in him that had brought him back to his mission: he had an *on* to the men who had trusted him, Embury and the others.

And now he was close to the Peace Faction, working for a member of it. He still, however, had to find out the organization's aims and how it worked and whether it was still effective. With four hundred members in prison, amongst them some of the men who would certainly be its leaders, it might already be smashed. He would have to consult again with Minato.

Madame Imamaru gave him no days off. Several times he drove her down to Nayora; she was hoping for a glimpse of Lily and he was hoping for the same of Natasha; both of them were disappointed. Once he drove her into Tokyo to visit an aunt; sitting up front in the big black car he felt conspicuous and resented, but no one threw stones at them; once again he marvelled at the restraint of the Japanese lower classes. And felt angry at their passive acceptance of the rigid system.

Though he had no days off, he did have most nights free. Sometimes General Imamaru appeared and stayed the night; he never sent for Okada and the latter only knew of his presence when told by Hara, the butler. On her nights when the general was not at home, Madame Imamaru spent the evening with her three children or, according to Hara, listened to her gramophone. One night Okada went out into the garden from his room at the back of the house and listened to the music coming from Madame Imamaru's bedroom. He was surprised to hear the saccharine strains of Guy Lombardo and his Royal Canadians. Okada all at once felt sorry for her and wondered what she dreamed of as she listened to 'Deep Purple'.

He found an old bicycle in the garage, repaired it and one night took off down the road for Nayora. There was no moon and the lamp on the bicycle was as weak as a newborn baby's stare: all it seemed to do was illuminate the whirling top of the front wheel. Occasional cars and trucks passed him, their headlamps hooded like drugged men's eyes, and twice he was almost run down.

When he reached the outskirts of the village he dismounted, wheeled the bicycle up into the pine forest and left it there. Then he went on foot down through the trees to the back of Natasha's villa. He had just stepped out of the blackness under the trees when he saw the dark shape come round the corner of the house. He froze, fearful of stepping back and treading on a twig; all he could hope for was that the man, whoever he was, would not see him against the black background of the woods. The man stood for almost five minutes watching the back of the house; Okada, afraid to move, could feel the muscles in his legs tightening as with cramp. Then at last the man went back round the corner of the house and disappeared. Okada waited another couple of minutes, easing the ache in his legs, then cautiously, ready to turn and run if the man jumped him, he went down to the back door. He hesitated, then knocked gently.

Almost instantly, behind the locked door, Yuri said, 'Who is it?'

'Okada,' he whispered.

The door was opened at once and he slipped inside. Yuri said, 'We have been waiting for you every night. The mistress said you would come. She is in the living room with Madame Tolstoy.'

'Anyone else?'

'No.'

He went in to the front of the house. Natasha rose and came to him in a rush; he held her to him, still amazed at his feeling for her. Lily, playing solitaire, watched them approvingly, like a matchmaker.

When the two lovers had separated and sat down next to each other on a couch, holding hands, reluctant to let each other go, Lily said, 'And how is the general's wife?'

209

'She is not meek, as you said. Not in her own house.'

'Well, perhaps wives are different at home. Housewives often are, I'm told.' Told by husbands she had comforted. She had never been a housewife herself: a wife, yes, but never about the house. 'Still, she doesn't whip you, I hope?'

Okada was nervous, aware of the man outside the house: perhaps still there, but at the front. But he smiled for Lily's benefit: 'No, no whip. But a tongue that can lash, so the butler tells me.'

It was Lily's turn to smile. 'We all have tongues like that, Mr Fujita. Even Natasha at times, I'm sure.'

'But not now,' said Natasha, and took Okada upstairs to her room.

Once there he said, 'We're not going to bed with her right underneath us.'

'Why not? She knows why we came up here.'

'It's not just her.' He sat down on the bed, but didn't lie back. 'No, leave your clothes on . . . There's a man watching the house. I saw him as I came down through the trees at the back.'

She had undone three buttons of her blouse, but now she stopped. The anticipation on her face faded suddenly; she sat down beside him, began to do up the buttons. 'I know. They're the *kempei*. I didn't tell you – there was someone watching the house the last night you were here.'

'Why didn't you tell me?' He was angry with her, but it was only nerves that made him so.

'I didn't want to spoil the night. Darling—' She put a hand on his arm.

He relented, lifted her hand and kissed it. 'I'm sorry. But it's all getting too risky for you . . .'

'I can look after myself.' She had done so for more years than he had had to; but one didn't tell a man that, not if you loved him. 'And in a way, Lily is a protection.'

'You sure?' He told her about General Imamaru's father-in-law being a member of the Peace Faction and in prison. 'Maybe the *kempei* is keeping an eye on all of them, the general and Lily too.'

Natasha shook her head slowly. 'I'm not sure. Major Nagata tells me everyone in the village is being watched. Their suspicion of foreigners has got even worse.'

'What about Lily? Is she any more suspicious about me?'

'It's hard to tell. I don't think she believes everything we've told her.' They were speaking in low voices and in Japanese; Lily had not been told that Okada spoke English. 'I still don't know if she would be on our side or theirs if it came to a pinch.'

'Ours? You and me? Or the Americans?'

Natasha shook her head. 'I don't think she cares one way or another about who wins the war. She's a true neutral, she only cares for herself.'

He smiled at her out-of-character cynicism; but maybe she was just being honest, seeing something of her old self in her mother. He had the sense not to ask.

'Have you managed to transmit again?'

'Last night. I just told them there was nothing to report.'

'Did they have any message for me?'

'None. I thought they might have said something about the Japanese suspecting you're here in Japan. But not a word. Don't men like that care about their agents?' She was concerned for him, not for herself.

He made a wry grimace. 'How would I know?' He didn't say that he might never know; but the thought occurred to him. 'Have you got a pen and some paper up here? I want you to send another message when the coast is clear.'

She got him a fountain pen and some headed notepaper: Professor Keith Cairns, Faculty of Art, Tokyo University: the heading was in both Japanese and English. She said, 'Keith used to write to people all over the world. He was very highly regarded.'

He suddenly felt inferior to the dead Keith, and jealous of him. He said nothing, but immediately began writing his message, telling San Diego that he had discovered another member of the Peace Faction and naming Otozo Toshiaki. He did not state that he worked for the Toshiaki family; if the message were intercepted and the code broken, they would know where to come looking for him. Then he looked at Toshiaki's name, had second thoughts and crossed it out. Without the name the message had nothing new in it, was not worth sending. He tore up the notepaper, but as he did so he wondered whether he was more concerned with protecting Natasha's safety than doing his job.

'What's the matter?' said Natasha.

'Nothing.' He looked around, but there was no fire in the grate this evening. He gave her the scraps of paper. 'Burn that in the kitchen stove.'

'Do you want me to transmit?'

'No. Stay off the air till I've got something worthwhile sending.'

'But they'll wonder what's happened to us—'

'Let 'em wonder!' He put his arms round her, said very softly in English, 'Darling, you're more important to me than they are. With those *kempei* guys wandering around outside . . .'

She nodded, not in the least wanting to argue with him: she was his and she wanted to stay his. She kissed him. 'Do you want to go to bed now?'

He laughed softly, kissed her passionately; then let her go and stood up. 'I can't – not with Lily downstairs—'

She couldn't understand his modesty. She wondered how inhibited he would be if she lived in a Japanese house with its paper-thin walls.

They went downstairs and Lily said, 'So quick?'

'He was afraid you'd hear us,' said Natasha.

'Oh I'm sorry,' Lily told Okada. 'You should just ignore me, Mr Fujita. I've never been a voyeur, or whatever it is they call someone who listens in on lovemaking.'

Okada looked at mother and daughter and shook his head in wonder. One never heard conversations like this in Gardena. 'Are you two trying to embarrass me? I'm a nice moral boy from – Saipan—' He changed his birthplace just in time.

'And we wouldn't want you to change, would we, Natasha?' said Lily. 'But you must learn to take advantage of opportunity. These aren't ordinary times, Mr Fujita.'

'You can say that again,' said Okada.

Lily looked at him. 'That's an Americanism. I've never heard it in Japanese before.'

He almost floundered; but recovered. 'I heard the American guards say it on Saipan. Before I escaped.'

'Perhaps we'd better learn some more Americanisms,' said Natasha, trying to help with a frayed rope. 'The way the war is going.'

'I shouldn't try them around the village,' said Lily. 'Not with the *kempei* still here. They took away two Frenchmen last night.'

Lily was not enjoying her evacuation from Tokyo. She had been afraid each time the bombers came over: Nayora was safe from such threats. But she was a city woman, even though the city had been almost destroyed around her; the atmosphere in Nayora was sophisticated, but it was still just a village. Despite the danger and the devastation, Tokyo was still the centre of power; and she had enjoyed being close to that centre. It was not enough for General Imamaru to come every other night and give her second-hand accounts of what was going on. She had almost established a *salon* for the general and herself and now here she was in this backwater playing solitaire or, worse still, playing mother.

She gathered up her cards, held out a hand for Okada to kiss it. He did so, still feeling slightly ridiculous: this was something else that had never happened in Gardena. 'Goodnight, Mr Fujita. I'll be out tomorrow evening with the general, if you wish to visit Natasha. Frustration has never improved a woman's looks.'

A few minutes later, as he kissed Natasha goodnight just inside the back door, he whispered, 'Do you think Yuri is listening to us?'

She smiled in the darkness. 'Of course. Will you come tomorrow night?'

'I'll try.' He held her to him with something like desperation. He longed for the end of the war, but wondered if they would survive till then.

Next day Okada had to drive Madame Imamaru into Tokyo for a committee meeting of a soldiers' welfare organization. It was held at a mansion in Kanda, the university district. Okada knew that Madame Imamaru would be at the meeting for at least an hour. Not all the women of the committee had come in their own cars, but there were five other chauffeur-driven cars besides the Toshiaki Rolls-Royce. Okada asked one of the chauffeurs to keep an eye on his car and went down the street looking for a phone booth.

From there he called Minato. 'Can you talk?'

'Not really.' Minato wished Okada would not call him here at the office. He had been every night for the past week to the mail-drop, but there had been no message and he had begun to wonder if Okada had already been picked up. 'There has been no communication from you.'

Okada guessed there must be someone else in Minato's office. 'I'll do the talking, then. I've had to move out of Tokyo. I'm not sure when I can come in, so the mail-drop isn't much use to us. But we better keep it.'

Minato was trying to look relaxed as he sat back in his chair at his desk. But he was painfully aware of Nakasone at the desk opposite. He had been surprised at how Sagawa's death had affected Nakasone, as if the latter had belatedly discovered qualities in Sagawa that he had never previously suspected. Minato still felt no qualms about the killing of Sagawa: it had been as necessary as the killing of Mate Third Class Bateman in San Diego. But he had been required to show more regret at Sagawa's death than he had expected. And Nakasone had become quieter, almost suspiciously so; Minato had begun to wonder if he had been recruited by Colonel Hayashi to replace Sagawa.

'Keep digging on the Peace Faction,' said Okada. 'I've discovered another member of it, Otozo Toshiaki.'

'How did you find that out?'

At once Okada knew he had made a mistake. Dammit, he not only had to keep secret his whereabouts from the *kempei* but also from Minato.

'Pure chance.' Which was true. 'Maybe they're not all military men, but civilians. Diplomats, industrialists, men like that.'

'Perhaps,' said Minato. Nakasone had stopped writing whatever he had been working on, was sitting back in his chair and gazing out the window. And listening? 'Well, I'll attend to the matter as best I can. Goodbye.'

He hung up and looked across at Nakasone. The latter turned from his scrutiny of the patch of sky through the window and said, 'Has Colonel Hayashi asked you to lunch again?'

'No. Why?'

'He's asked me to go with him today. I haven't the slightest idea why.' But he looked smug, an expression Minato had never expected to see on Nakasone's cheerful face.

4 3

March passed, like a ragged, broken parade; and fickle April came in. Still unable to meet with Minato, with nothing to report to San Diego and therefore unwilling to risk Natasha's safety by transmitting while the *kempei* were still in Nayora, Okada began to feel he was already outside the war. Air raids continued, but there were no more fire-bombings; Okada, listening for news of the raids every day on Hara's radio, wondered if the generals had been shamed by the stories of destructions that the bomber crews must have taken back. It struck him that, since he had begun his mission, he knew the names of more Japanese generals than American.

Okinawa was invaded by the Americans, but the radio propagandists told the country that it was not a disaster: the enemy was just being drawn into the net set for it. Okada laughed when he heard it; then turned to find Hara standing right behind him. But the butler, too, was smiling.

'They think we'll believe anything they tell us. I wonder what Adolf Hitler is telling the Germans?'

'We should be careful,' said Okada, acting uneasy. 'If the general heard us—'

'Perhaps you're right,' said Hara, but was too old really to care.

Then Franklin Delano Roosevelt died. The radio announced his death, saying he had died from strain brought on by the losing of the war. He had been succeeded by a man named Harry S. Truman, a nobody who had once owned a haberdashery store: the snobbery in the announcer's tone was like a layer of static.

Okada had difficulty in remembering who the new President was. He dimly remembered the name: he had been Vice President, an office that Okada, like most voters of his age, had thought of as empty and ignored. He felt nothing at first about Roosevelt's death; it was the President who, by signing the Executive Order back in 1942, had declared he and other Nisei were not loyal Americans. He wondered what his father, smug in his bitterness at Blood Mountain, would think of Roosevelt's death.

When he was not polishing the Rolls-Royce or driving it, he was working in the garden, taking pride in how he was bringing order and neatness back to it. At the back of the house there was the tall tree that, at first, he had hardly remarked; now, as its wide leaves, almost a foot across, began to shine like large green plates, he looked at it again and remembered it. He had seen trees like it growing in southern Japan, down near Nagasaki.

'What do they call that tree?' he asked Hara.

'The phoenix tree. Don't ask me why. Perhaps it grows out of the ashes, I don't know. The master has a *bonsai* of it in his study.'

'The general?'

The butler pursed his lips, as if he had just tasted something sour. 'No. The master, Toshiaki-san. He loves this place, says it gives him the peace he has always wanted.'

'What sort of peace?'

Okada was cleaning curled leaves from the surface of the

216

pond. A golden carp glided beneath the tines of his bamboo rake, certain that he meant it no harm. A willow, still young with spring, hung like a fall of green droplets on the far side of the pond. Lichen-mottled rocks, grey-green, looking like half-buried mastodons trying to break out of the ground, bordered the still, green-reflecting water. The golden carp drifted slowly beneath a pattern of lily pads: even a thug's eye must have stopped to admire, if not to understand. There was a tranquillity in this garden that Okada had never experienced before; he could understand any man, except the most tortured, finding peace here. But was it the only sort of peace Otozo Toshiaki was seeking?

'He has worked hard all his life. When the war started in China –'

He thinks like Father, thought Okada. They were at war long before Pearl Harbor.

'– he went there and expanded his business, even though by then he could have sat back and let his sons carry on.'

'There are sons?' Okada had heard no mention of any Toshiaki children but Madame Imamaru.

'There were two. But they were fired up by the generals their father knew – they wanted to be soldiers. They are both dead, killed in the war. There is a shrine to them in the master's study. He keeps them to himself. The shrine in the twelve-*tatami* room is for his dead wife and other members of the family. The sons were his own special loss.'

'So he would wish the war to end? Is that why he is in prison?'

'You ask too many questions for a young man.'

'How else does a young man learn? When I am old like you' – he bowed his head – 'the questions will all have been answered.'

But Hara was too old to be flattered. 'There are questions that should never be asked, not by gardeners.' He meant *common* gardeners. He was a kindly man, but snobbery is bred into butlers. It is their best protection against disillusion with those they serve. 'Get on with your work.'

But Okada was not to be put down entirely. He looked about the garden. 'Perhaps all the answers are here in the trees and flowers and water and rocks.'

'Then find them there,' said Hara and went into the house, wondering what the world was coming to, that the young, and the common young at that, should have such confidence.

Each night he could get away, Okada went down to visit Natasha. Sometimes he missed her; Yuri would tell him that she had gone to a dinner party or a reception with Madame Tolstoy and the general. He would then get on his bicycle and start the long, gruelling ride back up the slopes, arriving home exhausted, frustrated (what was it doing to *his* looks? he wondered) and, unreasonably, cursing Natasha for not staying at home to wait for him. But on the nights when she *was* home, and Lily had gone out, the lovemaking, the mere being with her, made up for all the disappointment, the frustration and the long journey to Nayora and back.

Natasha would look at herself in the mirror. 'Do I look better now you've relieved my frustration?'

'You've bloomed.' So she had.

'So have you.' She put the hand-mirror in front of him, but all he saw was a man who seemed to have aged in the past few months.

April went out and the war situation got worse. On the second last day of the month, the Emperor's birthday, the news was broadcast that Japan's former ally, Benito Mussolini, was no longer *Il Duce*: he was dead. Nothing was said of how he had died: the war must be painted in only the best of light, no matter what horrible shadows there were in the truth. On 2 May Adolf Hitler was no longer *Der Feuhrer*: he, too, was dead. But again the manner of his dying was concealed.

The German embassy staff in Miyanoshita suddenly found themselves ostracized. When Germany unconditionally surrendered to the Allies on 7 May, the newspapers all at once broke out with criticism that bordered on hysteria. *Mainichi* was vitriolic in its bitter editorials, asking how Japan could ever have degraded itself to take sides with a nation that understood nothing of *bushido*, the warriors' code of honour. Japan now stood alone and the radio propaganda reached further into fantasy.

Hara came to him one day with two bamboo spears, handed

him one. 'We have to go down to the village and practise.'

'What for?'

'To fight the Americans when they come.'

Okada looked at the spear in his hand. 'With this? Against tanks and planes?'

'The war is lost. But we must die with honour.'

So Okada went down with the old butler to Miyanoshita and there, with other old men and peasant boys, some of them no more than twelve or fourteen, from the neighbouring farms, they went through the farce of a drill that seemed, to Okada, medieval. That night he went down to Nayora and, with Lily out of the house again, he took the risk of transmitting a report to the Aleutians. It was no more than a comment on the low morale in Japan, but at least the message let Embury and the others know that he and Natasha were still alive.

San Diego, through the Aleutians, had a message of its own: *We need more information Peace Faction. Progress unsatisfactory.*

Okada's reply was testy. *Both willing resign if replacements can be effected.*

'Now close it down,' he told Natasha. 'We're not going to risk our necks while they sit over there in California criticizing us.'

She got up and stood aside while he checked and cleaned the set as he did after every transmission. He still remembered how close they had come to losing the set because of Natasha's neglect of it. When he had hidden the set behind the segment of the cellar wall Natasha looked at him curiously. 'You've changed.'

'What do you mean?' Still angry with San Diego, he was too sharp with her.

'I'm not sure – it's almost as if you don't care any more. About the war, I mean.'

He *did* care, he told himself. But not about victory or defeat, only about those who were being sacrificed. Yet so far it had not occurred to him that he was becoming a pacifist, a conscientious objector. He would continue to fight the war, but only to hasten the end to the slaughter. He was neutral, as ready to fight for the old men and the peasant boys with their bamboo spears as for the American young men who would soon be landing here. He

219

was experiencing the conflict between *ninjo* and *giri*, between human feeling and duty; the classic Japanese struggled in him with the modern American. All he wished for was the death of the generals, on both sides.

'If San Diego knew that, they'd be worried.'

'Let's go to the mountains!' She was exclamatory again, roused to passion by her desire to keep him for herself. 'We'll be safe there—'

'What would we live on?' He took her hands in his. 'I've heard them talking in the drill squad up in Miyanoshita. You can't buy food in the country – money doesn't mean anything any more. It's all barter – you give me clothing, I'll give you food—'

'I have stacks of clothes—'

'Fancy stuff – you think a farmer's wife wants that? She'd take your fur coat – but what would we get for it? A week's supply of food, maybe. No—' He shook his head. 'At least while you stay here with Lily and I'm up with Madame Imamaru, we're both being fed. It's black market stuff, but an empty belly has no conscience. I think Confucius said that.'

'Confucius never had an empty belly in his life.' Natasha, like many women, was not worshipful of male philosophers. 'I still think we'd be safer in the mountains.'

'Safer, maybe, but hungrier. We stay here and trust to luck.'

'All right. Now let's go to bed.' It was an answer to all problems, at least for a while.

5

Next day Otozo Toshiaki came home to Miyanoshita. Like the other members of the Peace Faction he had spent only forty days in prison; since his release he had been in Nagasaki, six hundred miles to the south. There he had been in conference with several other members of the *zaibatsu*, the cartel that dominated the industrial and financial structure of Japan. He was a lesser member, he did not come from the Mitsui, Iwasaki or Sumitomo families, but he was respected and he was listened to.

Okada, sent down to Shizuoka to pick up Toshiaki as he came up by train from Nagasaki, knew nothing of what his master had been doing. Hara, his lined old face expanding with pleasure, went with him in the Rolls-Royce.

'It will be a pleasure to have the master back. It is never the same when a woman is head of the house.' General Imamaru might command an army or a corps, but in Hara the butler's eyes he was just a supernumerary in the house at Miyanoshita. 'I see you have put flowers in the vases.'

'Madame Imamaru made sure that I did.'

The train was late, as was to be expected; it was enough that the trains ran at all now. When Otozo Toshiaki got down from his compartment he was hot, sweaty and irritable. He was dressed in the normal civilian wartime uniform, but it was custom-tailored; instead of the usual cap, he wore a grey homburg. Okada, seeing him for the first time, guessed that in prewar days Toshiaki-san would have been a dandy. He had a round, well-fed face, a stomach that strained the buttons of his jacket and the air of a man who had just returned from an enjoyable vacation spoiled only by the crowded journey back.

'Who is our new driver?' he growled before he stepped into the Rolls-Royce.

Hara introduced Okada as Tamezo Fujita: 'He was a hero during the fire-bombing, master. The general rewarded him with this post.'

'Indeed?' said Toshiaki and Okada felt a black mark had just been painted against him.

'Fujita is also an excellent gardener. You will be pleased at what he has done.'

'Indeed?' said Toshiaki and Okada felt the black mark had been watered down to a light grey. He decided then and there that he would gain nothing by showing that he owed something to the general. From now he had to see that he was Toshiaki's man.

When they drove up to the house Toshiaki got out of the car and looked at the garden. It was a good day for a well-tended garden to be looked at. The sun was shining, heightening the colour of the early blooms, glinting on the pond; a prospecting breeze turned over the leaves of the trees, finding silver beneath the green; the white pebbled paths looked as if each pebble had been hand-placed. It was enough to have Okada forgiven for having been sponsored by General Imamaru.

'Excellent,' said Toshiaki and went inside to be greeted by his daughter and his grandchildren.

Two nights later Toshiaki had guests to dinner. They were all men, eight of them, and they arrived in cars that marked their wealth; a Rolls-Royce, several Mercedes-Benz, a Cadillac and a Packard pulled into the driveway with heavy dignity. The men were all elderly, geriatric period pieces who carried a whiff of the past, like a musty scent, with them as they creaked up the steps and into the house. They were all in civilian dress but the last one to arrive, a Navy officer.

'Who is he?' Okada, who was out in the drive supervising the parking of the cars, spoke to the driver of the naval staff car.

'Admiral Tajiri. I don't know what he's doing here.' The driver was middle-aged, looked like a reservist who had been called back into the Navy just to shuffle desk-bound admirals from one reception to another. 'We're not on official business.'

'He's got no aide with him?' Okada wondered where Minato was.

'Just himself, that's all. Where's the lavatory?'

Okada told him where the lavatory was, then went round to the small room beside the garage which was his living quarters. He had memorized the numbers of all the cars and he wrote them down. Then he sat on his bed mat, feet tucked beneath his knees, completely comfortable in a position he had fought against all his life. Unconsciously he was becoming more and more Japanese; what had started out to be protective camouflage had become a natural state. He sat there in the gathering darkness debating his next move. A long time later he would realize that in that half-hour he chose between duty and self.

At last he got up, stood for a moment till the circulation

flowed again in his legs. Then he went out into the garden, staying off the path, keeping to the soft earth where the plants and shrubs grew. He passed under the phoenix tree and moved in close to the main villa. Lights showed in what he knew was the twelve-*tatami* room and he could hear the murmur of voices.

He stopped beneath the open shutters of a window. He was not high enough to see into the room and see who was speaking, but that did not matter. What was being said was important, not who said it.

'We don't have much time.' The voice was querulous, that of a very old man. 'With Germany gone, it could be a matter of only weeks.'

'Is that your feeling?' Okada recognized that voice as Toshiaki's. 'The military feeling?'

'Opinion is divided.' That was a good firm voice, Admiral Tajiri's. 'There are some fanatics close to the Emperor who won't hear of any sort of peace proposal.'

'How does the Emperor himself feel?' That was another voice.

'Who knows?' said still another voice, dry and weary-sounding. 'Sometimes I feel we'd be better off with someone less exalted.'

Then Okada heard a footstep on the path that led round from the front of the house. He stiffened, saw the figures come round the corner of the villa. One was Madame Imamaru, clad in a dress kimono; the other was her young son, a boy of ten. Goddam, thought Okada, why isn't the little son-of-a-bitch in bed?

'You should walk in your garden at night,' Madame Imamaru was saying. 'The flowers smell different then. Smell them, now.'

The child took a deep sniff; his nose needed blowing. 'I can't smell them, mother.'

Okada eased himself sideways, glad of the soft wet earth beneath his shoes; he had watered the garden late this afternoon. He had slid in behind a tall rhododendron, the only thick growth so close to the villa. Madame Imamaru and her son paused on the other side of the bush, opposite the open window.

223

'Mother—'

'Hush,' said his mother.

Holy shit, thought Okada. She's spying on them too.

'Whatever the Emperor's opinions,' said Toshiaki, 'we have to see he is protected.'

Protected? Then the men inside were not plotting against the Emperor? If not, then what the hell were they up to? The questions buzzed so loudly in Okada's head that he wondered that Madame Imamaru could not hear them.

'Mother, I want to go inside—'

Madame Imamaru hissed with irritation, grabbed her son by the hand and almost dragged him back along the path and round the corner of the house. Okada relaxed, let out his breath. Then he heard Hara calling his name at the back of the house.

Cursing the butler, he went round to the kitchen. 'Where have you been?' demanded Hara. 'Never around when you're wanted—'

Conscious of his muddy shoes, Okada said, 'I've been down the driveway. One of the drivers was pissing on the camellias.'

'It's to be expected,' said Hara, as if chauffeurs were only good for urinating on plants. 'You are to go down to Nayora and pick up the general. His staff car has broken down.'

'Do I bring him back here or take him into Tokyo?'

'Into Tokyo. Come back here first thing in the morning. The master or Madame Imamaru may need you.' He looked down at Okada's shoes. 'Smarten yourself up. You look like a gardener.'

Okada smartened himself, tried to look like a chauffeur and, packing a razor, a toothbrush and a sleeping coat, drove the Rolls-Royce down to Nayora. The Peace Faction conference was still in progress behind him, but there would have been little chance of his learning more if he had stayed; at least he had something to discuss with Minato and, he hoped, something on which they might build. His luck just had to hold, that was all: he had to find Minato tonight.

When he drew up at the bottom of the path below Natasha's villa the staff car was there, its driver sitting sullenly in the front seat. 'The clutch has gone, completely. I've got to stay here all night with this damned wreck. You'd think a general would rate a decent car.'

'It's the war,' said Okada, grinning to himself, and went up the path and knocked on the front door. Natasha opened it. 'Good evening, Madame Cairns. I've come for General Imamaru.'

'*Madame Cairns?* Come in, you fool!' She pulled him into the hallway, kissed him with mouth so open he thought she was going to bite his lips off.

He struggled away. 'Careful! Where are the general and Lily?'

'In the living room.' She wiped the lipstick from his mouth and hers, took him by the hand and led him into the living room. 'Here is your chauffeur, general.'

Imamaru and Lily sat side by side on a sofa, as if posing for a family photograph. Lily smiled approvingly at Okada and even the general did not seem put out at having his chauffeur brought in here. He had just spent an hour in bed with Lily and post-coitally he always felt more benevolent than blue.

'Life at Miyanoshita seems to suit you, Mr Fujita,' said Lily.

'Why shouldn't it?' said Imamaru, who was not suited by life at Miyanoshita. 'Wait for me outside.'

Natasha went out with Okada, stood with him on the front verandah. Her hand dug into his, but she kept herself from clutching him to her. 'I could eat you piece by piece! I've been sitting out here so I shouldn't hear Lily and the general in bed—'

Okada was shocked into whispering in English, a moral language, 'You mean she's now bringing him here for *that*? What sort of mother is she?'

Natasha laughed. 'Oh, don't be silly! I'm not shocked by it – I just wish I didn't have to think about them up there in bed. It makes me think of you and me—'

'Easy!' An eagle's claw couldn't have worked harder on his hand.

'Come back tomorrow night—'

But when he left with General Imamaru she stood on the verandah for a moment, all thought of sex suddenly gone. She might sound like a whore, but she loved him with more than just her body. She had moved round this Eastern part of the world, but her world had always been small: a circle surrounding the man of the immediate moment. Now it had contracted even more: Tom Okada *was* her world. It seemed that her very life depended on him, yet she could ignore all the dangers that surrounded them. They were bearable: life without him was not.

Okada, his mind still on Natasha, drove carefully. But Imamaru wanted to be back in Tokyo in a hurry: 'Faster! You're not driving my wife now. Faster!'

Okada was a good driver, something he had learned most Japanese were not. He must have impressed Imamaru, because when they drew in before the mansion in the Palace district the general said, 'Excellent, excellent. Perhaps I should keep you as my driver.'

That was the last thing Okada wanted. 'I'd have to join the army for that, general.'

'You don't want to do that?'

'Not this late in the war, general.'

Imamaru was surprised at the frankness; but the memory of Lily still had him in a good humour and he laughed. 'You're a very intelligent young man, Fujita. I wonder how far you will go when the war is over?' He said it almost wistfully, as if he knew that defeated generals could not expect to go very far. Then he turned abruptly, said over his shoulder as he went up into the house, 'You'll find quarters at the back.'

Okada found the servants' quarters, introduced himself to an old man who didn't identify himself. He was shown into a small room in which there was another pallet, but no sign of another occupant. The general seemed to be short of full-time staff.

He waited till the old man had gone, then he left the Imamaru residence and hurried through the dark streets till he found a phone booth. His luck was still holding: he found Minato at the Staff College.

'I have to see you tonight. I've got to leave Tokyo again first thing in the morning.'

'It's late. I was in bed—' Then Minato at last caught the

urgency in Okada's voice. 'I'll meet you at the same place in half an hour.'

Okada made his way to the mail-drop under the elevated railroad tracks. The streets were comparatively deserted at this hour; it was time for the bombers to arrive, but so far the sirens hadn't sounded. Perhaps tonight everyone would get a good night's sleep.

The city still smelled dead; ash still occasionally floated like black blossoms in the spring night air. But no fires burned: the city was just a charred black hulk under the rising moon. Waiting amidst all the devastation, Okada became more and more depressed. He almost sighed with relief when Minato arrived.

'What's so urgent?' They began walking. Minato was wearing his uniform; he still felt uneasy at being in the company of a civilian. Or anyway a civilian who might be picked up at any moment by the *kempei*. 'Have you been questioned?'

'No. I feel safe enough where I am.' He debated whether it was time now to tell Minato where he was working; then decided against it. He had no exact reason for his doubts about Minato, but they were there and they worried him. 'But I've got some information on the Peace Faction.'

Minato looked at him curiously. 'How did *you* get it?'

'There's another agent working here, you must have guessed that. How do you think I get our information back to California?' There had always been an unspoken understanding that Okada controlled another agent, but no name or sex had ever been mentioned. 'In any case, the information came by pure accident.'

'Can you trust that sort of information?'

'Don't be pedantic. In this game you take everything luck brings you.' He sounded like an old hand. 'The point is, I've got more on the Faction.' He gave Otozo Toshiaki's name and the number-plates of the cars that had been at tonight's meeting in Miyanoshita. He did not mention Admiral Tajiri. 'Find out who owns those cars. You can do that better than I can.'

'Toshiaki? I don't know him.'

Okada didn't give too much away. 'I understand he's an

industrialist, big but not as big as the Mitsuis, people like that. But it's not just the names . . . The Faction seems to be trying to *protect* the Emperor, not hatch a plot *against* him.'

'Protect him from whom?'

'I don't know. The Army?'

'The Army wouldn't lead a coup against the Emperor.'

'Why not? They tried it before. Well, not a coup, but a mutiny. It was some time in the 1930s. 1936, I think. The February mutiny.'

He had read about it while he had been waiting at San Diego. Officers of the Army's 1st Division had wanted national policy changed, had sought a return to old *samurai* values. They had marched out of their barracks to murder 'the evil men about the Throne'. They had killed several Palace advisers, but never gone near the Emperor. The mutiny had lasted three days; then the leaders of it had surrendered. The leaders, mostly junior officers, had been executed; a number of generals were summarily retired. Okada, reading the reports on the mutiny, had been struck by the Emperor's part in the punishment of the rebels. The Son of Heaven had shown a determination for harsh justice.

Minato shook his head. 'No, it would be the businessmen, some of the *zaibatsu*.'

'Not these men.' Okada tapped the piece of paper he had given Minato. 'I tell you, they are trying to *protect* the Emperor. But why and who from? Maybe your pal Colonel Hayashi would know.'

'You don't think I'm going to ask him, do you?' Minato sounded dispirited.

Okada said quietly, 'You're not going to drop out of this mission are you?'

'What would you do, if I did? So long as I didn't betray you?'

'What the hell could I do?' Okada waved a hand helplessly. He stopped, leaned against a solid wall. It was a moment before he realized it was the front wall of the Marunouchi building; he was only thirty or forty yards from the other mail-drop, the one that he and Natasha no longer had to use. He sighed, took a risk, took Minato into his confidence: 'I've felt like it myself a couple of times. Dropping out, I mean. Does it hurt you, I mean to see the people, ordinary people, being killed, being burnt out of their homes? Last night, for the first time in years, I thought of my cousins down in Nagasaki. Remember them?'

'Isomura and Taro. I remember them.'

'They were good guys. They're probably making swords or bayonets or something that's being used against our guys somewhere—I don't know, maybe they're in the army or maybe they're dead. But I *liked* them and I think they liked me – at least they never did me any harm.'

'They were my friends at school, till we left and came to live in Tokyo. Then I lost touch with them.'

'It's people like them I'm seeing killed. This isn't war the way I imagined it. I'm on the wrong battlefield.'

'Is that belly talk?' Belly talk, *haragei*, was the practice of saying one thing and meaning something different. Politicians have practised it since they recognized that the populace occasionally had to be spoken to; the Japanese, generals and bureaucrats as well as politicians, had raised it to the level of an art. 'Belly talk for my benefit?'

So much for being honest. Okada felt a spasm of anger, but controlled it. He straightened up from leaning against the wall, said curtly, 'Forget it! I asked you – are you going to drop out?'

Minato had felt doubt taking him over like a cancer. He had come back to fight, even if only from a desk, for his homeland; he had wanted to be with his countrymen in the last dark days, to die with them if necessary. But now he had begun to wonder if his dying, or that of the vast majority of his countrymen, would be worthwhile. The militarists, never giving a hint of the truth to the ordinary people, as Okada had called them, were leading the country to destruction. They were professional patriots; he had been one himself. But now he found himself caring for the amateurs, the millions who had let themselves be led into this war that, even from the beginning, was never going to be won.

He wanted to drop out; but his answer would be at cross-purposes to Okada's question. So he answered with a question, which is a vocal way of saying nothing, another political art.

'What happens to me when the war is over? Do you think I can go on living here in Japan?'

'You can always go back to the States. You said you liked the life there.'

'I'm not like you, Tom. I'm Japanese.' He was telling Okada more than what he was saying, halfway to confessing the truth of his betrayal of his friend.

'So all that you told them in San Diego was bullshit?'

Yes. But all at once he could not face the shame of telling Okada. 'Now I'm back here I can see what I missed in those six years in America—'

'What?'

He thought a moment, spoke this time in Japanese as people crossed the square in front of the main station and came towards them. 'The discipline . . .' The people passed close by, two couples; one of the men lifted his head and nodded, as if discipline were a banner to be saluted. But, of course, discipline was a yoke that the militarists were using to drive people into the abyss. 'The proper values. The respect people have for each other. You don't get that in America, not in a democracy, not when everyone thinks he's equal to everyone else.'

Okada sighed with exasperation; they had argued like this when they had last been in Japan together. Respect was part of the hierarchical system; but it had another meaning in America. But the argument had got nowhere then and it would get nowhere now. 'Look, are you dropping out or not?'

'What about you?' They were like boys daring each other to some game. *If you do it, I'll do it . . .*

'No,' Okada said slowly. 'Like I said, I'm on the wrong battlefield. But if I drop out, I'll be admitting my father was right – even if Japan loses the war.'

'You're fighting him then, not Japan?'

'I'm fighting the Japan he believes in, the generals' Japan. I just wish our bombers would drop their fire-bombs on the generals. Now do we go on working together or do I tell San Diego you've had enough?'

'What if you tell them I've had enough and they tell you to kill me?'

230

'I wouldn't do it. Not unless you tried to kill me first.'

'I don't think I could ever do that.'

'If your neck was in danger, you might. You killed Sagawa.'

'That was different.' He still felt no remorse about Sagawa's death. 'I think we'd better say goodnight, Tamezo. I'll continue to work with you.'

Okada looked at him, then said quietly, 'We should have stayed friends, Kenji.'

Minato bowed; Okada did the same. Then they went their separate ways just as the sirens began to wail.

That night the Americans, for once answering a corporal's wishes, bombed the generals. Okada, the old butler and two maids hurried down to the concrete shelter dug beside the house. General Imamaru, wearing a blue sleeping kimono, came tumbling down the steps, pulling the door closed behind him. He switched on a flashlight and looked around.

'We're all here, Kawabe?'

'Yes, general.' The old man pushed the two maids into a corner to give the general more room to spread his bulk.

Imamaru sat down and for the first time Okada saw that he was carrying a sword. He placed it across his knees, looking for all the world like a man about to begin the ritual of *seppuku*. He saw Okada looking at the sword and ran his hand lovingly along its scabbard.

'My most precious possession, Fujita. It is over four hundred years old, a true *samurai* sword. Did you ever hear of Okada swords down on Saipan?'

'Yes, sir.' And all the way to California too. 'Do they still make such swords today?'

'A few, but not many. Quality has had to give way to quantity. Down in Nagasaki the Okada family is now turning out cheap swords for junior officers. Taro Okada told me himself how much it hurts him, but it must be done.' He drew the sword out of its scabbard, let the light play on its brilliant blade and decorated handle. The two maids cowered in their corner, as if he might try its sharpness on them. 'It's beautiful, is it not? One couldn't have something like that destroyed by a bomb.'

231

Okada remembered watching his grandfather, and his father's younger brother and cousins, at work in what had then been a small factory next door to the family home. He could not see that same small factory, a shrine to sword collectors, turning out cheap swords by the hundreds; suddenly, with a new respect for the family's tradition, he hoped the mass production was done elsewhere. He could still see his grandfather making offerings, as his ancestors had done for centuries, to the Shinto spirit shrine which stood beside his furnace. He did that each morning before he started; then he would go to work, treating a blade as slowly and carefully as if he might take a century to complete it. Two types of sword were made: the long blade, *tachi*, used in combat, and the short one, *wakizashi*, used for suicide. Okada wondered if General Imamaru had one of the latter but thought it prudent not to ask. With a bomb threatening to drop on their heads at any moment, it was not the time to ask a man, especially a general, if he had other means of ending his life.

The bombs began to fall close by. The ground shuddered and some dust fell from the concrete roof of the shelter. Okada, an ironist, wrapped his arms round his knees and smiled at how he seemed to be the bombers' only consistent target: they dropped bombs on him at both ends of the hierarchy.

'Why are you smiling, Fujita?' The general had his head on one side, as if listening for the approach of a particular bomb, one with his name on it. He had been asleep when the sirens had started and the effect of his evening with Lily had worn off: one couldn't feel benevolent towards bombers. The flashlight lit his face, turning it white and expressionless as a *noh* mask. 'Is something funny?'

'The bombs seem to be following me, general. My first night back in Tokyo . . .'

'It may be your last,' said Imamaru and switched off the flashlight in case his mask slipped.

The Americans bombed not only the generals. They also hit the villas of Cabinet ministers, noblemen, *zaibatsu* and a section of the Imperial Palace. They hit pagodas, temples and tombs and the mansion of Tokyo's leading *yakuza* boss. They showed true democracy in their aim: everyone was equal in their sights. It just so happened that the bottom end of the hierarchy, because there were so many of them and they could not afford deep concrete shelters, suffered the most casualties. The generals and their equals emerged from their shelters, looked at the ruins of their villas and made plans to move to their summer homes out of Tokyo. After all, summer was almost upon them.

The Rolls-Royce had suffered some damage, but nothing serious. Perhaps it looked better: some dents and holes in the bodywork, the shattered windscreen: it, too, had now been to war. Okada drove it back to Miyanoshita feeling less conspicuous in it, though some passing soldiers in a truck did jeer at him. But there was no real malice in their abuse: they were only filling time till the end of the war.

Seven

There was still snow on the peak of Blood Mountain, but it was no longer cold-looking, just an artificial frosting that was already hazy in the early summer sun. The wind had turned round, gradually easing into a cool breeze that soothed the cheeks that had been sliced by winter's scalpel. The ponderosa pines and, higher up, the lodgepoles had lightened their colour, showing more green; lower down, the Engleman spruces added life to the mountain. Beside the swift tumbling river the cottonwoods and quaking aspen shimmered in the sun, the gossip breeze running through their rippling heads.

It was a day when Chojiro Okada, a man aware of the seasons, should have felt much better than he did. The seasons in southern California were always smudged; here one could see Nature going through its cycle in the same distinct pattern as he had known in Japan. But everywhere he looked today he saw only headlines, heard the radio instead of the breeze.

'The war is going badly, Okada-san.' Even Yosuke Mazaki was depressed; fanaticism occasionally needs a little encouragement. 'There are rumours the Americans are to test a bomb bigger than anything ever made before.'

'Where do you get these rumours?' Chojiro Okada, never at home in America, had always lived in a small circle, where rumours die quickly for want of voices to carry them on.

'There is nothing definite, just rumours. The network has a man in New Mexico near a place called Los Alamos. Or rather it did have. He has been caught and locked up.'

Okada continued to be amazed at the organized network of spies. He was not a simple-minded man, but he had never been able to comprehend all the levels on which war was fought. He had been brought up on the tales of the *samurai* and still read them; he had avoided the stories of court intrigue, the breeding ground for spies, because he wanted illusion, not education. He was depressed now because he had come to realize that illusion never won wars.

'What sort of bomb?'

Mazaki shrugged. 'Who knows? I am not a scientific man. But it will be another barbarism – the Americans are masters at inventing those. Flame throwers, poison gas—'

Chojiro Okada didn't correct him: he was old enough to remember that it was the Germans who had first used poison gas, in what had been called the Great War. In that war Japan had fought against the Germans; or at least had sided with Britain and France. He had never examined Japan's aims in that conflict: better to keep the illusion.

'Have you heard from your son?'

Chojiro Okada took his time about answering. He had been troubled lately by intruding thoughts about his 'son'; he had once again begun to think of him as such. 'Nothing. Has the – the network had any word from Tokyo on him?'

'We hear nothing from Tokyo now.' The fanatic was being buried under a heap of neglect. 'They have abandoned us.'

'They are fighting for their lives, if one can believe the American propaganda.' Not so long ago he would never have entertained such a thought, let alone voiced it.

'What went wrong, Okada-san?' Mazaki said plaintively.

Chojiro Okada knew what had gone wrong: the generals' ambitions. He could now admit that to himself, but he couldn't admit it to this young man. 'Perhaps we relied too much on the Germans and the Italians. They shouldn't have surrendered.'

Mazaki nodded, brightening a little: pride had been saved from drowning in a sea of shame. Or anyway, it could still tread water. 'Yes. If they had only fought better—'

Chojiro Okada left him and walked down the camp road towards the huts. He could see his wife, Tsuchi, working in the vegetable garden amongst the beans and carrots he had planted. With Etsu and Masako settled in Chicago, writing home every week to say how much better life was in that city; with Tamezo not heard from at all, with her children gone, Tsuchi had retreated into herself. She and Chojiro hardly spoke to each other now: they were not at war, just growing strangers to each other. He paused in the middle of the road, looked across at her, wanted to call out her name as he had as a young man: he felt something he had never felt for her before. It was love, but he was too old, too glazed with bitterness, to recognize it.

He went on into the hut, closed the door behind him and stood stock still. Tears came to his eyes; he could not remember when he had last wept. He was weeping for all the joys that might have been, lost now and irretrievable. But worse, he felt an immeasurable shame for what he had done to his son Tamezo.

2

In San Diego three other men, not family members, were thinking of Tamezo Okada with concern.

'If the OSS gets into the act, they'll want to control Okada. And Minato and Mrs Cairns. The operation will get bigger and bigger and somewhere along the line Okada and the others will finish up being controlled by some guy at a desk in Washington.'

Irvine interrupted Embury. 'We're just chaps – guys – at a desk here in San Diego. We mustn't forget that. But I see your point. So far we've been able to run the operation without interference. The danger for Okada and the others is that, if the OSS takes over, where will it be run from? From Berne or from Washington or from here? Too many cooks in the kitchen—'

'And Okada gets stewed,' said Reilly. 'Or cooked. Whatever,' he added lamely as he saw his remark had got only a pained reaction from Embury and Irvine.

The end of the war in Europe had meant little to the three men; they had been fighting the war in the Pacific for too long. Men and matériel would be diverted from the European theatre, but they knew that meant little: the Pacific theatre was almost overrun with men and ships and planes. The worst effect was that, in their own particular field of Intelligence, there were now out-of-work organizations looking for employment. There were Nazi war criminals still to be traced in Europe, either to be brought to trial or to be used as agents against the Russians, who were already emerging as the new enemy; but there were more than enough men for those tasks. The rest, some of them senior men, now wanted to run the show in the Pacific as they had run it in Europe. After all, as they said, they had the *experience*.

'Experience!' Embury exclaimed. 'Most of them have been sitting on their arses in Berne, living the fat life . . . What the hell would they know about the Jap mentality?'

Irvine said nothing; there were times when he wondered how much Embury and Reilly knew about how the Japanese mind worked. He left it to Reilly to say, 'They've been dealing with the Jap mission in Berne for what? A year, two years?'

'What the hell would that have taught them about the way a Jap thinks? Jesus Christ, the OSS hardly ever spoke to them. They were too goddam busy winning the war in Europe.'

'I think we should somehow quash this idea of theirs of wanting to put more Nisei into Japan,' said Irvine. 'It will finish up with agents just getting in each other's way. We might lose Minato too. He's in a dangerous situation as it is, without having to change bosses so late in the piece. At least he can trust us.'

Embury and Reilly nodded, sure that Minato's trust was well placed.

'But our real concern is for Okada,' Irvine went on.

He was the real professional amongst them, more professional (or at least experienced) than the OSS men who wanted to come in and take over the operation: after all, he had been in espionage before the war had started. He did not like the idea that an agent of his (he would never admit it to the others, but he thought of Okada as his) should be placed in jeopardy. There was also Mrs Cairns to be considered; though, since he had never had any direct dealings with Mrs Cairns after she had taken her husband's place, his feelings towards her were more impersonal. Unlike Reilly, he had nothing against using a woman agent, but it helped if one could remember her. He had met her once, fleetingly, vaguely remembered her as beautiful; but he had taken little notice of her. Part of the reason, he now admitted to himself, had been snobbery. He had had the old English expatriate's attitude towards half-castes; one couldn't trust them. If he ever met Mrs Cairns again he must make his apologies to her, if only silently.

'And Mrs Cairns,' he added now. 'Why should we give them up? All three of them? Let's hang on to the operation.'

'How can we do that if Washington insists?' Reilly was shackled by procedure, it was what Annapolis had taught him.

Irvine, who did not have to bend the knee to Washington or Annapolis, looked at Embury, the ex-car salesman. 'When you were in business what did you do with bills you didn't want to pay immediately?'

Embury grinned. 'I'd wait thirty days and then query them.'

Irvine gestured at the letter on Reilly's desk. 'Let's wait thirty days and then query that.'

'What if they get impatient and fly out here?' said Reilly.

'We move our base,' said Embury. 'I've talked to Captain Fleming. He's sending us out to Guam. By the time OSS catch us up there we tell them we're still waiting on a further report from Okada, that we haven't heard from him for some time—'

'But what if they ask for the file?' said Reilly, who was uncomfortable telling lies: not because he was a good Catholic, who can lie with the best heathens, but because he was such a poor liar.

'His reports, if they come in, won't be entered in the file.' Irvine looked at Embury, who was still grinning. 'Am I being too devious and unscrupulous, Commander?'

'On the contrary,' said Embury. 'I was just wondering how you guys ever managed to lose the Colonies.'

Irvine smiled in reply, but he was thinking: Just don't let us lose Okada and Mrs Cairns and Minato.

'I think we should send these people back to their houses, major. They have no right to be out here watching this.'

Major Nagata sighed inwardly at Sergeant Ugaki's zeal. It was the sergeant who had arrested the two drunken French journalists for singing 'The Marseillaise' and there had been nothing Nagata could do but have them sent away for a stay in jail. Nagata had made some friends in Nayora: well, acquaintances: he was realistic enough to know that foreigners did not make friends with a secret police officer. He had been as polite and accommodating as he could be without arousing the suspicions of the four men working for him; when the war ended no one here at Nayora would be able to complain about his treatment of them. With his eye on the future he had established a one-man foreign ministry.

'Sergeant, if we send them back to their houses they will only look out of their windows. I don't have enough of you to supervise every window in the village. They are doing no harm where they are.'

'They are watching a military manoeuvre, major.'

Indeed they are, thought Nagata, and they must be laughing their heads off. Down on the beach, beyond the anti-invasion stakes that had been driven into the sands, a company of soldiers were preparing what Nagata thought must easily be the world's longest assault on an enemy. Several thousand balloons, each about the height of a small man, floated on their thin cables; attached to the cables, Nagata knew, were packages of incendiary bombs. In a few minutes the balloons were to be released and the winds, Japanese winds, that is, were to carry the bombs six thousand miles across the Pacific to the North American continent where they would run up against the Rocky Mountains, set fire to the forests and bring about such devastation that the Americans would sue for peace. Nagata himself was silently laughing at the mad desperation of it all.

'Sergeant, let's see it as a celebration. After all, that's what

balloons are for. Or they were when you and I were children—'
He was talking of a distant past, it seemed; Sergeant Ugaki just
looked blank. 'When the balloons go up, exhort all the spectators to cheer.'

Sergeant Ugaki looked dubious, but he bowed and went off
up towards the crowd standing on the path that ran the length of
the beach. Nagata looked back at the crowd, bowing to those
who were marked for future use; they bowed back, both sides
aware that each was making use of the other. The war had
reached the bargaining point, Nagata thought: at his level if not
at that of the generals.

He saw Madame Tolstoy and Mrs Cairns; his bow to them
was no more pronounced than to the others. Then he saw Mrs
Cairns smile at a young man standing just behind her; Nagata
wondered who the young man was that he should merit such a
friendly smile. The young man did bow, but Nagata, suddenly
suspicious, saw that the bow was almost satirical: it was certainly not respectful. He would have to find out who the stranger
was.

Then a shot was fired and he turned round as the first of the
balloons began to lift into the air. Soldiers ran along the beach to
release the cables; they stumbled in the sand and several of them
fell headlong. The crowd began to cheer, but the cheers were
ironic, heavy enough to have turned the breeze and blown the
balloons back over Japan. But the charge of the light balloons
was not to be denied; they soared out over the bay, rising on the
air currents like thousands of small suns. The wind caught them
and they sailed high into the air in clusters, a child's idea of
warfare. The soldiers cheered and the spectators responded in
mocking echo. The soldiers, deaf to nuances, as they are taught
to be, bowed to the spectators and they bowed back. It was all
very courtly, thought Nagata, like a medieval battle.

Up on the edge of the crowd Okada had looked at the
despatch of the balloons with the same wry amusement as
Nagata. Natasha, standing some yards away, had identified
Nagata with a nod of her head; and Okada had kept a wary eye
on the *kempei* officer. Natasha had told him Nagata was running
the village with a benevolent hand, but that some of his men

240

were still obsessed with their suspicion and hatred of foreigners.

Okada had brought Otozo Toshiaki down here to Nayora to lunch at the villa of another man Okada now knew belonged to the Peace Faction. Nobuaki Noguchi was a retired senior bureaucrat, a man in his eighties who suggested someone even older; Okada, who had seen him several times, would have been only half-surprised if someone had told him that Noguchi had served at the court of the Emperor Meiji. He was a close friend of Toshiaki and the latter had great respect for the old man.

Noguchi, wavering on frail legs, took Toshiaki's arm as the two old men turned from watching the departure of the balloons and began to walk back towards the Noguchi villa, one of the largest in the village. Okada walked behind them, ears pricked to their conversation.

'What next will they try?' Noguchi, despite his frailty, had a firm voice. 'We have the peasants with bamboo spears, now we're sending off balloons . . . Do you think we should start making slingshots?'

'I think we should start making definite plans,' said Toshiaki. 'Who else is coming to lunch today?'

'Tajiri. Just the three of us. Then I have to go in to see Prince Konoye tomorrow. Perhaps you would care to come with me?'

Toshiaki nodded. 'We'll go in my car. I shall call for you in the morning.'

Noguchi smiled a gap-toothed smile. 'Riding in a Rolls-Royce . . . There are so few pleasures left at my age.'

Toshiaki smiled. 'Perhaps I could invite a couple of geishas out here, girls suitable for men of our age?'

The two old men were enjoying the joke against their years. 'I hear that might not be so easy, to get a geisha. I understand there is now a black market for the best of them. Where have they all gone?'

'To the factories, I believe.'

'What a waste,' said Nobuaki Noguchi, whose only pleasure now was in remembering pleasure. They both chuckled, like old vultures who had had the choice of pickings. 'What a waste.'

They had reached the front of the Noguchi villa. As they did so a Navy staff car drew up and Okada pulled up sharply as he saw Minato jump out and hold open the door for Admiral Tajiri. The admiral bowed and smiled to Toshiaki and Noguchi, gestured at Minato.

'I brought Lieutenant Minato with me for the ride. I thought a little sea air might do him good – he's been tasting nothing but ashes for months. Come back in two hours, lieutenant. See if you can find a pretty girl amongst the foreigners.'

The three old men went up into the villa; they looked like pensioners entering a retirement home. If that's the Peace Faction, Okada thought, what price peace?

Then Minato said, 'Who are you?'

'I am Toshiaki-san's driver, sir.' Now Minato knew where to find him; but he didn't care any more. 'From Miyanoshita.'

He bowed and went to move away, but found himself facing a stout man in police uniform; it was a moment before he recognized Major Nagata. 'You know this man, lieutenant?'

'No,' said Minato. 'May I ask you to identify yourself?'

'Major Nagata. I am in charge of the police in this village. May I ask who you are, lieutenant?'

'Lieutenant Minato, aide to Admiral Tajiri. He is visiting Noguchi-san.'

Okada, standing close to Nagata, could almost hear the *kempei* officer's mind working; certainly his eyes showed it. 'We seem to have a lot of visitors today, lieutenant. Did they broadcast that the balloons would be going up?'

'No, major. I think it must just be coincidence that Admiral Tajiri came to Nayora today.'

'And you?' Nagata swung his head sharply towards Okada. 'What brought you here? Do you have a pass to enter the village?'

Okada could feel himself beginning to sweat under his clothes. The summer humidity along the coast was notorious; only those who liked to bathe in the sea or sail boats built houses in places like Nayora. Okada wished he were being interrogated in Miyanoshita, where the air was much cooler. And where he would be a good distance from Natasha.

'I am the driver for Toshiaki-san, of Miyanoshita, major. My master has the pass. He is visiting Noguchi-san.'

242

Nagata added another name to his list. He was collecting them like beads on a rosary; he often used Christian images, since in China, as he arrested missionaries, he had come to know their customs. Admiral Tajiri and Otozo Toshiaki were beads to be polished.

'Is there anywhere here, major, where I can buy some food?' said Minato.

'Unfortunately, no. All the food shops and cafés were closed up ages ago.' Nagata knew where some food could be bought on the black market, but it was not his place to direct a Navy officer to such a place. He tolerated those in Nayora who could afford to buy the black market food, though money had little value these days; he had noticed that most of the foreigners, as if sure that the war would be over before winter came again, had traded their heavy clothing to the local farmers for what provisions they could get. Not all of them had been successful in buying or bartering for food; many of them were on the point of starvation. It hurt him to think of them each time he sat down to his own adequate meal. 'The Navy should take care of you better, lieutenant.'

'If I may be so presumptuous' – Okada bowed. 'I have brought food with me from Miyanoshita, lieutenant. If you would allow a humble man like myself to share it with you—?'

'I would suggest that is a good idea, lieutenant,' said Nagata. 'In times like these it is patriotic to share what we have.'

'Perhaps you would care to join us, major?' said Minato; and Okada cursed him for his cheek.

'Ah no, I don't know what the driver has in his box, but I'm sure it is not some loaves and fishes. He doesn't look the sort of man capable of miracles. Do you know the fairy stories of the Christian Bible?'

'No,' said Minato, who was an atheist and therefore had to invent his own stories. 'Now if you will excuse us, major?'

He bowed and walked away, jerking his head at Okada for the latter to follow him. Okada bowed to Nagata and went after Minato, keeping a respectful couple of paces behind him. Major Nagata looked after them, marking them for future reference; but this late in the war small fry did not interest him. The

Americans would not reward him for presenting them with sprats.

Minato led Okada out to a small point that overlooked the bay. A few of the foreign colony were strolling nearby; they looked curiously at the naval officer and the civilian, but they knew better than to stop and stare. Farther back up the slope a side road ran up towards the main highway; a road-block had been set up and two soldiers, bayonets fixed in their rifles, lounged there. The closest living things to Minato and Okada were the gulls, which looked better fed than any of the humans.

'It's just rice and seaweed balls and an apple,' said Okada, offering his lunch-box. 'You took a risk, didn't you, asking him to join us? Or were you trying a bad joke?'

'He's *kempei*, isn't he?' Minato took some rice and a seaweed ball in his hand. 'I despise those bastards. They don't fight a war, they corrupt it.'

He's getting reckless, Okada thought, and that's dangerous. 'Did you check on the owners of those cars up at Toshiaki-san's house? It's been two weeks now.'

Minato closed his eyes, ran off a number of names from memory. Then he opened his eyes, took some more rice between his fingers. 'Can you remember those? Don't write them down. Someone may be watching us.'

Okada memorized the names. 'I've got them. I'll see the names go out on the radio tonight.'

'I've seen the full list of those who went to prison.' Minato looked out to sea, then back at Okada. 'Your uncle, Tamezo Okada, your namesake, is on the list.'

Okada remembered his uncle, his father's younger brother. He had been a quiet, gentle man, one, it had seemed, ill-suited to the making of swords and other weapons; the sort of man one expects to belong to a peace movement. But Okada was now too confused about the Peace Faction to be able to place any man in it.

'A sword maker? An arms manufacturer?'

Minato nodded. 'None of it makes sense.' Then he looked back at the village. 'Does your other agent live around here?'

Up above the village Okada could see Natasha's villa against the pines. But he looked right round him in mock inspection. He said in English. 'Here? Right under the noses of Major Nagata and the *kempei*?'

Minato was not fooled. 'He's around here somewhere, I'll bet. So you work for Toshiaki? An easy job?'

'Except for his daughter, who's a pain in the arse – General Imamaru's wife.'

Minato was impressed. 'You work in good company.'

'So do you. And what the hell's it got us? The names of some of the Peace Faction, but not a clue as to what they're up to.'

'Not so long ago you'd lost your enthusiasm. Are you getting to be a one hundred per cent American again, now the war is almost won?'

'All I want is to get the job done and go home.' And take Natasha with me: he flicked a glance up towards the house on the hill. 'Shove your neck out, try and find out from Admiral Tajiri what's going on.'

'My neck?' Minato took the half an apple Okada handed him. 'You want me to be a one hundred per cent American hero? If I'm caught, you can just head for the mountains and be safe.'

'You could give me away.' Okada bit into the apple.

'You still don't trust me, do you, Tamezo?'

But Minato was not angry or disappointed. He felt he had become totally discouraged about the future; he was betraying his country even with just his thoughts, but when the war was over and lost he would still be here, still Japanese. He had not begun to think of suicide; but who was there to expect it of him? It was an honourable act; not a despairing one, as the Americans thought of it. But his parents were dead, he had no close relatives: his name was his own. There was Admiral Tajiri who might expect him to save his honour; but the admiral had become so cynical that one could doubt Tajiri's own sense of honour. If he did commit suicide it *would* be out of despair, an American act.

'I don't know, Kenji,' said Okada honestly. 'I just wish to God our guys would come soon, get it over and done with! They're killing hundreds, maybe thousands, every goddam night with their raids—'

245

'Tamezo, don't be sentimental about those who are being killed—'

'I can't help it. I've worked amongst these people – they're not soldiers—'

'Be sensible. Most of them are doing war work. Tamezo, you can't pick and choose whom you're going to bomb in a crowd. And there's the psychological effect – the American generals know that if enough citizens are killed, maybe the rest of them, the survivors, will rise up and tell the Japanese generals the carnage has got to stop. War is no longer an exercise in chivalry—'

Okada turned away and looked out to sea. This was crazy: he was arguing for the Japanese people and Minato was defending the American generals. 'I shouldn't have come. Neither of us should have . . .'

'I had to,' said Minato. 'It was that or execution as a spy.'

Okada looked east across the North Pacific, stretching his gaze beyond its limit till imagination had to take over. It would be 9 p.m. on the West Coast now. The night shifts would be at work in Seattle and all the way south to San Diego; people would be sitting in front of their radios listening to Fred Allen or Jack Benny or Fibber McGee and Molly; he had forgotten what nights the programmes went out. If Japanese bombers had ever made it to the American mainland, bombed the hell out of Seattle and Portland and San Francisco and Los Angeles, would the citizens have risen up in wrath and demanded that the war be stopped?

He doubted it: at least not the first time or the second or even the third. But after nine months of continual bombing? Yes, Minato was right. The general would have heard from the citizens, the ordinary people. The difference, of course, was that the American people expected to be heard from. Respect from the hierarchy was contrary to the American character.

'Okay,' he said, 'we go on as we've been doing. Get what you can out of Admiral Tajiri and I'll find out what's happening around Toshiaki.'

Minato too was looking out to sea. 'Remember when we used to go down to Redondo Beach as kids?'

Okada remembered, felt a sudden rush of nostalgia for old times and an old friendship. 'Maybe it'll happen again. Your kids and mine.' But he knew that it never would.

He closed up his lunch box, stood up and bowed. He went off back to the village and Minato continued to sit on his rock and stare out to sea. He was thinking of America, wondering where he would be now if he had not come back to Japan with his parents sixteen years ago. But to contemplate what might have been is an exercise for old, or anyway older men. When young it just becomes an exercise in self-pity. He was not yet reduced to that.

Up in the villa on the hill Natasha, at her bedroom window, had been observing the two men through binoculars. It had been a moment or two before she had recognized Lieutenant Minato; it had taken her only another moment to recognize that he must be another of Okada's agents. Then she had swung the glasses back towards the village and seen Major Nagata standing outside the police station also observing the two figures out on the point.

4

'I have had word from Tokyo,' said Sergeant Ugaki. 'There will be another visit tonight by the Radio Interception unit. Their van will be here at nine o'clock.'

'Good,' said Major Nagata; but thought the exercise was pointless. 'See that no word gets out about the visit.'

'Of course, major,' said Ugaki and looked at Sergeant Masuda at his desk on the other side of the room. The village police station had been designed to hold no more than two policemen and two overnight prisoners; now it was accommodating six policemen, Major Nagata, to give himself the private office to which his rank entitled him, had taken over the single cell. 'Did you hear that instruction, Sergeant Masuda?'

'I am an oyster,' said Masuda, who was a blabbermouth and knew it. 'Not a word goes out of this office. Do you want me to meet the unit when it arrives?'

'No,' said Ugaki, conscious of his own rank; village policemen were several rungs down the ladder below *kempei*. 'I shall
do that. How many people in the village have radios?'

'Only the diplomats,' said Masuda. 'All registered.'

'Do you suspect any of them of having short wave radios?'

Masuda shook his head. 'They all know the consequences.
They prefer to live here instead of in prison. Well, it's time I did
my rounds.'

'Are you looking for an outbreak of crime?' said Nagata from
his cell.

Sergeant Masuda smiled at the major's humour, which always left him uneasy, put on his cap and, with his peculiar
loose-kneed walk, went out to warn his villagers, *his* people, to
be careful tonight when the Radio Interception unit came
snooping.

He made his round unhurriedly, stopping to chat with
people, saluting others, passing the word discreetly and knowing that his information would be treated with discretion. His
last call was at the Cairns villa on the hill; but no one appeared to
be at home. He went round to the back of the house, but even
the kitchen door was locked. Ah well, he had no reason to think
that Mrs Cairns might have a short-wave radio. He had just
wanted to see her, speak a few words to her. Beautiful women
were long-spaced events in his life.

5

'I went looking for you just after lunch,' said Natasha, 'but you
must have gone back to Miyanoshita with Toshiaki.'

'We left immediately after lunch,' said Okada. 'Where are
Lily and Yuri?'

'Yuri's been gone all day – she's taken my fur coat up to the
farms to try and barter it for some food.'

'Are things so bad?' Okada was surprised. 'I thought Lily
could keep you well supplied.'

'The black market is getting tougher. General Imamaru is
getting extra out of army rations, but we can't always have it

delivered here. He thinks it doesn't look good in front of the foreigners.'

'I wouldn't have thought he cared a hoot for what foreigners thought.'

'He's changing – or so Lily says. I think she's afraid he may toss her over.'

'Where is she tonight?'

'She's in Tokyo with the general. She'll be home later. She doesn't stay there any more, not since the general's house was burnt out.'

'We better start transmitting then.'

They went down to the basement, where Okada gave her his encoded message. He had had a busy afternoon, taking Toshiaki back to Miyanoshita, then driving Madame Imamaru up to Goro to have tea with the wife of the Russian ambassador; the Russians, quite sensibly, had withdrawn to the mountains from Tokyo, not wishing to be the victims of their Allies' bombs. While he waited for Madame Imamaru Okada had encoded tonight's message, but his memory was not clear on the code and it had been full of gaps. It had been nine o'clock before, cycling hard, he had got down here to the Cairns villa.

Natasha took the message, sat down at the Morse key. 'Is this a list of names?'

'Yes.'

'Did you get them from your friend Lieutenant Minato?'

'That's none of your business!' Then he drew in his sharp tongue. 'Sorry, I didn't mean that. It's just – well, the less you know the better.'

'You think so? If something happened to you—' She stopped, horrified by the thought; then she went on, 'Wouldn't he want to use me to send his messages?'

'How did you get onto him?'

'I met him weeks ago at a dinner party in Tokyo. I saw the two of you today out there on the point – you were talking like old friends.'

Like old friends? 'We're just two guys working at the same game. Come, start transmitting.'

249

His tone was too sharp, but it was born out of concern for her. He did not want the operation complicated. The less she knew about Minato the better; to hell with what happened to the operation if he himself was captured. She had to be protected as best he knew how. And one way was for Minato never to meet her.

She looked at him, not hurt but puzzled. Then she turned to the key and tapped out her call signal. And Lily said from the top of the steps leading out of the basement, 'I'd close that down if I were you. There's a Radio Interception unit in the village.'

Natasha's fingers came down hard on the key, stayed there. She looked at her mother, unafraid, like a brazen schoolgirl caught smoking or looking at dirty pictures. 'You have no right to spy on me!'

'Spy?' Lily glanced at the radio. 'That's an appropriate word in the circumstances.'

Okada was busy putting away the radio and closing up the wall. 'You better get upstairs, Natasha, keep an eye out. If they come up towards the house, give me the word and I'll go out the back way. I'll wait up in the trees to see what happens.'

Natasha kissed him quickly. She went up the stairs, determined to push Lily out of the way if she had to. But Lily had already turned, was going through to the front of the house. Natasha ran after her, but was too late to prevent her mother opening the front door and going out on to the verandah. Natasha followed her, almost on the run.

'I'll kill you if you let them know where Tamezo is!'

'Sit down,' said Lily calmly, settling herself into one of the cane chairs. 'We'll sit here and chat for a while, as we always do on a summer evening.'

They had not sat out here once. Natasha eased herself gingerly into a chair, taking the one nearest the open front door; she would fly through the house to warn Tom at the first hint of danger. Over the past month she had begun to feel at ease with Lily and now she was sitting close to the enemy.

'Would you really kill for him?' said Lily.

'Yes!'

250

'Don't be so fierce, child.' In her own ears Lily sounded more grandmaternal than maternal; she would have to do better than this. 'If those men from the Interception Unit come up here, they are going to be very suspicious if you're acting so highly strung.'

'How do you expect me to feel?' But Natasha tried to calm down. She had sailed sedately through life up till now, living in the present tense, never tense about the past or future. Men had told her she was a balm for their nerves as well as their organs. 'You're going to betray us—'

Lily sighed: motherhood really was a burden. No wonder she had run away from it all those years ago. 'Natasha, how long have you been doing this? Acting as a spy?'

Natasha, one eye down the path for approaching danger, said, 'Ever since my husband died.'

'Whom do you work for?'

'The Americans.'

'Not the Chinese? Or the Russians? Or some group here in Japan?'

'The Chinese? Chiang Kai-Sek? Or the Communists? Why should I work for them?'

'Your grandmother was Chinese. Still, as you say, why should you work for them?' She herself never had. 'And not the Russians, not like Richard Sorge?'

'No. What group here in Japan would I work for?'

'There's the Peace Faction.' But Lily had only heard Imamaru mention it, she knew nothing about it. 'So it's the Americans. Well, perhaps you can put in a good word for your mother when they come. How much are they paying you?'

'Nothing.' Natasha's eyes had become accustomed to the moonlight. Down in the village, at the corner of two streets, she could see the van, its direction finder moving slowly, almost inexorably, on its roof; its slow circling mesmerized her for a moment, but she dragged her eyes away. 'They're paying me nothing.'

Lily tut-tutted. 'To work for *nothing* – that's worse than treason.'

'I'm not committing treason.' The van had begun to move up

the street towards the villa. 'You forget – you neglected to give me a country.'

'I left that to your father,' said Lily primly; a mother wasn't expected to do everything. To give birth was enough without having to give nationality. 'What about Tamezo?'

'He's an American, a Nisei.' At once Natasha wanted to bite her tongue.

'Nisei? What's that?' But Lily wasn't interested in the answer. The van had pulled up at the bottom of the garden path and someone was getting out of the front seat. 'Here are your friends. Keep your mouth shut and let me do the talking.'

The shadowed figure coming up the garden path materialized into Major Nagata. 'Enjoying the evening air, ladies?'

Natasha, not enjoying it in the least, was as still as the night itself. She could feel sweat running down her, turning cold on her. She tried to say good evening, but her tongue was a piece of flannel in her dry mouth. She was not so much frightened as despairing: she could be taken but she must never allow them to take Tom.

'There is little else to enjoy, major,' said Lily.

True, thought Nagata; but didn't voice it. He had no doubts that Madame Tolstoy was concerned only for herself; but it would be foolish to tell her that he too was selfish. 'At least the evening air comes free. One doesn't need to go to the black market for it.'

Behind him the direction finder had stopped moving on the roof of the van; one arm pointed directly up the path like a sniper's rifle barrel. Natasha tried to tell herself that meant nothing, the radio was no longer working; but reason had turned to mincemeat. She heard herself say, 'Are you looking for black marketeers, major?'

Nagata laughed, a social sound. 'The jails would be overflowing, Mrs Cairns, if we took in all the people who buy and sell on the black market. No' – He gestured behind him. 'Our friends from Tokyo are looking for illegal radios.'

'There is nothing illegal in this house, major,' said Lily. 'General Imamaru would never allow it.'

Natasha went weak with relief. She had fully expected Lily to denounce her and Tom; now she was overwhelmed by something she had never felt before. Filial love? Daughter looked at mother; but mother, as if afraid of too much sudden devotion, wasn't looking at daughter. Instead she was looking almost sternly at Major Nagata.

'I think the general would appreciate it, major, if you told your friends in the van they should not waste their time pointing that thing in this direction.' She made it sound obscene.

Nagata recognized he was being dismissed. He had hoped to be invited to stay: a little *saké*, a little chat; it would have rounded off the day. 'Of course, Madame Tolstoy. They are only doing their job, but they do tend to get a little over-zealous. It's the times.'

'We all suffer from them,' said Lily but sounded insufferable.

Don't push him too far! Natasha thought. She gave Nagata a smile, a small going-away present. 'Goodnight, major. We appreciate that it was you who called on us and not them. We feel you're one of us now.'

Nagata bowed, went down the path wondering if Mrs Cairns had been giving him some message. He waved the van on and walked on down into the village. The two women, Madame Tolstoy and her daughter, were working together: of that he was certain. But at what and for whom? He would have to get Mrs Cairns alone (the thought momentarily thrilled him, but in another context) and question her. He would ask her if she knew the young man who was Otozo Toshiaki's driver and, if she did know him, what was his connection with Admiral Tajiri's aide. As for what Madame Tolstoy knew, the possibilities there were endless, but he could not see himself questioning her, not while she was General Imamaru's mistress.

'Why didn't you betray us?' Natasha said to Lily.

'I'm no fool.' She was no sentimentalist, either: 'Holding up a flag when a ship is sinking is a waste of time. One should be learning to swim . . . Go up and bring Tamezo back to the house.'

Natasha stood up, looked steadily at her mother. Then, making up her mind that Lily had to be trusted sooner or later,

253

she went quickly through the house and up through the garden to the pines. Okada stepped out of the shadows and she stumbled into his arms.

He held her to him, could feel her trembling. He was amazed at his own feelings. It excited him sexually to have her close to him; but this was something more. He felt a certain peace, but it was that felt by a man standing still in a minefield. He was, he guessed, more in love than he had ever expected to be.

Natasha's trembling subsided; her body became less fragile, more sensual. But there was no time for that sort of thing. 'They've gone,' she said. 'Major Nagata was with them – I thought Lily was going to give us away—'

'She didn't?' It was a stupid question; but he had forgotten Lily for the moment. 'Where is she? Gone with Nagata?'

'She's down in the house. She wants to see us.'

She took his hand and led him down to the house. Lily was waiting for them in the living room, looking commanding and demanding: a real madame. Or madam, thought Okada, who had known one or two in Los Angeles.

'You have a lot of explaining to do, Mr Fujita. Or should I now call you Mr Okada, since we're supposed to be getting down to brass tacks?'

'How far can we trust you?' said Okada.

Lily smiled. 'That's for you to answer, not me. All I can promise you is that I shan't let any harm come to Natasha.'

'Thank you,' said Natasha sincerely, 'mother.'

Lily shuddered delicately. '*Lily*, please . . . Tell me as much as you want to, Mr Okada. You're an American Japanese, I take it?'

Okada told her as much as he dared: about parachuting into Japan, linking up with Natasha, sending messages out regularly on the radio. He did not tell her about Minato. 'My specific mission is to find out what I can about the Peace Faction.'

'She mentioned it when we were out on the verandah,' said Natasha.

Okada's interest quickened. 'What do you know about it?'

'I have just heard the general mention it, that's all. He seemed to know a lot about it, but he wouldn't tell me.'

Okada was not sure whether to believe her or not. With her eye always to the main chance, she would not neglect any opportunity to build ammunition, or insurance, for the future; as soon as the Americans arrived she would switch sides as easily as she switched her wardrobe. She sat unperturbed, waiting for his next question.

'The general evidently doesn't tell his wife much about it,' he said, hoping that might prompt her, in her vanity, to show that a mistress was always better informed than a wife. 'I saw her once spying on a meeting at her father's house. He belongs to the Faction.'

'Madame Imamaru would only be listening for gossip,' said Lily. 'She hasn't the brains for any sort of intrigue.'

He knew at once that she was right. He had worried about Madame Imamaru for a day or two after he had seen her eavesdropping, but the more he had come to know her the more he had realized she was a silly woman who fed on rumour and tittle-tattle. Anything she had gleaned from her eavesdropping on her father's meeting would not have been for political purposes but for her own reputation as a source of private information. He was beginning to wonder if some of the loosest tongues in a war were not to be found amongst the top heads.

'Time's running out,' he said. 'If the Peace Faction is going to do anything, it's got to do it soon. Otherwise Japan is going to finish up a wasteland from north to south.'

'You sound concerned for this country.'

He hadn't realized that was so; but it was true. 'I don't want to see any more slaughter. I'm sick of it. Every night there are raids on the big cities – the radio never tells us how many die, but I can guess it's in the thousands.'

'Why do you want to stop that if it's going to win the war for the Americans?' She thought war was stupid; but once something was started it should be finished properly. 'They didn't start all this slaughter.'

I'm arguing with this mercenary whore against my own countrymen, Okada thought. He gave up, said, 'If you can, try and get something out of the general on the Faction. Anything.

He's there at the top – he must know as well as anyone that the best thing is to sue for peace.'

'I'm not so sure,' said Lily. 'He's been admitted to the inner circle – he had an audience with the Emperor last week. He's strutting around as if the Son of Heaven has asked him to be his foster-father.'

'He'd chop your head off if he heard you being as disrespect-ful of the Emperor as that.'

'He may try to chop it off anyway,' she said unworriedly; she had never been afraid of swordsmen, in bed or not. 'He sent me home early this evening without any reason. But don't worry about me. You two are in more danger than I am. You are taking a great risk using that radio downstairs.'

Natasha had sat silent during the conversation between Lily and Okada. She had slowly, almost reluctantly, come to trust Lily. She had also come to accept that she was Lily's daughter: the acceptance in the heart had not been as easy as in the mind. She felt no swelling of love nor even a warm feeling towards the cool older woman; but Lily had come in from being a stranger to being someone to whom she now owed a debt. Natasha felt no resentment at being indebted to her; on the contrary she almost welcomed it. It made them mother and daughter, she thought. As if family ties were no more than a form of debt collection. She was handicapped by the fact that she had never seen a family *being* a family.

'We can't stop now,' she said. She had a debt to Keith, too, but she hardly admitted that to herself. Thinking of Keith, she looked guiltily at Tom. 'But if you drop out . . .'

'No,' he said after a pause. He felt he was in a crazy Hall of Mirrors; he was bewildered by reflections of himself. He wanted to run away from the war; but what would that achieve? He felt a mad urge to go down to the basement and broadcast a long harangue against the bombing of the civilian areas. But the Radio Interception unit would be on to him before he was halfway through all he wanted to say. He would be executed by the Japanese as a spy and disowned by the Americans as a radical soft-in-the-head nut. Neither side would give him any credit for conscience. 'No, we'll keep transmitting.'

'If you are found out, I shall disown you,' said Lily.

'You did that to me a long time ago,' said Natasha with some of the old asperity.

Lily winced inwardly as conscience, a hitherto unrecognized weakness, pricked her. Dammit, motherhood was worse than she'd imagined. For once she did not trust herself to answer and she rose abruptly and swept out of the room. Gone like a madam, thought Okada.

Natasha took him to the back door. 'You don't want to stay and go to bed?'

'Not tonight. I'm impotent—'

'Not for *that*.' Though she would have welcomed some lovemaking; if nothing else, it took one's mind off other things. 'Just to comfort each other—'

He put his arms round her, kissed her gently on the lips. 'Sweetheart, just thinking about you is enough comfort. There's nothing I'd like better than to stay, but I've got a ten-mile ride uphill on my bicycle—'

She smiled, kissed him just as gently in return. 'I'm selfish. When the war is over, can we have a year-long honeymoon?'

On the long ride back to Miyanoshita he thought of a honeymoon with Natasha. It was a way of filling in the dark hour or more though several times he had to rise from the saddle.

Eight

'Lieutenant,' said Colonel Hayashi, 'why didn't you and Admiral Tajiri go down to Hiroshima as planned?'

Minato wondered how Hayashi knew of the plan; the visit to Hiroshima had not been announced. 'I thought the Emperor's visit was supposed to have been secret, sir?'

'It was, lieutenant.' Hayashi smiled, but said no more.

'Well, you must know, then, that the admiral didn't go to Hiroshima because the Emperor didn't go.'

'You were fortunate then. *Mutsu* might have blown up while you were there.'

The battleship *Mutsu* had blown up in Hiroshima harbour two weeks before; at 39,000 tons, it was larger than any ship sunk by the Americans in combat. Because there had been few crew on board there had been few casualties; it had been announced that the explosion was an accident due to a spark firing the ship's magazine. Rumour had it that the blowing-up of *Mutsu* was an act of protest by Navy personnel, but Minato knew that so far the Navy police and the civilian Special Higher Police had made no arrests. Nonetheless the accident, or sabotage, had had its shock waves travel as far north as Tokyo.

'Was that an accident, colonel, as they are saying?' He felt sure that if anyone knew anything about the explosion it would be Hayashi.

'No.' Hayashi's tone was curt, but he said nothing more to enlighten Minato.

He had called Minato this morning to ask him to lunch again at the Army Club. Minato had dutifully reported the invitation to Admiral Tajiri and been told to accept. Lunch this time, Minato had noted, was more austere than on his previous visit;

food rationing was now being extended to the privileged, at least in their clubs. Perhaps it was the thin gruely soup, the stringy seaweed balls and the chicken that tasted like crow that had made conversation over the table desultory and left Minato wondering why he had been invited. When lunch was finished Hayashi rose as abruptly as before and marched out of the club, with Minato hurrying to catch up with him.

'Weak! Spineless!' Hayashi had snapped and it was a moment or two before Minato guessed that he was referring to the club's members and not its food.

They marched south, down past the Imperial Guards barracks across the moat on their right, past the secret police headquarters on their left (Minato breathed a sigh of relief as they went past without slackening of step), then turned west and south again into the East Garden of the Imperial Palace. The guards at the gates saluted Hayashi, and he and Minato passed through without being questioned. Minato, puzzled, uneasy, kept the silence that had prevailed throughout their brisk walk. He was beginning to wonder if Colonel Hayashi was more than slightly mad.

Minato had never been in the East Garden, though he knew it was not the most private of the Imperial gardens. They passed the Chamberlain's Palace, turned west again, crossed a bridge and skirted Maple Leaf Hill. Here there were guards posted all along the path at regular intervals; they all seemed to know Hayashi and saluted him. Hayashi slowed his step at last and Minato, mind now almost feverish, wondered if he had been led into some sort of ambush.

They passed the villa of the Crown Prince, went through another gate, where the guards again saluted Hayashi, and came into the Fukiage Gardens. Through the trees on his left Minato could see the Palace Shrine and beyond it the Inner Palace. For one wild moment Minato wondered if Hayashi was going to take him before the Emperor himself. Here he was, a junior naval officer, in the Emperor's own private park and he hadn't the faintest idea why.

'Are you on the Emperor's staff, sir?' The question struggled out of a hoarse, dry throat.

'We are all on the Emperor's staff,' said Hayashi and smiled for the first time since lunch. 'Even the street sweeper in the farthest village.'

It sounded like a line from a medieval play, but Minato nodded. The gravel path crunched beneath his feet like eggshells breaking. On the Calabash Pond mallard, teal and a Mandarin duck cruised at ease, heads gleaming like jewels in the bright sun. The gardens, as beautifully kept as ever even in wartime, were a green oasis and Minato suddenly wished he belonged to the inner circle that could retreat here.

'Do the Navy Staff believe the blowing up of *Mutsu* was an accident? Even a man like Admiral Tajiri?' Hayashi saw Minato's hesitancy and he smiled again; or rather he bared his teeth. 'Oh, I know you report everything I say to him, lieutenant.'

Minato took a risk: 'Then why do you ask such questions, colonel?'

'Have you ever played *Go*, lieutenant?'

Minato had played it at the Academy, but never seriously. It was a game that required patience and, having very little and not wanting to lose, he had preferred not to play when avoidable.

'It's a mixture, like most board games, of mathematical calculation and intuition. Occasionally one must take chances. That way one often wins the game more easily.'

'Are we playing a game now, sir?'

Hayashi looked impressed rather than annoyed. 'Yes, I think we are, lieutenant. Are they talking of surrender over at Navy Staff?'

'In what way, sir?' Minato, still puzzled but a little less afraid, made a cautious move in the game.

'You must know that things are not going well for us.' They had begun to walk along the path between the Emperor's Library and the Concubines' Pavilion. Minato had heard of the latter and knew that it was now where the Empress and her ladies lived; he was surprised to see that it was an English-style country house, an unlikely nest for concubines. 'But in the field our soldiers are dying like heroes of old. No sacrifice in the name of the Emperor is too much for them.'

Minato felt he was listening to a soft-voiced political speech, but he just nodded in agreement. A peacock, tail spread, crossed the path in front of them, an aberration in the circumstances.

'How would they feel if they knew that back here at home there was much less determination to win?'

Minato did not ask the obvious question: *But can we win?* He could see that Hayashi, for all his soft voice and now slow walk, was a tightly controlled bundle of nerves and passion. He felt that the colonel was on the point of taking him into his confidence, but one out-of-step remark and he would lose contact with Hayashi forever. It was not too bizarre that he might even lose his head. He knew that other heads, in other times, had rolled in these gardens.

'The Emperor—' Hayashi nodded towards the library on a small hill on their left. It was a squat concrete building and looked, to Minato's eyes, like a fort; which it was. The Emperor had moved out of his palace into the library as the war progressed; buried deep in the hill was a large air-raid bunker. Minato knew that Adolf Hitler had committed suicide in his bunker in Berlin and wondered, a treasonable thought, if the Emperor might do the same if Japan lost the war.

'The Emperor is being wrongly advised,' said Hayashi. 'You were in America all those years – do the Americans expect him to surrender?'

Minato felt he was hardly in a position to speak for Washington; he had known virtually nothing of what went on there. But he felt he could speak for the American people he had met on the West Coast and at the Military Language School in Minnesota: 'They see the Emperor as a fanatic, colonel. In the best sense,' he added hurriedly. 'A fanatical patriot.'

'As he is, as he is.' Hayashi's voice was still low, but it had a fiercely vehement note to it. 'He must not be talked into surrendering! He must throw out the spineless traitors!'

'Sir, do you think Admiral Tajiri is one of those traitors?' It was a daring question, but he correctly guessed that Hayashi was in the mood to answer it.

'Of course! Did you know that Lieutenant Sagawa worked for me?' Hayashi had paused in his walk, as if his passion had

261

made him lose step; but now he resumed it, still at the same leisurely pace. 'Unofficially, of course.'

'No, sir, I didn't.' His voice was steady, but his throat was dry. 'Was he killed because he was working for you?'

Hayashi shrugged, as if he neither knew nor cared: 'Perhaps. But he believed what I told him – that there must be no surrender on the part of the Emperor.'

'Colonel Hayashi, are you asking me to take Sagawa's place?'

Hayashi turned his head, looked squarely at Minato; he pulled up abruptly and Minato had to turn round. 'Yes. I am looking for young officers who still have national pride, who still revere the Emperor and what he means to our country. I have others – I need more.'

'Sir, you are asking me to betray Admiral Tajiri.'

'I am asking you to see that the Emperor is not betrayed.'

A crane rose out of the shallows of the pond, flapped on heavy creaking wings across to the other side. It was almost as if Hayashi had stage-managed the appearance of the large bird; he could not produce the Emperor, but he could display the symbol of him. There was an ancient phrase, 'The Emperor lives above the clouds like a crane'; on those rare occasions when he issued an edict to the nation, his command was known as 'The Voice of the Crane'. Minato felt himself being drawn towards an abyss. But he knew he would never have another opportunity like this to get to the heart of the matter, to find out how the Peace Faction was operating.

'I take it that Admiral Tajiri and the Peace Faction want peace at any price?'

'The Admiral has told you about the Faction?'

'A little.' Tajiri had told him nothing.

Hayashi shook his head. 'Believe only half of what he tells you. They are not what they seem. They believe they are protecting the Emperor, but they will only degrade him. That imprisonment of their members was all show, nothing more, designed to impress the Americans if and when they come. That's all they accept, that the Americans will come and must be collaborated with.'

Minato could not bring himself to believe that Admiral

262

Tajiri, a patriot, even if a cynic, could ever be a collaborator. Before he had left America he had seen newsreels of what had happened to French collaborators after Paris had been liberated; he could not see the admiral, an honourable man, ever placing himself in that position. But obviously the Peace Faction was working towards some sort of compromise when the enemy finally came.

'What can I do, sir? I'm a very junior officer—'

'Rank doesn't matter.' But Hayashi's magnanimity sounded hollow; he was as rigidly held in the hierarchy as the Emperor himself. The nation might fall, but not position. 'There are others besides myself with sufficient authority . . .' Minato wondered who they might be. He looked around the gardens, but no conspirators lurked there, at least not obvious ones. There were guards, court flunkeys, palace bureaucrats, all moving intently about their business; but none of them, as far as Minato could observe, was covertly watching him and the colonel. 'All we need is a nucleus. We don't need an army to get to see the Emperor. We have entrée.'

'Does the Peace Faction have entrée?'

'Yes,' said Hayashi bitterly. 'They have had it for years. That is our only handicap, that we learned too late what they are trying to do.'

'I wish you'd tell me more, colonel.'

'I'll tell you more when I know you are on our side. I can see that for the moment you have your doubts. In my day young men jumped at the chance to serve the Emperor.'

'If you spoke for the Emperor, sir, I'd have no hesitation. But—'

'I speak for the Throne.' Which was different, and Hayashi knew it.

'Are you not afraid that I'll report to Admiral Tajiri what's been said?'

'I told you, lieutenant, in such a game as we're playing, one must take risks, must put a bet on intuition. The day before he died Lieutenant Sagawa reported to me that he suspected you were not what you seemed. He was killed before he could confirm it.'

Despite the warm day Minato felt a chill. 'Sagawa was mistaken, sir. He was an ass-kisser, as the Americans say. He would tell his superiors anything to get himself noticed.'

There was a glint of anger in Hayashi's eyes. 'Don't go too far, lieutenant—'

'I am only defending myself, sir. Lieutenant Sagawa had no proof of anything against me. He resented me because I'd come back and was promoted over him to become Admiral Tajiri's favourite. I owe a great debt to the admiral.'

'You owe a greater one to the Emperor. I don't think I am mistaken in my intuition, lieutenant. For your own reasons, whatever they are, you want to be more than just the aide to an admiral, the messenger boy for a tired old man. Perhaps it was all that time in America – ambition has got to you. Come, I'll see you out of the gardens, since you have no pass.'

As abruptly as on their previous meeting he turned and strode off, leaving Minato to hurry to catch up with him. At the West Gate he gestured to the guards that Minato was to be allowed out, returned Minato's salute and turned quickly on his heel and went back through the gardens, heading in a south-easterly direction. Minato tried to remember what buildings lay there, but could think only of the Inner Palace. Hayashi had the look of a man completely at home in his surroundings. He certainly did not look afraid, which was how Minato himself felt.

But as he walked back to the Navy building he made up his mind he would not report everything that had been said to Admiral Tajiri. The *Go* game was just beginning and Colonel Hayashi had left the next move to him. The game would be over if he brought Admiral Tajiri into it.

2

July came in, humid as a hothouse; people wilted and so did morale. The war continued to go badly; the radio no longer tried to hide the truth, though it did not tell all of it. Bombers came almost every night; the cities were turned to rubble. Food

264

became even more scarce than before; people began to wonder if they would die of starvation before the bombs got them. They waited for some word from the Emperor, but he and his ministers and his generals were desperately seeking, through Moscow and Berne, a way to honourable surrender. Ears turned westwards for an encouraging reply, which never came; they did not hear the explosion to the east where, in the New Mexico desert, a giant cloud boiled up, the shape of which had never been seen before.

Okada drove the Rolls-Royce, polished it, tended the Toshiaki garden. He had planted some carrots, beans and cabbages and they had flourished; the Toshiaki household at least had vegetables on its menu and even Madame Imamaru was appreciative. He had cleaned out the garden at the back of the Cairns villa in Nayora, working at night, and planted the same vegetables there, leaving Yuri to tend them; women are always appreciative of a good provider and Natasha and Lily were no exception. Their expression of gratitude was only spoiled by Lily's remarking that it was a pity he was not also a fisherman.

He managed to get down to Nayora at least one night a week; he was developing into a moderate marathon cyclist. Lily saw General Imamaru much less frequently now and, against the grain and all her history, had become a chaperone, though a tolerant one. She read or did needlework, two pursuits she had always avoided, but she remained in character: she read pornographic novels and sewed classical scenes full of erotic love. She smiled indulgently, but not lewdly, when Okada and Natasha went up to Natasha's bedroom; she had already begun to think of herself as a mother-in-law, a thought that at first gave her a migraine. Okada, overcoming his modesty, and Natasha made love in the big bed in her room and talked about their future. Or rather she did: he just answered her questions.

'I want a week, a month, somewhere alone with you. America is so big – are there any places where one can be alone?'

'Wyoming. There's marvellous country there called the Grand Tetons. I'll take you there.' But not to Blood Mountain.

'Will I find you so different back in your own country?'

She stroked his face and his shoulders, prospector's fingers: she was looking for what made her love him so much. But she knew it was not just the physical side of him; she had learned from experience that that was the easiest attraction. Keith, in this very bed, had once told her that love was death's brother; she had not known what he meant and had been afraid to show her ignorance. But gradually she had come to know that even in the happiness of love there was pain; fear that the happiness could not last. Love was a strength when one was desolate; and Tom, without speaking of love, had a strength that she could draw on. He was, and would remain, part-mystery to her; as Keith had been. But that, perhaps, was part of the essence of love.

'Probably.' He kissed her, wondering how different *she* would be in America. But he felt certain she would survive in the melting-pot.

'Don't change, please—' She kissed him.

He drew her down on to him, opening her. Lovemaking, as distinct from love, doesn't require honest answers.

The Radio Interception Unit had moved on to other areas— 'They are still looking for spies,' Major Nagata had said to Natasha. 'As if it mattered any more.' Natasha sent out a weekly transmission, but she and Okada began to feel they were tap-tapping their messages into outer space: these days there seemed to be no reaction at all from San Diego to what they reported.

'They don't care any more,' said Okada. 'Why do we bother?'

But they continued the transmissions. Okada went into Tokyo twice to see Minato, getting permission, through Hara the butler, from Toshiaki-san on the pretext that he wanted to see how an ageing aunt was faring in the bombing raids. He and Minato walked through the summer twilight in Shiba Park, a battered ruin of an oasis but still preferable to the charred devastation of the inner city. The park was crowded, people coming out of their holes in the ground like troglodytes to lap at the faded green of the gardens; the Japanese are the most private of crowds and no one looked at the two tall young men, the Navy officer and the civilian. Okada and Minato felt reasonably safe.

'Colonel Hayashi is trying to recruit me,' Minato said at their first meeting. 'I'm not sure what he has in mind, but it's some sort of conspiracy to protect the Emperor.'

'Are you going to go in with him?'

'I could be digging my grave. Everything in Japan is just a big grave now, we're all tumbling into it.' He was depressed, unutterably sad for his country. 'So I suppose I have nothing to lose.'

'Is he so close to the Emperor?'

'I think so. He's only a colonel and, as far as I know, he has no nobleman's rank. But he's *there*, in that inner circle. He knows all about the Peace Faction too.'

'Then it's worth a try. We've just come up against a brick wall about the Faction.'

'Are they pressing you from San Diego about me?'

'Yes.' It was a lie; but he was the control. He determined on one last gamble, though all the gambling would be done by Minato. 'Take up Hayashi's offer.'

Minato was no fool; he knew who was being pushed off the cliff. He also had begun to think about the Emperor: 'What if I get in there and I decide that I'm all for the Emperor? I still honour him, despite the fact that he's backed the generals.'

Okada had felt the other influences of Japan working on him; but he could not revere the Emperor. The Son of Heaven meant no more to him than a President of the United States; and he knew how fallible the latter could be.

'Just let me know, that's all I ask. If I know where you stand, I'll know where I stand.' He sighed, managed a slight smile. 'I guess I'm putting my trust in you.'

In the distance a siren wailed, its warning taken up by another and another. The crowd in the park began to hurry, then to run. It swept by the two young men, who stood in its tumbling current as if debating whether to go with its flow. Then they shook hands and turned in opposite directions. Minato went against the current, back towards the Staff College. Okada noted wrily that it was he, the American, who went with the crowd flowing towards the shelters.

In the next two weeks Okada saw Minato once more. The

latter was now a secret protégé of Colonel Hayashi. 'What makes me feel ashamed is that I can't tell Admiral Tajiri.'

'When the war is over, Kenji, you can repay all your debts.'

'It may be too late.'

They had met again in Shiba Park, late in the evening. Most of the park crowd had gone home, getting ready for the expected night raids; they were counting the days to the last bomb. It disturbed Okada, some of the old rebel rising in him again, that there was no sign of any resistance to the continuance of the war, no outcry for surrender to the Americans. The old rigidity, despite all the battering, still existed: the lower orders still waited on their superiors to tell them what the decisions would be. No new *shogun* strode out to lead a revolution.

'Hayashi is a fanatic,' said Minato. 'I think he'll kill the Emperor rather than let him surrender. Then he'll commit *seppuku* and expect everyone with him to do likewise.'

'Who's with him?'

'Two junior officers, a major and a captain.' Minato gave their names. They meant nothing to Okada and he guessed they would mean nothing to San Diego. 'But there are others, men with higher rank. I'm still trying to find out who they are.'

'Get me those names and then I'll send them to Embury. He's not going to be interested in majors and captains.'

'Have you given him Hayashi's name?'

'Yes, but I got no reaction. So maybe they're unimpressed by him too.'

'They shouldn't be. He's more than what he seems.' Then Minato added in frustration, 'But it's like trying to write a profile on a shadow. Everyone just clams up when I ask questions about him.'

Okada was having almost the same amount of frustration in trying for more information on the Peace Faction. Like the Japanese citizens he was just waiting for the end of the war; it must come soon and the Peace Faction was beginning to appear unnecessary. Otozo Toshiaki rarely went out nowadays, staying close to his house and garden, as if he had settled on his own personal peace.

One day at the end of July he paused in his walk along the meandering path and watched Okada raking up petals that had fallen from the flowers of the phoenix tree. Okada bowed towards the old man, but respectfully waited till he was addressed. He no longer consciously had to prompt himself in the routine; nor did he feel his old impatience, wanting to speak first. He was *thinking* Japanese.

'You take great care of that tree, Okada. Why it more than the others?'

Okada had not been aware that he tended the phoenix any more carefully than he did the cherry, the maples, or any of the other trees; it was a sturdy giant that needed no gardener. But he humoured the old man: 'Perhaps I am fascinated by its history, Toshiaki-*san*. Hara tells me it is over two hundred years old.'

'It is older than that.' Toshiaki put up an umbrella against the hot sun. He wore a dark blue kimono and sandals, looked like an old man sunk reluctantly into retirement. His belly had fallen, so that it looked like a half-filled waterbag; his jowls were now just extra creases in a face that had turned lugubrious. 'It was planted *three* hundred years ago. A clan lord lived here in the time of Shogun Iemitsu. When the *Shogun* drove out all the foreigners and closed Japan to the world, the clan lord planted that tree and said it would continue to grow till Japan was opened up to the world again. He was wrong, of course – it had stopped growing long before the American Perry came to Japan. But it has survived, it is still as strong and healthy as ever.'

'If it were burnt down, would it grow again? Is that why it's called the phoenix tree, because it can grow out of its own ashes?'

The sun reflected from the white path made Toshiaki's face a bland mask. 'I thought you'd know that, if you worked in a sawmill on Saipan. Or did you just kill trees and not nurse them?'

Okada knew he had made a mistake. He said, hoping it was true, 'I don't think there are any phoenix trees on Saipan, Toshiaki-*san*. The climate isn't right. I know certain trees won't grow again if they have been burnt – pines, for instance. The eucalyptus does – it will grow again after even the worst fire.'

'Perhaps we should have planted eucalyptus in Tokyo.' Toshiaki seemed to make the remark to himself; Okada stayed silent. The old man looked around his garden, then walked on. 'Take care of all the trees, Okada. Something must be allowed to survive.'

Next day Okada was once again in the garden when he heard an American voice coming from the main house. He stood stockstill, at first thinking he had imagined the voice; but the voice was real, a little distorted but calm and steady and understandable. It spoke in English, then began again in carefully accented Japanese.

Okada stepped closer to the house, stood outside the open windows of Toshiaki's study. He knew there was no short-wave radio in the villa; this voice was coming through on the medium-wave band; that meant it was probably being heard all over Japan. There would be nothing that the Radio Interception units could do to stop the message:

'. . . One alternative is prompt and utter destruction . . . Centuries of sweat and toil will be brought to naught in a cataclysmic end . . . The other alternative is the end of war . . .'

Okada, intent on trying to catch every word, did not hear the soft footsteps on the *tatami* mats in the study. Then he looked up and saw Otozo Toshiaki standing at the window, looking down at him from under the raised shutter.

'Did you understand all that, Fujita?'

Okada hesitated, went to bow his head, then changed his mind. Goddam-it, Japan had been led into this war while all the people's heads had been buried in obsequious bows. He straightened up, looked directly at the old man.

'Yes, Toshiaki-san. What I saw on Saipan is going to be repeated here in Japan, only worse. The Americans somehow intend to wipe us off the face of the earth.'

Toshiaki stared down at Okada; it was impossible to tell what he thought of the younger man's remark. Then he said, 'Come inside.'

270

Okada went round to the back of the house, took off his garden clogs and, barefoot, went through the house towards Toshiaki's study. On his way he passed Hara, who looked at him askance and at the dirty footmarks Okada made on the *tatami* mats; but the butler did not try to stop him and he knocked on the study door, slid it back and entered. He bowed politely, then straightened up. He sensed he had somehow turned a corner, one, he suspected, that Toshiaki himself had not seen till now.

The study was less austere than the rest of the house. Paintings hung on the four walls; small pieces of sculpture and a large ceramic vase stood in the corners. Books were stacked in neat piles on a table against one wall, arranged so that they looked like part of the decoration of the room. There was a small shrine in an alcove to one side of the door, its tiny headstones looking like pages broken from a stone notebook. On the low table in the centre of the room was the *bonsai* of the phoenix tree. The radio, on the floor beneath the window, looked as out of place as a neon sign. But, Okada remarked, it was what had brought him into this room. All the treasures, the Sesson and the Kano paintings, the *bonsai*, the shrine, might be timeless, and invaluable, but none of them had the immediate value of the bakelite-encased radio. It held the voice that controlled the future.

Toshiaki stood with his hands folded in the sleeves of his kimono. He gazed steadily at Okada and for a moment the latter thought the old man had had second thoughts, was going to dismiss him without a word. Toshiaki, indeed, had had second thoughts; and a third. He was uncomfortable in the presence of young people; he was never visited by the ghost of his own youth. But, apart from the two maids, both young and both stupid, there was no youngster in the house. True, there were his grandchildren, but they were too young. To talk on the level of children would be to admit to senility. He had never given any value to innocence.

'Why should I choose a gardener?' he said suddenly and rhetorically.

Okada knew the question was not meant to be as simple as it

sounded. He tried to look intelligent, something he had too often had to disguise.

'Am I being chosen for something, Toshiaki-*san?*'

'Perhaps you're not a gardener at all? Nor a chauffeur, nor a sawmill worker.'

'Only temporarily, sir.' He'd been led to the corner by Toshiaki's order to come into the house; he put a metaphorical foot round it. 'I studied law.'

'Where?'

'The University of California at Los Angeles.'

'You studied American law?'

'Yes, sir. My father wanted to do business with the Americans and he thought I should know their law.' That was partly true; the rest was not. 'He not only owned a sawmill on Saipan, but a sugar plantation too. But war broke out and I had to return home to Saipan.'

'You should have had a commission in the army, a young man of your education.'

Okada kept to the same line as he had with General Imamaru: 'The army didn't have much regard for us Saipanese, sir. We're just looked upon as colonials.'

Toshiaki nodded. 'I understand the English think the same way about the Australians. It's natural,' he added, and Okada wondered if he should feel insulted or comforted. Then Toshiaki abruptly smiled, as if highly pleased with himself. 'Then I chose right, didn't I?'

Okada wondered exactly who had chosen him: Lily, General Imamaru, Madame Imamaru? Certainly not Otozo Toshiaki.

But the old man was talking of his choice for the future: 'If we are to save Japan, after what the Americans have threatened on that—' He nodded at the radio. 'If we are to save it, we have to save it for the young like yourself. You'll be the phoenix tree, not old men like me.'

Managers from the Toshiaki factories had been coming to the villa once a week for the past nine months; but none of them had been young men. Middle-aged and worried-looking, they showed the leprosy of their production figures; the bombed-out factories were producing only a fraction of what was needed.

They had not looked like men of the future. Okada, tasting irony, wondered if he was going to be apprenticed to the Toshiaki empire.

'It will be an honour, Toshiaki-san. But what terms will the Americans allow us?' He wanted to ask: *What terms will you ask from the Americans?* But barefooted gardeners, dirt-stained and sweaty, did not ask such questions, not even gardeners who were lawyers in another life. Still, he had turned the corner and answers lay along the road ahead.

'That will depend on how our ministers play their cards. What cards they have,' he added morosely: he had seen their hand.

Okada said nothing. In America a young man might have led the conversation further with more questions; but not here, not if he was to be pushed back round the corner again. He would have to be patient, never an American virtue.

'We shall be going into Tokyo again,' said Toshiaki. 'There are meetings that will have to be held now . . . Do you understand the American mind, Okada?'

Once upon a time he had thought he did . . . 'Only partly, sir.'

'Are they devious?'

'No, sir. They are very honest and simpleminded.' In both their beliefs and their bigotries; but he didn't add that. He was certain now that the Japanese here in the homeland had never really cared what happened to the Nisei in America. 'They just don't understand the rest of the world, that's all.'

'I think I may engage you as my American adviser.' Toshiaki smiled at the thought of asking his gardener, even an educated one, for advice. The old order had not yet collapsed that far. 'You speak English, I take it?'

'Yes, sir.' It was a strange sensation: he could feel himself slowly returning to his true self.

'Then I must keep you close by me for when the Americans come.'

'The general has no time for me any more,' said Lily. 'Now he is commander of the First Area Army, he has to devote all his time to losing the war.'

'You sound bitter,' said Natasha.

'It's this gruel we have to eat.' Lily grimaced at the thin mess in her bowl. Yuri went out every day now scavenging for food; it was her efforts that kept the three women just above the starvation level of most of the others in Nayora. But Lily was not unappreciative, she just did not like being reminded of her childhood. 'Let's hope the Americans bring food.'

'You *are* bitter,' said Natasha.

Lily laughed that one away. 'A sensible woman is never bitter about anything a man does. I gave the General one of the best years of my life—' She had done that with at least another dozen men; her best years had always been spent with men. 'I'm a little put out because this is the first time I do not have another man to move on to. One should always have someone in reserve.'

I'm a novice compared to her, thought Natasha; and was glad. 'Preferably with more money or more rank.'

'Of course,' said Lily and beamed at her daughter with approval.

But Natasha, though joking, was suddenly in no mood for jokes. With the end of the war so imminent, would Tom desert her? She knew as well as Lily the unreliability of men, even those truly in love: they did not have the total commitment that a woman could give. Lily would not concern herself with love; she had long since passed that commitment. But Natasha knew that love was necessary to herself: she had found it, twice, with Keith and with Tom. If she lost it, she would go on seeking it; but there would never be a man held in reserve. If she lost Tom, it would be a long long time before she found love again.

'Things must get better soon,' said Lily, swallowing the rice gruel. The American generals, who would also be rich, could not come soon enough.

'So you think they will be interested in us?' Natasha said *us*, but she did not mean to include herself. 'We're outsiders. Half-castes.'

'That's what appeals to men. They think we're only half-moral.' Morality had never appealed to her, but she knew it was some sort of yardstick. 'But you have Tom. You have no need to worry.'

'I hope not.' She was ashamed of her doubt of Tom, but self-preservation had always been an enemy of love. She had been steeped in it till she had met Keith.

Then they heard the knock at the front door. Both paused in their eating, waited while Yuri went along the hallway to the door. Then they heard Major Nagata asking for Natasha.

She got up at once, went into the living room and waited for Yuri to bring him in. Lily followed her, like a good chaperone. Nagata came in, smiled when he saw both women. To meet with two beautiful women was better than to meet with one; one woman's principal attraction was the possibility of going to bed with her. He knew there was no possibility of that with either Mrs Cairns or Madame Tolstoy.

'Ladies—' He bowed, more with a boulevardier's panache than Japanese politeness. Soon he hoped to be seeing American films again, watching Melvyn Douglas and Charles Boyer courting the ladies. He was sure of his future, was already thinking of the trivia that would enhance it. 'I'm afraid I have bad news.'

Natasha felt herself tense: something had happened to Tom! But Lily, who took bad and good news with the same phlegmatic swallowing, merely said, 'I'd be surprised if you had good news, major.'

Nagata had to admire her; he was coming to see more in her than in the daughter. At least she would be more experienced. 'You will have to leave the house, and quickly. The Radio Interception Unit picked up a short-wave radio last night.'

'What makes you think we have such a radio?' Natasha was calm again, now that she knew Tom was in no danger.

275

Nagata smiled again: he was their friend, didn't they know that? 'It's not what *I* think, Mrs Cairns. The unit didn't get a direct fix on the radio, but the band was narrow, covering this part of the hill. It closed down just as they picked it up.'

Okada had been down here last night, but the transmission had lasted only a couple of minutes. He had sent a short report on the reaction to the warning broadcast yesterday by the Americans; they hadn't known the Radio Interception Unit was in the vicinity and they had been miraculously fortunate that they had not been on the air longer. She wondered why there had been no knock on the door last night.

As if in answer to her unspoken question Nagata said, 'They came to me because I am in charge of the village. I told them who your patron was, Madame Tolstoy—' Again the boulevardier's bow. 'They saw my point. They went back to Tokyo, leaving it to my discretion. But my sergeant, Sergeant Ugaki, is making a nuisance of himself. He's very ambitious. Behind my back, he got in touch with our headquarters in Tokyo. They have ordered me to arrest you for questioning.'

'Are you going to?'

'How can I do that to you?' He made a poor show of looking hurt; he wasn't a bad actor, but there were some expressions beyond him. 'You must leave at once. I have sent Sergeant Ugaki on a wild goose chase further down the coast, but he will be back within the hour. So please pack and get out of Nayora.'

'But we have nowhere to go!'

Nagata looked at Lily. 'I'm sure General Imamaru can accommodate you.'

'Of course.' Lily was that best of mistresses, never hysterical. 'Unfortunately we have no transport.'

'Ah, I cannot help you there. As you know, we are reduced to a motorcycle and I had to give that to Sergeant Ugaki to get rid of him.'

Lily had never seen herself on a motorcycle. She had always been a whore with dignity.

'However, there is a train for Tokyo in just under the hour – if, of course, it is on time. I shall have Sergeant Masuda carry your bags up to the station. I know he can be trusted, he's been protecting you for so long.' He smiled, to show what an indulgent secret policeman he was.

It took Natasha and Lily only five minutes to pack. Or rather it took Yuri five minutes to pack for them: left to their own choice of what to take with them they would still be in the house when the train went through the station. Their wardrobes had been their identity for so long: to leave behind a favourite coat was like leaving behind both arms.

'Go downstairs and wait,' Yuri ordered. 'I shall stay in the house and join you when you have found a place.' Or better still, she told herself, I'll stay here till the war is over. The villa could be taken over by *anyone*. She was house-proud, at the risk perhaps of her life.

Nagata had gone to fetch Sergeant Masuda. When they returned the village sergeant folded himself in two in his bow, so pleased was he to be of some real help to Mrs Cairns. He was fighting the war for his villagers: if the enemy should be those from Tokyo, it couldn't be helped. He picked up the two suitcases, headed out the back door and up through the pine forest, stopping every few yards to caution Lily as she stumbled through the shadows after him.

Natasha said goodbye to Yuri. 'I'll let you know where I am as soon as we're settled. You can join us—'

'Only if there are no bombs. Be careful.'

'You too.' On an impulse Natasha kissed her on the cheek. The old woman put her hand to her cheek and held it there, as if holding the kiss in place. She waited till Natasha had gone out the back door, then she dropped her head and wept. She had done the same when Cairns-san had died, though Natasha had not seen those tears, either.

Major Nagata followed Natasha out into the back garden. 'Telephone me at the police station, say you are my daughter.'

Somehow she had not thought of his having any family. 'You've helped us enough, major.'

'You may be able to help me.' One never knew how much the Americans would demand. 'If you meet the Americans before I do, tell them how I protected your radio.'

'What radio, major?'

277

He smiled. 'What a pity we didn't meet sooner, Mrs Cairns. Under my teaching you would have made a marvellous spy. Good luck.'

She hurried up through the pine forest, catching up with Lily and Sergeant Masuda as they reached the highway and the side path that ran up towards the railroad station. 'We'd better take the bags from here, sergeant. We don't want someone reporting you tomorrow, that you helped us leave Nayora.'

Masuda protested, but weakly. Wars, even small personal ones, should be fought intelligently. 'If you insist—'

He said goodbye to them, bowed and went back down the moonlit path into the blackness of the pines, looking as if he would at any moment, with his peculiar loose-kneed gait, flop to the ground like an elderly hound. Which would have been apt: he had always shown a hound's simple devotion to Natasha.

'We have male friends at all the lower levels,' said Lily. 'Now let's hope we still have one at the highest.'

'Do you think the general will welcome us?'

'Not with a twenty-one gun-salute.'

'If he won't have us at all, could you blackmail him somehow?' She had not intended to think that way; but like mother, like daughter. Lily was a bad, if sensible, example.

'What could I blackmail him with? Infidelity to his wife? That's no sin in Japan. It's like an Englishman playing cricket.'

They waited for the train, which was half-an-hour late. Natasha paced up and down, thinking of Tom, worrying about him, willing him to appear out of the darkness, saddle-sore but loving, on his bicycle. She would have to phone him at the Toshiaki villa, but there was no phone here on the station. She was a bundle of nerves by the time the train came in and Lily, nerveless, had to bundle her aboard. They stood in the crowded darkness, smelling the ill-health of the near-starving, and said nothing to each other during the slow journey into Tokyo.

They found a taxi outside the main station, shared it with four other people; Lily, sounding imperious and therefore impressive when she gave their address, insisted that she and Natasha should be dropped off first. When the taxi drew up outside the ruins of the Imamaru mansion, the other passengers

278

were suitably impressed. They wished the two women good-night in polite tones, then abused them quietly as they were driven off in the taxi.

Lily and Natasha stood in the driveway inside the gates; there was no soldier on guard now. Natasha was not sure what she had expected to see. On her visits to Tokyo she had been shocked at the bomb damage she had seen; but she had not been to the city now for several months. She was standing in a wasteland that looked no better for being seen at night; the moonlight turned the shadows into open graves. The mansion was a heap of rubble, all its timbers gone for firewood; the smaller house, Lily's, seemed to have disappeared altogether. There were craters in the driveway and paths; the ponds in the garden had become one small lake rank with weeds. The devastation stretched away on either side; the neighbourhood was past history. The smell of death, of old graves opened, was heavier than the smell of the shrubs and flowers that had survived.

A woman appeared in front of them, one shadow moving out of another. 'You can't come here – get away—'

'Is that you, Yone? It's Madame Tolstoy.'

The woman raised her face to the moonlight; a dead mask that suddenly cracked in a surprised smile. 'Madame Tolstoy! We never thought we'd see you again—'

'Where is General Imamaru?'

'Oh, he never comes here now—' As if Lily should understand that generals never visited lost battlefields. 'He stays at his headquarters, in the Dai Ichi building. There's no one here but—' She named four of the staff. Then she added sourly, 'And the riff-raff. One has to be careful of them. Thieves, beggars . . . I tell them that if they touch us, the general will send soldiers. They laugh, but they haven't touched us so far.'

Natasha could now see the figures in the gardens, dim shapes amongst the shrubs and trees, still as iron birds. All at once, despite the warm night, she shivered, felt the chill of menace.

'Where are you living?' said Lily.

'In the shelter, Madame Tolstoy.'

'Is there room for me and my niece?'

'Of course.' But there was no enthusiastic welcome in the

279

woman's voice. She did, however, take Lily's suitcase from her, though she left Natasha to carry her own.

They moved up the driveway, turned onto a side path that led to the steps going down to the shelter. At the head of the steps stood two men and a young woman. The moonlight was behind them, but their very silhouettes were threatening.

'Who are you?' The thicker of the two men had a voice like an animal's growl.

'Out of the way,' said Yone, but her voice was hesitant, afraid.

'Who I am is no business of yours,' said Lily. She opened her handbag and took out a gun. 'If you want to make trouble, I'll shoot you. If you're not gone from here by the morning, I'll have the *yakuza* remove you.'

Natasha saw the three silhouetted figures stiffen. She had felt herself go rigid when Lily produced the gun. She had seen violence – a man stabbed close by her in Hong Kong, police beating up another man here in Tokyo, (at a distance) bombs falling on a town. Yet to see Lily with a gun in her hand threatening to shoot a man was a violence that shook her; though her whole adult life had been a game of chance, she had never expected that someone might have to be killed in order that she be protected. She knew that Lily would be protecting herself as much as her; perhaps it was the means, the gun, that she had least expected. Lily had always seemed to her someone who would save herself by her wits.

The spokesman growled something obscene, then he and his companions turned and shuffled off through the debris of the mansion. Yone giggled with relief. 'Oh, that was telling them, madame. Especially the bit about the *yakuza*.'

'I want you to go to Osachi Cho first thing in the morning and ask him to send someone here to get rid of these people.'

Even Natasha had heard of Osachi Cho, the top *yakuza* boss in Tokyo. She knew that she should not be surprised that Lily knew him: Lily would have no scruples in choosing the right people to know. But even Yone seemed not quite able to believe that Madame Tolstoy should actually call on a gangster for help.

'I thought you were just joking—'

Lily smiled; but it was not a joking smile. 'I can see, Yone, that you need a mistress to run this shelter properly.'

4

'Tell me where your mistress and Madame Tolstoy have gone,' said Sergeant Ugaki.

'I don't know,' said Yuri. 'I've already told you that. They left while I was out trying to buy food—'

'Where is the radio hidden?'

'What radio?'

Ugaki had already been all over the house and down into the cellar, but had found no sign of a radio. He lit a cigarette, his second last; he would have to go back to the Italians tomorrow and ask for more; he had no idea where they got their supply but so long as they bribed him with a packet a week he didn't enquire. He puffed on the cigarette, then held the glowing butt close to Yuri's face.

'You know what radio I mean—'

'No, no!'

Then he pressed the lighted end of the cigarette against Yuri's throat. She screamed with pain, then fainted. He looked down at her, finished the cigarette, dropped the butt on the mat beside Yuri's head and ground it out. By rights he should burn the villa down, but the traitorous bastard Major Nagata would be sure to report him to Tokyo.

He went back to the police station and Major Nagata said, 'Where have you been?'

'Up at the Cairns house. I was interrogating the house-keeper.'

'I told you, Sergeant Ugaki, I had already done that. Don't you think I'm competent enough to do that?'

'Of course, major.' Ugaki could feel himself bubbling inside. The other traitorous bastard, Sergeant Masuda, was in the next room listening to all this.

'The women Cairns and Tolstoy have disappeared. They have probably gone to Tokyo. I shall inform headquarters of that and let them look for them. Our concern, Sergeant Ugaki, is to see that no more foreigners leave Nayora without permission.'

'Yes, sir.' The other foreigners, Ugaki was sure, were not spies.

'You seem upset that Mrs Cairns and Madame Tolstoy managed to leave us.'

'Yes, sir. I think they are spies, especially the Tolstoy woman.'

'Sergeant, do you think the war is lost or still to be won?'

'Still to be won, sir.'

Ugaki was a religious fanatic, Nagata thought: it was a pity he had no other religion but patriotism. 'If it's still to be won, then General Imamaru would not be pleased with us if he knew we were chasing his protégée as a spy.'

'Protégée, sir?'

'Madame Tolstoy.' *Stupid*; but he bit off that word. 'What would you call her? Relax, Sergeant Ugaki. Go out and make the other foreigners uncomfortable. We're still winning the war, aren't we?'

5

'Your cousin wants you,' said Madame Imamaru.

'My cousin?' Someone from Nagasaki? But how would they have known he was here.

'Some girl. I hope she *is* your cousin, Fujita. It is bad enough having your relatives telephone you here. But to have one of your girlfriends—'

'I'm sorry, Madame Imamaru. It must be urgent— I've told the family never to phone me—'

'Take it on the kitchen phone.'

It was unfortunate that it had been Madame Imamaru who had answered the call. Hara, the butler, had gone into Miyanoshita to see a doctor about his arthritis; the maids were in the laundry doing the washing; the children were at school and Otozo Toshiaki was sitting under the phoenix tree reading.

Madame Imamaru worshipped the phone; it was an instrument of gossip, the exercise that kept her in condition. There was only one line to the villa and she did not want it taken up by a call from the gardener's relatives.

Okada kicked off his clogs, went into the kitchen and took the phone off the wall. Madame Imamaru had come out to the garden to speak to him, then gone back in through the front door. There were two other phones in the house, one in Toshiaki's study and the other in the main hallway. He knew that she would not be able to resist listening in on the conversation, at least for the first minute or so. But the risk had to be taken; one couldn't work for a gossip and expect deaf ears.

He jumped into what he hoped was Natasha's ear: 'Cousin Etsu? How is Aunt Tsuchi?'

Natasha guessed at once that they were being overheard. 'She's fine. She's here with me in Tokyo, at her old house. She wants to see you. She has some family matters she wants to discuss with you.'

Okada heard the phone being quietly replaced somewhere else in the house. He had to admire how quickly Natasha had caught this warning; but then how many other times had she had to be alert to warnings? He had never questioned her very much about her life before she had married Keith Cairns; indeed, he had not questioned her about her life with Cairns; he knew the low threshold of his own jealousy. But some day he knew he would need to know all about her. In the meantime, an obviously experienced target of eavesdroppers, she had put no flea in the ear of Madame Tolstoy.

'I'll come in tonight.' Madame Imamaru had come to the kitchen door. 'Tell Aunt Tsuchi not to worry.'

He hung up, thanked Madame Imamaru for the use of the phone, then asked permission to go into Tokyo that evening.

'You will have to ask Toshiaki-san. He will probably say yes – you appear to be a favourite of his. What does he talk to you about?' *A common gardener and chauffeur?* He wondered why she didn't use the words.

'Just things in general, madame. I think he just likes to talk to someone young. There are no young men left in Miyanoshita.'

'So I've noticed. You're very fortunate, aren't you?'

'Being a Saipanese, madame, is not to be fortunate.' Shove that one up your kimono, he thought. He thoroughly disliked this plump, self-centred, scandal-mongering woman; even Lily Tolstoy was preferable. But he bowed respectfully as he went out of the kitchen. 'Everyone looks down on us.'

She nodded, agreeing with him and everyone's attitude towards the Saipanese. Though she could not remember ever having met one before. Her husband had brought home silks, jewels, paintings, furniture; but this Fujita was the first living souvenir. If all the Saipanese were as brash as this one, it was no wonder they were looked down upon. Sakichi was brash, but he was not from Saipan and he was a general.

Toshiaki was reading *Gone With The Wind*, a book that showed the follies of a headstrong woman. If the heroine was typical of all American women, the voters had been wise in never electing a woman President.

He saw Fujita approaching him. 'Are all American women like Scarlett O'Hara?'

Okada had never read the book, but had seen the English-woman Vivien Leigh in the movie. 'All women are alike, aren't they, Toshiaki-san?'

Toshiaki shook his head at the innocence of young men. He closed the book; he had reached the chapter that described the burning of Atlanta. If Americans could do that to each other, why should anyone expect them to be more merciful towards the Japanese? 'I have to go into Tokyo this afternoon, Fujita. We shall be staying overnight.'

Okada bowed gratefully. 'I was about to ask permission to visit my aunt. Now perhaps I can be excused for an hour this evening?'

'This aunt – how does she survive in Tokyo?'

Aunt Lily would survive in hell. 'I don't know, sir. Some women are indomitable.'

'Like certain trees?' Toshiaki nodded at the phoenix tree behind him. 'I like your word, indomitable. Some women one couldn't chop down with an axe.' He thought fondly of his wife, a slender reed; then looked up towards the villa and saw his daughter, a plump thornbush. 'I shall be staying with Admiral Tajiri. You will probably have to sleep in the car. I understand there are looters in the city these days. Though how one could loot a Rolls-Royce, I really don't know.'

They drove into Tokyo that afternoon. There was a lot of military traffic; and there were people still fleeing the city, their trucks and cars piled high with furniture and luggage. Okada glanced at Toshiaki in the rear-vision mirror; the old man looked out at the passing traffic and the desolation on either side of the road with sad resignation. It struck Okada then that maybe it was only the old men of Japan who could afford to be fatalistic.

He had been directed to drop Toshiaki at the Dai Ichi Insurance building. He knew that the First Area Army was headquartered in the building; he also knew that the Peace Faction had offices there. He was chafed by the thought that he was so close to what San Diego would obviously call the heart of things but could do nothing about entering the building. A private citizen's chauffeur (the gardener had been left at Miyanoshita) would not get past the bottom step of the entrance.

'Come back for me in two hours,' said Toshiaki through the speaking-tube. 'Go and take care of your aunt.'

The old man got out of the car. He was dressed today in Western style: a double-breasted navy blue suit that was now too big for him, a homburg hat. He looked like a banker, thought Okada, whose overdraft was bigger than his customers'. He went up into the building and in the foyer met Admiral Tajiri and General Imamaru, each tailed by an aide.

'I wonder if Dai Ichi would issue insurance on all of us?' said Tajiri. 'Do you think we should all ride up in the one lift or spread the risk and travel separately?'

The three men, with their aides, got into the lift reserved for senior officers. General Imamaru stood next to his father-in-law. His bulk and his self-esteem filled his uniform till the seams were stretched. Toshiaki thought his son-in-law looked like a general just beginning a war, not ending one.

'Your wife and children are missing you,' said Toshiaki. He

was always formal with his son-in-law; to be familiar with him would have been both a pain and an embarrassment. 'They wish you could come home for a night.'

'I'm too busy,' said Imamaru, looking pleased and proud. 'There aren't enough hours in the day.'

For what? Toshiaki wondered.

'Come to my office for a moment,' said Imamaru. 'There is something the admiral has just told me.'

They got off the lift at Imamaru's floor, went into his office, leaving the two aides outside. Imamaru's aide looked at Lieutenant Minato.

'What did your man tell mine?'

'I don't know.' But Minato could guess what information Tajiri had passed on. He decided, however, to act ignorant. 'I've given up trying to guess what's going on. Everyone's running around in circles.'

In the inner office Imamaru had gone behind his desk, stood there with legs apart and fists resting on the desk. He reminded Toshiaki of Benito Mussolini in his poses on Roman balconies.

'Tell Toshiaki-san what you told me, admiral.'

Tajiri had sat down, as if being on his feet for more than a few minutes exhausted him. He took off his horn-rimmed glasses to polish them and with their removal his face seemed to shrink.

'Something has happened down in Hiroshima,' he said. 'We don't know what yet. All the lines are out, but calls have been coming in from towns close to Hiroshima. Nobody seems to know anything, the calls are more questions than statements. But one call came in from Matsuyama, that is a hundred miles away across the Inland Sea, saying they'd seen a tremendous flash of light. We suspect the worst – the Americans have dropped an atomic bomb.'

'What's an atomic bomb?' said Toshiaki.

'I understand our scientists have known of the principle of it for some time. They were working on it up till a few months ago. Then there was a bad accident, some physicists and the building they were working in were blown up, and the project was abandoned. I don't understand it myself—' He sounded weary; what would the old *samurai* have made of war today?

'But I gather that one bomb can do the damage of a hundred ordinary bombs. Or even worse.'

It was beyond Toshiaki's comprehension too. He shook his head and looked at his son-in-law, the military man. 'If they do have such a bomb, what are you going to fight it with?'

'Spirit,' said Imamaru, looking more than ever like Mussolini.

He's gone soft in the head, thought Toshiaki. But he said, 'That's good to hear.'

Tajiri rose from his chair. 'Let me know, general, if you hear anything more. I'll do the same for you. If we are going to be blasted into oblivion, I think I'd like to know. It would be educational to have one eye open on Judgment Day, as the Christians call it.'

He and Toshiaki left him and went down to Prince Konoye's suite of offices on the fourth floor. Minato rode down with them in the lift, was introduced by Tajiri to Toshiaki. 'Lieutenant Minato is collating all the information for me on Hiroshima. Did you tell Lieutenant Nakasone to call you here?'

'Yes, sir,' said Minato. 'I'll bring it to you in the meeting as soon as I hear from him.'

'Tell him to listen to the short-wave radio. The Americans may be broadcasting something about it. In the meantime' – Tajiri paused outside the outer door to Konoye's offices – 'in the meantime we'll see what can be done about the peace. If there is to be any.'

Nine

The Rolls-Royce stood amidst the wreckage of the Imamaru grounds like a galleon that had run aground on a volcanic rock coast.

'You can't stay here,' said Okada.

'We'll be all right,' said Lily. 'All the riff-raff have gone. If they come back, I have my gun and a box of ammunition.'

Okada didn't want Natasha around where guns might be going off, even one fired by her mother. 'What are you going to do if the *kempei* come here. Shoot them, too?'

'But where do we go, then?' said Natasha.

'Perhaps Madame Imamaru would give us a bed up at Miyanoshita?' Lily's smile looked like a weapon in itself. 'Tom, let's be realistic. The war is almost over. All we have to do is stay out of the way for a few days. Wherever we'd go in Tokyo, we'd be noticed – we're not Japanese. Even ordinary people might attack us, just because we're foreign-looking. At least here the general's staff won't harm us.'

'I still think you'd be safer out of Tokyo.' He looked about him, as if he might see a signpost. He wanted Natasha safely away from the danger of their situation. She was a spy by default: not even a mercenary. She had no commitment to either side; she would always be an outsider, no matter what the circumstances might be. She had become a spy because of Keith Cairns, had remained one because of himself. He had to find a way out for her.

Then suddenly he had a wild idea, one that he voiced before he tried to kill it with reason: 'If I could get you travel passes, would you go to Nagasaki?'

'Nagasaki? What's there?'

'My father's family, an uncle and some cousins. I can't get in touch with them, they don't know I'm here. And they'd be suspicious if they did know. But I have a friend who knows them well—'

'Will you come with us?' said Natasha.

'I can't, not right away. You'll be safe down there from the *kempei*.' He hoped they would be safe from the family; already he was beginning to doubt the idea. But he could think of nowhere else to send them. 'You say you trust Major Nagata. But what if the *kempei* has arrested him? He'd save his own neck before he'd save yours.'

'We'd be trusting strangers,' said Lily. 'How do you know your relatives don't hate foreigners? What do they do?'

'They make swords and bayonets.'

Both women laughed, peals of merriment that brought heads popping up out of holes in the grounds like an upsurge of moles. Even Okada had to grin.

'My Uncle Tamezo is a very gentle man.' Or was. 'An artist. I've also learned he is a member of the Peace Faction.'

Natasha had sobered, looked at Okada with new interest. 'You're one of *those* Okadas? Keith had one of their swords—'

Keith would have. He wondered when they would ever get rid of his ghost. 'What did he do with it? You never showed it to me—'

'It's at the university, in their collection.'

Then there was the crunch of footsteps on the gravel path behind them. Okada turned and saw the familiar figure coming towards them with its rolling swagger, a new derby hat on the cannonball head.

'Koga-san, what a pleasant surprise!' But he was past surprise.

But Koga wasn't; he looked at Okada with his eyebrows lifted comically. Then he bowed to Lily. 'Madame Tolstoy, Cho-san sent me. He said you needed help. I am Koga.'

Lily recognized an underling when sent one. 'Thank Cho-san and tell him his help is no longer needed. You may go.'

Only Okada saw the dragons snarl on Koga's hands. The burly man bowed and turned to go. Then Okada said, 'Koga-san, perhaps you can help. Madame Tolstoy and Mrs Cairns need travel passes to go to Nagasaki.'

Koga looked at the three of them, then directly at Okada. 'I wondered why you never came back to the docks.'

'I work for a friend of Madame Tolstoy's.' *Well, not exactly a friend. The father of the wife of Lily's patron.* 'I've been sent here to take them to the station to go to Nagasaki. But they have no travel passes.'

Koga, one eye on the arrogant half-Chinese bitch, said, 'How could I get passes?'

'Not you,' said Okada, wanting to punch the bastard in the mouth. 'Cho-san. He would do it as a favour to General Imamaru. The general himself could arrange for them, but he is so busy we can't reach him.'

Koga hesitated. Like everyone else he wondered who the new king would be when the Americans came; they might think no more of Cho-san than they had of their own *yakuza*, Capone-san. But then again they might find him useful, in which case Koga himself would still be in a job. He would not be if somehow he offended Cho-san or any of Cho-san's friends.

'I can arrange the passes. I'll bring them here within an hour.'

'Thank you, Koga.' Lily gave him a smile that made him change his mind about the Chinese, the whites and bitches. She had started her climb up the ladder dealing with men like him.

Okada looked at his watch. 'I have to get back, just in case my master has finished his meeting. Perhaps I can give you a lift, Koga-san?'

Koga looked at the Rolls-Royce, his eyes flickering for a moment with delight. 'It will save time.'

'I don't know what time the train leaves for Nagasaki,' Okada said to Natasha and Lily. 'I better drive you to the station now. Koga-san can bring you the passes there.'

The two women had not unpacked; their bags were in the boot of the Rolls-Royce within two minutes. Okada drove out of the desolate grounds with Koga sitting beside him stiff and straight as a cartoon equerry and Natasha and Lily seemingly haughty and elegant in the back. But Okada, glancing in the rear-vision mirror, could see the strain in Natasha's face, the worry in her dark eyes. Lily, face calm and expressionless, might have been on her way to a reception at the Imperial Palace.

'Cho-san has a motor car like this,' said Koga.

'Do you ride in it with him?'

Koga shook his head: he was a foot-soldier, always would be. 'Drop me here. I shall be at the main station within an hour with the passes.'

He got out of the car, took off his hat and bowed to the two women. Okada looked after him as he went rolling down a side street, then he glanced around at the devastation. 'I'm glad to see the gangsters got bombed as well.'

'Don't sound like a pious priest,' said Lily. 'The Americans were not selective when they dropped their bombs.'

Okada reluctantly agreed with her, but he thought that, for a whore, she sounded too pious.

22

'I am afraid there is no mistake, general,' said Colonel Nitobe, running a nervous finger along his moustache. 'Sergeant Ugaki found nothing the first time he went to the villa in Nayora – Madame Tolstoy and her niece, Mrs Cairns, had already fled. But he went back a second time—'

'A persistent man,' said General Imamaru; but cursed the zeal of the *kempei*. 'He is to be commended.'

'Yes, sir,' said Nitobe, still unsure of the general's reaction to what he had been told. 'Sergeant Ugaki found the radio hidden behind a section of the wall in the villa's cellar. He arrested Mrs Cairns' servant and tried to interrogate her—'

'Tried?'

'Unfortunately, the woman appears to have died. A heart attack.'

Imamaru had heard rumours of how often people died while under interrogation by the *kempei*.

In the outer office Major Nagata and Sergeant Ugaki sat stiffly upright against a wall while the room itself seemed to be a quaking jelly of movement as army personnel came and went in what seemed to Nagata an aimless flurry, not panic-stricken but bewildered. He and Ugaki had heard the news as soon as they had entered the Dai Ichi building, that physicists at the Imperial University had confirmed that the Americans had dropped at atom bomb on Hiroshima. Nagata had no idea what an atom bomb was, but snatches of conversation and the dazed look on the faces passing in and out of the room told him that the bomb was more terrible than anything one could imagine. Hiroshima, it seemed, had been completely destroyed.

Perhaps the Americans would drop an atom bomb on Tokyo; he would half welcome it. He was sitting next to a bomb right now, this stupidly zealous idiot, Ugaki. The upstart had bypassed him and called Colonel Nitobe direct to tell him he had found the radio in the cellar of Mrs Cairns' villa. Nitobe, a man with a better sense of protocol than the ambitious sergeant, had asked to speak to Nagata. From then on there had been nothing Nagata could do but bring Ugaki with him into Tokyo.

'You have made a mistake, Ugaki,' he had said on the journey into the city. 'General Imamaru will have your head for what you are suggesting about Madame Tolstoy.'

'I am prepared to risk that,' said Ugaki. 'We should be working for the Emperor, not General Imamaru.'

Let the gods protect me from patriots and zealots, thought Nagata. But he feared the gods had been too late.

In the inner office General Imamaru was cursing what the gods had done to him. He had come back to Japan resigned to being banished to some remote command, perhaps even back to Hokkaido where his father had come from; he had stretched out his stay in Tokyo by cultivation of the proper contacts and by taking advantage of the uncertainty that had taken hold of the desk generals in the Army high command. Then, almost by default, he had been given command of the First Area Army, was, in effect, one of those responsible for the protection of the Emperor. He was, he admitted to himself, responsible for much more than that, but the figure of the Emperor concentrated his ego and satisfaction with the post. And now the dalliance with Lily was threatening to ruin all that.

'We suspect that Madame Tolstoy and Mrs Cairns had an accomplice,' said Colonel Nitobe. He had stopped scratching his moustache, had begun to sense that the general was not going to have his head. He respected General Imamaru for his understanding that women, in war as in life, should not allow the priorities to be shuffled. 'A male accomplice. The radio was in good condition, as if it had been properly serviced. Women are not good at those sort of things.'

'You seem to know a lot about women, colonel.'

'Only professionally, sir. Did Madame Tolstoy or Mrs Cairns ever introduce you to someone whom you might suspect was in league with them?'

Imamaru thought of Fujita, the educated Saipanese who hadn't wanted to join the army. Suddenly he was brusque: 'I don't have the time to do your detective work for you, colonel. There are more important things – this bomb on Hiroshima—'

'Yes, sir.' The hand went back to the moustache. 'May we have your permission to arrest Madame Tolstoy and Mrs Cairns? We shall be discreet—'

'Yes,' Imamaru snapped. All at once he had the feeling that spies, even one you had slept with, were no longer important. The war was lost and it had not been lost because of anything that Lily or her niece might have contributed. 'Yes, arrest them!'

Nitobe saluted, bowed and went out of the office, glad to escape. He nodded to Nagata and Ugaki and led them out into the corridor. The long hallway seethed with movement and murmuring; nothing inspires the bureaucracy of an army more than defeat right on its doorstep. Victory is almost always distant and therefore makes only ripples, not waves. Colonel Nitobe, unconcerned with the larger issues of the war, a true secret policeman, drew Nagata and Ugaki into a short hall that led to a washroom. The washroom, or its toilets, seemed to be unusually busy at the moment. The bladder, thought Nagata, is a useful barometer of the nerves.

'We can arrest the women,' said Nitobe. 'The general doesn't object. We also have to look for the third person, the man. Have you any ideas, Major Nagata?'

'Yes, colonel.' Nagata had been weighing up his choices; he did not have many. He could find himself arrested by his own force, the *kempei*, before the Americans got here; the *kempei* would not save its prisoners to hand over to the conquerors. 'I think we should look at a man named Fujita. He is chauffeur for Otozo Toshiaki.'

'General Imamaru's father-in-law?' Nitobe's moustache seemed to follow his eyebrows in surprise. 'The plot thickens.'

I wish it were thick enough to choke you and Ugaki, thought Nagata.

'Otozo Toshiaki is here in the building,' said Sergeant Ugaki; he was almost incandescent with fervour and excitement. 'He's at a meeting with Prince Konoye.'

'We can't just walk in *there*.' Nagata wondered how Ugaki knew so much; he was a minefield of information. 'The prince would have us thrown out immediately.'

'We wait downstairs for Toshiaki-san's motor car to come for him. It's a Rolls-Royce, easy to recognize.'

'Of course we'll do that,' said Colonel Nitobe, angry at the presumptuousness of Major Nagata's underling. If they all survived into the peace, he would have to watch out, for fear that the sergeants would take over. 'See to it at once, Major Nagata.'

'Shall we arrest Toshiaki-san too?' Nagata was dispirited enough to attempt a sick joke.

'I'll leave that to you,' said Colonel Nitobe, like a good superior, and departed on that note of wisdom.

3

As the Rolls-Royce drew up, Otozo Toshiaki, Admiral Tajiri and Lieutenant Minato came out of the Dai Ichi building. Okada got out of the car and stood holding open the door while Toshiaki and the admiral said some last words to each other.

Major Nagata, another good superior, looked at Sergeant Ugaki. 'There is your man, sergeant – Fujita. Go and arrest him.'

Ugaki was not the idiot Nagata thought he was. 'Now, sir? With his master and Admiral Tajiri there beside him? Right out here in front of the passers-by?'

'There's no time to waste,' said Nagata with a sort of sad enjoyment at the situation. 'The war may be over tomorrow.'

Sergeant Ugaki stood still for a moment and Nagata thought he was going to refuse to move. Then he gave a slight bow of the head and crossed to the small group beside the Rolls-Royce.

He saluted Admiral Tajiri, said something that Nagata, standing some distance away, did not catch. But there was no mistaking the effect on the four men. Okada and Minato said nothing, but it seemed to Nagata, who remarked it with satisfaction, that the two old men leaned in on Ugaki as if about to crush him between them. Then Ugaki, a wise inferior, not in the least an idiot, nodded towards Nagata. The latter sighed and advanced on the group.

'I am Major Nagata,' he said and bowed to the two old men.

'Your sergeant has just made an accusation against Toshiaki-san's chauffeur, that he is wanted for questioning as a spy. What do you know of this, major?'

'Sergeant Ugaki has enough evidence for Colonel Nitobe to order the investigation.' Nagata was not going to carry all the responsibility for this stupid exercise.

'What evidence, sergeant?' said Toshiaki.

Ugaki told of finding the radio in Mrs Cairns' villa, of Major Nagata's suspicion that Mrs Cairns and Fujita knew each other. Then he looked at Minato and said, 'Lieutenant Minato was also observed in conversation with Fujita out at Nayora. I saw that myself and so did Major Nagata.'

Nagata sighed again, this time inwardly, and said, 'That is so, Toshiaki-san. Perhaps Lieutenant Minato will explain why he shared the lunch of a chauffeur.'

Okada had stood on the outskirts of the small group, almost ignored; for one wild moment he had thought of running, then reason told him he would get no more than fifty yards before being captured; there were soldiers all round him, all of them armed. So he stood very still, feeling despair creeping through him, and waited for Kenji Minato to betray him.

295

'What have you to say, lieutenant?' said Tajiri. 'Sharing a working man's lunch is no crime, but what did you talk about?'

Minato looked at Okada: there was no recognition in the black eyes, Okada could have been a stranger. Then he looked back at Admiral Tajiri. 'We talked about the war, sir. I have met no working men since I came back to Japan. I wanted to know what people outside military circles thought. It was the sort of thing I did regularly in the United States.'

Okada kept rigid control of himself; but it was only a brittle shell, inside he was weak with relief. He bowed his head to Minato, aware that Major Nagata was watching him; but Tajiri and Toshiaki were also watching him and they saw his bow as the proper acknowledgment of a man who had told the truth.

'Do you have any complaint about your chauffeur?' Tajiri said to Toshiaki and the latter, after a glance at Okada, shook his head. The admiral then looked at Nagata. 'I think that should be all, major. Give Colonel Nitobe my compliments.'

Nagata knew when to back off: his neck had to be saved till the Americans came. 'I shall do that, sir. My apologies for disturbing you and Toshiaki-san.'

He marched off without a glance at Sergeant Ugaki; the latter was left stranded for a moment, then he bowed to Tajiri and Toshiaki and hurried after the major. Tajiri looked after the *kempei* with sour amusement.

'What are they going to do when the war is over? No one to spy on—' But he knew the question was rhetorical: none knew better than he that whoever was in power would always need spies. Even anarchists spied on each other.

The two old men said goodbye, got into their respective cars and were driven off. Minato and Okada had not glanced at each other after Nagata and Ugaki had departed; they were protected by the system, an admiral's aide did not recognize a rich man's servant. But Okada, now driving the Rolls-Royce, glanced in the rear-vision mirror and saw the rich man watching him closely.

'I am staying in Tokyo this evening,' Toshiaki said through the speaking tube. 'Drive out to Shibuya-ku, I shall be staying at a friend's house.'

'But what if the Americans should drop another bomb like

that on Hiroshima, Toshiaki-san?' He pushed aside the sliding window that separated the front seat from the rear. He had heard enough of the damage done to Hiroshima, though news was still sketchy. He was concerned for the old man's safety. 'You should find somewhere more out of town, sir.'

Toshiaki recognized the concern and the sincerity of it. 'Thank you, Fujita. But I don't think the Americans will drop an atom bomb on Tokyo. I have a feeling their politicians don't want the Emperor obliterated. But then perhaps you would know that better than I.'

Okada slowed the car, drove carefully round a danger spot where the road had caved in. 'I'm not sure what you mean, Toshiaki-san.'

'Come now, Fujita. You are more than you claim to be. Are you indeed a spy?'

Driving a big car along a pot-holed road, with your back to your interrogator, and with only a distorted glimpse of him in your rear-vision mirror, is not the best of situations in which to plead any innocence. Even the *kempei*, he guessed, would interrogate you face to face.

He drew the car into the side of the road. 'With your permission, Toshiaki-san, I should like to stop for a moment.'

'Of course.' Toshiaki fingered one of the white roses in the silver vase by the side window. The summer flowers were wilting, even though it was only early August; perhaps it was an omen. 'Turn round so that I can look at you.'

Okada turned round, slid back further the glass that separated him from Toshiaki. This, he supposed, was what the Catholics he had known would call a confessional. 'I have been working for the Americans, Toshiaki-san. I am a Japanese-American, a Nisei.'

'Are you going to tell me more?' Toshiaki said after a moment's silence.

Okada, after a slight hesitation, told him how he had been sent here. He mentioned neither Minato nor Natasha, but Toshiaki had a memory for names. 'Sergeant Ugaki said something about a Mrs Cairns, who lives in Nayora. Do you know her?'

'No, sir.' He was surprised to find that it hurt him to lie to the old man.

'Did you come to Miyanoshita to spy on me or General Imamaru?'

'No, sir. That was pure accident. Madame Tolstoy, the general's friend, recommended me.'

'Why should Madame Tolstoy recommend you? Is she a spy, too?'

'No, sir. I understand she is a woman who knows where good servants are to be found. I hope I've been a good servant, sir.'

Toshiaki smiled. 'Excellent, Fujita. But should that excuse you being a spy?' He touched the rose again; a petal came loose in his fingers. He looked out at the hot humid day; there might be a thunderstorm tonight. He always thought of the tumult and pyrotechnics of a thunderstorm as one of Nature's bowel movements: it cleared the air. Within the next week there would be a military and political thunderstorm that might take years to clear the air. He crushed the rose petal in his hand, said quietly, 'Drive me to my friend's house, Fujita. Then I think you had better disappear.'

'How will you get back to Miyanoshita, sir?' It no longer surprised Okada that his immediate concern was for the old man's welfare.

Toshiaki smiled. 'You speak like an adopted son. Thank you, Fujita. Now drive on, leave me and the car at my friend's house and find your own way back to town. Or wherever you plan to go.'

Five minutes later the Rolls-Royce drew up outside a gate set in a high yellow brick wall. Okada got out, opened the door for Toshiaki. 'I am very grateful, sir. I am in your debt.'

Toshiaki shook his head. 'No, Fujita, let there be no question of *giri*. I believe you Americans don't understand that principle.'

'I understand it, sir. My father tried to teach it to me.'

'Tried?' Toshiaki nodded in sympathy with the absent father. 'Tell me, will the Americans ruin our country when they take it over?'

'I don't know, sir. They are not experienced conquerors.'

298

'Perhaps the phoenix tree will tell us in years to come. It has survived all the dynasties. Unfortunately, I shan't be here to read what the tree has to say.'

Okada felt suddenly chilled: was the old man talking of suicide? But he forbore to ask. 'Goodbye, Toshiaki-san. And thank you.'

'For what? It is no effort to be magnanimous in defeat, Fujita. Or didn't you know we have lost the war?'

'Yes, sir. I knew it months ago.'

'I knew it years ago. Goodbye, Fujita.'

Okada turned abruptly and went hurrying down the street. At the corner he stopped and looked back. Toshiaki still stood outside the high wall; in the bright glare he looked no more substantial than a pale shadow cast against the yellow bricks. When he opened the gate in the wall he seemed to melt, rather than walk, through it.

It struck Okada that he felt sadder at this moment than when he had said goodbye to his own father.

4)

Okada reached the main railway station five minutes before the train for Nagasaki was due to depart. He had run half the distance in from Shibuya-ku, but managed to catch a bus for the last part of the journey. He was hot, sweaty and afraid that he might have missed Natasha and Lily.

They were standing in the main hall of the station still waiting on Koga and the travel passes. Well-dressed, each with an expensive, if now somewhat battered, suitcase, they were the target of surreptitious glances from the throng that swirled round them. Lily, long impervious to disapproving stares, had the calm, isolated look of a woman blind to crowds: it is a quality empresses and high-class whores have in common. Natasha, however, was aware of the stares; it seemed to her that in the time since she had last been in the city, the attitude of its ordinary citizens had changed. It was as if they were taking a last look at a life that was gone forever, or would be within the next few days, and the look had little charity in it. Natasha had never felt so *foreign*, not even in the dangerous days of the anti-foreigners hysteria.

She started as Okada touched her arm; then fell into his arms. 'Oh Tom! I thought I'd never see you again—' The thought had dropped into her mind only then; she caught her breath at the horror of it. 'Are you coming with us?'

'Yes. Where's Koga?'

'Not here, as you can plainly see,' said Lily tartly. If one was to be banished to the provinces, one should not be kept waiting. 'I should have gone to Osachi Cho myself and demanded the passes. Underlings are always unreliable.'

As if to prove her wrong, Koga emerged from the crowd. He looked hot and uncomfortable and, after he had bowed, took off his derby hat and fanned himself with it. He held out an envelope that was stained with sweat from his fingers. Okada noticed that the big beefy hand was shaking; Koga was a beaten, nervous man. Even the dragon on the back of the hand looked cowed.

'Cho-san's compliments, Madame Tolstoy. He wishes he were going with you to the south.' He looked as if he wished that he, too, were going with them.

'I'll get your tickets,' said Okada and took the passes and hurried across to the ticket window. He pushed in at the head of the line, apologizing profusely but not caring whether anyone accepted his apologies; he could hear the announcement that the train for Nagasaki was about to depart in three minutes. 'Three first class tickets to Nagasaki.'

'Single or return?' The ticket clerk had no interest in refugees fleeing the capital; or else he just liked making sick jokes. 'Passes?'

'Single.' Okada flashed the passes, one of them folded over so that it looked as if he was holding three passes. The ticket clerk just glanced at Okada's hand and passed over the tickets. Okada pushed money at him, didn't wait for change and ran back to Natasha and Lily. 'Hurry!'

He grabbed the two suitcases, jerked his head in farewell and thanks to Koga, and pushed the two women ahead of him

300

towards the train. It was beginning to move even as he pushed the suitcases on and jumped in after Natasha and Lily. He slammed the door shut and leaned against it. He was out of condition, mentally, emotionally and physically.

Natasha pressed his hand, restrained herself from kissing him. She could not believe her luck that he was coming with them; bereft of him, she had shut her mind against tomorrow and Nagasaki. It was as if she were stepping off the edge of her world and she had not cared about a parachute. She had trusted to luck, as she always had, and luck once again had been unbelievably good to her. She said a quick prayer of thanks, which would have pleased the French nuns.

The train, even in first class, was crowded. Okada pushed a way through the crowded corridor. Nobody gave way obligingly; he was handicapped by the two suitcases and the fact that he was escorting two non-Japanese women. At the end of the corridor he set the suitcases up in a corner and gestured to Natasha and Lily.

'I'm afraid that's it. I sense a certain antagonism towards you two. We don't want any fights, not all the way to Nagasaki.'

Lily looked back along the corridor of faces all turned to her and Natasha in open resentment, even hate. She had the sense to submerge her usual arrogance; for the first time in her life she wished she was not so well dressed. She sat down on one of the suitcases, all at once feeling hopeless and, yes, a little afraid. She felt like a camp follower with no more camps to follow; they had all been destroyed. She looked up at her daughter and for the first time felt a maternal apprehension. It was a day of firsts for her.

Natasha sat down beside her. 'Lily, I've never seen you look glum before—' Her tone was filial; Okada, listening to her, was touched. 'We'll be all right now that Tom is with us—'

'How do we know his uncle will welcome us? Look at those people—' She nodded at the faces in the corridor. 'Perhaps he'll feel the same about us. We're outsiders.'

'But I'm not,' said Okada, trying to sound reassuring. 'I'm family.'

Still, he had his own doubts. He was an American spy, albeit

301

one who was running away from his duties; perhaps even Embury and the others would consider him a traitor, or at best a deserter. He felt guilt about that; or (the Japanese in him dominating) shame. He had reduced the war to personal terms: his revulsion at the slaughter, his concern for Natasha's safety. He anticipated that his uncle would condemn his desertion, even if it was of the enemy; but he hoped that, if his uncle believed in the Peace Faction, then he would understand a nephew who wanted peace above all else. He stared out of the window at the passing countryside, which, if nothing else did, looked peaceful.

The journey was painfully slow. Four times the train stopped to wait for the track ahead of it to be repaired; half a dozen times it pulled into sidings to allow other trains to pass on the single line that remained. At Osaka, during an hour's stop in the early hours of the morning, Okada went looking for a phone.

Minato did not appreciate being dragged out of bed at the Staff College so early. 'Where are you?'

'In Osaka, on my way to Nagasaki. I'm with Mrs Cairns and Madame Tolstoy.'

'Madame Tolstoy? General Imamaru's woman?'

'Yes, she is Mrs Cairns's aunt. There's no time to explain. I had to leave, Kenji—' They were the friends of old; he used the intimate address. 'Toshiaki-san knows what I am, but he let me go. Is Admiral Tajiri suspicious of you?'

'It is difficult to tell. Suspicious or disappointed, I don't know which.' At six o'clock in the morning Minato did not care if the operator on the switchboard was listening, as he probably was. He had become reckless, wanted everything to end in a hurry, no matter how disastrously. Japan was finished and he felt an unutterable sadness, one he could not state even to Okada. 'Be careful, Tamezo. Give my respects to your uncle.'

'I'll call you from Nagasaki. Good luck, Kenji.'

He went back to Natasha and Lily, who were still sitting on their suitcases in the corner of the corridor, afraid of losing their places. He had brought them tin cups of tea and some rice cakes; they ate like the famished women that they were. Lily

302

said, with no resignation but tartly, 'I suppose we shall have to get used to such fare.'

'My uncle should be a wealthy man,' said Okada. 'I don't think the rich have gone hungry in this war, have they?'

'Crumbs from a rich man's table – is that what we're going to get?' But Lily was not ungrateful, just uncommonly hungry. She had never eaten much, to keep her figure; now she wanted to stuff herself, to look like Madame Imamaru. 'Is he a moral man?'

'Who knows?' said Okada. 'He is an armaments manufacturer.'

It was another forty-eight hours before they reached Nagasaki. Three times they had to change trains; chaos had taken over the timetables and the tracks. At Okayama they were taken up through the mountains and across to the northern coast; Okada learned that no traffic, rail or road, was being allowed near Hiroshima. On the last change-over he managed to get seats in a compartment for Natasha and Lily, but had to content himself with a cramped space in the corridor.

There was a six-hour delay while they waited for a ferry to cross the Kammon Straits. Okada watched the fishing boats putting out to sea, following the routine of centuries; the fish had to be caught, as if the sea issued its own command. Natasha stood beside him holding his hand, oblivious of the stares of disapproval of such public intimacy.

'Perhaps we should get off here, find a place in the mountains.'

'You suggested that once before. There'd be no peace for us up there. I remember the mountain people from when I lived in Nagasaki before the war. They are almost a different race, they hate the people from the cities. You and Lily would—' He shook his head. He didn't know if the peasants stoned outsiders, but it was possible. He squeezed her hand. 'We'll be safer in Nagasaki.'

The train arrived in the city at nine o'clock on Thursday morning. It ran slowly down the Urakami valley and Okada looked out for familiar landmarks. There was evidence of bombing, but Nagasaki seemed to have fared better than Tokyo; the city was still much as Okada had remembered it. By the time he and Natasha and Lily emerged from the main station he felt reasonably certain of his whereabouts. It was almost, but not quite, like coming home.

He managed to get a taxi, which took him and the two women to the Okada home on Sasuke Street. But the home was now occupied by four families, seemingly all living in each other's laps. Okada-san, they said, now lived up on the hill on the Unzen road – 'a big white house with an ornamental gate.' Tamezo Okada sounded as if he were indeed rich.

When the taxi deposited them outside the Okada house, Okada saw that his uncle had risen not only geographically but financially. The house was a small mansion set in a spacious garden; the ornamental gate might have been the entrance to a temple. Even Lily was impressed and brightened visibly.

But she said warily, 'Let's hope we are made welcome.'

Tamezo Okada was coldly polite to the two women, but he welcomed his nephew warmly. 'Tamezo! How splendid to see you back— Have the Americans landed so soon?'

'Only this one, uncle.' Okada had been meticulously formal, bowing low before putting out his hand to take the one his uncle offered him. 'I have to explain something to you . . . May my fiancée and her aunt have some tea while you and I talk? We have come all the way from Tokyo.'

Tamezo Okada had been jovial when he had asked if the Americans had already landed; he had been so pleased to see his nephew he had not bothered to examine why the young man should be here before the war was ended. Now he looked seriously at Okada, realizing the situation was like a badly-cut diamond, the facets were all wrong. Then he looked at the two women, the Eurasians, the outsiders, and Okada, watching his uncle closely, saw the older man's face close up.

Tamezo Okada, however, was a polite host. 'If you have come all the way from Tokyo, with the trains as they are, the ladies must want to bathe.'

He summoned a servant who took away the grateful Natasha and Lily. Then he led Okada into a small four-tatami room and gestured to him to sit down. Okada sank to the floor and his uncle nodded approvingly.

304

'You haven't forgotten how to sit.'

'I've only learned it again while I've been here in Japan.' Another servant had brought tea and Tamezo Okada served it without ceremony. 'That is what I have to explain.'

'First, how is your father?'

'I haven't seen him in two years. My sisters wrote and told me he and my mother were well.'

'You speak as if in the past. Have you been a prisoner of war and escaped?'

'No, uncle.' He sipped his tea. He had always known it would not be easy to explain his position to his uncle, but now it seemed to be growing more difficult by the moment. Tamezo Okada's welcoming mood was cooling, there was a formality about him that Okada could not remember from the old days. In those days, of course, Grandfather Okada had been head of the family. He put down his cup, not wanting to betray any nervousness by rattling it, and said, 'I landed here in Japan last February as an intelligence agent for the American Navy.'

'An intelligence—? You mean a spy?'

'Yes. I was sent here to find out the aims of the Peace Faction and who was behind it.'

Tamezo Okada had a long bony face that had dropped and softened about the jowls since his nephew had seen him last. He had a shock of grey hair that seemed to explode out of his skull, eyes that had once been pensive and now appeared calculating; the only physical feature about him that had not changed were his long craftsman's hands with the broadened fingertips. He was dressed in a dark blue kimono that failed to hide the belly he had developed. Wealth had made its mark on him: he made money now rather than works of art. Behind him a ceremonial sword, a family treasure that Okada remembered, hung on a wall like an artefact of another generation.

'What did you find out about the Peace Faction?'

'Only that you were a member of it and had been to prison because of it.'

'Is that why you are here?'

'No, I came here hoping you would let us stay till the war is over. It will only be a few days.'

'How do you know that?'

'On the way down here I kept hearing bits and pieces about what happened in Hiroshima. That city has been completely wiped out and tens of thousands of people killed. If they do that again, if they drop a bomb on Nagasaki or Osaka or somewhere else, even Tokyo, do you think the people will want the war to go on?'

Tamezo Okada had already considered that question and knew the answer. But he would not give his nephew the benefit of what he knew. 'If you are so sure the war is over, why have you come to me?'

'Because the *kempei* are investigating me. My employer, Toshiaki-san, told me to run away.'

'Otozo Toshiaki? You have infiltrated well – you must be a very good spy.'

'No, uncle, I'm a poor one. I've learned practically nothing and I'm not sure America is going the right way about winning the war.'

'Oh, they are going the right way about winning.' For a moment the older man let down his guard. 'For the short term, yes.'

Okada hesitated, then said, 'With all respect, uncle, can't the Peace Faction do something to end the war before another atom bomb is dropped? The Americans are waiting to hear from you.'

Tamezo Okada smiled, but it had no humour or warmth in it. 'You misunderstand our motives. To that extent we have been successful.'

Okada, tired, dirty, hungry, all at once was in no mood or condition for argument or cross-examination. He was, he decided, not only a poor spy but would have made a poor lawyer. 'May we stay here?'

'No.' The answer was blunt. 'We are on opposite sides, Tamezo.'

He's just like Father, Okada thought with despair, still believing in the Japanese cause.

Tamezo Okada stood up. 'I am going to call the *kempei*.'

Okada threw off his tiredness, was on his feet in one swift

306

movement, his legs exploding beneath him like a spring. 'You can't do that – I'm your nephew, your brother's son!'

'Unless your father has changed, he would understand what I'm about to do. He used to write our father and me, tell us how he believed in what Japan was doing. When he hears what I have done, he will understand.'

The system still stood: Okada had forgotten the fact. Everything must be sacrificed to the *on*, even sons and nephews.

He stepped back to the doorway of the small room, stood blocking it. He looked over his shoulder, saw the telephone on the small table against the wall in the large outer room. There was no sign of any servants or of Natasha and Lily.

Suddenly he shouted at the top of his voice, something he had never done in an Okada house, not even the one in Gardena, California. 'Natasha – Lily! Get dressed – get down here – quick!' Without meaning to, he had shouted in English: the tongue had its own panic. 'Hurry!'

Tamezo Okada closed his eyes: whether at the ear-splitting shout or the rebellion of his nephew, it was difficult to tell. Three servants, a man and two women, came running from the back of the house. Natasha, wrapped in a towel, appeared at the head of the stairs that led to the upper floor.

'Tom! What's wrong?'

'Get dressed! Hurry!' He was unreasonably angry that she and Lily had spent so long in the bath, yet they had been no more than ten minutes upstairs. 'We've got to get out of here!'

Natasha asked no more questions: she caught at once the urgency, even the fear, in Okada's voice. She disappeared, calling out to Lily, and Okada backed out into the big room, crossed to the phone and tore out its cord. Tamezo Okada had come to the doorway of the inner room, stood looking implacably at his nephew.

'You won't get away, Tamezo—'

'Where are the other phones? There must be others here—'

The older man said nothing. Okada looked wildly around, saw the glass case against the far wall of the big room. He ran to it, kicked in the glass and grabbed one of the swords displayed in the case. He remembered the display from the other Okada

307

house, a priceless collection of the family's craft; he looked at the short sword in his hand, saw that it was a *wakizashi*, the instrument for ritual suicide. But he was not going to use it for that purpose.

He crossed quickly to the manservant, held the sword against the man's chest. 'Where are the other phones?'

'Don't harm my servants!' Tamezo Okada snapped. 'There are two telephones upstairs and another two down here.'

Okada waited till Natasha and Lily, dressed, puzzled and distraught, came downstairs. 'Do you still have your gun, Lily?'

Lily took it from her handbag. 'Am I expected to shoot someone with it?' She sounded calm but didn't look it.

'Yes – if anyone moves—' He raced upstairs, found the phones and tore out their cables. Then he ran downstairs, found the other phones and disconnected them. When he came back into the big room he saw that no one had moved: Lily, a woman with a sense of the proper target, was pointing the gun directly at Tamezo Okada.

Okada looked at his uncle, gestured helplessly; he could not hate the older man. 'I'm sorry we couldn't see eye to eye. Whatever happened to you? You were once a peaceful man – my favourite—'

'You had better go.' Tamezo Okada did not want to be reminded of what he had once been. Wealth and importance are a congratulatory mirror; only bankruptcy and banishment could crack it. He still had hope, even if it was no more substantial than a snowflake.

'Do you have a car?' But Tamezo Okada refused to answer. He turned his back, as if daring Lily to shoot him. Okada turned the *wakizashi* on the servant. 'Is there a car? Where are the keys?'

The man was not prepared to commit suicide, not at someone else's hand. 'The car is out in the garage. The keys are in it.'

'What about our bags?' said Natasha. 'They are still upstairs —'

'Forget them!' Okada could feel himself crumbling; the sword shook in his hand. He looked at his uncle, wanting to say goodbye; he could feel the family bonds still encircling him, no matter how loosely. But Tamezo Okada was not interested in farewells or family bonds: his back was a wall. Okada sighed, gestured to the servant. 'Take us out to the car.'

It was a Packard, polished and well-kept: a successful man's car. All Okada could remember from his time with the family was an old Ford. He got in, started up the engine; the fuel gauge showed *full*, but he knew from experience with the Rolls-Royce that the gas-bags mounted on the rear often made the gauge unreliable. Still, the car would at least get them down off the mountain, even if he had to let it coast.

He looked at his watch: it was 10.30. He put the sword on the seat beside him, let off the brake and drove the car out of the garage and out through the ornamental gates, which had been opened for him by the servant. Natasha and Lily sat in the back of the car; he still wore his Toshiaki uniform cap and he might have been a chauffeur taking two elegant ladies out to morning tea. He turned the car north, down the hill towards the city. He had no idea where he was heading, only that he had to put as much distance as possible between them and Nagasaki.

Ten

The previous night Commander Embury and Lieutenant Irvine had flown over from Guam to the neighbouring island of Tinian. They had heard of the bomb raid on Hiroshima on the previous Monday and knew some of the details as seen from *Enola Gay*, the B-29 that had dropped the atom bomb. Fifteen miles from the bomb drop the *Enola Gay* had leapt like a wild horse in the sky as the blast had followed it. The sky for a hundred miles around had lit up as if another sun had burst on the world. A great cloud had mushroomed, as Embury and Irvine heard it described, and flattened out at the top as if against an invisible ceiling. One of the flight crew had entered in the flight log the stark exclamation, 'My God!'; but it had not been the Second Coming. Observation planes had flown over Hiroshima later in the day and came back with reports of devastation that hardly anyone could believe.

And now a second raid was planned. Embury and Irvine flew over with a Navy observer party to Tinian; but being Navy and not Air Force they were kept at a distance; there are wars within wars. Still, the Navy could not be kept entirely out of the picture when history was being made. The Russians were massing on the Manchurian border and were expected to cross it at any hour. The Americans had to win the war before the Russians got to Tokyo first.

Embury and Irvine stood on the tarmac watching the second bomb being loaded into the bay of *Bock's Car*, the B-29 that was to carry it. With the whimsy of a juvenile witch, someone had named the two bombs Thin Boy and Fat Boy. It had been explained to Embury and Irvine that there was a difference between the first and second bombs: the one dropped on

Hiroshima had been charged with uranium, this one had a plutonium base. Neither man understood the scientific significance of the difference; but the blast of Fat Boy, they were told, was expected to be three times that of Thin Boy. The message, it was assumed, would be three times as emphatic for the Japanese.

Embury had been shocked, but not horrified, at the stories of what Thin Boy had done to Hiroshima. He had no sympathy for the Japanese; they deserved whatever was coming to them. He had read the reports that had come back on the sufferings of American prisoners-of-war who had survived and been rescued. The Bataan death march, he thought, merited any sort of retribution. Irvine, for his part, remembered the rape and massacre of Nanking the year he had arrived in the East and, more personally, he remembered that his mother and father had died in the rape of Hong Kong, his mother literally raped to death. He too watched the bomb being loaded with no feeling of conscience about what it might do.

Except: 'I hope it doesn't land anywhere near Tom Okada. Where's it to be dropped?'

'Kokura, on the north coast of Kyushu – that's five or six hundred miles from Tokyo. He'll be safe.'

'Is there a secondary target, in case they don't make Kokura?'

'Nagasaki.'

Bock's Car took off at 1.56 a.m. Tokyo time. If all went well, it would be over its target at 8.30 a.m.

But all did not go well. For some extraordinary reason radio silence from headquarters on Tinian was broken; but if Japanese radio monitors heard the thirty minutes' transmission and deduced anything from it, no planes were sent up to intercept *Bock's Car*. Two and a half hours out of Tinian a red warning light flashed that all firing circuits on Fat Boy were closed: for one awful moment it looked as if the bomb was going to explode in the plane. The crew sweated for another half-hour before it was found that a faulty switch had triggered the false alarm. Well into daylight, just after 8 a.m., the B-29 rendezvoused off the southern tip of Japan with one of its two escorting camera planes; but it spent another forty minutes circling looking for the second camera plane and could not find it. At a few minutes before 9 a.m. Major Sweeney, the *Bock's Car* pilot, headed for Kokura, hoping that all the gremlins had now gone home to roost.

But war, like life and love, was never meant to be easy. When *Bock's Car* arrived over Kokura on what was otherwise a morning of excellent visibility, the bombardier could not see his aiming point, which was obscured by thick smoke from factory chimneys: a cynical anti-environmentalist would say years later that Kokura that morning was saved by pollution. The B-29 made three runs over the city, but each time the bombardier could not see his aiming point and announced 'No drop'. By then anti-aircraft guns were finding the range of the circling plane and fighters were taking off from nearby fields. Major Sweeney, aware now that his fuel was running low, that he would not get *Bock's Car* back to Tinian but would have to land either on Iwo Jima or Okinawa, turned south towards the secondary target, Nagasaki.

At 10.58 a.m., from a height of 11,000 feet, Fat Boy was dropped. It drifted down on its parachute towards the bowl-shaped valley of the Urakami, towards the railway line and the road that ran north-east towards Isahaya.

23

'Did you know that *Madame Butterfly* was set in Nagasaki?' said Natasha.

'Earth-shattering,' said Lily; then added like a real mother, 'Don't chatter.'

Natasha, uncommonly for her, was all nerves. Okada had driven the car down into the city, found his way through its maze of streets and now they were out of the valley, on top of a hill and about to begin the long drive north. For more than twenty minutes she had been clenching her fists; twice they had passed police cars and she had held her breath, waiting for the cars to turn and chase them. She had made almost inane remarks about points they had passed; even in her own ears she had sounded like a frightened child. She was almost grateful for Lily's sudden asperity; it made her feel better to know that she was not the only one who was afraid. Even Tom, in the front seat, looked nervous.

'What's the matter?'

He was craning his head to look out of the car and up at the sky. 'I think there's an air raid. The anti-aircraft guns are firing.'

'Can you see any American planes?'

'No.' He saw a glint in the sky, but then he had to concentrate on driving down the long winding road. There was little traffic heading north, but a steady stream coming towards Nagasaki. 'I think we better get out of here just in case they start bombing this road.'

He put his foot down, took the car at speed round the long curve of a hill. A minute later they heard the ear-splitting bang somewhere behind them beyond the hills. Okada went deaf with it: for a moment he lost all orientation as he sped through an utterly silent world. At the same time the world turned blue-white, bleached momentarily by the blinding light that burst up from the hills behind the speeding Packard; the dark-blue road, the yellow-and-green fields, the emerald trees, all suddenly were just images on a strange photo negative, no longer three-dimensional. Then colour came rushing back, the blinding glare faded; a huge wind rushed by overhead and the car wavered on the narrow road in a vacuum. Miraculously the gas-bags at the rear neither collapsed nor exploded; and equally miraculously Okada managed to keep the car on the road despite the fact that the steering felt like a stick of jelly in his trembling hands. He gasped for breath, took in nothing and for a moment thought he was going to pass out. Then air came hurtling back at the car, into it; the women's hair blew out and their faces contorted as if they were drowning in an invisible wave. Then, just as suddenly as it had happened, the blast and its effects were gone.

Okada did not slow the car. He knew another atom bomb had been dropped; he did not want to wait to see its effect. He took a quick glance back and saw the giant cloud, fiery at its base, rising into the air; it was the most terrifying sight he had ever seen, etched in memory's eye for ever. He did not look at it again.

They had been saved by the hills that surrounded Nagasaki; the bowl of the Urakami Valley kept the blast within a two-mile strip. Within those limits the city was reduced to crushed rubble. On the hill facing the valley Tamezo Okada, standing in his garden, died instantly. With him died 40,000 other citizens of Nagasaki.

His nephew and the two women with him, the enemies of the homeland, drove on to safety, escaping even the radiation that spread out to inflict itself on those who knew or saw nothing of the infection that was to maim or kill them in the months to come.

3

'Where are you?' said Minato.

'Yamaguchi. We've run out of gas and we've just about run out of money too. Madame Tolstoy is trying to hock her diamond rings. We've got to get out of here, Kenji. I mean this city, any city. God knows where the Americans are going to drop their next atom bomb. What are they trying to do? Flatten the whole of Japan?'

Minato remarked *the Americans*: Okada sounded as if he had become totally neutral. 'If you can get the gasoline, or get on a train, I think you should go up into the mountains or come back here to Tokyo. The feeling is that the Americans won't drop an atom bomb on Tokyo. The word from Berne in Switzerland is that the Americans want to spare the Emperor.'

'I'm not taking the women to the mountains. Up there anything could happen to them. We'll try and come back to Tokyo, hole up there till it's all over. It can only be a day or two now.' He was silent for a moment, then he said, 'Are you all right? Has our friend Nagata been back to you?'

'Not yet.' They had been talking guardedly, but Minato was reasonably sure that no operator on the Navy switchboard was eavesdropping on them. Since the dropping of the second atom bomb on Nagasaki this morning it seemed that every phone in every ministry in the capital had been off its hook; Okada had told Minato he had had to wait twenty-five minutes before he had managed to get through. In pre-phone times, Minato mused, disaster had spread more leisurely. 'But anything may happen in the next day or so. It's time for honour and revenge —' He looked up to see Lieutenant Nakasone standing in the doorway of their office. 'I have to go. Call me later if you can.'

In Yamaguchi, almost five hundred miles away, Okada wondered why Minato suddenly had to hang up. And what had he meant by 'It's time for honour and revenge'? Was he in danger, was he contemplating suicide? He came out of the phone booth and Natasha, sharp-eyed with love, saw at once the concern on his face.

'What's the matter?'

'I think our other agent is in some sort of danger.' So far he had told her nothing of Minato, on the hopeful premise that the less she knew, the safer she would be. 'I've got to get back to Tokyo.'

'We all have to get back there. I feel safer there – or anyway, safer than I do here.'

They were standing by the stranded Packard in a narrow street on the outskirts of the town. Nobody had stopped to stare at them, but they were aware of the curious and hostile glances of those passing by. It seemed to Okada that only apathy was saving them; the news from Hiroshima was already widespread and whispers had come up the line of what had happened at Nagasaki three hours ago. Once they got used to the idea that the war was over, the apathy might abruptly turn to last-minute anger, a last blow at foreigners.

He waited for her to ask about his other agent, but she didn't. She was no longer a spy; the war was won but not yet over. She was interested only in herself and him. And, he guessed, Lily.

Then Lily, trying to look humble and inconspicuous, an effort that made her look almost epileptic, came round the corner. She held up a bare-fingered hand.

315

'He took all my rings and paid me two hundred yen, take it or leave it, he said. They were worth thousands. He said he would have given me more for a bag of rice. Rice more valuable than diamonds – who would have believed it?' She didn't. Still, she was philosophical: 'But then I never believed that beggars could not be choosers . . .'

'We're going back to Tokyo,' said Natasha. 'As soon as Tom fills up the car.'

'Good,' said Lily, who had never been one for the provinces, having escaped them years before. 'Get the petrol, Tamezo, and let's get back to civilization as soon as possible.'

It wasn't easy to buy gasoline and have the bags refilled; but Okada found a garage owner who still had enough hope of the future to take a bribe. Half an hour later they were heading over the mountains to the north coast road, having been told that all roads past Hiroshima on the south coast were blocked to traffic. Farmers worked in their fields, bringing in the harvest; in the villages washing hung on the lines, children played in yards; priests sat outside a temple, eyes closed against the sun (or against the future? Okada wondered). The landscape looked as tranquil as a Noami print.

Okada drove carefully but steadily, intent on saving fuel but determined to get back to Tokyo as soon as possible. He had started on this trip to Nagasaki concerned only with Natasha's safety; gradually he had become protective of Lily too. The feeling for Natasha had come out of love, a love so deep that he had become a little afraid of its depths; the regard for Lily's safety had come from natural charity and a growing, reluctant admiration for the woman's resilience. Now he was heading back to Tokyo concerned for Minato's safety, but also out of a sense of debt. He owed a *giri* to Kenji Minato: he had gone over to the Japanese side to that extent.

4

'Time for honour and revenge?' said Nakasone. 'Which is your choice, Minato?'

Nakasone had changed since his recruitment by Colonel Hayashi. If Japan was on the verge of defeat, no one would have known it from Nakasone's demeanour. He had just discovered he was a *samurai*; or a reasonable facsimile thereof. He no longer looked cheerful but pompously zealous. It didn't suit him, Minato thought.

'I shall follow Admiral Tajiri's course,' said Minato cautiously. 'Won't that be the honourable thing to do?'

'No.' Nakasone sat down: stiffly, as if at attention. 'He and the others in the Peace Faction think they are doing the honourable thing, but they are wrong.'

'What do you know about the Faction?'

'More than you, obviously.' Nakasone had become cunning, a trait that had never spoiled him before his conversion. 'I thought the admiral would have taken you into his confidence.'

He's jealous, thought Minato. That's why he's gone over to Colonel Hayashi, all because of petty jealousy. He tried a cautious feint: 'If Colonel Hayashi is still true to habit, I don't think he will have taken you into his confidence.'

Smugness took away all the familiarity of Nakasone's features. 'We all know what the colonel's plans are. We are ready to act at any moment.'

'Does the Emperor know what you intend doing?'

For a moment there was a crack in the smugness. 'You know the colonel's plans?'

It had been a shot in the dark; but Minato put his neck out into the same dark: 'Yes.'

'Does Admiral Tajiri know?'

'Perhaps you should ask him. You seem to think he hasn't taken me into his confidence.'

Nakasone's self-confidence had gone; he looked like a man who wished there had been some self-torture, such as biting one's tongue. 'You spoke of honour. What we are doing is for the honour of Yamato.'

They, whoever they were, were living in the ancient past: Nakasone had just used the ancient name of Japan, the word used by the blindly chauvinistic. Minato had to restrain himself from shaking his head at such foolish patriotism. He could understand *seppuku*: he knew there would be a lot of that in the next few days. But that would be from personal shame in defeat: it would have nothing to do with the honour of Japan, or Yamato.

He stood up. 'All I can say is, may the Emperor be saved from your efforts at honour.'

For a moment it looked as if Nakasone would spring at him. He jerked up from his chair, drew a deep hissing breath; then abruptly he swung round and was gone. Minato felt himself shaking, felt suddenly at a loss, alone and afraid. As a youth, a new recruit in the Navy, he had prayed for stoicism, even fatalism. Now all he prayed for was peace and a release from all obligations.

Then the buzzer on his desk rang: the admiral wanted to see him. He went into Tajiri's office. The old man stood at the window, looking out through the criss-cross of tape holding the glass from shattering; the taping was so thick that he gave the appearance of peering through a spy-hole. He said without turning round, 'They are discussing surrendering over at the Palace, Minato. Does that please you?'

'Yes, sir.'

Tajiri turned round. 'You're honest, at least. All the other young men have been holding their tongues, waiting for the old men to tell them what to say. You're not with Lieutenant Nakasone and the rest of Colonel Hayashi's fanatics?'

'No, sir. Is the Peace Faction over at the Palace? Should you not be with them?'

Tajiri smiled. 'Minato, you have never really understood what we are about, have you? We have never been interested in promoting peace, only in preparing for it.'

Minato looked puzzled and knew it showed.

'Ah Minato, you always misunderstood us, didn't you? I wonder if the Americans had hopes of us?' Minato let the question remain unanswered. Tajiri didn't look at him, so the question could have been no more than rhetorical. 'We were meant to be the scapegoats, Minato, never anything more than that.'

'Scapegoats?' He knew he sounded stupid; but he felt stupid.

318

'If we lost the war, as we have, we were meant to take the blame for starting it. We are the scapegoats for the Emperor. It was not his idea, but Koichi Kido's, the Lord Privy Seal. Shigeru Yoshida and Prince Konoye have been its leaders – perhaps I am also one, but I have been modest about my responsibility for it. We were all volunteers, none of us was dragooned into the Faction. We are a mixture – Army men, Navy men, industrialists, bureaucrats, palace officials. Personally, I've always thought there were too many of us. I'm not sure how many hundreds of us there are. Will the Americans believe that it took so many of us to start a war? They are planning to have war criminal trials of the Germans, but how many are they going to charge? Hundreds? Perhaps, but most of those will be the small people who massacred prisoners or ran the concentration camps. We'll have some of those, surely—' He shook his head sadly. 'Not all of us fought the war in a civilized way, Minato.'

'Is there a civilized way, sir?' In his own ears Minato sounded like Okada.

'You, a career officer, asking such a question? Of course there is. War is part of civilization. Only fools think otherwise. We started this war because the rest of Asia needed to be civilized.'

'So when the Americans come, you and the rest of the Peace Faction will take the blame? Then what will happen to the Emperor?'

'That, I gather, is the cause of all the debate over at the Palace. The Emperor wants to surrender at once, to save further destruction and killing. War Minister Anami is arguing that we must strike a hard bargain.'

'What would you argue for, sir, if you were over at the Palace?'

Tajiri took off his glasses, polished them with a silk handkerchief. He was almost blind without them, but his insight was perfect. 'I should be watching Colonel Hayashi. He is plotting a coup d'état, to isolate the Emperor, or worse, he is plotting to kill His Majesty. Either way he and the people around him want no surrender. They are madmen, they want the whole of the nation to become *samurai*, to die for the Emperor. They want us to continue the fight from the Spirit World. What ghosts have ever won a war?' Tajiri put on his glasses, came round his desk, stood in front of Minato. There was an intimacy about the stance, like that of father and son. 'You're wondering why I told you all this?'

'Yes, sir.'

'Did Colonel Hayashi ever try to recruit you?'

The *Go* game had taken a turn he had not expected: Admiral Tajiri was a third player. 'Yes, sir.'

'I want you to enlist with him.'

Minato hesitated, then said, 'He may be suspicious of me, Tajiri-san. I mean if I suddenly change my mind and say I want to join him. Lieutenant Nakasone is one of his supporters and Nakasone knows how I feel.'

'You'll just have to act more fanatical than the young idiot. I suspect that you are on the Americans' side, that they did indeed turn you around and sent you back here as a spy. That man Fujita is Tamezo Okada, is he not? You have been working together, am I not right?'

Minato was not surprised that he had been found out, or almost; he was surprised that Admiral Tajiri seemed neither disappointed in nor angry with him. 'Are you going to turn me over to the *kempei*, sir?'

'What would be the point of that? The secret police are now being used to spy on bigger game than you, Minato. No, you are my man, my pawn, if you like.' The *Go* game had changed utterly, Minato thought. He was both a player and a piece; but he had no control of strategy or tactics. 'You will report to Colonel Hayashi this evening.'

'You want me just to walk in and volunteer, sir?'

Tajiri shook his head, the light winking on his glasses. 'We must be a little more subtle than that. I shall give you a note for the colonel pleading with him to abandon his plot. You can tell him that you know what is in the note. He'll ask your opinion – he's that sort of man. He has only contempt for the weak and he thinks people like me are weak. You can agree with him. If he says that Nakasone has reported adversely on you, you can say that you have never been interested in another junior officer's opinion of you. Hayashi likes arrogance – so long as you are not arrogant towards him.'

Minato was impressed. 'How long have you been studying the colonel, sir?'

'Ah, only a short time. Only since you reported to me that he was interested in you. I'm a quick study, Minato.'

'How long have you been studying me?'

Tajiri smiled avuncularly. 'From the day you returned to work for me. I suspected from the first day that you might have come back to work for the Americans. I kept you here because sooner or later I thought you might be useful. Now you can be.'

'What do I do if Colonel Hayashi does accept me? Why can't you have him arrested?'

'Because he is working with, or for, someone in the Royal Household. We don't know who and we may never know. But Colonel Hayashi is the man who is going to stage the coup or, at worst, kill the Emperor. You can kill if the occasion calls for it, can't you, Minato?'

'What makes you think that, sir? Before I went to America, you told me that good spies should always avoid killing.'

'When you escaped from the Americans, you killed one of their men. Oh yes, we got reports on your escape. The Americans planned it well – one never expected them to be so ruthlessly competent.'

'That killing wasn't planned.'

'But you did kill him. How did you feel afterwards?'

He still felt no regrets: 'That it was necessary.'

'And Lieutenant Sagawa – did you kill him? Never mind, don't tell me. He was betraying me by working for Colonel Hayashi.'

Some admirals rise to the top because of their flotation, lightweights who manage never to be sunk. Tajiri, who looked as if he could not command a skiff, had reached his rank because not even the seniority system had been able to torpedo his shrewdness. No one was safe from his assessment of them.

'Are you asking me to kill Colonel Hayashi, sir?'

'If necessary. For the Emperor's sake, not mine. You still

have your *on* to the Emperor. I think I have read you right, Minato, have I not?'

Minato closed his eyes as if he had been hit, opened them and sighed. Tradition was in his blood, like leukaemia; but he didn't feel diseased, only saddened. It is not always a joy to find one is more honourable than one expected.

'Yes, sir.'

Eleven

Okada and the two women reached Tokyo on the Saturday morning, forty-eight hours after leaving Nagasaki. Twice more along the way they had run out of fuel; twice more Okada had had to go looking for garage owners who could be bribed into selling gasoline. Money was running short and Lily's small jewel case was being eyed by Okada as if it were a food basket.

'I am going to finish up penniless,' said Lily.

'It will only be temporary,' said Natasha. 'I have confidence in you, mum.'

Lily squirmed: she would rather be a pauper than a mum. But she returned Natasha's smile, feeling love seeping through her like an incontinent bladder.

Okada, choosing an obvious hide-out as perhaps the safest, drove straight to the ruins of General Imamaru's mansion. He deposited the two women and their baggage there, then drove the Packard into the centre of town and parked it near Hibiya Park. It was the best place to abandon it; for a day or two, till the police became suspicious, it would be taken for the car of someone of importance doing business at one of the nearby ministries.

As he passed the Navy building on his way back to the Imamaru residence he was tempted to ask for permission to go in and see Lieutenant Minato. He called Minato six times along their route, but each time had been told he was not available. He was worried, certain now that Minato had been arrested. But he could not walk into the lions' den and ask if Daniel had been eaten.

He stopped by a phone and rang Minato's office; but again there was no answer. When he reached the Imamaru place Lily and Natasha were already installed in the air raid cellar beneath the ruins.

'We have to share, of course, with the servants,' said Lily. 'There are four of them. I could ask them to move out and sleep somewhere in the garden, but I don't think that would be diplomatic. They have welcomed us back only because I am such a good mistress.' She had been a good mistress to both master and servants; better than anyone, an intelligent whore knows the impermanency of her position; one builds support at both ends of the scale. 'We shall have to be careful of the riff-raff. They are still here.'

'Give me your gun.'

Okada took the Mauser and went up the cellar steps and into the garden. He had no trouble finding the riff-raff; they came out of the ruins like rats. There were a dozen of them, eight men and four women; Okada was glad there were no children. They stared menacingly at him, but he recognized the menace of the group: individually, they were wary and afraid of him, especially when they saw the gun in his hand.

'I work for General Imamaru at his country place. He has told me I have to kick out all of you. You have five minutes to pack up and go.'

'Tell General Imamaru to go fuck himself.'

He was a little man, but he would be tough, Okada thought: he was all bone and sinew and meanness. Okada raised the gun and pointed it at his close-cropped head.

'Do you want to come with me and tell that to the general? Or do you want me to blow your head off?'

The man was tough; but he hadn't survived in his tough world by being foolhardy. He stared at Okada; then he turned and went back into the ruins of the mansion. Okada, controlling the expansion that threatened to burst his chest, aware of the weakness in the hand that held his gun, stood stock-still: it was the best, indeed the only way of asserting his own menace. The man came back out of the ruins with a sack; the others were following his example and gathering up their possessions. The leader gave Okada one last hard look, spat contemptuously, and walked off down the driveway. The others followed him, silent and resigned, no longer menacing. More survivors, thought Okada.

There was a crunch of gravel behind him; he spun round, the gun coming up of its own accord. But it was Natasha, pulling up sharply as the gun almost jabbed into her stomach. 'Put it down!'

He lowered the gun with embarrassment. The *wakizashi* sword was with Natasha's suitcase: he was collecting an arsenal, or anyway borrowing it. Natasha said, 'Would you have shot him? I heard what you said.'

'I don't know,' he said honestly. 'Not in cold blood. But if he had jumped me—' They were speaking in English; it was their lovers' language. 'Yes, I suppose I would have. In the back of my mind was what they might do to you . . .'

'You'd kill for me?' She was touched; she looked at the gun as if it were a talisman. 'I suppose it had to come some day . . .'

'What?'

'Nothing.' She was thinking of the life she had led, beginning to see it for the first time in perspective. She had lived dangerously and never really realized it. She touched his arm in the gathering summer dusk. 'I wish we could go to bed.'

He grinned, shook his head at her cure for all ills. 'Here? We couldn't find a soft spot. You'd be all bruises.'

'Not if you were underneath.'

'You'd get gravel-rash on your knees.'

It was silly talk: sex may raise other things but not the level of wit. But it eased the tension that surrounded them; there had been none between them. They walked arm in arm around the ruined garden, past the shrubs that turned into heaps of ash, past the crippled iron birds, the beheaded stone lions. In one of the ponds a dead carp floated like a bloated, faded flower; a disturbed arrangement of white pebbles now looked like an obscene scrawl. But, blind with love, they saw nothing that disturbed them. It was Saturday night, young lovers' night, the last Saturday night of the war.

Sunday morning Okada, with one of the women servants, went looking for food. But they were in a rich district, where there was no *tonarigumi* to dole out rations of food. He went

325

back to Lily, asked her for another donation from her jewel-box.

'You'll bankrupt me,' she said, but gave him a gold bracelet that should have bought an emperor's banquet. 'Get the best possible price for it. It has sentimental value,' she said and looked almost wistful. 'My first rich client.'

Okada went down alone to the docks, walking through the almost deserted ruins of the city, glad of the exercise; his legs felt as if they had not been used for the past week. Several of the docks had been repaired and were operating; he found Koga without much difficulty. The *yakuza* had come back to his true domain: the Americans would bring their ships in here, would be looking for a dock boss.

'Back from Nagasaki? I thought the bomb would have got you.'

He hadn't expected humour, even bad humour, from Koga. But he humoured the burly thug, smiled. 'I knew when to duck. I'm looking for food, Koga.' No Koga-san now; it had been established they were equals. 'Enough for seven people for a few days.'

Koga bunched a fist; but he was only admiring the dragon dimpled by his knuckles. 'I've had them retattooed, changed their snarls to smiles to greet the Americans. You're asking for a lot of food. How much will you pay?'

'What will you give me for that?' Okada held out the gold bracelet, wishing he had been able to find a pawnbroker first. 'Give me the food I want and a thousand yen change.'

'You must think I own the Bank of Tokyo.'

'Talk to your boss, Cho-san, if you haven't got the money. But I'm sure you have.'

Koga didn't haggle any further. He went away, came back with a small handcart on which were two boxes and a sack. He threw a tarpaulin over the cart. 'Fish and rice. And 900 yen change – I'm charging you for the cart.'

'You're a crook, Koga.'

'I know,' said Koga, and raised his fists to let the dragons smile.

Okada pulled the cart back through the streets to the Im-

326

amaru residence. No one took any notice of him; he was part of what was now the everyday scene. But he still did not see himself as Japanese: the image that came to mind was pictures in old copies of *Life* magazine showing Okies fleeing the Dust Bowl in the Thirties. They had had brokendown jaloppies instead of handcarts; but they had been refugees, though no one had ever called them that. He was a refugee, though he was not quite sure what he was fleeing from.

The servants cooked the rice and fish and Okada, Natasha and Lily had their first good meal in days. In the afternoon Okada, restless and suddenly homesick, asked Lily to point out where General Imamaru's study had been when the house had still stood. Under the wreckage he found what he was looking for: paper, pen and ink. He wrote two letters, one to his sisters in English, one to his parents in Japanese characters. It might be weeks before the letters reached his family, but in them he told where he was and, guardedly, what he had been doing. He finished the letter to his parents with the admission to his father: *I am more Japanese than I had supposed*. It was a plea for reunion, but he had little hope that Chojiro Okada would respond.

He sat on the chipped steps of the mansion and Natasha, who had left him alone while he wrote, at last came and sat beside him. 'There's something on your mind, Tom. I noticed it last night – you were so restless in your sleep.'

He nodded; then decided to take her into his confidence. He told her all about Kenji Minato, beginning with their boyhood friendship and ending with his last sight of Minato outside the Dai Ichi building. 'He protected me that day. He could have given me away, but he didn't. What I'm afraid of is that they have arrested him. He could be dead.'

She touched his hand sympathetically. 'There's nothing you can do. We just have to wait.'

Which is what they did through the rest of the day and all through Monday. The servants went out and came back with rumours; people were saying they had heard the Americans broadcasting on short-wave that the war was over. Passers-by sometimes paused by the gates and looked up the driveway at the small group moving about amongst the ruins; but the passers-by were not riff-raff, as Lily had called them, and they still respected the privacy of General Imamaru's residence even if it looked like nothing more than a tiny battlefield. Old habits died hard, thought Okada, and wondered which ones the Americans would try to kill first.

Tuesday morning it rained pamphlets. American B-29s flew over the city and dropped over a million leaflets; for a few minutes the sky was alive with what looked to be gently falling gulls. People, expecting bombs, cowered at first; then the leaflets were fluttering down amongst them and they rushed to pick them up. A couple drifted down into the Imamaru garden and Okada picked them up. He handed one to Natasha and Lily.

'That's it.' He looked tired and drawn, but his eyes had brightened when he read the message. 'The government have offered to surrender.'

The strain of the past few days drained out of the women's faces; in the background the servants were suddenly cheerful. But no one danced or sang; though out in the street they heard what sounded like a shout of joy. Then it seemed that a vast hush of expectancy settled on the city as the citizens waited for the government announcement that the surrender was official.

But within an hour the civilian police were patrolling the streets telling everyone they should turn in the leaflets. By noon most of the pamphlets had been collected; Okada sent a servant out into the street to hand over to a passing policeman the two leaflets he had picked up. It was Natasha, the one foreigner who had lived in Japan the longest of the three of them, who guessed the reason for the collection of the leaflets.

'If the government has surrendered, they don't want the Americans announcing it first. That would be the Emperor's duty.'

'The Emperor won't make an announcement like that,' said Lily. She believed in the divinity of no man, but she knew how Imamaru had always spoken of the Emperor as if he were a god. She said waspishly, 'That would destroy the myth, that he lives above the clouds like a crane. The Voice of the Crane isn't going to make any surrender announcement.'

Natasha looked at Okada for a comment, but he didn't seem to have heard what she and Lily had said. He wandered away from them and she left him alone; she saw him as a soldier who, now that it was at last a fact, could not quite believe in the end of the war. Then a chilling thought struck her: what if he saw the end of the war as the end of their romance? Had he kept something from her, was there a wife and perhaps children back in America?

She went to him at once, but even as he turned towards her and put out his hands to take her, she knew her fears were groundless. He loved her and she had nothing to worry about. Except: 'I have to go looking for Kenji Minato,' he said.

'You can't!' Her fingers tore at his hands.

'I have to. I have a *giri* to him—'

'You don't! Damn you men – you're always thinking of duty—' She almost wept with anger at him. 'You have a duty to me!'

'Of course I have. But you and Lily are safe – no one is going to come looking for you now—'

'It's not my safety I'm thinking of – it's yours!' She wanted to fight him, to pound her feelings into him with her fists.

But he held her by the wrists now. 'It's no use, Natasha – I've got to go and find out what's happened to him. If I don't find out, I'll spend the rest of my life wondering if I could have saved him—'

'And if something happens to you, what about me? Do I spend the rest of my life grieving for you? Mother!' She looked past him, at Lily standing watching them in the driveway. 'Try and talk to him!'

If the cry of 'mother!' disturbed Lily, she showed no sign of it. She had expected that some time, sooner or later, Natasha would turn to her for help in some situation; she had come to know that they were closer in feeling than either of them had yet admitted. She was suddenly maternal, which, now that she had surrendered to it, was no worse than pretending to love a man. Better, even.

But she knew men better than her daughter did: 'If he's so pig-headed, it's better to let him go. He'll never forgive you—'

Women, thought Okada, they can turn any argument against you. But he was grateful for Lily's backhanded help: 'Look after her, Lily. I'll be back as soon as I can – I promise to be careful. I'm as scared for my neck as she is—'

He went quickly, not even embracing Natasha; he knew she would cling to him and he would have to hurt her to free himself. He heard her cry out, but he didn't look back. Nor did he look ahead, at least not to the prospect that he might be arrested. He put that thought out of his mind and plunged on, a step at a time.

2

He went first to the Staff College: it seemed to be the safest place to begin his search for Minato. It was a long walk, almost three miles; no buses or street-cars appeared to be running; the city had come to a standstill waiting for the surrender announcement. He hurried, sometimes breaking into a run. When he arrived at the Staff College, he was stopped by a guard; but the guard was not officious, the war was over and this civilian didn't look dangerous. He put in a call for Lieutenant Minato; the word came back that Lieutenant Minato had not reported in for the past six days. Okada felt sick, certain now that his friend (he thought of him as he had thought of him of old) was dead.

He went back to the centre of the city. He stood opposite the Navy building for an hour, hoping for a miracle, that he might catch a glimpse of Minato going in or coming. But miracles need faith and he had none.

He debated a dozen ways of approach; in the end, out of desperation, he chose the boldest. He crossed the street and presented himself to the guards on the door. 'I wish to see Admiral Tajiri.'

The two guards looked at him, a shabby civilian wishing to see an admiral, as if they hadn't heard correctly. But he persisted, fearful but determined now that he was here on the doorstep: 'I have a message from Otozo Toshiaki for the admiral. Please tell him I must see him.'

The Toshiaki name meant nothing to the guards; but one of them had a little more intelligence than the other. He sensed that this civilian was something more than he looked; strange things had been going on in the past few days. He called to someone inside the lobby and an nco came out. Okada patiently explained that he had an important message for Admiral Tajiri that had to be delivered personally.

'Tell the admiral my name is Fujita. He will know me.' He felt sure that Tajiri, an Intelligence chief, would not forget a name.

Five minutes later, under the suspicious escort of the nco, he was shown into Admiral Tajiri's office. Okada, on his way through, noticed that the admiral's outer office was empty.

When the nco had gone, Tajiri said, 'I admire your initiative, Mr Okada. It is Okada, isn't it, not Fujita? Have you really come with a message from Toshiaki-san or from the Americans?'

'I'm too humble a personage for the Americans to use as a messenger, sir. I am just a corporal in the US Army, Corporal Tamezo Okada.'

'With the war over, do you presume we meet as equals?'

'No, sir.' It was difficult to tell whether Tajiri was antagonistic or receptive towards him. Perhaps he was just playing him along before calling for the guards to come and arrest him. 'I am here to ask a favour of you, to tell me what has happened to Lieutenant Minato.'

'Why your concern for Minato?'

'We were boyhood friends, sir. We still are – I think. I have a *giri* to him.'

Tajiri was silent for a moment, then he said, 'Doesn't this strike you as bizarre? You, an enemy agent, a humble personage as you describe yourself, coming in here to plead for information about one of my aides?'

'Yes, sir, the thought occurred to me. But I've read history – in the last days of a war all sorts of strange things happen.'

'True.' Tajiri knew the ironies and comedies of history,

better than this young man did. There were lessons to be learned in history, but they had only made him cynical. 'Did you learn much about us? I mean, as a spy?'

'No, sir.' What he had learned had influenced himself, not the course of the war. 'But that's all unimportant now, isn't it? I'm concerned only for Lieutenant Minato.'

'So am I.' Tajiri got up, went to the window. He stood there a moment, then he slowly, almost abstractedly began to peel the strips of tape from the glass. There would be no more bombing. Smoke was drifting up from fires in the neighbourhood; ministries were burning their papers. He looked down the street towards the Imperial Palace. 'He was here till last night. We have not gone home, none of us.' He gestured towards the camp bed, neatly made as if for inspection, in a corner of his office. 'We have been waiting for something to happen.'

'I telephoned here several times, sir. Minato never answered.'

'I had all his calls monitored. No, I was not looking for you, corporal. Forgive me for saying so, but you are unimportant.'

Okada was relieved, suddenly felt safe. 'Thank you, sir.'

Tajiri smiled, but tiredly. 'You have a sense of humour, corporal. But that is little help in times like these. Especially in regard to Lieutenant Minato. I was waiting on a certain phone call for him and I gave instructions that he was unavailable for all other calls. The one we were waiting on came last night.' He turned back to the grimy, smeared window. 'He is somewhere over there, in the Palace.'

'On the Emperor's staff?' Okada could not keep the surprise out of his voice.

Tajiri shook his head. 'On the staff of a fanatical patriot named Colonel Hayashi. I have been waiting on a call all day from Minato, but there has been none. He may be dead, and if he is, someone more important may also die.'

The Emperor? But Okada did not venture the name. He was, as he had said, a humble personage; he could not imagine what intrigue went on at the very top. Kings and presidents were assassinated; but there was no monarch or president anywhere in the world who had the almost divine impregnability of

Emperor Hirohito. Kings were killed out of revenge or spite, but never as scapegoats.

'How do we find out what has happened to him, sir?'

'How, indeed? One would think that someone of my rank would have access—' His voice trailed off. In a day or two, when the Americans came, rank would be a burden. 'My views are too well known to Colonel Hayashi and his gang—'

'Haven't you talked to others, sir? I mean of your rank?'

'Of course. But opinions at the top are never clear-cut, corporal, didn't you know that? Not now, not when we are defeated. We are squabbling amongst ourselves as we never did when we were winning. Everyone has his own idea of how we should surrender.'

It was a moment before Okada said, 'Could I get into the Palace?'

Tajiri shook his head in wonder. 'Is that the American in you, Okada?'

'It could be, sir. *Lèse-majesté* has always been one of our virtues. I know it sounds bizarre, to use your word, sir—'

Tajiri up till now had been little more than academically interested in the Japanese-American, sizing up what sort of man a rival intelligence agency had sent here. It had surprised him to hear the young man speak of *giri*; he hadn't expected that sense of honour to come out of an American education. Now, for the first time, he looked at Okada as an instrument who could be used. He knew the small histories within the larger frame of chronicles; those, for instance, of the world's secret services. He knew the story of the legendary Sidney Reilly of the British Secret Service; more recently there had been Richard Sorge, the German-born Russian spy, who had operated here in Tokyo for nine years before he was arrested and eventually hanged. Nothing was really bizarre in the secret world of espionage.

'How did you come here to Japan?'

Okada told him briefly.

Tajiri nodded. 'An adventurous entry. Why shouldn't the adventure end right at the heart of things? Yes, Okada, you could get into the Palace. Would it go against your dignity to impersonate a Japanese naval officer?'

He said it with a smile, but Okada knew the old man was not joking. 'No, sir, not in the circumstances.'

'What would you like to be? A lieutenant, a commander? You're too young to be an admiral, I'm afraid. Our navy is like navies everywhere, it reserves privilege for the elderly.'

'Commander will do, sir. I'll never make anything like that rank in the US Army.'

Once committed to what he had in mind, Admiral Tajiri lost no time in putting it into effect. It was not easy to find a uniform to fit Okada, but Tajiri's orderly, a wizened middle-aged man, was a born valet and therefore not to be beaten in the search for proper dress, even for a stranger. He came back in half an hour with three uniforms. In the meantime Okada and Tajiri, the American corporal and the Japanese admiral, had established respect for each other. Which is as difficult as establishing any feeling between the young and the old.

One of the uniform jackets fitted perfectly; the pants of another were comfortable, if a little tight round the hips. 'Very presentable,' said Tajiri, who had been a dandy when young but knew that elderly dandies looked pathetic. 'You look better than some staff members I've had.'

He had written a note to General Mori, commander of the Imperial Guards, and signed a pass. 'That will get you into the palace compound. You have to make sure you are not taken before General Mori – we are not sure whether he is part of the coup or not.' He spread out a map of the Imperial compound. 'Colonel Hayashi has a private office somewhere in the Imperial Household building. If Minato is still alive, he'll be somewhere close by, I should think. The time for the coup, if it's to come, will be within the next few hours. The plotters aren't going to be spread all over Tokyo.' He looked up from the map, then began to fold it carefully. 'I asked Lieutenant Minato this question – are you prepared to kill?'

It had never occurred to him that he might have to kill.

'If Minato is dead, it may be necessary for you to kill Colonel Hayashi. For Japan's sake and, who knows, the Americans', too.'

Minato heard the sirens go and wondered if, after all, the Americans were going to drop an atom bomb on Tokyo. He had never felt so depressed; the bomb would be welcome. He knew the details now of what the new bombs had done to Hiroshima and Nagasaki; little had been told to the general public, but one of the drawbacks to Intelligence is that it can't be deaf to horrors. He knew that the bomb blast was something more horrific than anyone had previously imagined, that whole blocks of the cities had been reduced to ash in seconds. It almost pleased him to think that in a few minutes he would be nothing but ash. Cremation was preferable to cutting open one's belly and then cutting one's throat.

He had been a virtual prisoner since he had come here last night to Colonel Hayashi's office in the Imperial Household building. He had first come to see the colonel last Thursday; Hayashi had greeted him coldly and suspiciously. 'Lieutenant Nakasone has told me about your attitude towards us, Minato.'

'Lieutenant Nakasone was only guessing, sir. He was never very good at Intelligence work.' Be arrogant, Admiral Tajiri had advised; and it proved easy. Humility is harder; but he knew that. 'Does a good conspirator confide in underlings? Nakasone is junior to me.'

'Only by a hair's breadth.' But Hayashi seemed amused, although his face didn't alter; it was like talking to a mask, Minato thought. 'What made you change your mind?'

'Circumstances, sir. When you spoke to me last I still had hopes, faint ones but still hopes, that we could come out of the war honourably. We shan't now, not if Yamato is allowed to surrender in the name of the Emperor.'

'Are you prepared for any sacrifice?' Only the fact that he kept talking showed that Hayashi was prepared to listen: his face showed nothing.

'Any sacrifice you ask for, colonel.'

Hayashi remained impassive and unmoving; then he nodded.

'Come back when I send for you. Just remember – when you come back, you may not leave here again.'

'Do I tell Admiral Tajiri, sir? Has the *Go* game finished?'

'All games are finished, lieutenant.'

So Minato had been sent for last night. Others in the plot had come and gone throughout the night; the office, like all other offices in the Household building, was a throbbing pulse. Except, Minato thought, that all the blood in this office was diseased. Even the once-genial Nakasone was now almost unrecognizable, a puppet in the stylized theatre of *bunraku*. He didn't speak at all to Minato, but acknowledged his presence with a stiff bow of his head, a silent suspicious manikin. Several times Minato thought of getting up and walking out, but he knew that once he left the palace compound he would not be able to return. Hayashi, a true leader of conspiracy, showed no trust: he had confiscated the passes of his late recruits.

Minato heard the American bombs begin to fall over the east: no atom bomb was being delivered tonight. He sighed, feeling disappointed. He stood up from the narrow, stiff-backed chair where he had been sitting for the last hour, like some job applicant (but the job was assassination), and walked out into the corridor. And saw Okada, dressed in naval uniform, coming towards him, escorted by one of the soldiers of the Imperial Guard. He moved quickly down the corridor towards them.

'I'll take over now,' he told the guard. 'I presume this officer is looking for Colonel Hayashi.'

The guard went back along the corridor and Minato, nodding to Okada, turned and led the way in the opposite direction, past Hayashi's office and out through a door at the far end to a terrace that looked up at the dark mound of Maple Leaf Hill. There had been a thick summer mist since late afternoon and there was no sight of the moon, only a pale diffusion of light that added a theatrical artificiality to the gardens.

'Why are you here? How did you get that uniform?'

You can't tell a man you have come to save his life; or Okada couldn't. He didn't know whether it was the American or the Japanese in him that held him back. He just answered the second question: 'Admiral Tajiri put me into this uniform.

336

When he didn't hear from you, he thought the worst—'

'I couldn't use a phone. Hayashi has had someone sitting on the phone day and night. The phones in all the other offices are monitored by the Palace switchboard. It seems no one is trusted—'

Soldiers were moving in small groups along the paths; it seemed that the entire Imperial Guards Division was being deployed. Water was being poured on fires that had been used to burn documents all day; steam and smoke rose in the sultry night air like mist from a swamp. In the blackout voices had a quick, nervous pitch to them.

'Where's the Emperor?' Okada could not find his bearings, though he had studied the map in Tajiri's office. There is no compass for a republican suddenly sent to save a monarch. Though he would have been just as much at a loss had he been sent to the White House to rescue a President. Especially one he knew nothing of, Harry S. Truman.

'Over in the Imperial Library. He's been living there for most of the war, rather than in the Palace.'

'Where's Colonel Hayashi?'

'Up at the Guards' headquarters, trying to get General Mori's support. There are other officers over at Army headquarters in the Dai Ichi building, trying to talk General Imamaru and the other generals into supporting them.'

'Who's the ring leader? Hayashi?'

'No. The rumour is that it's a royal prince, but I haven't sighted him. It's like trying to pin down mad ghosts. Maybe that's what will save the Emperor – the plotters are all hysterical, running round in circles.'

'I think we should get out of here, trust to luck they'll keep running around in circles.'

Minato shook his head. 'I can't, Okada. I am committed.'

Even as he spoke they saw the big Daimler come round the curve in the path, past the ruins of the Phoenix Hall, the Crown Prince's villa and the other buildings that had been burned down on the night of 25 May when B-29s had come on a tightly targeted incendiary raid. The car pulled up and the Emperor, in field marshal's uniform, got out and came up the steps and went

337

into the Household building. Minato and Okada, standing in the shadows, bowed low, but neither the Emperor nor his chamberlains looked at them.

'What's he doing here?'

'The audience hall is upstairs. There is a team from Japan National Broadcasting waiting up there for him – he's going to record the surrender announcement.'

'Now is your chance to tell him, or one of his officials, what Hayashi and the others are planning.'

Minato looked at him as if he didn't understand how Okada could be so unintelligent. 'Who is going to take notice of a lowly lieutenant saying there is a plot against the Emperor? It would be sacrilege in the eyes of some of those court officials even to mention such a thing. And what proof do I have? That I'm a part of the plot? I'd have a sword or a bullet through me in less than a minute. I can't go near the Emperor. What I have to do is stop Hayashi and his madmen from getting near him!'

Okada heard the rising note in Minato's voice, felt the sudden tension in the other's body. 'Settle down, Kenji—'

'You must get out of here! The admiral should never have sent you looking for me—'

'He didn't send me. I asked to come.'

For a moment Minato looked as if he were about to weep. He had spent so many years alone, he was suddenly afraid of friendship like this. He was not afraid of any *giri* it might lay on him; he just could not bear the weight of the emotion he felt. Okada, looking at him, realized for the first time how lonely his friend had been.

'Aah—!' It was almost a sob. All his adult life he had practised self-control and now he was losing it. He put out a hand and Okada took it. 'Tamezo—'

'We'll get out of here safely,' Okada said softly. A platoon of Imperial Guards had drawn up alongside the Daimler at the bottom of the steps. But were they there to protect the Emperor or take him into custody?

'I hope so,' said Minato equally softly. He had regained control of himself; it was as if there was something more than death to wish for. He now felt concerned for Okada's safety and

338

that all at once gave him something to live for. 'Stay here.'

He went back inside to see what was happening in Hayashi's office. Okada remained where he was in the shadows on the terrace; no one appeared to take any notice of him. There was so much movement now in the Palace compound that no one was checking on possible intruders. A covey of chamberlains, all dressed alike in drab blue wartime jackets buttoned to the neck, looking like a squad of cleaners, came swooping up the steps and into the building, bureaucrats looking for more paper to peck at. Two officers on bicycles pedalled furiously by on the path below, almost running into the platoon of Guards and spattering them with gravel as they swerved to avoid them. The bombers had gone, the raid had been no more than a reminder that the Americans could come and go when they wished, and a heavy silence had settled on the city, broken only by the occasional bell of a fire engine. Okada even heard a night-bird cry somewhere up on Maple Leaf Hill.

Minato came back. 'Colonel Hayashi is still up at Guards' Headquarters. But things are worsening – it looks as if some of the Guards officers are supporting him. If the Guards take over the palace, no other troops will be able to get in from the outside. All the Guards will have to do is hold the bridges over the moat.'

Okada's hand strayed of its own accord to the holster at his belt; Admiral Tajiri had insisted that he wear a gun. 'If the Guards all go over to Hayashi's side, who's on our side here in the Palace?'

'A few officers on the Emperor's personal staff. The chamberlains. You and I.'

Half an hour later the Emperor emerged from the building, went quickly down the steps, got into the Daimler and was driven away. The platoon of soldiers did not move other than to snap to attention; watching them, Okada let out a sigh of relief. But he knew that the night was far from over.

In the next hour Minato went back to Hayashi's office several times, to find out if there had been any new developments and to let Nakasone and the other officers there see that he had not deserted. No one asked him where he had been; when there are

339

more than two plotters, conspiracy is difficult to regiment. Except that everyone in the office looked so strained and nervous, the atmosphere might have been farcical. Already word had come in that two of the officers, on their way to influence yet another general outside the Palace, were still inside the compound, mending punctures on their bicycles. So far the coup was running on wobbly wheels.

When Minato went back to the office for the third time Nakasone stood in front of him in the doorway. 'We should go upstairs now!'

Minato tried to look both enthusiastic and cautious, an expression not easy for someone who had tried for so long to hide his feelings. 'But why? We should wait for Colonel Hayashi.'

'The Emperor has made his recording – we should make sure they haven't already smuggled it out.' Nakasone looked out of his depth already; he hadn't the stamina for fanaticism. 'If it is broadcast tomorrow, we must all die of shame!'

'We shall die,' said Minato, trying to sound coldly fatalistic. 'But with honour, not shame. I shall help you die, Nakasone, if you are afraid to do it yourself.'

Nakasone gave him a murderous, not a suicidal, look and went back into the office.

Minato had returned to join Okada on the terrace when the shot rang out from the northern end of the compound, from the Imperial Guards' headquarters. The platoon, standing easy at the bottom of the steps, stiffened to attention, though not in parade ground fashion. For a moment there seemed to be utter silence; one could imagine men all over the compound waiting tensely for the volley of shots to follow. But none came. Then the officer in charge of the platoon snapped an order and the soldiers formed neat ranks.

'We'd better go inside,' said Minato.

'I can't! Someone might recognize me—' Then Okada realized he was an absolute stranger here in the Palace; there would be no Major Nagata or other secret police to point the finger at him. 'Who am I supposed to be if someone asks.'

'The man your pass says, Commander Kita. Tell them you're

on Admiral Ito's staff – he's down at Yokosuka. Tell them you support them, that the word has spread . . . Can you act the fanatic?'

Okada had always ridiculed fanaticism, and now he was being asked to impersonate it. But irony had been piled upon irony ever since he had come to Tokyo.

They went into the building. Okada, passing rooms along the corridor, was surprised to see how Western were the furnishings: there were heavy desks, upholstered chairs and sofas: bureaucrats, he guessed, liked their comfort. Only Hayashi's office was austere and Japanese; but he had expected that. What he did not expect was the sight of the man himself as he came bursting into the office.

The front of the colonel's uniform was drenched in blood; his face and hands were spattered with it. But he was not the one who was wounded: 'We've killed the Guards' commander! The Guards are now with us!'

If that were true, Minato knew that the night was lost: there would be murder and suicide that would turn the Palace into a blood-bath. There were shouts and a wild babble of voices. No one seemed to notice Okada as those in the office swept out after Hayashi, rushing along the corridor towards the upper floor.

Okada, all his interest focussed on Hayashi, hadn't heard what was being shouted. 'Where are they going?'

'Upstairs to look for the Emperor's surrender recording!' Minato was out in the corridor, uncertain of what to do next. Especially as at that moment a mob of soldiers, some of them looking half-drunk, burst in at the far end of the corridor.

The mob came running down the corridor, some of them peeling off into the offices. Chamberlains came to doorways to look in fearful bewilderment; the corridor of secretive whispers was now an alley of bedlam. But they had a moment to take it in before they were pushed back into their offices; some of the older ones fell backwards and the soldiers trampled over them as they plunged in to smash the furniture. One chamberlain cried out as he saw his beloved files tossed out of an open window; but a rabble never knows the difference between

341

tabulations and toilet paper. They wipe their arses on both and the world goes down the drain.

The first of the soldiers reached Minato and Okada. It was the latter who reacted quicker. 'Upstairs! Follow Colonel Hayashi!'

The mob swept by and Okada and Minato, the latter a little slow to move at first, fought their way through the current and out on to the terrace. 'Where to now?'

'To the Library!' Minato was prepared for a last-ditch stand. 'The Emperor will have gone back there!'

The paths were busy with soldiers running aimlessly as if on training runs. It struck Okada as he ran down a path after Minato that he had gone back in time: he was back in the Middle Ages, Kublai Khan was just across the water. He was racing through the dark summer night to save an emperor: a twentieth century American playing at being a *samurai*. He suddenly laughed out aloud, but he felt no mirth or excitement. He ran straight into a soldier who was standing in the middle of the path relieving himself of the *saké* and beer he had been drinking. The soldier fell over with a yell, cut off in mid-stream.

Okada and Minato crossed the moat by a causeway, came to a gate that led to the enclosure where stood the Pavilion of Concubines and the Imperial Library. Two soldiers stepped into the middle of the gateway, rifles raised.

'We've come to warn the Emperor!' Minato was out of breath, could say no more and held his sides.

Okada all at once realized he was supposed to be a commander. 'Out of our way! We must get to the Emperor!'

These two were loyal Guards: one of them raised his rifle and Okada heard the bolt slide back. Then beside him Minato fired his pistol, twice; both soldiers went down. Okada stood stock-still for a moment with shock: he still could not quite believe what was happening, that he was in the middle of it. But he was: and he came out of his shock and ran after Minato through the gateway.

There were shouts behind them as they left the driveway and ran beneath the trees. More shots rang out, but it was impossible to tell where they came from. Then they ran out from under the trees and Minato pulled up sharply and Okada almost cannoned into him. The Library loomed up ahead, a low concrete building on a low hill, looking more like a fort than a repository of learning.

'The Emperor has his living quarters in a bunker in the hill,' said Minato. He was still gasping for breath and his words came out separately as if he were testing his voice. 'We must get in there somehow!'

Okada looked up the slight hill. He could see the soldiers at their posts, a dozen of them; he knew there must be more somewhere out of sight. At the sound of the shots chamberlains came out of the building, but were at once pushed back inside by a Guards officer. If the Guards were in revolt, the order had not yet got through to these immediately surrounding the Emperor; they were taking up defensive positions, two machine-guns had been mounted. For the moment the Emperor looked safe.

Okada was surprised at the breadth of his thinking. Up till now he had been thinking in purely personal terms; true, he had been a spy working in a wide context, but he had never really been able to see himself as contributing much to winning the war. The war was won now: or lost; he was in no man's land, looking both ways. But if the peace was to be won, the Emperor had to be allowed to surrender with dignity. Though he did not know it, governments were arguing that point thousands of miles away. But the Japanese in him told him something that the Western statesmen, with their prejudices and refusal to accept any standards but their own, might never admit. The Emperor, whether he remained divine or not, was the focal point of Japan and it would need him, at least for the immediate future. Okada had no idea what the Son of Heaven would say in his surrender broadcast, but the Japanese people had to hear it.

'Never mind the Emperor. If he's made his recording, someone will have taken it away to broadcast it tomorrow. We have to stop Hayashi and his gang getting to it first. We have to kill Hayashi.'

Minato was silent for a moment; he had stopped breathing, as if Okada had taken his breath away with his suggestion. Then he said admiringly, his voice steady now, 'You're truly Japanese.'

'No,' said Okada, smiling, all at once feeling at ease now the decision had been made, 'there have been some excellent American killers.' It disturbed him, however, that the only ones he could think of were outlaws and John Wilkes Booth.

'Do we go looking for him or wait here for him?' It did not strike Minato as strange that he should look to Okada for the lead. He had been relieved of the need for decision. He listened for the sound of footsteps on the driveway, but there was none. 'They must have gone elsewhere looking for the recording.'

'Where else would they go? Where would the technicians have taken it for broadcasting?'

'Possibly to the Japan Broadcasting Corporation's building. But more likely to the Dai Ichi Insurance building. They have an emergency station there in the basement – and they would be right underneath the Area Army's headquarters. I don't think General Imamaru is involved in any plot – he would see that Hayashi didn't get into the building.'

'Then we'll go there – just to make sure.'

They had perhaps a mile to go. Okada saw two officers coming up the driveway on bicycles; he ran out from under the trees and stood in front of them. He presented his pistol. 'Gentleman, I need your bicycles.'

They were Guards officers, both junior lieutenants, neither of them prepared to die for a piece of army equipment. They handed over the bicycles without argument, but demurred when Okada asked for their guns.

'Gentlemen, your guns are needed in the cause of Japan.' He could not imagine his speaking like this in English; but the pompous formality came easily to his tongue in Japanese. *Samurai* had spoken like this and he was one of them, at least for tonight.

He and Minato took the guns, mounted the bicycles and rode off down the driveway. The moon had risen, the mist had gone and they rode through the Fukiage Gardens like lovers on a romantic spin, past the ponds where the water reflected the moon like polished shields, past the platoons of soldiers now

344

seemingly strolling aimlessly like night-time pleasure-seekers, out through the gates and across the moat and down the road that led past the bomb-shattered ministries. Traffic was coming and going, but it was all military traffic: the populace was at home waiting for the end of the world.

As they pulled up outside the Dai Ichi building, Minato paused and put his hand on Okada's arm. The intimacy was against his whole nature; not even as an American schoolboy had he made such gestures. But now he was neither Japanese nor American but a friend.

'Tom—' He spoke softly in English, the language of their boyhood. 'Don't come any farther. You don't have to risk your life for this—'

'I think I do, Ken. You're not going in there on your own.'

'Tom, I'm not worth following. I tricked you – and those officers in San Diego. I didn't come home to spy – I came back to fight for Japan—'

Okada suddenly felt sick; not with fear but at his friend's betrayal. 'Jesus! But why did you pick me to come with you?'

Minato felt equally sick; but with shame. 'I could think of no one else. I guess I thought I might even convince you that you were wrong about Japan . . .' He stopped, looked about him. Japan was in ruins, brought there by the militarists and the ambitions of greedy men. Fires burned over to the east, a reminder of the holocaust that might come if the Emperor was not allowed to surrender. 'You were not wrong. I've learned that since I came back. But I'm still Japanese, not American.'

Okada could not shape his feelings into any coherence. He felt angry, betrayed; yet all at once he felt pity for Minato. Before he could find words that might have forgiven Minato, two lorries and a car came round the far corner of the building. The three vehicles jerked to a halt and soldiers and officers fell out of them. In the bright moonlight Okada recognized their leader. It was Hayashi, waving a pistol, looking like a figure in some raw propaganda poster.

The officers and soldiers, thirty or forty of them, surged up the steps. The sentries outside the building fired two or three shots, but they were overwhelmed in a moment; the mob

345

plunged in over them. Okada and Minato looked at each other; for a moment Minato expected Okada to turn away. But he didn't. He just said, 'Come on!' and ran up the steps. Minato, on the verge of tears, followed him.

Once inside the building the soldiers didn't appear to know where to go next; the mob folded in on itself like a crushed bladder. Hayashi, with Nakasone and other officers grouped around him, shouted at the soldiers, but no one heard him. Then he fired his pistol: plaster fell from the ceiling on to his shoulders like bird-lime.

'To the basement! Take the radio station!'

But when they all turned towards the steps that led down out of the lobby, Minato was standing there, his own and the Guards officer's gun menacing Hayashi. Okada had not noticed Minato slip away from him; he was as surprised as Hayashi and the others to see Minato blocking the way to the basement.

Minato had acted instinctively: the Emperor, or anyway the Emperor's words, had to be saved. But only when he looked past Hayashi and saw Okada, did he realize he could do nothing to save his friend. But it was too late now.

It was Nakasone, not Hayashi, who shot Minato. Minato fired both his pistols and Nakasone spun round and fell to the ground. But Minato was already dying, the hole in his throat spewing blood. He looked around as if bemused at what had happened to him; he looked straight at Okada but didn't see him, his eyes blind with death. Then he fell backwards and hit the marble floor with a thump.

In an instant Okada was standing over him. He fired from the hip at Hayashi, hit him in the face; the colonel fell back against the officers behind him. The young officers held him, looking down at him as if they could not believe how the current had suddenly changed. The soldiers, rifles raised and aimed from the hip at Okada, looked equally at a loss. Then there was a bellow from the back of the lobby.

General Imamaru had stepped out of a lift. He stood there, arms akimbo, with only two aides beside him, both of them looking far less confident and authoritative than he. Imamaru strode forward; as far as Okada could see he was unarmed. One of the officers still holding the body of Hayashi, a major, raised his pistol. Okada raised one gun.

'Shoot the general, major, and you die with him.'

Imamaru had pulled up; it seemed that up till this moment he had not noticed Okada. He looked at the latter, then back at the major. There was no fear in his broad face; he had been defeated in the field as an army commander, but here in the lobby of a pre-war insurance building, a most unlikely last battleground, he had reached the end of the road. He would die more gloriously than from the blade of a *wakizashi* sword.

The major stared at Imamaru; his finger twitched on the trigger. But he knew their cause was already lost; killing General Imamaru would achieve nothing. He put down his pistol and with that the soldiers around him lowered their rifles.

Still keeping his own pistol raised, Okada backed towards the general. 'They were trying to take over the radio station, General Imamaru. I believe they have killed General Mori.'

'I know that.' Then Imamaru's fatalistic mask cracked; he looked at Okada with the amazement no general should ever show. 'Fujita – how did you get here?'

'Ah, general—' Okada looked at the body of Minato sprawled on the lobby floor, the head in a pool of blood, the legs and arms twisted awkwardly. He shut his eyes against the sight: it was no way to remember his friend. 'That's a question my father is going to ask. And I may not be able to answer him either.'

4 \

At noon that day the Emperor broadcast Japan's surrender. Okada, Natasha and Lily went down to the Imperial Plaza, outside the south-eastern gate to the Palace, and there in the huge, thronged square they listened to the high-pitched voice declaring that, for Japan, the war was at an end. Okada watched the crowd from the edge of the square, marvelling still at these people to whom, no matter how distantly, he belonged. As the Emperor's voice broke the vast stillness the crowd bowed its

347

head; a ripple ran over the dark human lake like a passing breeze. Nobody really understood the Emperor's actual words: he spoke in the language reserved for the Son of Heaven, an antique tongue, almost Chinese. A commentator came on the air immediately the Emperor's speech was finished; but no one needed him to tell what they all knew. Okada saw the dulled, stiffened faces begin to crack as tears rolled down the sick, sunken cheeks; then as he looked at it, the mask of Japan crumbled. Men and women dropped to their knees and beat their heads against the ground.

'Oh no!' Natasha clutched Okada's arm.

Close by them a man drew a knife, shouted something that could have been a prayer or a curse, and drove the blade into his chest. On the far side of the crowd a shot rang out; then another, much nearer. Okada turned his head and saw the man, half his head blown away, the gun still in his hand, still standing in the crowd, unable to fall because of the press of bodies.

'Let us go home,' said a man to his wife and children, 'and eat stones and drink gall.'

Okada looked at Lily, who had remained impassive throughout the speech and its aftermath. 'You're not moved by any of this, Lily?'

'Yes,' she said; but it was not she who had surrendered. So far she had not fought the Americans; or tried to be an ally of theirs. They would arrive tomorrow, and tomorrow, as she said she had always said (though she hadn't), was the first day of the future. 'I think we should go back to General Imamaru's. But not to eat stones and drink gall. Did you tell him last night that I was with you?'

'No, Lily. He had too much else on his mind.'

'I suppose so,' said Lily, but sounded as if she wondered what else could have engaged the general. She was not unintelligent, just self-centred – a good survivor. She washed her hands of the war and said, 'Let's go home.'

Natasha looked at her with affection. 'You're incorrigible, mother.'

'I know,' said Lily. 'And don't call me mother.'

Next day it was announced that there would be a disposal of

goods. Over the next few weeks ten billion dollars' worth of assets, from trucks to toilet bowls, banknotes to blasting powder, disappeared, most of it to syndicates being repaid for past services. It was possibly the first time in history when the looters were those who had been defeated.

Okada, leaving Natasha and Lily, the outsiders still, at the Imamaru residence, went to one of the hand-out depots and there saw Koga. The *yakuza* was supervising the loading of five trucks.

'For Cho-san,' he explained cheerfully. He was wearing a new derby hat, worn rakishly; he looked like an overweight pugilist starting out a career as a music-hall comedian. Then he thought he had better explain further: 'Cho-san wants to make sure the workers get their proper share.'

'I'll bet,' said Okada in English, safe now in his own tongue.

He managed to collect three blankets, some tinned fish, tea and a small bag of rice; he went home laden, wondering what he would take out of the first American PX when it was set up. In the afternoon he went to the Navy Building and asked to see Admiral Tajiri. He was still wearing the naval commander's uniform and the lieutenant on the desk looked at him sadly.

'Didn't you know, commander? The admiral committed *seppuku* immediately after the Emperor's speech.'

Okada went out of the building, sad and angry at the suicide of the old man. If the good were dying with the bad, who would be left to lead? Standing there outside the building he thought again of Kenji Minato and tears came to his eyes. But perhaps Minato was more comfortable where he was, with the spirits: he might never have been comfortable in the world of mirrors that would be the immediate future of Japan.

The Americans were slow to arrive. Paperwork, protocol and policy had to be paid lip service; lips worked overtime at General MacArthur's headquarters in Manila, where negotiations took place. The rains came and Japan looked as if it might be washed away before the victors could lay claim to it.

Then, two weeks after the surrender, the Americans began to arrive. It seemed that the first of them had all been chosen for their size; they towered over the polite welcoming party. They

349

were awkward, both arrogant and affable: it was the first time they had conquered another nation's homeland on their own. The Japanese showed their adaptability, looked the more at ease, expressed their admiration at the speed with which the Americans organized themselves. Japanese ladies waited to be raped, but were saved by their more professional sisters. An enterprising police chief had organized a corporation, the Recreation and Amusement Association; geishas, bar girls and brothel-keepers flocked to the colours, the American colours. The *samurai* had been replaced by a different swordsman.

Okada found US Navy headquarters and found Lieutenant-Commander Embury there. 'Goddam,' said Embury, 'you're still alive! We'd given up hope.'

'I didn't contribute much, sir. I might just as well have stayed in San Diego.' But he didn't believe that. If nothing else, he had found Natasha here in Japan.

'It doesn't matter. We won, didn't we? What's with that uniform? Did you have to join the Japs? Sorry, the Japanese.'

'In a way.'

He felt curiously out of touch with Embury, almost as if he would have to learn how to be an American again. He stayed at Navy HQ for an hour, was issued with a letter to Army HQ detailing who he was. He said goodbye to Embury, said he would be back to put in a full report, and went out to find Army headquarters.

'You mean,' said the lieutenant he faced, 'you've been here in Japan for the past six months? Christ, how was it?'

'Not very comfortable. Especially during the bombing.'

'Yeah, we gave 'em hell, didn't we? Well, glad to see you survived. I suppose you want to get out of the uniform and back into ours, eh?'

Okada went to the supply store and was issued with a uniform that fitted and a set of corporal's stripes. 'You want to burn this outfit?' said the supply sergeant, holding up the Japanese naval uniform.

'No,' said Okada. 'I'll keep it for old times' sake.'

Natasha had no uniform to establish her identity in the days to come; nor in the years to come. 'Will they accept me in America?'

'It's supposed to be a melting pot,' said Lily, who had no melting point.

The two women had patiently waited out the days at the Imamaru mansion, sitting amongst the ruins like sirens who had lost their voices. Lily had phoned General Imamaru at his headquarters; he had been polite, but that was all. She had shown no bitterness that she had been dumped as his mistress; she was a true professional, knew the chances one took in her game. Another game was beginning with the arrival of the Americans.

'You wouldn't come to America with Tom and me?'

'Not as a mother-in-law. If I find a rich American general—'

'Lily, I'm sure all the American generals, especially the rich ones, are married.'

'Well, a rich colonel—' Okada had told her that army rank meant nothing in America. 'Don't worry about me, Natasha. I'll get by, and when everything is working again I'll come and visit you.'

'Tom and me and the grandchildren.' She was building dreams, the easiest of constructions in a new peace.

'Don't ruin the prospect,' said Lily, who would never be a grandmother, no matter how many grandchildren she might be presented with. 'Let's look on the bright side.'

Which she always would, though not with blind optimism: one just needed the light of the bright side to illuminate the pitfalls.

Natasha kissed her on the cheek. 'I love you, mother.'

For a moment Lily almost did melt. She put a hand on Natasha's, looked at the beauty she and (almost forgotten) Henry had produced. For the first time she could remember, she could think of nothing to say. All she could do was press her daughter's hand and hope that America and Tamezo would treat her well.

Next day, in the uniform of the conquerors, with money in his pocket and Natasha on his arm, Okada went by train and bus out to Miyanoshita. They walked up the drive, past the garden that was already showing signs of neglect. Hara, the butler, came out to greet them.

'Toshiaki-san and Madame Imamaru and the family have gone down to join the general in Tokyo. The general thought they should all be there to greet the Americans.' He had shown no surprise that Okada should be in an American uniform. Either Otozo Toshiaki had told him who Okada really was or he was past surprise: his was the face of Japan, Okada decided, that would never change.

'I only came to say goodbye to Toshiaki-san.' But he had already done that and perhaps it was better that it should not be repeated. The old man's life was over; it would be cruel to pour salt into his grave. 'I should like to show my fiancée the garden.'

'Of course.' Hara hesitated, then bowed: Okada was still the gardener, though in the victors' uniform. He bowed to the uniform, which was the proper thing. 'Summer is almost over.'

He went back into the house and Okada led Natasha round to the phoenix tree. The flowers had fallen and lay like cracked lemon-yellow plates in a circle round the tree. The rains had stopped two days ago, but the earth still steamed in the hot sun. Haze softened the neighbouring hills and it was difficult to believe that less than fifty miles away one of the world's biggest cities lay in ruins and heaps of sodden ash. But there had always been peace, of a sort, here in the mountains.

Okada led Natasha in under the shade of the tree, put his arm round her waist. He saw the look in her eye and, smiling, shook his head. 'No, not here. We'll find a hotel somewhere, with a big thick mattress.'

'We could go back to my house in Nayora.'

'No.' He was finished with the ghost of Keith Cairns. 'We're going to make a fresh start.'

She understood. Love is blind; but a voice can still be read. 'I'll have to make a new start in America. Will it be difficult?'

He watched a flower spiral down from the phoenix tree. 'It may be. For both of us. But we won't be the only ones.'